Repression

Nataya

Copyright pending

<u>*Dedication*</u>

This book is dedicated to my mother, Pamela. When I was a child, I'd go through my mother's things to find out what she had been writing about. Knowing a piece of her that she didn't verbally discuss with me made me secure in my own ways...made me feel relatable.

My mother kept a transparent folder of her writings under her mattress and to this day, I'm not sure what made me check that hiding spot...but I'm glad I did. When I told her that I wanted to be a writer, she told me that she had some things she had written back in the day and I responded with, "I know. I found them." She told me to stay out of her shit and stop being nosy but also, I should write daily if that is what I truly wanted.

Mom, I write because of you. I express myself in this form of creation and even though no parent is perfect, you taught me how to save myself. You made me but you've also given me the ability to make myself.

That's love.

Acknowledgement

I'd like to acknowledge a friend and old coworker of mine, Julia Hall. We became friends shortly after meeting one another and she was instantly nice to me. Julia was one of the many people who had been ready and excited to read this novel. She asked me could she be the editor and wanted to do it free of charge. I offered to at least take her to lunch to express my gratitude. It was the least I could do.

Being how Julia was supposed to be my editor and since she is no longer with us, this book is written as is. This is my very first novel and I can move differently next time but as of now, it doesn't feel right allowing someone else do something I wanted my friend to do. This novel resembles each and every one of us: perfectly imperfect.

Julia, you will be missed by many. You fought hard and remained strong throughout your battle. You were so pleasant to others throughout your pain and I pray your soul is at peace.

<u>Prologue</u>

February 10, 2004

Dear Joyce,

I wanted to write to you because I knew this would be the only way you would listen to what I had to say. Things have gotten crazy over the last few months and I wish something different would've happen.

I wish I could hug you. All of the times I was rude or mean to you, I wish I could take them back and say nicer things instead. I wish I could've been more like you.

I'm…different now. You know where I am. These people here make you different. No one is happy and everyone walks around as if they are never leaving. We're stuck. One girl tried to jump on me and when I stabbed her, they told me that I was a threat to everyone.

They make me take medicine. At first, I tried hiding it under my tongue because I knew what they were doing to me. But, one of the ladies caught on and they forced me to swallow the pills.

The medicine makes me feel like I'm spinning and unable to talk. Most of the time, I just go to sleep and hope that the feeling goes away when I wake up. I think everyone here must take medicine. It's just weird. A lot of the people here shouldn't really be here.

I know you probably don't want to hear from me after the way I treated you but I just wanted to let you know that I'm leaving this place. I'm getting out of here and I'm coming to be with you. I miss you more than I've ever missed anyone before.

Mom, I know you're reading this. Give this to Joyce. It belongs to her.

I wish we could breathe in the mirror together just one last time. I've loved us since the belly. I'll love us forever.

Love, Mary.

Chapter 1: Mary

June 25, 1999

"*M*ary! Mary!! I know you hear me calling you, child!"

That's mama. I know it's time to go in but dang, I wanted to keep playing! Why do mamas and papas always want to ruin fun just as soon as it starts getting good? What if I went in their room at night to ruin the nasty stuff they think we don't know about? I think I'll do that tonight if mama doesn't stop yelling my name like she's crazy!

"What mama?!? I'm down by the water feedin' these greedy ducks!" It seemed like the ducks had a way of understanding me. Whenever I was feeling sad, they would get closer to where I always sat near the water. Every day there were the same 4 hungry ones.

Rocksi was my favorite. She's black all over, has a pretty green patch around her eye and a cracked beak. Mama always says she can spot a hurt soul and Rocksi seems to have been hurt in some kind of cruel way. Must have had a hard life. Rocks are hard…so I named her Rocksi.

Spending time by the lake is a happy place for me. The first time mama let us sit down here, the smell made my stomach hurt. There's not much to do around here but since we started hanging with the ducks every day, it doesn't smell too bad anymore. Mama will end up putting us to work with some chores if we hang around the house all day.

Taking a deep breath in and holding it for a few seconds, I close my eyes and imagine that I'm Rocksi. The water feels good and dripping off of my feathers. My friends are all here and we race for bread knowing that we'll all get fed. The sun is burning my beak. Inhale…exhale…inhale…and dive!

"Who you think you sassin' little girl?! Don't forget, I brought you in this world and I don't mind taking you out!" she says.

Even though I know she wouldn't do it, this was her favorite line. She was sweet most of the time but would turn crazy if needed. Whenever she would get upset, it meant that the other person deserved it.

Lovette Anne Marks was the most beautiful woman I've ever seen. Her hair looked as if it were the perfect sunset with long tight burnt orange curls. The red freckles going across her face were the prettiest thing about her.

Mama is loved by so many people, so I figured each freckle represents how many people love her. One day, I took a red marker and tried to make me some freckles. Mama laughed, gave me this long talk about loving myself the way God made me and some other mess. Then, she made me wash my face.

My feet are dirty and my nail polish is chipping badly. I hate wearing shoes. Who wants their feet covered all day? These things need to breathe sometimes. The grass tickles my toes with every step I take closer to home. I'm not ready to go inside. I'll just walk a little slower.

Bending down to swat a mosquito off of my leg, I sit. I lie down. My hair hugs the grass. The sun has decided to rest for the day and the clouds start to look upset. I'd be upset too if I had to be up there all day with nothing to do.

"Who are you mad at?" I know talking to the clouds sound silly but maybe she needs someone to talk to. There is a feeling that comes over her. The darker she becomes, it's clear the pain gets worse. She screams and I lie still. Tears from her face meet mine. I knew she was angry. Let me go before my mother comes after me.

Jumping up and running towards the house, I remember. This house has been in our family for so long. It's so old but still pretty. Mama said something like her grandparents lived here. Now, that has to be like super old!

The house is big and white with every shutter painted red. Cherry red. The door matched the pretty red. I loved the way mama would decorate the house during Christmas. Probably why she had the shutters painted red to match the holiday. Who knows? Seems like that would be one of her crazy reasons.

Stepping up the four steps and opening the door, the smell of peach cobbler rushes up my nose. My stomach starts talking. She tells me to follow the scent.

"Mary, I know you heard me calling you! We go through the same mess every day! If you can't learn to be here at this table on time, then you can forget about spending time down by the lake with those ducks!"

She made my stomach shut up quick with all that yelling. "Makes no sense how everyone can be in here on time but YOU!"

"Sorry, mama." That's all it took. She forgives so easily. Next, she'll tell me to wash up before papa gets to the table.

"Now, go upstairs and clean up before your papa comes down." I knew it. Papa was more than likely upstairs shaving. Daily. Not sure what kind of hair grows daily but he sure does a lot of shaving.

10 steps. The stairwell vanity. I've always thought that this was a weird place to have one of these but, of course, it's another one of mama's ideas. Running my right hand over its cherry wood glossy frame, I pause. Wiping the dust from my hands and onto my dress, I sit and stare. Moving my curls from my face, my right hand meets my reflection.

"Go get ready for dinner!" His voice booms and makes me jump. Hitting my knee on the table, I stand up in pain.

"I'm going!"

Joseph Marks, Sr. wasn't the most handsome man, but I guess mama still loves him anyway. She always tells me that it isn't about what someone looks like but what they have on the inside that makes them a good person. I kind of don't understand because mama is so pretty and I just don't think daddy would've wanted to marry an ugly woman. Doesn't make sense to me but whatever. All I know is that when I finally get a husband, he has to be handsome.

Papa was a very tall and large man. He made the whole family seemed so small. Sometimes, people thought that mama was one of our sisters because of how short she was compared to daddy. People would always tell her that she didn't look her age. Papa had the palest skin with hair that always looked like he put too much stuff in it. Not sure what stuff he uses but maybe he should stop because it doesn't smell good either.

Ignoring the bathroom, I stop at one of the guest bedrooms. Joyce. She's been sick for days and a part of me has been sick with her. My stomach aches sometimes during the day and I know she's in pain. I'm not supposed to go in there but something in me just needs to see her right now. Touching the doorknob and pushing open the door, the creak is so loud.

"Mary, you're not supposed to come in here! They're gonna be upset. Just go!" Joyce struggles with the words in between holding her stomach. Seeing her like this always makes me feel sad. It hurts to know that she's hurting and there's nothing I can do.

"I won't be long. Just wanted to make sure you were okay," I say. Sitting on the bed and hugging my sister, she smells weird.

"I've missed you down by the water today. You should've seen Rocksi being greedy as always. Do you feel any better yet?" She's going to say she does, but I know she doesn't. Anything to get me out of this room before we are caught.

"I do. Now, go before we both get in trouble." The tears in her eyes lets me know that she doesn't really want me to leave. One falls and she turns her head quickly as if she were ashamed for me to see her cry. When I leave this room, I feel like I'll be leaving myself behind.

Closing the door, I run to the bathroom before one of them starts hollering again. Letting the water run a little longer to cover up the sounds of me crying, I wish hard that Joyce feels better tomorrow.

As soon as I get to the dinner table, Joey is already there with an upset look on his face. You'd think I've done something to him to make him hate me the way he does.

"We always have to wait on you. Why can't you ever be on time so we can eat? You don't even have any friends, so I don't know what could be holdin' you up every single day," says Joey.

See. Another reason why I know he hates me. Every day he has to make it his business to say something mean to me. Not sure how everyone else's big brothers treat them but I'm sure it's not like this. If he keeps on, I'm gonna make sure mama knows what is under his bed. Our father hears all of this, says nothing but nods his head as if he agrees with Joey.

Sticking my tongue out, I reply, "You don't know if I have friends or not, so shut the f…"

Out of nowhere, I feel something swing around from behind me and hit me right on the lips.

"Mary Marks, you better watch mouth before I wash it out with soap!"

"But mama…" My lips sting.

"Don't but mama me. Mind your manners in this house. If you don't have anything nice to say, keep it to yourself!" Of course, she would hear what I said and not what Joey had said to me first.

Looking over, he has the biggest grin on his face. Papa had been sitting here the whole time and never said anything. He never says anything to help me. I'm starting to think he hates me too. Meanwhile, mama headed upstairs with a food tray for Joyce and we wait for her to return.

"Now, everyone bow your heads and let's say grace." In unison, "God is great, God is good…Amen."

Chicken, peas and mashed potatoes. Again. Boy, am I tired of eating the same thing, but I know Mama will more than likely have my tail for complaining about food.

"When will Joyce be able to eat dinner with us again?" Papa looks up at mama and she looks at me.

"Eat your food. Joyce will be back at the table when she is feeling better," says mama.

"If whatever she has isn't contagious, I don't see why she can't sit at the table with us. It won't hurt her. She's up in that dark old room alone." I felt like crying. It wasn't fair to her.

"I know you're concerned about your sister. It's only right, baby. I'm concerned about her as well but she has to stay in bed in order for her to get better. She will feel better and before you know it, everything will be back to normal." Although it wasn't what I wanted to hear, mama's words made me feel a little better.

"Papa," Joey swallows his food and spit flies from his mouth as soon as he starts talking again.

"Can I spend the night with Tommy tomorrow? His parents said it's okay with them if it's okay with y'all." The wet food lands on me. A clump of chewed up peas and mashed potatoes right on my wrist. Upset, I wipe it off and wait for them to respond to his question. Of course, they will let him to stay the night. He always gets his way.

"Yes, just make sure you've done your chores before you leave," says papa.

Nobody tells Joey to stop talking and to finish his food. So many unfair things always happen but I know as soon as I try to say anything, I'll be told to hush. He smirks at me and continues to eat his food.

He's probably not even going to Tommy's house. He's probably going to hang out at that old shed to smoke cigarettes.

****

One day last month, Joyce and Mary were riding their new bikes down the long dirt road beside the house. They had stopped dressing so much alike recently but that day, they both had decided to wear pink dresses to match the pink bicycles Lovette had gotten them. It was Joyce's idea to add on purple hair ribbons with white polka dots and to wear white flip flops. Mary hadn't been a fan of ribbons but the look on Joyce's face of excitement was enough to make her wear it.

During the ride, Joyce started to complain. "Mary,

how much longer before we get where we're going? My legs hurt and I need a break!" This was who Joyce was. It wasn't long before she'd keep asking about where they were headed.

"We'll be there in just a few more minutes. Remember what I said. Keep quiet and do everything I do" said Mary. Even though she may have questioned some of the things Mary had asked her to do, Joyce was always willing to go along with everything.

Leading them into an open field, Mary spots the single old shed surrounded by neglected land. The windows were busted out and looked as if the wind was going to send it away at any given moment.

"Get off of your bike and follow me," instructed Mary.

Dropping the bikes and whispering for her sister to keep quiet, Mary slowly walked up to the shed with Joyce following. The first step's noise was loud enough to give away their presence. Placing her hand over Joyce's mouth without looking at her, Mary could sense the terror she knew her sister had felt.

"Be quiet and be still," she whispered. Joyce nodded her head with her eyes still wide. Her saliva coats Mary's hand. Gross by its contact, she snatches her hand away and wipes it on her dress in disgust.

Waiting for him to come out hollering that he's caught them spying, neither of them move. When enough time has passed, Mary leads Joyce over to the window. She finally is able to show her sister what she's known for a while now.

It's Joey. He's standing up in a corner drinking out of a red cup. He was always filthy as if his parents didn't have multiple bathrooms for him to shower in. Wearing an old raggedy t-shirt and ripped up jeans, he scratches the back of his head. Putting his drink down on the floor, he lights a cigarette and coughs. Another thing he managed to keep hidden from his parents. Mary and Joyce both wait for what Mary knows is about to happen next.

"Mary, why did you bring me here? I don't want to spend all day looking at Joey do stupid boy stuff. Let's go," whispered Joyce.

Staring at her with a face that says, "Shut up and wait," he walks to the middle of the room that has an old brown rug in place. Bending down to pull at the shaggy ends, Joey sits in a squatting position. Tossing his halfway smoked cigarette in the dirty corner, he moves the rug to the side and pulls up the floor door. When he walks down inside, Joyce gasps as they watch the door shut.

****

"You hear me girl? I think we need to get your ears checked because I've never had to repeat myself so much!" Looking up at mama, she continues.

"Go clean your plate and get ready for bed."

I'm the he only one left sitting at the table, I get up and do what I'm told.

Chapter 2: Mary

July 8, 1999

There's knocking at the door. Looking over to the window, the sun isn't even awake yet. Staring back towards the ceiling and wrapping my blanket tighter around me, I wait for the sound of mama's slippers to scurry downstairs. After a couple of minutes, there's still no sound of slippers. There's no sound of water running, so she can't be in the shower. The knocking becomes louder, and then screaming begins.

Joyce runs over to my bed, jumps behind me and presses her back against the wall. "Should we go see who it is?" My sister had her brave moments, but they didn't always happen at the right time. Right now wasn't one of those times for her to be brave.

"No, let mama go first. Go to your safe place."

"Joseph Marks! Open this damn door before I kick it in!" the voice booms. Both of us jump and Joyce runs back to her side of the room. Rolling over in my bed and dropping to the floor, I scoot under my safe place. Taking a deep breath in, all of the dust makes me sneeze.

Now, I regret not cleaning under here as good as I should have. Pushing the blanket up and looking towards the door, those pink slippers quickly run by. Before she can get all the way down the steps, the unwanted guest has started to invite themselves in. The banging ends and is followed by a loud crash.

"Where is Joey?!" A male's voice screams along

with the sound of the front door meeting the hardwood floor. "You have 3 seconds to tell me where that no-good son of yours is before it gets ugly in here!" Not sure who could be this upset so early in the morning, but he definitely means business.

What has Joey has gotten himself into now? Whatever it is, I'm sure he did it. Papa usually leaves for work before everyone wakes up and I begin to get scared for mama being downstairs alone with this crazy person.

"MY DOOR! You couldn't wait a few seconds for me to put some clothes on and get down here?! Now, who's gonna pay for this to get fixed? And what is this nonsense about Joey so early in the morning?" Her voice is shaking and the screams only get louder. I hear her struggling to pick the door up only for it to fall again.

"You're drunk. You need to leave. If you want to speak to Joey, you can when his father gets home," says mama.

I can't let mama be down there too long by herself. "Stay here and don't move unless you hear one of us scream for help. If we do, go into their room and call papa to come home." Sliding from underneath the bed and heading towards the door, I quietly make my way downstairs.

The vanity makes me stop. My palms are sweaty and my hair is a mess. My right eye begins to twitch and there is a pain in my bottom lip. "We don't have time for this right now, Mary. Go help mama," I whisper. Tip toeing down the rest of the stairs, there is a hole staring back at me where the front door used to be.

Will. Fat belly, baldheaded Will. He works with papa and is always drunk. His hands are in his pockets and there's water dripping from all over him but it's not raining outside.

"I want to speak with him now! Quite frankly, this doesn't concern you, so I would advise you to get your husband and son home now so we can settle this matter!" Will is always loud. So much for using inside voices.

"Now, you know Joe works early in the morning. The same place you should be! Either tell me what's going on or get the hell out before I call the police!" says Mama while backing up into her plant and knocking it over. Dirt spills everywhere and the pot breaks into tiny pieces. Dropping to the floor after trying to catch it, she begins to cry.

Mr. Baldheaded Will stops pacing, looks down at mama and walks towards her. Making my way down the last step, I walk towards the both of them. Mama is still on the floor and holds her hand up to stop me.

"This doesn't concern you. Everything is fine. Now, go on back upstairs and get yourself cleaned up for breakfast." Standing still and refusing to leave her with this looney bird, she gives up and tosses dirt at his pants.

Turning to look at me, he pauses. The look on his face doesn't seem angry anymore. He just stares at me and doesn't say anything. My heart starts to beat really fast and I'm sure they both can hear it. "Do you know where your brother is, Joyce? Shit. I meant Mary."

"She doesn't know where he is, so get the hell on

somewhere!" screamed mama.

Ignoring her, he walks over to me and bends down in my face. His breath smells so bad that it forces me to take a step back. Turning my head away from the smell, Joyce is standing next to the vanity. Will follows my head movement to see what I'm looking at. "Is Joey up there?" he whispers.

Before I could answer, Papa walks through the hole.

"Will, in my office. Now."

****

"Were you scared, Mary?" Looking up from the bathroom sink, Joyce is standing in the doorway with swollen eyes. She sniffles and keeps talking. "What did Joey do? Where is he at?"

Joey sneaks out in the middle of the night almost every night, so there are a number of places he could be. I'm sure he'll be here any minute now trying to sneak his way back in.

"Scared? For mama, yes. I'm sure papa will fix everything. Don't worry about it," I say.

The sun has finally decided to get out of bed and is shining through the bathroom on my shoulder. Walking over towards the window, I open it. Taking in its morning breath, the breeze pushes my hair back. Lying my head on the windowsill, a touch on my back makes me jump.

"Do you want to look in the mirror today?" whispers Joyce.

Lifting my head up and looking back towards the mirror, I nod. We both stand in front of the sink. I stare and then the sweating begins. It's hard to breathe and my throat feels tight. My head tells me to let some air in and to look away but my heart tells me to keep staring. Her hand touches my shoulder and she turns towards our reflection.

"You have to breathe, Mary." We haven't done this together in a long time. Taking my hand, she repeats herself. "You have to breathe, or the same thing will happen like last time," said Joyce.

"Does your head hurt yet?" Joyce asks. This always happens. It's the same feeling every time we do this. Forcing myself to blink, my knees feel weak. Stumbling into the shower curtain, she catches me before I fall in.

"We have to be careful," she whispers.

"Okay, you're right. Who knows what he'll do if he finds out again?" I say.

"Find out what?" Look who's home. Looking as if he has just got done rolling around with a bunch of pigs, Joey stands in the doorway and is dirty as usual. I just don't understand why someone would want to go around looking like that all the time.

"Nothing" we both say at the same time. He stares as if he doesn't believe us.

"It doesn't look like nothing in here. Tell me or I'm going to tell them what you're up here doing." Joey is just about as smart as a bag of rocks. Doesn't know what we're are doing but he's willing to go make up a story. What an idiot.

"None of your business, so just leave. I'm using the bathroom." I try to close the door in Joey's face. Sticking his foot in the crack of the door, he pushes it back open.

"You think you can just do whatever you want, huh? You're just a child. You better tell me or..."

"OR WHAT?!?" I scream at the top of my lungs. He constantly bothers me for no reason. Breathing hard, I lower my voice so that Mama can't hear, "If you don't get out of here, I'll tell them about that stupid shed you keep going to."

The look on his face told me that Mama and Papa didn't know about it. Looking past the dirt, his skin turns pale. Now that I know this is one of his secrets, I wish I would have said this a long time ago. Maybe he would've been left me alone.

His bright blue eyes stare me down for a few seconds and for a moment, he looked like the devil himself. The hair on my arms stand up and before I know it, Joey has his hands around my neck. The more I struggle to get free, the tighter he squeezes. Falling to the floor and clawing at his face, I feel his skin roll up underneath my nails.

He's going to kill me. My eyes begin to burn. I can hear Joyce screaming for help.

"JOEY, LET GO! MAMA! PAPA! HELP! HELP!!" screams Joyce. It's as if no one hears her.

Trying my best to kick the floor as hard as I can, the

smell of burning bacon instantly hits me and I hear the slippers scurry. He starts to jerk my neck around and bangs my head on the black and white tile. Over...and over...and over again.

Mama. She struggles to pull Joey off me with the help of Joyce beating on his back as if it were a drum. He finally gives. The air slowly comes back through my throat and I can't stop coughing. My chest burns so bad and my ears hurt.

Jumping up as if nothing just happened, Joey runs out of the bathroom and down the stairs. The cries of mama and Joyce force me to keep my eyes shut from seeing their faces. The look I know they will have will only make me feel worse. Rolling over on my side and touching the back of my head, it's wet. Forcing myself to finally open my eyes, the tiles have gained another color.

"Mama, we have to take her to the hospital!" screams Joyce. My whole body hurts. We argue all the time but not once has Joey attacked me like this. Yea, he can be a bully but he's never hit me. My ears are ringing so loud and my leg begins to jerk. The cries have gotten quiet and the ringing in my ears has gotten even louder.

Where's papa? Did he not hear all of this going on? My tears come down even harder than before. Why was it so hard for him to see me as one of the other kids? I've seen him smile at Mama and have fun with Joey and Joyce but it's like I'm invisible. The beating Joey just gave me was invisible to him. Why wasn't papa up here?!

Scooping me up from the floor, Mama takes me to the bedroom and softly puts me in my bed.

"Mama, I'm sorry you burned the bacon because of me." The look in her eyes told me how much she was hurting.

"Don't you be sorry. You've been through a lot only in a morning's time. Bacon isn't that good anyway." She was always so gentle. Oh, and she loved bacon, so I knew she was only saying that to make me feel better. Kissing me on the forehead, she moves my hair out of my face. "Don't move. I'll be right back."

Sitting up in my bed, Joyce comes to sit next to me. Putting her head on my shoulder, she doesn't say anything. She's still crying. Walking back in the door, Mama gives me that look when I've done something I wasn't supposed to do.

"I thought I told you not to move. Joey put a whoopin' on you and you need to lie down in bed for a while." Placing a bowl of water on the floor and wringing out a washcloth, she wipes my face. I point to the back of my head for her to look at.

"I've called Dr. Oar to come over immediately to look at that. Baby, tell me what happened?" said mama.

Before I could answer her question, Joey's screams begin to echo throughout the house. Staring me in the eyes, mama doesn't move.

"Why is Joey downstairs screaming?"

"Don't worry about it. Now, place your hands in this bowl and tell me what happened," she said.

The water turns light red and pieces of Joey's face

float from under my nails. Picking up a piece of his skin, I rub it in between my fingers. It's rubbery and sticky.

Counting how many pieces are in the bowl, there are seven. There won't ever be a next time he hurts me again. 7 scratches on his face to remind him to never touch me again. I'll probably rub some dirt in his sores while he sleeps to make sure.

"We can talk about it later but you're not moving from this bed for the rest of the day" says mama. Her voice sounds so tired but she managed to laugh before talking again.

"I remember the first school dance I went to. Your grandmother and grandfather had a fit, child! Thought about clawing at this one girl just like you had."

Mama told the best stories from when she was younger. Using a washcloth, she gently washed my hands and pressed it against the back of my head.

Taking a towel to dry me off, I felt as if I would pass out just from her pressing on my head. Placing a bandage over it until the doctor was able to come look at it, she paused and said nothing for a few seconds.

Taking the bowl from me and getting up from her knees, we all lie down in the bed together. With me in the middle, she squeezes me tight and keeps talking.

****

December 17th, 1981

Out of all the high school boys, Lovette wanted

none of them. They were immature and just wanted to play around too much. All of them were gross and acted as if they were still in elementary school. But, all of them wanted her and would stop at nothing to have a chance. This was their senior year and the annual "Winter Wonderland" dance was this weekend.

Unsure if she was going to attend the dance, she had yet to choose someone to go with. It's high school; no one goes to dances alone or they'd risk people thinking they were a loser for the next few weeks. Either she would have a date or she wouldn't go at all.

"Heyyyyy, Love. How you doin', sweetheart?" Closing her locker and sucking her teeth, she already knew which annoying person it was. Michael O'Conner. Mike was handsome and had the prettiest smile but he had a horrible reputation when it came to dating. The school year had just started a few months ago and he had already had at least 4 girlfriends. Rubbing his face and pressing his charm, he leaned against the locker and smiled even harder.

"What do you want, Mike?" said Lovette while clearly annoyed. He may have been good looking but Lovette wouldn't let him know that. He had enough females telling him that daily and the last thing she needed was for him to think she was anything like the other girls.

"Awww, Love. Don't be like that! I was just coming to see who you were going to the dance with. You know everyone is going. So, I hope you are too."

Looking up at his 6'3 frame and taking in his scent, she thought about being nicer to him for a change but then shook the thought off quickly.

"Why do you care? I'm sure you already have your date picked out" said Lovette. Mike's smile quickly turned upside down. She had assumed the same thing he had assumed about her. Being that they both were two of the most popular people in school, both just knew the other had a date already.

"Actually, I don't. If you haven't found a date yet, I'd like to take you. I already know what you think of me but it's just prom. We can go as friends and if you still decide that I'm whatever person you already think I am, I won't bother you again. Nothing wrong with gaining an extra friend, right?" He had laid it on thick. Even though he was used to getting his way with most females, Lovette still made him nervous and she could hear it in his voice.

Many girls had certain reputations throughout Brightfield-Heights High. There was a sophomore named Sharon who would have sex with any boy who wanted to have sex with her. The craziest part of the rumors about her is that she never denied doing those things. It was as if she wanted everyone to know and think that she was involved in everything people said about her.

Then, there was Brenda. Brenda did everything except actual intercourse. Somehow, she convinced herself that it meant she was still holy because of it and that it wasn't a sin. Somebody must've fallen asleep during that part in Sunday school.

But, Lovette? No one had any type of dirt on her because she hadn't done anything worth talking about. Most people would consider her stuck up until they got to know her but, that was it. She was different in Mike's eyes and all he wanted was a chance to show her he wasn't as bad like people had thought he was.

Mike had a crush on Lovette ever since he first saw her walk into a math class they shared last year. She stumbled in wearing a bright yellow sundress and her curly orange hair sat perfectly on her freckled shoulders. As soon as her books went crashing towards the floor, Mike was the first one out of his seat to help. She thanked him and sat down in her seat without even looking him in the face. Breaking his thoughts from the past, she started laughing.

"So, you're telling me that Mr. Player himself doesn't have a date yet? Hmph!" said Lovette while still laughing at the same time. She didn't have a date and did want to go to prom. Before she could think about it any longer, she spit the words out he had wanted to hear.

"Listen, if I go as your date, don't expect for me to do anything with you. We're going as friends and that's it. You can pick me up at 6:30. I hope you had already planned on wearing black and call me before you come."

Quickly writing down her number and address, she shoved a piece of paper into his hands and walked off towards her next class. The one-minute bell had rung and she refused to be late. Feeling as if he had just won the lottery, Mike walked off to class with his chest puffed out.

The next day, all Mike could think about was taking Lovette as his date. He didn't want to say or do anything stupid to ruin his chances of at least gaining her as a friend. Once she gotten to know him instead of listening to what everyone else had to say, maybe she'd change her mind about him.

*As soon as the final bell rang for the daily
dismissal, he ran home to get ready. Meanwhile, Lovette
had second thoughts about going to the dance but she
didn't have a way to call and cancel. She had given Mike
her number but didn't think to ask for his.*

*"Lovette, you told the boy you'd go with him. So,
don't go backing out on him now. Plus, do you want to sit
here all night bored with me? I wish I could go out and
have fun like you. Mom and dad both treat me like a baby"
complained Lovette's younger sister, Iris.*

*Iris was Lovette's best friend and the smartest 12
year old in the neighborhood. Sometimes she would help
older kids do their homework and in return, they paid her.
Iris would save all of her money and hardly ever spent a
dime.*

*"Iris, you'll be going to dances before you know it.
I guess I won't be a bummer and get dressed." Swirling
towards the mirror, Lovette held up a black gown with
silver straps. Holding it up to her as if she were skeptical
about the choice, she asks what her sister thought about the
dress. Giving her a thumbs up, Iris ran out of the room.*

"The silver heels will go perfect," whispered
Lovette.

*Placing the final bobby pin in her hair and applying
another coat of lip gloss, the doorbell rings. Lovette had
told him to call before he was on the way. Boys never pay
attention. Running downstairs and bumping into the vanity,
a thread from her dress snagged the corner. Being careful*

not to rip her dress, she removed it and continued downstairs trying to catch the door before her mother or father got to it. She had been a couple of seconds too late.

"Why is that stupid vanity right there?!" shouted Lovette.

"Hush child, that vanity reveals true reflections," said her mother, Trudy. Turning back towards the door, she kept talking.

"You might be looking for someone next door," said Trudy. She closed the door without waiting for a response and turned around to head back to cooking dinner.

This is what she was afraid of. This is why she had wanted Mike to call her before he was on the way over. Paw was sitting in the living room and hadn't moved from his chair. Mike rang the doorbell again.

"Mom, he's my date to the dance." The look on her mother's face confirmed what Lovette suspected for so long.

"THAT BOY IS ALMOST AS BLACK AS YOUR DRESS!! You couldn't find someone else?! Why would you do this, Lovette??" That's all Paw needed to hear and he was out of his seat joining us in the foyer. While they both continued to ramble on, she stopped them both so she could have a turn to talk.

"Mom, Dad...you both said I could go to the dance tonight but never said anything about with who. Why does it even matter?! I'm the one going to the dance with him!

Plus, mom, I wish you'd stop acting like you aren't half Black yourself. Everyone knows that you were adopted. Yes, I know that grandma and grandpa aren't your real parents. Just because your skin is as light as it is, doesn't mean you can ignore what you really are."

Lovette felt the sting of a hundred bees come down on her face. This was the first time her mother had ever hit her and everyone stood in silence. Iris had seen and heard everything. She ran upstairs and shut her door while their father walked off without saying a word. Running out of the door, Lovette left her mother screaming for her to come back but all had been ignored. Meanwhile, Mike had already started to walk away.

Catching up to him and trying to catch her breath at the same time, "Mike, I'm sorry for all of that. I'm sure you heard most, if not all of it. The way she thinks...the way they think, that's not how I think. I've always suspected they had issues like this but they've never blatantly said the things they've said tonight."

"Is this why you asked me to call before I came?" Looking in his face, she could tell his feelings were hurt but he tried his best to hide it. Even though she didn't like him like he liked her, she still didn't want to see him sad. Especially if it had anything to do with her.

"Yes. My plan was to meet you at the end of the dirt road but even then, I'm pretty sure they would have insisted on meeting you anyway. Ya know, just to see who is taking their daughter out for the first time and all" replied Lovette. "But boys have to be so hardheaded and not follow directions." Giving him the side eye while sucking

her teeth, he stopped walking.

"Hardheaded? That's funny." Holding up the paper she had handed him yesterday, "Explain to me how I could've called a six digit phone number." Walking up to him and taking it out of his hands, Lovette had accidentally given him an incomplete phone number. It had been one digit too short.

"I went to call you and saw you hadn't written down the full number. At first, I thought you might have done it on purpose. Ya know, because you think I'm this or that. Anyway, I just decided to come over hoping you'd still want to go. As far as what I heard, it's okay. Believe it or not, I'm used to being judged before people get to know me," he continued.

Lovette had seen a side of Mike that she hadn't allowed herself to see before. She was wrapped up in what everyone else said about him that she didn't take the time to get to know him herself. Taking his hand into hers and looking him in the eyes, Mike got nervous.

"I know this started off weird and unexpected but can we make the night better from here on out?" said Lovette. Mike agreed and they both walked towards the school.

****

Waking up to a sandwich on the nightstand and Joyce drooling on my arm, mama had written a little note along with lunch.

"Dr. Oar came and patched up your head. So, be

gentle and STAY IN BED!!"

I don't remember falling asleep and I definitely don't remember the doctor stitching my head up. Pushing Joyce off my shoulder and sitting up in my bed with the worst headache, Joey is standing in the doorway. Along with the scratches I made, he has a new purple eye the size of a golf ball.

"I'm sorry for hurting you and I'll never do it again."

His face is blank and when he realizes I don't know what to say, he walks off to his room. At least I now know why he was screaming downstairs.

Chapter 3: "You knew the rules."

July 8, 1999

It was still dark out and Joseph had forgotten his briefcase at home. The day would be hectic without it and he just knew it would mysteriously end up missing. Pulling up to the house, there had been a familiar red pickup truck parked in his usual spot. Getting out of the car and walking up the front steps, there were wet footprints. Looking up to see a hole in the doorway, Lovette was on the floor in tears.

"She doesn't know where he is, so get the hell on somewhere!" shouted Lovette.

Barging into the house, Joseph interrupts the moment. "Will, in my office. Now."

Whispering but yet still maintaining an angry tone through clenched teeth, Joseph maintained to keep his voice to a level that his family wouldn't hear.

"What the HELL are you doing in my home? Did you touch my wife? Because if you did..." Holding up his hand and smirking, Will stopped him from making a threat he would regret later. Joseph didn't need to add fuel to this fire.

"Joseph, don't. You and I both know how terrible this could end. I've managed to calm down a bit. Your daughter helped. She has a pleasant face. Nothing like yours. Now, where is your son? I don't have all day and honestly, I'd like to get out of these clothes. I took a piss by

your lake and managed to slip in the damn thing. Almost killed myself. You should have that a fence around that thing. As nice as this house is, seems like you'd be able to afford one..."

Will had been out all night drinking with some friends. He'd been avoiding his wife due to her finding out about his numerous affairs. He was more surprised that it took her this long to even catch on. He had practically cheated right in front of her face.

Anyway, he wasn't ready to face her. She may have been a little gullible but Caron was a good woman. She didn't deserve the things Will had done to her. They'd been married for seventeen years and had only given birth to one child, Frankie.

"As you already have concluded, I'm just returning home. Apparently, my son isn't here. That still gives you no right to disrupt my household, break down my door and scare my family. You could've waited but you're too damn drunk to even think straight. What is the problem?" Joseph was becoming more and more angry. Not only did Will break into his home and frighten his family, Joey was missing and he had to be back at work soon.

Slurring his words, Will explained himself. "I know my household situation may be the talk of the town. It takes no time for everyone to pass around what they think they know. Anyhow, I skipped going home last night and went out for some drinks at the bar. I may be a little tipsy, but whatever. You've been here before. Don't forget that."

Will had decided to catch up with a few old friends at one of the town's most popular bars, Swooney's. It had helped him temporarily forget about the issues he had to face. Knowing he couldn't go home just yet, he knew there was one woman that he could always call. Brenda. He had convinced himself that he was done with all of the other women except for her. She knew exactly how he was feeling at all times and was more than just an affair. He had fallen in love with her.

Drinking his last beer at exactly closing time, Will made his way over to Brenda's house. He had been drinking and driving for so long, it seemed easier to do while under the influence. Somehow, he managed to escape being caught. Being in jail was the last place he needed to be.

Pulling up in the driveway, the house was completely dark except for the kitchen window. Brenda had given him a key a few months ago, so getting in this late would be no problem. Stumbling past the microwave, the time read 2:21 am. She'd definitely be sleep.

As soon as he reached the hallway, his phone rang. Caron. He couldn't talk to her right now. He was here and this is where he needed to be for the time being. Picking up the phone and hearing her voice asking him to come home would only make him feel guilty. Guilt was the last thing he wanted to feel at the moment. He just wanted to be with Brenda and deal with the issues tomorrow...or another day but just not right now.

Ignoring the call and staring at the phone, he let it go to voicemail. Sliding down the wall and having a seat on the floor, he waited for whatever message she would leave. His phone dinged and he listened to the message Caron left him.

"Will, you need to get home now! This isn't about us. It's about your daughter! Get here now!"

That's all he needed to hear. He loved Brenda but he loved his daughter even more.

Leaving the house in a hurry without letting Brenda know he had stopped by, Will rushed home to see what the fuss was about. He had called Caron back several times but it would only go straight to voicemail. The thoughts of whatever could be going on with Frankie made him sweat. He had just hoped she was okay. Whatever else it was couldn't be that big of an issue.

Will had started thinking maybe Caron was lying. Up until a few days ago, she had been desperate for him to talk to her about the affairs. It was definitely possible she'd go as low as using their daughter to make him come home. Slowing the car down, Will thought about turning back around to go back to Brenda's but if something were truly wrong with Frankie, he wouldn't be able to forgive himself.

Finally arriving home, there was a bike lying in the yard that didn't belong to Frankie. Opening the door, Frankie and Caron are seated in the living room. With a confused look on his face, Will walked over and stood in front of both of them.

"Well, is someone going to tell me what is going on?" he asked.

"Go ahead and tell your father what you were doing. Don't be quiet now. You were making a lot of noise

when I got here! SPEAK UP AND TELL HIM!" screamed Caron.

Walking to the liquor cabinet, Will opened up the vodka and poured himself a glass. He had felt his buzz dying down and there was no need in becoming sober when Caron was screaming like a mad woman.

"Since she'd rather sit here and cry like it's going to get her out of trouble! I guess it's on me to tell you. I come home to your daughter upstairs with Joey in her bedroom! He's like a brother to you, Frankie! I didn't want to call Lovette and get into it with her. Will, you need to fix this," said Caron.

Will stopped in his tracks and turned to look at his daughter. Frankie had shame written all over her face. Dropping her head and beginning to apologize, he cut her off mid-sentence.

"Where is he?! In my house, Frankie?! Have you lost your mind?! YOU'RE ONLY FIFTEEN! You still play with baby dolls for Christ's sake!"

Turning to Caron, Will continued to scream. "And where the hell were you?! It's almost 3 in the morning and you weren't even home to monitor our daughter!"

Pacing back and forth between the kitchen and living room, Will felt his chest getting tighter and tighter. Joseph knew the rules and one had just been broken.

"How dare you question where I was and you weren't here either!! Oh yea, was it the 20 year old this time? Or some random hooker you followed home after the

bar? Oh, must've been Brenda. Yea, Brenda. The one you fell in love with. You were planning to sleep at her place tonight, huh?"

Caron had him cornered. The look on his face proved that he didn't know she knew exactly who he had been with. Will ignored her for the moment and directed himself towards his daughter.

"Frankie, go to your room. Your mother and I need to talk. We'll deal with you later." Waiting to hear the closing of Frankie's door, Will responded.

"Regardless of where I was, I was already out. There should've been at least one of us here and if you wanted to leave out, you could've dropped her off at your mother's house. Now, look! Our daughter was left alone and has had sex!" shouted Mike.

Even though Frankie's situation was important, his ego had been bruised. Although he had constantly cheated on her, he still loved Caron. The thought of her being with someone else did hurt but if she had, he deserved it.

"Yea, go ahead and blame me. I don't even care where you've been or who you've been doing it with. You just need to speak with Joseph about Joey before it causes problems within me and Lovette's friendship. Oh, and take some clothes with you. Unless you're here to remove your things, I don't want you hanging around here anymore. Put Brenda's key to good use," sneered Caron.

That stopped him in his tracks. He cared for Caron but deep down he had only wanted to know how she knew about the key. Deciding to act quick, Will headed for their *bedroom and packed his things. She already knew everything and there was no need in denying it.*

Bumping into everything for almost an hour, Will finally got everything he needed at the moment. Brenda had been asking him to move in for the past few months, so he knew showing up with his bags would make her happy. Grabbing the liquor bottle and rushing out, he got into his truck and left. He'd first stop at Joseph's house.

"...and that's why I'm here, Joseph. You didn't stick to your part of things. Your son had sex with my daughter!" Will hadn't slept since the day before, so the alcohol and plus being tired had started weighing down on him. Trying not to nod off, he stood up and started pacing around Joseph's office.

Joseph hadn't seen his son since after dinner last night. Joey had gone up bed and that was the last time he had saw him. He had a history of sneaking out but it had been awhile and he thought his son had learned from being punished. He had touched the one girl he had grown up with and this alone had Joseph steaming. Trying to calm down, Joseph responded.

"I think you know that this has to be a big misunderstanding. Joey and Frankie are like siblings. He's never even shown any interest in her," said Joseph. There was no point in Joseph returning back to the office today. Will wasn't in his right mind and the family had needed him home.

"You better hope this is a misunderstanding but we'll get to the bottom of everything. I'll be out of the office today, as you can see. I'll talk to my daughter but keep your

son away from her," said Will.

Will stormed out of the office and started up his car. Meanwhile, he had managed to miss Joey by seconds. He had quietly snuck into the house and made his way upstairs.

Leaving out behind him, Joseph went out in the garage to search for his tools. The front door didn't seem too badly damaged and he figured he could fix it himself. Will would compensate him if he found any damages beyond what he could repair. Shaking his head and entering the garage, a feeling of grief came over him due to the things that could happen from the can his son had just opened. Will was clearly still intoxicated but that didn't mean Joseph would take his threat lightly.

Back in the house, Joey had heard his sister in the bathroom talking. "Okay, you're right. Who knows what he'll do if he finds out again?" said Mary.

"Find out what?" questioned Joey.

The both of them had gone back and forth about Mary not telling him what she had been up to in the bathroom. Before he knew it, she was in his face.

"If you don't get out of here, I'll tell them about that stupid shed you keep going to." The shed. He hadn't known that Mary knew about it. His veins felt cold and the blood flowing through them felt like they had become frozen.

He had no idea how she had known about it. The only one who knew was…their father. Joey knew for sure *that his father wouldn't tell her. Shaking his head to rid thinking beyond this moment, before he knew it… "darkness".*

He had his hands wrapped around Mary's throat. The voice in his head told him to squeeze harder. She needed to be silenced. Although she could make no noise, she still fought back by clawing at his face. The scratches made his skin sting and it had angered him even more. Instantly, he had switched to banging her head against the floor.

"Kill her. She knows too much for someone who barely knows anything at all. Finish this, Joey" the voices kept whispering. He could never control the voices once things had gotten to a certain point. She had to go. This wasn't up to him anymore.

Running up the stairs to see what the commotion was about, Lovette was met by Joey's back facing the bathroom door. All she could see under him were Mary's fuzzy socks and her head being thrown around as if she were a ragdoll.

Trying her best to pull him off of her, he finally released his hold. There was a puddle of blood under her child's head and her body was still. For a moment, she just knew she was dead until Mary rolled over. Dropping to her knees and sobbing like a baby, Lovette had felt helpless.

Leaving quickly out of the bathroom as if he didn't care what he had just done to his sister, Joey headed downstairs.

"You shouldn't have come home. You're not

welcome here. Just leave, Joey." The voices wouldn't stop. Pounding himself on the side of his head, he headed for the back door. As soon as he stepped outside, Joseph looked up from the garage and immediately stood up from the ground. Just the person he had needed to see.

"WHERE IN THE HELL HAVE YOU BEEN? AND WHERE DO YOU THINK YOU'RE GOING?!" Joey stood still and dared not move.

"Come down the rest of the path and face me man to man...since that is what you are now, right? Since you make your own decisions at fifteen now, huh?" Joey continued to be quiet and didn't move an inch. "SPEAK UP, NOW!"

Making an instant decision to run back in the house, Joseph chased after his son. Joey hadn't had a chance to make it to the foyer before Joseph had caught him by the back of his neck. Snatching him with the quickness, Joseph had slammed him face first into the wall. Screaming as if he were dying, Joey tried his best to fight back.

"Do you have any idea what kind of position you put me in? DO YOU?! I've had you repeat me the rules several times and you've looked me in my face agreeing that you understood. Frankie?! Out of all the girls in school, you just had to be caught with her?! You know better!" With that being said, Joseph spun his son around to face him.

"Dad, I didn't..." Before Joey could complete his sentence, his father had come down with several blows to his face and chest. Joey's pained screams echoed throughout the house. Walking down the stairs and past the
pg. 44

altercation as if it were nonexistent, Lovette walked into the kitchen to fix a bowl of water to tend to Mary. He was her son but the condition her daughter was in, she needed her more at the moment.

"Don't you move!" Leaving his son against the wall, Joseph entered the kitchen to let his wife know what had just happened. Feeling his presence and turning around to face him, Lovette had blood on her that wasn't once there. Her eyes were red from crying.

"I walked in on Joey attacking Mary. She's in pretty bad shape. I just called Dr. Oar to come look at her. I'm sure she's gonna need a few stitches in the back of her head" said Lovette.

She had sounded and looked exhausted. Putting the bowl down and hugging her, Joseph responded. The anger he had just released had begun to consume him all over again.

"Will's unexpected visit was because Joey was caught in Frankie's room," said Joseph.

Staring in space as if she didn't hear what her husband had just told her, Lovette released herself from his hold and proceeded to go tend to Mary.

Walking back out in the hall, Joey was in the same position. "Dad…" Cutting him off before he could finish his sentence, Joseph held up his hand and spoke.

"When your sister is feeling well, you will apologize. Also, if you ever place a finger on anyone in this house again, consider that your last day on earth. Go up to

your room and so help me God, if you step foot out of this house without my knowledge..."

Staring face to face and almost nose to nose, Joey was confused but he also knew not to go against anything his father had just demanded of him. Dismissing his son to his bedroom, Joseph went back outside to get started on fixing the front door.

Meanwhile, Lovette had been telling a story that she knew would relax her child. Out of all her children, Mary had been the most like Lovette. She had cherished these moments because childhood was very short. Before she knew it, the children would be grown and the house would feel empty without them. As soon Mary had drifted off to sleep, Joseph had entered the bedroom with Dr. Oar.

"I'm just gonna give her something to numb the pain and she may sleep for a while with this one" mumbled the doctor. The gash on the back of Mary's head was ugly but nothing he couldn't fix. Placing the last stitch and slipping off the latex gloves, he sighed before talking again.

"It doesn't look infected and she should feel better within a couple of days. I'll leave something for the pain in case she starts complaining. Use these to keep it covered for the next day" he said while handing Lovette some gauze pads. "If she complains of dizziness, give me a call. She needs to rest for the next couple of days, so make her stay in bed."

Joseph walked Dr. Oar to the driveway while Lovette went to clean up the mess in the bathroom. Getting the mop and her cleaning products, Lovette wept. Her tears met the puddle of blood on the floor and it made her cry even harder. Her son was acting out and her daughter was in pain. Letting her tears only last a minute, she refused to let it consume her. Finishing the floor, she closed the bathroom and headed to speak with Joey.

Pushing open her son's bedroom door, he sat on the edge of his bed with his head hung. Hearing the door open didn't make him budge and he kept his eyes towards the floor.

"Stand up and look at me," demanded Lovette. Instantly standing to his feet, Joey looked down into his mother's eyes.

"What in the world were you thinking? How could you do something like that to your sister?! What did she say? What did she do for you to do such a thing to her? It's been a long time since you've…" and stopping herself, she knew what it was.

"Have you been taking your medicine?" Staring off as if he heard nothing she said, Lovette screamed. "Answer me!"

Walking over to the dresser next to his bed, Joey pulled out his prescription bottle. It had been full. He hadn't taken his meds for almost two weeks. Lovette wanted to scream at him some more but she knew this would do her son no good. Instantly, she felt bad for ignoring the signs that this could've been a possibility.

"I know it gets hard but you need those, baby. What do you remember?" asked Lovette. She walked over and embraced her oldest child. Pulling away from her, he did exactly what she knew he would.

The process. Pacing. Shaking. Sit. Stand. Sit. Stand. Head drop and then, the tears. This happened every time Joey tried to remember. Sometimes he would eventually remember but when he did, it would be too late. It hurt her heart that he had to deal with this.

He had started the medicine about 8 months ago when Lovette noticed how much he would lash out over minor things. If the girls were playing too loud or if dinner wasn't what he had wanted, things would spiral out of control quick.

Before Joey started the medicine, therapy had been suggested but during his second visit, Joey threatened to kill his therapist in her sleep. One morning, she woke up to her front door being wide open. After that, she had refused to continue their sessions and Lovette had been scared to make him see anyone else.

The medicine had seemed to be working. The bi-polar episodes and blackouts had reduced significantly. Although he still snuck out of the house often, peace in the household was worth not punishing him for breaking that one rule. Somehow, trading doing what he wanted for a calm environment was worth it to Lovette.

"I know you don't know what all just happened but I need you to do as I say. When your sister is feeling better, apologize for hurting her. Tell her you'll never do it again. I'm sorry I didn't catch this sooner. Take your medicine immediately, okay? I'll get that face cleaned up as well," said Lovette.

Standing in the doorway to his sister's room, Joey watched Mary as she read a piece of paper. Looking up at
pg. 48

him, her skin was pale and looked as if she had seen someone who had risen from the dead.

"I'm sorry for hurting you and I'll never do it again," said Joey. He showed no emotion at all.

Lovette heard the apology and watched him walk towards his bedroom. She didn't stop her husband from attacking her son and weighed heavy on her. Joey's condition was still fairly new and she knew that Joseph lashed out without thinking. She had been so fixed on Mary that she didn't care for her own child who had no control over what he had just done. If she ever felt like a bad parent, today had been that day.

Chapter 4: Joey

July 8, 1999

Lovette and Joseph had decided to turn in to bed early. The kids were in their rooms and only Joey was wide awake. He had plans to hang out with his friends for the night. Waiting on their signal, a rock hit the bedroom window's glass. They were here.

Placing his black hoodie over his short dark curls, Joey quietly exited the bedroom. It was just after 12 am and he knew his parents would be sleep by now. Finally reaching the back door and grabbing his father's extra set of keys, he was met by Tommy and Jaxon. Both boys been his best friends since kindergarten.

"What took you so long, slow poke? Your parents haven't gone to bed yet?" said Jaxon while playfully punching him in the arm. Jaxon had been the only one who had decided to ride his bike. Tommy and Joey both were on foot and all three were headed to hang out at a nearby lake with some of their other friends.

Lake Peele had been one of the best spots for teenagers to hang out. Most of the time, someone would sneak in alcohol for them and they would all hang out until the sun came up. Once morning time showed its face, they'd all rush back home trying to be back before their parents knew they were gone.

"Look what I scored, fellas." Pulling a big plastic bag out of his sweater, Jaxon held it up. Pot. Joey had done

it before but he came home smelling like it and Lovette caught him attempting to sneak snacks up to his room. She made him swear he'd never do it again followed by a lecture of how it was the beginning of him being hooked on drugs, going to jail and being a criminal for the rest of his life. She had convinced him all of these things would happen if he continued to smoke marijuana. His mother sure did know how to convince him quickly.

"I'll pass tonight. I just want to hang out for a while," replied Joey. Both boys shrugged their shoulders and agreed it would be more for them had he not wanted any.

"Let's stop at Frankie's before we go there. I'll be quick. I'm trying to convince her to come out tonight but she's being a chicken. Her mom isn't home and she's being a stick in the mud following her rules. I told her I'd stop by before heading to the lake," said Jaxon.

Frankie was one of Joey's friends and Jaxon's "thing of the month." He had warned her about him but she thought she knew best and still continued to see Jaxon. The gut feeling that Joey got from hearing her name told him not to go but he had just turned down drugs from his closest friends, so he didn't want continue going against everything they had wanted to do tonight.

Agreeing to take a quick stop by her house, they all headed there. As soon as they had reached her yard, Jaxon dropped his bike in the yard and knocked on the front door. With Tommy and Joey behind him, Frankie answered the door in nothing but her underwear and bra.

"Shit, Jaxon! You could've told me you weren't

going to be alone!" Slamming the door and running upstairs to throw some clothes on, all three of them laughed on the porch. Frankie was a slim girl but the camel toe she had going on down south couldn't have been more hilarious.

Coming back to the door with an embarrassed look on her face, she rolled her eyes and let them all three inside the house. Her parents had been clearly stuck in the 70's. The furniture had been outdated and it even smelled the way it looked. Everything was either brown, orange, green or yellow. It had definitely been sore on the eyes.

"I hope you didn't come to try and get me to come out tonight. I already told you I ain't going so don't bother asking. Oh, and y'all can't stay long." Rolling her eyes again and sucking her teeth, Frankie plopped down on the couch and continued eating her popcorn. She had been watching "Friends" and the episode when Ross had issues with knowing how to flirt had been airing.

"Why are you watching this corny mess? You could be hanging out by the lake with us. Let me talk to you for a second." Jaxon tickled her and led her upstairs. As soon as they got to the top, he hollered down at Tommy and Joey.

"Hey, one of y'all come up here and be on the lookout just in case one of her parents comes home and sit on the steps just in case. We'll be quick." Jaxon winked at them, laughed and closed her bedroom door.

"Man, hurry up and don't take all night! I could've stayed home for this. Keep it in your pants!" shouted Joey. He sat in the middle of the staircase while Tommy sat near the back door. Not even 15 minutes had passed before they

both heard the front door open and shut.

*"YOUR MOM IS HOME!" shouted Joey while
laughing and running past Frankie's mother, Caron.
Meanwhile, Tommy had slipped out the back door and they
both made a run for their own houses. They wouldn't make
it to the lake tonight and at this point, Joey no longer cared
to.*

*Hollering like a mad woman, Caron shouted for
Frankie to come downstairs. Pushing Jaxon in her closet
and motioning for him to be quiet, she put back on her
clothes and ran downstairs.*

****

*A few minutes into his jog home, the voices started.
"Go. You haven't been in a while. No one will know that
you were there," they whispered. Shaking his head trying
to rid the thoughts, Joey knew he shouldn't go. He had only
visited a few times and that was because he had followed
his dad there. This had been the reason he found out about
the shed.*

*"Go see her. You haven't visited in a while. I'm
sure she'd want to see you." Joey pulled out a pack of
cigarettes and lit one. Taking a long pull, he turned around
and headed towards the open field. Finally reaching the
building, he went inside and sat in the only chair in the
single room.*

*Still sitting in the chair, the voices told him to open
the floor door. Slapping the side of his head, he began to
scream.*

"Get out! I can think for myself! I don't need you here! GET OUT!!" Accidentally hitting himself in the nose, it began to bleed and Joey blacked out.

When he finally came to, he hadn't been sure how long he was knocked out. The sun had come up and he had been in the chair the entire time. His lip had been covered in blood that now looked brown.

Staring at the floor, Joey pulled the rug out of the way only to see that the door had a new padlock. Becoming anxious, he pulled his father's set of keys out of his pocket and one by one, he tried each key. None of them had fit.

"I'LL FIND A WAY TO GET TO YOU!" he screamed. Going into a rage, he slammed his fists on the door and stormed out of the shed heading for home.

****

The next thing Joey had remembered, his father had him pinned up against a wall just past the foyer. His face was smashed against the wall and Joseph was furious.

"Do you have any idea what kind of position you put me in? DO YOU?! I've had you repeat me the rules several times and you've looked me in my face agreeing that you understood. Frankie?! Out of all the girls in school, you just had to touch her! You know better!"

Joey was confused. He hadn't touched Frankie at all or let alone speak to her. He remember that he was given a list of rules to follow when it came to his father's business but he hadn't gone against any of them.

Joseph spun his son around to face him and as soon

as Joey tried to tell him he didn't touch Frankie, his father began hitting him. Between the attacks, Lovette had come downstairs. Walking past them as if she didn't see what was happening, Joey was saddened at the fact his mother didn't come to his rescue. His father had never come down on him so hard to the point where he had to place hands on him.

Screaming at his son not to move, Joseph stormed off in the kitchen. Standing against the wall, Joey silently wept. He hadn't done anything for his father to treat him in such a harsh way. He wasn't sure what Frankie had told her parents but he need to make things clear. The hard part about everything was that he had a hard time remembering things sometimes. Sometimes, he didn't remember things at all.

Several minutes had passed before his father stormed back out in the hallway. "When your sister is feeling well, you will apologize. Also, if you ever place a finger on anyone in this house again, consider that your last day on earth. Go up to your room and so help me God, if you step foot out of this house without my knowledge..." threatened Joseph.

Joey was shocked and confused. His father told him he had been physical with someone and this couldn't be any further away from the truth. He hadn't hurt Frankie, Tommy or Jaxon. Did he hurt his mother? Is that why she came downstairs with blood on her? And why did he have to apologize to his sister? Was she the one he had hurt? His thoughts were rushing and the faster they became, the more he would become confused. Joseph demanded he go upstairs at once and Joey made himself disappear.

Entering his room, Joey sat at the edge of his bed. All he had wanted to do was go hang with his friends and come back home before his parents realized he had been missing. Instead, it turned into him being attacked by his father and having to apologize to his sister.

Moments later, Lovette walked into the room disturbing his thoughts. "Stand up and look at me," she ordered. Following her demand, he stood up and looked directly into her eyes. The next few moments were filled with many questions from Lovette trying to figure out what had happened between Joey and Mary. The confused look and his recent behavior had eventually set off a light bulb in Lovette's head.

Taking a pause from her interrogation, she whispered, "Have you been taking your medicine?" When Lovette wasn't satisfied with his response time, she shouted for him to answer her.

The scream made him shutter and he instantly remembered he had stopped taking the medicine a couple of weeks ago because he didn't like the way they made him feel. He had stopped hanging out with his friends and instead, he would be sitting in his room for hours. Most of the time, the room would be dark and he would just sit there. The voices had stopped but it brought on plenty of sadness.

Walking over to the nightstand, he handed his mother the container. The next few moments involved his mother hugging him and asking him to try and remember what had happened. It had been a fail and resulted in him he crying from so much confusion.

Lovette told him to take his medicine and how he still needed to apologize to his sister. He and Mary didn't get a long much but he had never hit her before. The possibility of him hurting her upset him. He did as he was told and headed to apologize.

As soon as he got to the bedroom door, Mary was sitting up reading something. For a moment, he thought about just leaving and never coming back. The way his dad had treated him today, there would be no chance anyone would miss him.

Staring at her for the next couple of seconds, Mary looked up at him and the shocked look on her face told him that he had done something awful to her. Doing as both of his parents had instructed, he apologized and walked away.

Chapter 5: "Ps: Invitation Only."

October 30, 1999

Lovette had been running around all day as if she were a chicken with its head cut off in an attempt to get everything situated for one of her favorite events: The Mark's Halloween masquerade. This had been her second favorite time of the year, Christmas being first.

This would be the seventh year she would host the event and it gave her a natural high. Although help had been hired, nothing pleased her more to add her own touch to things. Everything had been a bit stressful in the house for the past few months and a good party would help loosen the tension.

With multiple people in and out of the house all day, it was hard to keep up with who was who and who was supposed to be doing what. Normally, the same people were hired but a few new faces were in the mix.

Stepping outside to take a moment to breathe, Lovette had noticed Mary sitting on her swing set. She began to kick her feet in order to swing higher and as soon as Lovette was satisfied that her child was content, she turned to walk back into the house.

"PUSH ME HIGHER!" yelled Mary. Stopping Lovette in her tracks, she didn't bother to turn around. Taking a deep breath in and holding back her tears, she continued on back into the house. Guest would be here soon and there was still a lot she had to do. Today would be a good day.

Constantly bumping into people, Lovette made her way to the backyard. The scenery was nothing short of amazing. The dark yet enticing decorations made it easier to be out in the humid night-time in Shawford, Alabama.

The lights were a sight to see and would be the main attraction once the sun decided to retire for the evening. She threw these parties inside and out for those who wanted the beauty throughout the night. Plus, all of the liquor being passed around would make them all feel as if they needed to take in the night's air at some point.

Walking up from behind and catching his wife in her usual party gaze, Joseph placed his hands on her hips and his chin inside the crook of her neck. He felt her tense up and then soon relaxed once she realized it had been him.

"I enjoy seeing how happy all of this makes you. Just wishing my clever wife would take heed to my advice, apply her talent and start her own business. The work speaks for itself," whispered Joseph.

Time after time, he had tried to convince Lovette to start a party planning business to occupy her time but she constantly refused. He didn't want to pressure her into doing anything she didn't want to do but every time he saw how much she loved planning parties, he couldn't help but think it would do her some good to have her own business. She could have something of her very own.

"Ha! How many years has it been and you're still singing that same ol' tune? Is this my husband's attempt at pushing me to work so he can stop paying for all of the shoes he claims I don't wear? Tisk tisk." Turning around and smiling into his face, Lovette's smile turned into laughter.

"I'll cut back on the shopping if you promise to never mention running a business again. Anyway, you know I enjoy being home with you and the kids. Starting a business would take me away from that. Who would do all of the cleaning and cleaning? You? Yea right!"

Joseph leaned down and Lovette stood on the tips of her toes. Closing the significant space between the two, they kissed.

"Now, I need your height. I don't feel like falling off that raggedy ladder tonight," said Lovette.

"Oh, I just dropped the kids off with Lacy. Mary had a hard time getting off of the swing, as usual. Then, she had a hard time getting out of the car. I think we need to rethink…" and before he could finish his sentence, Lovette had cut him off.

"Joe…let us just enjoy the night. Mary will be okay. We can revisit this tomorrow but just not tonight." With that being said, Joseph nodded his head and accepted his wife's wishes; something he had always done.

The both of them walked back inside and stopped to admire the dining room table's spread. Lovette had loved to go all out for her guests. After all, the party consisted of people she and Joseph felt were important.

Lovette had been expecting exactly 50 guests and everything just needed to be perfect. The menu had a list of

"Thanksgiving-like" items that she had wanted everyone to enjoy and to leave without feeling hungry.

A long row of masks were aligned against the unlit fireplace. Lovette took her time to create some just for those who may have wanted one custom made by her or simply forgot to bring one.

There were 5 rules to her masquerade that everyone knew and had to abide by: 1) All guests must wear a mask. 2) Everyone had to present their invitation. No invitation meant no entry. 3) Remember your number. 4) Confidentiality. 5) No children were allowed.

"Everything is perfect. You can stop obsessing now and go get ready," mumbled Joseph. Even though he suggested this, he knew his wife wouldn't make a move unless she was ready. She had to make sure that everything was in place and ready for their guests. He was just along for the ride, as usual.

"Oh hush. I was just making sure. Jasmine, can you make sure those decorations are secured over there? I don't want anything falling on someone's head," hollered Lovette.

Slowly but surely, the help she had hired had finished setting up and started to disappear. It was now 6:45 pm and the guests would start arriving within the next hour or so. Every party they had would remind Lovette just how she met Joseph.

****

December 18, 1982

"Are you enjoying yourself, Love? You seem real standoff-ish. If what happened earlier is bothering you, I've already forgotten about it. Can't control how people feel about me, ya know?" said Mike.

Lovette had zoned out during their first slow dance together that she didn't realize how much Mike had been talking. She snapped out of it and instantly felt bad because she didn't want him to think she wasn't enjoying herself.

"Oh no, I'm fine. Sorry. I just didn't like the way they treated you. You aren't so bad," replied Lovette while grinning at Mike. That had been the truth; Mike had been a gentleman and was really nice. Still, she wasn't completely convinced of his full intentions. She didn't get a negative gut feeling about him but she didn't want to let her guard down just yet. Anyway, they were just friends.

"It's okay. That was bold of you to step up to them like that. Because, in my household? My mama would slap what we call 'the black off of me' or 'knocked me into next week' had I said anything against what she had already made final." The both of them busted out laughing at his remark.

As soon as Lovette heard her favorite song blare out over the speakers, Mike instantly started dancing. To her surprise, he had some pretty cool moves.

"Go! Dance without me. I'm going to get some punch," she shouted over the music.

"You sure? I mean, we came together. Wouldn't that be rude?" Mike yelled back. Lovette shooed him away and with that, he blended in with the crowd and danced

away to the song. Lovette wouldn't dare embarrass herself in an attempt to dance. She had been good at many things but dancing to such an upbeat song hadn't been her thing.

Making her way over to the punch bowl, she had noticed a group of five girls in a circle staring at her. As soon as they noticed she had caught them staring, they all turned away and started back with their conversation.

Lovette knew who each one of them were. They were always together and always talked about everyone around them. She knew they were probably gossiping about the fact she had come to the dance with Mike.

Wanting to make the night more interesting, Lovette decided to give the girls what they had wanted: attention. As soon as she headed their way, the wolf pack leader named Jennie smiled.

Jennie was a tall and stocky tanned girl who wore more make up than a clown. Her hair was shoulder length and way too blonde. The nerve of her to decide to wear a huge ruffled yellow dress only made her look that much more like a banana. This alone made Lovette laugh out loud.

"Hey, Lovette! Did you come by yourself? It's such a shame that a pretty face like yours couldn't find a date!" With that comment, the pack began to howl. Brenda had been a part of the group and had been the only one who didn't laugh. Her and Lovette weren't that close as friends but they've gotten along during a few classroom assignments. She had thought Brenda was kind of nice despite her reputation.

Before she could call Jennie the bitch she was, Lovette decided to take the funnier yet embarrassing approach.

"No, I actually have a date. I'm with Michael O'Conner. You know him right? Oh, yea! You have the biggest crush on him and he won't give you the time of day right? Such a waste of a mediocre face chasing after someone who doesn't want you." The look on Jennie's face was enough satisfaction for Lovette. The pack's jaws looked as if they were about to touch the ground at any second.

"Oh, I came over here to ask why you all were staring but I got my answer. Instead of worrying about who I came with, do you not realize that you're standing in a group of girls with no date in sight?" Lovette was on a roll. She knew the only reason Jennie decided to be rude was because of Mike. They had no previous issues before the dance. All of this over a boy!

Jennie's face was red as flames. Walking up to Lovette so close that she could smell the tons of hairspray Jennie had used, she whispered.

"Listen bitch, the only reason you're even here with him is because he only wants one thing from you. If I had really wanted to come with him tonight, I would've. I just hate that he let you step out of the house in such a tacky dress." With that being said, Jennie tilted her drink onto Lovette's bosom.

Ignoring the cold drink dripping down her skin, Lovette reached up and snatched Jennie by the hair as soon as she had turned to walk away. The pack jumped against the wall and watched. Jennie stumbled back and fell to the floor and the impact pushed a few dancers out of the way.

Before Jennie could even attempt to get back up, Lovette dumped her drink on Jennie. Quickly removing herself from the group, Lovette headed back to the other side of the gym before one of the teachers could get to them. On the way, she had heard Jennie screaming and still lying on the floor.

Rushing to the bathroom while still looking behind her, the teachers had made their way to see what the fuss was. Before she could turn back around, Lovette had bumped into an extremely tall guy. Well, everyone had been tall compared to her. Turning around and looking down at her, it was Joseph. "Football Jock Joe".

"If I didn't know any better, I'd think you just asked me for a dance," said Joseph. His voice was deep and carried well, so there was no need for him to holler over the music. Lovette was annoyed that he was in the way of her bathroom escape. Instead of noticing how aggravated she was, he continued talking.

"Um, I don't mean to pry but does the girl over there screaming have something to do with why your chest is covered in punch?" asked Joseph.

"How about minding your business and getting out of my way?!" shouted Lovette. Moving around him and making it to the bathroom, she looked back to Joseph and felt bad. He didn't deserve for her to have been that rude to him. Going into the bathroom and cleaning herself up, she had decided she would apologize to him.

Exiting the bathroom, she had managed to bump into someone else. The night was staring to get annoying for her and she couldn't wait to leave.

"Lovette. I was looking all over for you. Are you okay? You're wet. Wait, Jennie…" said Mike. He had been putting the clues together just as Joseph had did.

"Yes, Jennie was me. I mean, I did that. Well, she started first and I just finished it. Where is she?" replied Lovette while scanning the room for the wolf. She had been nervous that she was going to get caught and kicked out of the dance or worse, suspended from school. She hadn't been in any real trouble before and this would be just the thing to make her parents ground her even longer after running off with Mike.

"She left and of course, her crew followed her on out. I'd leave if I were her. She looked even more like a clown after you poured your drink on her. I don't know much about make up but I'm just glad you don't need it like she does," said Mike while the both of them laughed.

Peeping around Mike as he kept talking, Lovette caught a glimpse of Joseph staring at her. The look on his face was hard to read. She didn't know if he was upset that she was rude to him or if he was feeling some way about her being with Mike.

"Hey, Mike? Can you give me a second? I'll be right back." He nodded his head slightly confused and Lovette walked away towards Joseph.

"Hey, I'm sorry about that. I was just in the middle of something and didn't mean to be rude. I'm Lovette by the

way." Sticking out her hand, Joseph just stared at her. With no expression at all, he replied.

"I know who you are. Apology accepted. Did you come with Mike? If so, you might want to get back to your 'boyfriend' because he's looking a little pissed over there." Turning around, Mike had been looking at them the entire time and was leaning against the wall looking aggravated.

"Yes, I'm with him. I mean, we came to the dance together as friends. Anyway, I just wanted to say sorry. That's it." Before he could say anything else, Lovette turned around and walked off.

Approaching Mike, his facial expression had softened. "I had bumped into him earlier and wanted to apologize for being rude," explained Lovette. Mike waved it off as if it were nothing.

"Do you want to get out of here? We can go to Baker's. It's kind of lame in here anyway." That had pleased Mike. He had wanted to hang out with Lovette outside of a school event anyway.

****

Lovette was in awe of herself. Staring into her full length mirror, she was pleased with the dress Joseph had picked out for her. Not often did she let him pick out her clothing but he had an eye for a beautiful black dress. The black satin strapless fabric hugged her frame perfectly. Her hair had been straightened and laid perfectly on her shoulders and back. The simple and yet stunning gold heels pulled the mask into the whole outfit.

Satisfied with her beauty, she had picked up her mask and pulled it over her eyelids. It had been especially made to match her dress. With tons of gold glitter and black lace as a trim, she had loved her creation. Everything about her reflection was magnificent.

Making her way towards the staircase, she could hear the laughter and chatter. Guests had begun to arrive while she was busy getting ready. As soon as her presence became visible, Joseph calmed everyone and got their attention.

"And this is why my wife will live forever. We speak her name and she graces us with her late yet most pleasant presence. Everyone, your elegant hostess." With that, everyone in the foyer looked up to Lovette standing next to the stairwell vanity, smiled and clapped.

While walking down the rest of the stairs, Lovette laughed at her husband's silly introduction, kissed him and began to greet her guests.

"Thank you, everyone, for coming out tonight. As always, enjoy yourselves! Enjoy the food, music, outside scenery and enjoy what the night has for us all!" said Lovette.

The attire in the house was amazing. Everyone had worn black of some sort but added their own touch, just as Lovette had done. Joseph wore a sleek long sleeve black button up shirt with slacks to match. He had chosen to wear the cufflinks Lovette had gotten them for their 5th wedding anniversary. The gold attention to his wrist glistened with his engraved initials.

Making her way over to the front entrance, Lovette picked up the bowl that contained the signed invitations. Each one had a number on the back and she carefully took her time counting them to make sure everyone had been in attendance. "46…47…48…49…," she whispered. Almost everyone had shown up.

Turning around to face the crowd throughout the home. She began to make her speech. Stopping one of the champagne servers of the evening, Lovette grabbed a glass and tapped it to gain her guest's attention.

"As you all know, this happens to be one of my favorite events. I'm pleased to announce that everyone was able to make it tonight. I hope you all are enjoying yourselves so far and continue to do so throughout the night. We have some new faces but most have been hanging around for years. If you haven't had the chance to meet the mayor, Conrad Price, he's not here and you won't be meeting him tonight." The house erupted in laughter.

"I hope everyone has remembered their numbers on the back of the invitations. With that being said, if numbers 1-10 could make your way to your labeled door," said Lovette while pointing to the first guest room just past the foyer. It had "1-10" labeled in silver calligraphy on top of the door's black matte decorating paper.

With champagne in their hands, four men and five women walked towards the door and willingly entered. Staring at her husband, Joseph hesitated. He had been number 1. They had always entered the same room together and this time, Lovette had purposely given him a different number. Not breaking her stare, Joseph gave her a faint grin and entered the room.

"The rest of you can do as you please, for now. I suggest taking a look outside. It's beautiful in here but the view out there is even more amazing. Plus, it had cost my husband a pretty penny, so get his money's worth!" Everyone laughed and spread out throughout the house to enjoy the evening.

Lovette took the moment alone to go upstairs to her bedroom and call Lacy. It had been awhile and she had wanted to check on the kids.

"Hey, Lace! Was just calling to check on the kids. Is everything okay? Good. Is Joey still out with his friends? Okay. We told him he needed to be back by 10, so if he isn't back by then, just give one of us a call. And Lace? Thanks again for keeping them tonight. Talk to you later." Hanging up the phone and turning around to leave out of the room, Lovette gasped.

"You scared the mess out of me!" she said. Grinning from ear to ear as if she were a Cheshire cat, she embraced the tall figure. Repositioning his mask and sitting on the bed, he replied.

"That's what makes the evening even more fun. How've you been? As always, I've missed you." Pulling out his specially marked invitation labeled "Master Bedroom", he handed it to Lovette.

"I assume you had made only one of these or are we expecting more guests?" he questioned. Walking over to close and lock the bedroom door, Lovette turned back towards him and straddled his lap.

"We've waited long enough for this moment. Remember this?" Grabbing both sides of his face and kissing him so deep to prove how much she had missed him, Mike flipped her over on her back and removed his mask.

Chapter 6: Invitation Only-Part II

October 30, 1999

Zipping up his pants, it had dawned on Mike to ask about their private session. It was hard for him to decide to even partake in such a bold event.

"Love? Does Joseph know about this?" Mike was so caught up in the moment that he hadn't cared to ask her beforehand. Loving her that much made him forget about most things when they were in the moment.

"Would it have made a difference? Would you had denied me if I told you this wasn't signed off by him?" replied Lovette with a worried look on her face. She had been used to having Mike wrapped around her finger and the sudden question concerned her. Had she started something that would jeopardize him ever wanting to come back? Tons of questions started to flood her mind. She couldn't risk losing him again.

Sitting down on the bed, Mike caught her concerned look. Picking her chin up and turning her head towards him, his tone softened.

"Hey, I'm not going anywhere. I just want to make sure we go about everything the right way. I don't want any bad blood between anyone. It's been enough of that for a lifetime. Maybe we should head back down and join the rest of the party," said Mike.

His confirmation had lightened up her mood.

Standing up to fix herself, Lovette smiled and kissed him as if she'd never get the chance again. As soon as he had exited the room, Lovette sat and waited it out for a while. They didn't need to be seen leaving the room together.

****

March 14, 1982

"Are you sure your parents are gonna be gone the whole weekend?" whispered Lovette. Mike's house was empty and she had no idea why she still felt the need to whisper. She had told her parents that she was staying the weekend with her best friend, Jade.

Since Jade's parents were into church heavy, Lovette's parents just took her word and never questioned how legit her story was. And well, she would be spending the weekend with Jade. Just not this specific weekend.

They had started dating just a little after going to the dance together. Spending time with him had made Lovette instantly fall for him. He wasn't what she had made him out to be. There was a lot more to him other than just being handsome and popular.

Mike's parents' house was nothing short of magnificent. The one story home didn't have much color to it but it was clean and up to date. The paintings on the walls had to have been expensive or at least they looked to be.

Mr. O'Conner had his own private medical practice and Mrs. O'Conner spent some of her days as his receptionist and other days she would assist at school events. She had been a consistent member of the PTA at Bright-field Heights and pretty much everyone knew who she was.

"Yea, so stop worrying. We're fine. It's their anniversary weekend, so they'll be busy enjoying themselves," said Mike. He continued to show her around the house while Lovette was in awe. He was an only child so there wasn't much for him to show her. Ending up at his bedroom, he opened the door and Lovette busted out laughing. With a confused look on his face, she began to explain herself.

"Your room is very nice but the teddy bear sitting over there kind of threw me off." Sitting in a chair in the corner was his childhood stuffed animal, Bozi. Bozi had been given to him by his grandmother.

When Mike was 11 years old, his grandmother had been killed by a drunk driver. One morning, she was checking her mailbox and the driver swerved and pinned her against the house.

Mike had spent the summer with her and had been in the window watching the whole thing. The driver fled but was picked up within an hour. He hadn't been the registered owner of the vehicle and Mike was able to identify him when questioned by the police. Bozi was one of the few things he had left to remind him of her.

"Sorry, I didn't know. I didn't mean to laugh. It sounds like y'all were very close. She must've been a really awesome grandmother." Lovette had felt bad for laughing. He shrugged it off and told her it was okay. She had also felt a sense of trust from him. Up until now, he hadn't told *her too much about himself.*

Quickly changing the dark mood, Lovette turned on his stereo. Jumping on him as he sat on the bed and straddling his lap, she held both sides of his face in her palms. For a while, they both just stared at one another without saying a word. She had felt his body temperature rise and it made her even more excited.

This had been the moment she knew. Before he could say it, she beat him to it. "I love you." Repeating how the feeling was mutual, he flipped her on her back.

"Wait. Do you have a condom?" said Lovette in between taking deep breaths.

"No, but I want you bad. You said you were a virgin and I'm clean. My dad is a doctor, ya know? I'll pull out in time." Flashing his smile that she couldn't resist and kissing her even more, Lovette gave in to him.

Instantly, she felt like she could be in his arms forever. Mike would be her forever and to know he felt the same made things only that much better.

****

Getting herself together, Lovette went and joined the rest of the party. She knew her disappearing act would be noticeable. Taking the moment to stop at the stairwell vanity, Lovette sat.

The music and the laughter became heavy in the background. She had done this. She had made people happy. Gathering them together to fulfill something that hadn't dare to do on their own. Before she could turn to leave, Joseph had appeared beside her in the reflection.

"Why didn't we go into the same room this time? We've always gone in the same room. Were you with him?" whispered Joseph. He wasn't angry with her but he had known the answers to his questions before she had even responded. After all she had gone through, he could never fully be mad at her.

"How was the room this time? Did they exceed your expectations? I was skeptical about the red head. For a moment, I thought she was going to back out and go home. I saw her eyes widen when the door opened." With that being said, Lovette laughed and turned towards her husband.

"Let's go back to the party." Straightening his collar and kissing him on the cheek, Lovette took his hand and rejoined the guests. She hadn't answered any of his questions and hadn't planned on doing so.

As soon as they entered the foyer, the red head walked up to them. "Mr. Marks, your cuff links. You left them in the room." Joseph's face turned bright red. Lovette instantly knew that her husband had enjoyed carrot top. She had specifically picked her out for him.

"Thank you," replied Joseph while avoiding contact.

"I knew you liked MY red hair but eventually, I had a hunch of your infatuation. You're welcome," whispered Lovette.

The help had cleaned the room and switched the

numbers. The same as before, Lovette announced for numbers 11-20 to enter the room and so on throughout the night. Every time the group came out of the room, the satisfaction on their faces had let her know that this night was a success. Mike had disappeared throughout the night but Lovette knew where she could find him.

Walking down the stepping-stones towards the lake, she saw his figure sitting near the edge on the wooden bench. Mike had become even more handsome since the last time she saw him. The older he got, the better he looked. He knew to dress in all black but somehow, he had picked out the perfect color tie: gold. Handing him a glass of scotch, Lovette sat next to him and sat quiet for a while.

"Why are you still with him?" said Mike breaking the silence. He was full of surprises tonight. He had never asked Lovette this question. There was an understanding and Mike knew this from the beginning.

Slightly shocked by his question, Lovette took a big gulp of her drink before speaking. "You know I can't. The kids. The money. Believe it or not, I actually have love for him, too. You're still with Monica but questioning me..."

"You've always been the one. You know I love your kids as if they were my own. You don't love Joseph the way you love me. I asked you why you were still with him and not once did you mention being IN love." Lovette could feel the tension thickening quick and she knew deep down, he was right. She couldn't and wouldn't argue it.

"Mike, I'm sorry. Had I known it would've come to this..."Lovette stammered. She knew she had just hurt him and didn't know what else to say.

"What?! You would've never had a private room with me? Or you never would've started this? You talk about your children but did you forget about our own child?!" said Mike. His voice was agitated and was just above a level of a whisper.

Instantly, he had regretted his words. He knew the damage he had just caused and he couldn't take it back. The horrified look on Lovette's face made his throat tighten and become dry.

"Love, I'm so sorry. I didn't mean to…"

Before he could finish, she got up and walked back towards the house. Without turning around, she forced out her demand.

"Go home, Mike."

Watching her frame become smaller and smaller, she disappeared into the back of the house. Mike felt like he had completely lost her. He couldn't control his emotions at the moment and this might've been the last time he would see her. Obeying her command, Mike headed to his parent's house.

Chapter 7: Mary

"How was school today, Mary?"

She always started the session off like this. She didn't care how school was. Nobody ever cared how things were going for me. They had decided something was wrong with me and that was it.

"The same as every other day, Ms. Carle. Boring." I wasn't here by choice. Papa had finally convinced mama that I had needed to "talk to somebody" about the issues they say I have. They say I'm confused and won't listen. The thing is, neither one of them had bothered to ever listen to me. They do way too much talking but none of any listening.

"Something must've happened. You had to have learned something today. Did you make any new friends?" said Ms. Carle. She had been sitting in a tan leather chair across from me. Today's choice of shoes had been red with a pointy toe.

The only thing I had looked forward to during these meetings were seeing her shoes. She had never worn the same pair twice yet. Must be making a lot of money to afford these shoes with no husband.

"Where do you get your shoes from?" I needed to know. One day soon, I'd be wearing stuff like her. She had on a black pair of pants with a black and white polka dot shirt. Her hair was up in a bun and she had the prettiest dark skin I had ever seen. She had always smelled like roses and the funny thing was, she had always written down her notes with a black pen that had a rose at the end of it.

"These were a gift. Now, back to you. Can you tell me one thing that you've learned in school today?" Letting out a sigh, I figured she would keep on until I gave her an answer. Out of all the sessions we've had, she could've thought of some better questions to ask me. This was getting old really quick. With a grin on my face and crossing my arms, I knew exactly what I had learned today.

"I learned that my math teacher Mr. Sumner was having an affair with Mr. Jackson. It's going around the whole school. Hmph. Two men. Go figure." The look on her face did enough to make me cackle.

"Now, Mary. You know you shouldn't go around spreading rumors like that. Even if it's true, you shouldn't spread things like that around. What they do is their business." Writing down my behavior for today in her notebook, she made eye contact again. I've disgusted her. Mission accomplished.

"Okay, sorry. Please don't tell my parents that. I was only joking." But I wasn't. Mr. Sumner and Mr. Jackson had gotten caught in bed together. Mr. Sumner's wife came home early from work one day and had walked in on them together.

The whole school found out because an eighth grader, Joshua Tatum, lives right next door and saw Mrs. Sumner running out of the house behind Mr. Jackson with a knife. I saw her coming into the building I'm in last week. I guess she's started her own sessions. Seems to me that Mr. Sumner should be the one in here. He's the one who's confused since can't choose between a man and a woman.

"Forget it even happened. How are things going at home?" I knew this question was next. Getting up from the couch, I decided to walk towards the curtains. Every foot tap against the hardwood floor sounded as if the whole world could hear my movements.

The sun felt good coming through the windows. It had been a while since I had played outside. The ducks had stopped coming by every day and they started to get boring anyway.

Joyce never had to come to these sessions. Just me. It wasn't fair that she got to stay home and she had always been with me through most things. I really didn't deserve to be here. The more I thought about it, the angrier I became.

"Why isn't Joyce here with me? Why do I constantly have to come alone?" Ms. Carle heard my questions but just stared at me. This was the same stare people would give me when I mentioned my sister and I had become sick of it.

"Are you going to answer me or are we going to play the staring game now?"

"Have you asked your parents why she isn't here?" she replied. This was her game. She had been good at answering my questions with a question when she didn't want to answer them. My parents paid someone to ask me questions when they could ask me them for free.

"Can we just take a break? I have to use the bathroom." I had needed to get away from her for a while. The bathroom was the only place she'd let me go alone.

She nodded for me to go. I hadn't used the bathroom since school let out, so I really did need to go. Plus, the orange scented hand soap smelled so good.

Flushing the toilet and pressing the soap pump, the mirror calls me and...the sweating begins. Trying to turn away, the hold is stronger than it has ever been. A loud knock on the door forces me to blink and the right side of my head begins to throb.

"I'll be out in just a minute!" As soon as I opened the door, a short plump woman is standing there with her arms crossed. Her eyes were crossed harder than her arms and I just knew she had to be seeing two of me. I instantly giggle.

Looking annoyed that I had laughed at her, she moved around and went into the bathroom slamming it shut. Maybe she'll see two toilets and pee in the wrong one!

Walking back down the hall, I hear Ms. Carle on the telephone talking to someone in a hushed tone. Standing stiffer than Joey's dirty socks outside of her door, I put those listening skills that she nags about to use.

"She asked about Joyce. We talked about this last week. It's been way too long for this. One time wasn't enough, Mrs. Marks. Mary is a special case. No, it isn't for me to tell her. You two are her parents and there's no better people to hear that from. Hiding the truth from her will only delay her progress."

"She needs to know what reality is and isn't. The only way I will agree to initiate that topic is if it's in a family session. She doesn't need to hear that kind of information for the 'first time' without a family filled environment. If you still want to pick her up early, I'll let her know."

Tell me what about Joyce? It must be the reason why she gets to stay home while they drag me to this place twice a week. Whatever the reason for her not having to come, I'd just have to play her same game so they would stop making me come. As soon as Ms. Carle hung up the phone, I walked back in her office and sat back on the ugly pea green couch.

"Aren't you going to ask me if I heard your phone conversation?" I ask. Giving her the side eye, I'm sure she already knows I had heard exactly what she had said.

"Well, did you hear my telephone call?" She was nervous. I knew it was her job to show no emotion but I could feel it. Last month, I had heard one of the other ladies that work here crying and Ms. Carle walked over to her office. I heard her telling her that their clients weren't supposed to see them get emotional. Deciding to make her sweat it out a little more, I reply "no" and smile.

"Okay, well, your parents will pick you up a little early today, so the three of you can talk. We'll meet again on Thursday. In the meantime, make sure you're writing in your journal whenever you feel like it. Especially the moments when you feel really happy or maybe even really sad," said Ms. Carle.

Feelings. Everyone had always wanted me to write down my feelings. No matter what I had written down in the notebook, I still had to come to this place. I asked mama when I could stop coming and she told me "when you're better." I'm not sick and I'm not broken. I'm as best as I can be.

Ms. Carle kept going on and on up until there was a knock at her door. Cracking the door and peeping in, it was mama.

"Hey. I hope I didn't interrupt. Mary, you ready?" Mama looked like she had been crying. Her eyes were red and she kept sniffling. Before I could ask what was wrong, she continued, "Go on and head downstairs. Your papa is in the car waiting."

Almost tripping over my feet, I couldn't have run out of the office fast enough. Papa said he was going to take me to get some new shoes today since I had been doing okay in therapy these past two weeks. I hope Ms. Carle really doesn't tell them what I said about Mr. Sumner. I had convinced him to get me and Joyce a pair of high top Converse sneakers.

As soon as I got to the car, papa got out and opened the door for me. Joyce was in the backseat. I was happy to see her but still upset that she didn't have to do sessions with me. We've always done everything together.

"Hey, Mary. How did it go?" whispered Joyce. Papa had just buckled in the driver seat and we waited for mama to come down. She had her hair in a ponytail and was wearing a white and blue striped shirt with jeans. She had done this on purpose because I had been wearing the exact same thing. She had still wanted to wearing matching clothes and we were almost 12 years old.

"Would you rather switch places with me?" I snap and say with an attitude. Instantly making her feel bad, I apologize.

"Sorry, I just hate having to go by myself. I don't see the point of all of this." Papa had been staring at me in the rear view mirror with a funny look on his face. The same look he always gave me.

"You don't have to be such a bitch about it! It's not my fault they make you go!" shouted Joyce. Ms. Goody had finally cursed. She had never cursed before, especially at me. Mama and papa have both caught me swearing a couple of times and threatened to do stuff but the worst would only be mama popping me on the lips.

Before I could say a curse word or two back to her, mama opened the door and slid in the car. As soon as she closed the door, it seemed like a bucket of water poured from the sky out of nowhere. The rain was beating against the car as if it were trying to get inside. Finally getting to leave this stupid place, papa cranked up the car and headed home. Mama didn't say a word the whole car ride.

"I don't feel like being in this car with you anymore. You've changed. We used to have fun and stuff but now, all you do is whine about going to therapy. Did you ever stop to think if you really needed to go?" said Joyce. Papa had just stopped at a red light and an old woman had just started crossing the street. Her shoulders were leaning forward and she had a hump in her back. She walked slower than a slug moving along.

Before I knew it, Joyce had crawled over to my side of the backseat, opened the door and leaped from the car. Mama turned around and screamed as if she had been struck upside the head.

"Mary! Have you lost your mind?! CLOSE THE CAR DOOR THIS INSTANT!" As soon as Joyce heard mama scream, she started running down the street towards the ice cream shop.

"Mama! Joyce is getting away! She's such a big baby about everything!" I said. Joyce had never acted this way before. She had cursed for the first time and now she was trying to run away. Taking off my seatbelt, I had no other choice but to go after her. Papa had already gotten out of the car with mama on his heels.

The rain slapped me in the face and stung my skin trying to catch up to Joyce. Cars were swerving and slamming on their brakes trying not to hit the both of us. Horns were blaring and a man had the nerve to roll down his window screaming.

I was fast at running but she was even faster. Turning around to see where mama and papa were, they were closer than I had thought. I turned back around and Joyce ran inside of Freddy's ice cream shop.

"Mary! STOP! You're gonna get hit!" screamed mama.

They didn't understand. Nobody ever did. I didn't want Joyce mad at me. Running into Freddy' behind her, butt-face Beetle was standing behind the cash register looking butt-faced as usual. He was one of Joey's weird friends.

"Where is Joyce?" I screamed. Beetle had the worst acne and had a mouth full of metal. His braces always had food stuck in them but somehow, Freddy still gave him a job in his place. He was standing behind the counter with a confused look on his face and said nothing.

"HELLO?! Didn't you hear what I just said?! She just ran in here, so where is she?!" He stood there and still said nothing. I had the urge to jump over the counter and jack him up by the collar if he didn't start talking within the next few seconds.

Before I could carry out my thoughts, mama and papa both busted through the door and were panting.

"Mary! You can't just run out in the middle of traffic! You could've been hit and killed! What were you thinking?!" shouted papa. His face was bright red and he was soaking wet, just like me and mama were. He had on a white button up shirt, a bright red tie and those black fancy pants. He was so wet, that you could see his skin through his white shirt.

"Joyce ran in here and this bozo won't tell me where she is! I bet she's behind the counter hiding" I said. Before mama or papa could stop me, I jumped up on top of the blue countertop to see if Beetle had helped her hide. Just as I was about to jump down to look under the counter, papa caught be by the back of my jacket and pulled me down from the countertop.

"Mary, let's go. NOW!" he shouted. He went from looking tired to angry. "It's pouring down outside and you've led your mother and I in here on nonsense! We're leaving!" His voice had become deep and his eyes were bigger than an owl's eyes

"I'm not going anywhere until Joyce comes out!" Screaming at the top of my lungs, I begin to yell her name. "Tell them! Tell them she ran in here! I'm not leaving without my sister! She looks JUST like me and has on the exact same thing!" Yanking away from papa's grip, I move to the table near the door and sit down. I wasn't leaving without her.

"Sir? ....ma'am? Ummm. I didn't see anyone that looks like her come in here. To be honest, we haven't had many customers through here today. Could be because of the rain. Yesterday was prettier. Although, I do love the rain because it seems to calm to body. Do you all like the rain? Statics say that..."

"DO WE LOOK LIKE WE WANT TO TALK ABOUT THE RAIN, BEETLE?! Just tell us where Joyce is so we can go!" I had had enough of this. Maybe she had ran out the back door. If she did, she was probably long gone by now.

"Joseph, can you please go get the car and pull it around front before someone steals it or we get a ticket?" Mama's voice had become way too calm. Taking a napkin off of the counter and wiping her face, she sat down at the table with me. Storming out of the store, papa did what she had asked him to do.

"Mary, by the time your daddy has brought the car around to the front of the store, you better be out of this chair and ready to go home. I don't want to hear another word. Sit there and argue with me another second longer and I'll whoop your behind right here in front of Beetle. I said we're leaving and that's that."

Her voice was low and she didn't even blink. For a moment, I thought about running towards the back door to see if Joyce had run outside. But, the look on her face was enough for me to stay glued to my seat. Honking the horn, papa was outside.

"Now, get up and walk out of here or I'll drag you out myself." Not saying another word, I headed back towards the car where papa was waiting with my door open. Smiling as if she didn't just run away, Joyce patted the seat and motioned for me to get in.

Chapter 8: The Talk.

February 26, 2001

Joseph had put up with enough. His wife's happiness meant the world to him but he could no longer allow her to stifle the truth. He was soaking wet and it only angered him even more.

Lovette had looked over to him a few times during the car ride but he had refused to break his stare on the rainy road. Looking into her eyes would only make him continue to do things her way. Pulling into the driveway, he hadn't yet calmed down but he still had taken the time to open the car doors for his wife and daughter.

He had hurt for his daughter daily. Because she was the only family member unable to accept what had happened, this had constantly bothered him.

****

May 3, 1999

"Mary, wake up. My stomach is hurting sooooo bad! Mary! Get up!" yelled Joyce. The terrible pains had started right after dinner but she thought it was just their father's cooking that upset her stomach. Joseph wasn't the world's best cook but once in a while, he would step in the kitchen to give his wife a break. Hoping the pain would go away, Joyce decided not to tell anyone and went to bed.

"Well, what do you want me to do?! I was over here

having a dream about Tom Cruise and just as he was about to kiss me, here you come messing stuff up! I better be able to fall asleep at the exact same part or you owe me a date with Tom," whispered Mary.

Looking over at the alarm clock, it was 1:47 am. Sighing and rolling over to face Joyce, she was sitting in the middle of the floor between their beds.

"He isn't even that hot! Now, go get mama before my stomach explodes!" hollered Joyce. Before Mary could react to the insult about Tom, she had thrown her legs across her bed and stood up. Standing up too quick and losing her balance, Mary had fallen over onto Joyce.

"Ouch! Get OFF! You saw me sitting here and still fell over on me," said Joyce. She pushed Mary off of her and stood up but was still hunched over in pain. Mary managed to get up and flick on the light. As soon as she noticed the red smudge on the light switch, she had swiveled around to face her sister. Joyce's brand new white pajama shorts were covered in blood.

Mary couldn't find the words to say. Her eyes were glued to Joyce's shorts. Eventually, Joyce looked down to see what her sister had been staring at. Feeling stuck the same way Mary had been, Joyce eventually began to cry.

Lovette had just sat them both down about a week ago to talk about what a menstrual cycle was but neither one of them thought they would get it so soon. Just as Mary was about to go get their mother, Lovette had pushed the door open to see what the noise was about.

"What's going on in here? It's almost 2 in the

morning," whispered Lovette. Mary had still been silent and Joyce continued to weep.

"What's the matter, Joyce?! Were you two in here fighting? Mary, what happened to...?" As soon as she looked down to see the stain on her daughter's shorts, she instantly calmed down and smiled.

"Awww, baby, it's okay! Remember the talk I had with y'all last week? Well, I had the talk just in time because it's happening to you! You're turning into a young woman now, Joyce. Honey, don't cry. This is a good thing! Well, sort of. Besides the stupid cramps and hormones, but you'll be fine. Your body is working as it should. You're gonna be fine," said Lovette as she hugged her daughter.

Lovette had decided to talk to them because she had noticed the girls had begun to get curves and now had to wear a bra. She knew that their first period was just moments away and didn't want it to alarm them. They had known what a cycle was but she knew she had to go in depth with the topic. They both had listened and took to it better than she thought they would.

"Mama, I ruined my bed and my new pajamas!" cried Joyce. "Please, don't tell papa. I don't want him knowing," she said in between sniffles. Mary had been stuck in the same place the entire time before she had noticed the blood was still on her hand. Running out of the room to wash it off, she was in disbelief that her sister had started her period already.

Scrubbing her hands while grossed out, she dried them off and sat on the toilet to release her full bladder. She was still shocked that Joyce had gotten her period. The *thought of her having to wear those pads made her giggle. The ones mama wore were huge and looked uncomfortable. Taking some tissue to wipe herself, Joyce stood up and pressed the flush handle. Looking down into the bowl, she caught a glimpse of the red toilet tissue being sucked down the toilet.*

"MAMA!!!" screamed Mary. Her hands began to sweat and her stomach was in a knot. She hadn't moved an inch away from the toilet when Lovette came running in the bathroom with Joyce right behind her.

"Wait...YOU GOT YOURS TOO?! Both of you in the same day?!" shouted Lovette. She was happy and felt a little sad at the same time. The emotions were going to be all over the place in the house from now on. The girls were still young but were headed to their teenage years soon. She knew this mix could sometimes cause more tension.

"What's going on in here?! And why does everyone keep screeching?" Joseph had gotten out of the bed and was staring at the girls through a fuzzy vision. He didn't have to go in to work today and was thankful because they had interrupted his sleep.

"Oh, it's nothing. The girls saw some spiders and we got them. You can go back to bed. Everything is good here," lied Lovette. Since the girls didn't want their father to know just yet or even at all, she would wait as long as she could to tell him.

She had felt the exact same way the first time her period had started but, unfortunately, her mother blabbed it all to her dad the exact same day. He bought her a carton of chocolate ice cream and a big bag of pads. Lovette just knew she'd die from his gesture. Satisfied with her answer, Joseph shook his head and headed back to bed.

Waiting on the sound of her husband closing the bedroom door, she turned her attention back towards her daughters. To the outside world, they had the exact same face and were always referred to as a set. To Lovette, they were two completely different people who were easy to tell apart. They had been born together but were nothing alike. All of this was why she would've never guessed that they would start their periods on the exact same day. She wondered if...

Shaking her head, she rid herself from thinking way too deep into this. Comforting the girls and helping them clean up Joyce's bed was all she needed to worry about right now. As soon as they had finished putting new sheets on her bed, Joyce went to go take a quick shower. Getting dressed in new clothes, she had instantly felt better. The only thing bothering her was the thick padding under her.

"So, who wants ice cream?!" said Lovette. If getting ice cream at 2 o'clock in the morning was one of the perks of starting their cycle, Mary thought she was going to love this thing besides the horrible pad she had to wear. They followed their mother to the kitchen and all grabbed spoons.

"Mama, why did Joyce's stomach hurt and mine didn't? I've heard of most girls cramping but why didn't I?" said Mary.

"Well, some girls just don't. Everyone's bodies are different. Trust me; it's a good thing. Sometimes I cramp and sometimes I don't. Hopefully you don't ever experience

cramps and I hope Joyce's cramps will lighten up. Even better, I hope they go away," replied Lovette.

She was eating this bonding moment up. Her heart was full and grateful because she had been able to experience these moments with her daughters at the same time. This would be something that they both would remember and it had included her.

"I'm going to schedule an appointment for the both of you tomorrow," mumbled Lovette through a mouthful of ice cream. They all had taken turns digging into the carton until everyone had decided that they all had eaten enough.

"As far as school, you both can stay home for a couple of days and I'll let your teachers know. Eventually, I am going to have to tell your father. He does need to know. It's important to him too." The looks on both of their faces were completely over the topic. They knew it was only a matter of time before she had told him anyway.

"Tell dad what?" said Joey. He had just walked up to the kitchen when he heard his mother and sisters talking. He was wearing a dark hoodie, jeans and sneakers. Joey had snuck back into the house almost undetected. Lovette thought he had been in his bedroom the entire time.

"Never mind that. Where have you been?" questioned Lovette. She didn't want to upset him but as her mother, she had every right to know where he kept sneaking off to. He didn't appear to have done any drugs or drank alcohol, which was a plus, but she just couldn't understand why he would sneak out so much on school nights. Weekends made more sense to her.

"I just went on a walk. I woke up feeling like I couldn't breathe. I knew you were sleeping, so I didn't want to wake you and dad. Sorry," said Joey. He had appeared to be telling the truth and Lovette believed him.

"Next time you need some air, let someone know. We have a lot of land but anyone could walk up at any time or even an animal could try to attack you. It's not safe being alone out in the night, Joey. Okay?" She knew her son was dealing with a lot mentally and didn't want to add any extra stress on him. The last thing she needed was to trigger him. He nodded his head.

"Are you hungry? We just about ate all of the ice cream but I can fix you a sandwich," said Lovette. Shaking his head, Joey went up to his room and got back into bed.

"Mama, what's really wrong with Joey? I know he has to take medicine and stuff, but why?" asked Joyce.

Lovette and Joseph had both told the girls that Joey had to see a therapist before and that he takes medication but they avoided telling them exactly what was going on with him. They didn't want to alarm or scare the girls. They had agreed that the less they knew, the better things would be.

"You both know he just needs a little medicine to help him get through the day," said Lovette. She was tempted to tell them the full truth but couldn't bring herself to do it. She had a habit of sheltering them from the world's truth. All she ever wanted to do was to protect them from feeling disappointed, scared and any type of pain that she had once felt.

"Anyway, it's late. You both should get your beauty rest. Not that you NEED it. Y'all were blessed with your mama's good genes but don't tell your papa that," said Lovette while laughing. She winked at them both and motioned for them to head on up to bed.

****

Storming into the house, they followed Joseph into the living room and sat without saying a word. He had told them both that it was time for them to sit down and all talk again as a family again.

Mary had almost gotten them killed today running through traffic and it had been the breaking point for Joseph. He didn't care how his wife felt about this any longer. The truth needed to be embedded into Mary.

****

May 24, 1999

"Wait, are you sure? I don't get it. She's a healthy little girl? How can this be?" sobbed Lovette. The tears hadn't stopped since the doctor had called them back into the office about Joyce. Her nerves had been a wreck ever since the call. She wouldn't reveal anything over the phone, so to Lovette, this had to have been a bad sign.

"We just haven't seen anything like this before. At first, we thought Joyce had just gotten her menstrual cycle a little early. It's very common but she's been bleeding for 3 weeks now. We've run several tests along with researching her symptoms but we haven't come across a solution, treatment or cure yet."

"I'm sorry, Mr. and Mrs. Marks. We won't give up on her. We just have to keep her comfortable and as less stressed as possible. I have a feeling we're close to results," said the doctor. The look Lovette had given Dr. Johnson made her feel a bit uneasy.

"Sorry? You're sorry? My child is weak and hardly eats. Her skin is so pale and her body aches. She's 20 pounds lighter than her identical sister! 20 pounds! She's lost all of that weight in 3 weeks! Do you know that I haven't been able to hug my baby in over a week?!"

"The thought of touching her and putting her through pain is one of the scariest things ever. The worst part is, I can't help ease her pain one bit! So, no. I don't want to hear apologies. I want results! I want her to be able to get back up and play with her sister. I don't care what it costs or what you have to do but I can't keep watching my baby get worse each day. It's killing me!" shouted Lovette.

Joseph knew that his wife was in pain and one of the ways to get some frustration out was to speak on her feelings. He didn't want to make the doctor feel uncomfortable but everyone also needed to know how his family had been feeling about all of this. Silencing her would only make her mad at him and that's the last thing he had wanted. Reaching over to hug her, she continued to cry but calmed a little more.

"I know this is hard to accept but I promise we are working hard to help her. Continue to give her the prescribed medicine and she needs to stay in bed as much as possible," replied Dr. Johnson. She had felt for them.

She had just started her career and this was the first case she had no answers to.

Dr. Johnson had been staying up late nights to figure out what the problem had ben. Joyce's situation had grown on her as if she had been one of her own family members. Not knowing what else to do, Lovette grabbed Joseph's hand and they both headed home to be with their children.

****

"Joey, come downstairs! We all need to have a family talk," shouted Joseph from the bottom of the stairwell. Running to meet his father, Joey felt as if he was in trouble. Thinking on the past couple weeks, he couldn't remember doing anything in school and he had actually stopped sneaking out as much.

Everyone had been in the living room and waited on what Joseph had to say next. He had been so upset that he hadn't even bothered to change his wet clothes yet. The couch pillow beneath him had started soaking up the water from his clothes and left a wet spot.

"Me and your mother take most of the responsibility in why things have been the way they are," said Joseph. Lovette had lifted her head from looking at the floor and had given Joseph the worst death stare he had ever seen. She didn't know exactly where he was going with this conversation but hopefully staring at him would stop him in his tracks.

"Things have been hard for a while now. A terrible thing happened and we've avoided talking about it with the

pg. 99

both of you. Joey, you've been handling it the best way you can and I'm proud of you, son. I haven't always been the perfect dad towards you and for that, I'll always apologize."

Joseph had thought of the first and only time he had ever hit his son. Eventually, his associate, Will, had gotten the truth out of his daughter and let Joseph know that his son wasn't the one fooling around with Frankie. This had bothered him ever since it happened and he hadn't forgiven himself for the treatment he had shown Joey. Joey said nothing but they had all continued to listen to Joseph.

"We lost Joyce in one of the worst ways possible. We all miss her very much and I would do anything to bring her back but, unfortunately, that's not possible," he explained. The look on Lovette's face had made him pause but the expression he gave her back let her know that she better not had interfered with what he was trying to do.

"Papa, Joyce just went upstairs to take a nap. I mean, yea we lost her but you found her when you pulled the car around. She told me that she didn't feel like hearing you yell at us for running out of the car like that," said Mary. She hadn't grasped what her father was trying to tell her and just wanted the conversation to be over with.

Staring at his innocent child's face, for a moment, he had thought about dropping the topic. He had remembered how tragic this had been for Mary when it happened and since she was unable to accept it, this meant that he would have to hurt her all over again.

But, he couldn't keep denying the truth. Lovette had suggested they go about it this way and it wasn't helping

Mary at all.

****

June 26, 1999

The sun had just come up and the smell of Lovette's cooking had awaken her husband. The kids were still sleep, surprisingly. Putting his house coat on, he stopped at the guest bedroom to check on Joyce. Usually, she would be the first one up and needed help with changing her bedding and padding.

Pushing the bedroom door open, Joseph was witnessing his daughter gagging on her own blood. It had spread all over her pillows, face and t-shirts. The amount of blood he was staring at made his veins jump. He'd never seen anything like it before. Fear took over him and he had stood still for a few seconds while she continued to suffer. Before he could react to help her, Mary had pushed him to the side and entered in the room.

"JOYCE! MAMA, JOYCE NEEDS HELP! PAPA, DO SOMETHING!" Hearing Mary's screams and Joyce's constant gurgle had made him snap out of his trance. Scooping up Joyce's limp body, he ran downstairs past Lovette and headed for the front door.

"Get the car keys! She needs to be taken to the hospital! Hurry up, Lovette! She's throwing up blood!" hollered Joseph. Joyce's body had begun to convulse. Lying her down in the backseat, Mary tried to get in with her.

"NO! Go back in the house with Joey and wait

here!" Refusing to leave her sister, Mary sat in protest and didn't move. Not having the time to fight with his daughter, he let her be. Running out of the house with the keys and Joey running behind her, Lovette jumped in the passenger seat and the whole family headed to the hospital.

"Hold on, baby! WHAT HAPPENED TO HER, JOSEPH?! Just hold on! Just hold on a little longer. Everything is gonna be okay. Just hold on...just hold on...just hold on," repeated Lovette.

She hadn't bothered putting her seatbelt on and was on her knees facing her children. Joyce had stopped jerking around and was now unconscious. Jumping into the backseat, Lovette checked to see if Joyce was still breathing. Nothing.

"Joe! She's not breathing! Speed this damn car up now!" screamed Lovette. "Come on, honey. Mama's got you. Everything is going to be okay." Mary and Joey were silent while their mother tried to help their sister. They were both in shock at what was happening. Joyce was sick for a while but no one thought it would get this bad, especially so soon.

Pulling into the emergency room entrance, Joseph ran to go get the doctors. Lovette couldn't believe that this was happening. All of this started from the girls getting their menstrual cycles and the next moment, they were being told that Joyce was ill and the bleeding couldn't be stopped. She had wished that this had been happening to her instead of her youngest child.

The doctors came out to get Joyce and the family watched the hectic scene disappear down the corridor.

Lovette was covered in her baby's blood but she wouldn't dare leave Joyce in the hospital. She'd be here waiting on her to wake up and come home. They had all been sitting in the waiting room waiting for an update. Joseph couldn't sit and kept pacing back and forth.

"Mama, when is someone going to tell us what is happening to Joyce? It feels like it's been forever," said Mary. It had only been an hour but just as Mary had asked the question, 2 doctors entered the waiting room as if they had heard her. Heading towards the family, Lovette stood up and Joseph stopped pacing to stand next to his wife.

"Mr. and Mrs. Marks. Please, have a seat," said the first doctor. Motioning them to have a seat, Lovette stood still. Joseph had felt the same. Looking at one another, both doctors proceeded to explain what had happened.

"We took your daughter back to the operating room. She had lost a significant amount of blood loss due to her prior condition and vomited blood as well. We tried several times to revive her but unfortunately, we were unsuccessful. I'm very sorry for your loss and if there's anything we can do, please let us know," said the other doctor.

"Wait...no," whispered Lovette. She had just kissed her child good night with hopes of seeing her in the morning. Joyce wasn't feeling well but she was smiling and still looked hopeful. Lovette's head began to throb and her chest started pounding.

"Unsuccessful?!" screamed Joseph. "I just held my child and you're telling me she's no longer ALIVE?!" He *had felt as if his heart had been ripped from his chest. Lovette had collapsed in the chair behind her and sobbed so bad that her body began to shake terribly.*

Sitting beside her and trying his best to hold Lovette, Joseph had felt like he failed them both. Maybe he should've checked on her earlier. Maybe he should've driven faster to the hospital. So many scenarios on how he could've saved his daughter flooded his head. The doctors had offered their condolences for the last time and gave the family their privacy.

Joseph and Lovette were too torn and focused on one another to even think about their other two children who sat right beside them. Joey said nothing but hung his head and cried for his sister. He hadn't always been the best brother to Joyce and Mary but he still loved them. He would often sneak in to check on Joyce as well even though they weren't supposed to.

Mary had heard exactly what the doctors said but still waited on her parents to speak. Revive? She didn't know what that had meant but hearing papa say she was no longer alive must've meant that Joyce was dead. Mary didn't know much about death besides it meaning you never get to see someone again.

Walking over to her parents, Mary placed her hand on her mother's shoulder. It had taken a while for Lovette to even notice she was standing there. She couldn't control the crying and didn't care to. She had just lost one of the people she loved the most and there was nothing she could do to bring her back.

Both of them embraced their child and cried even

more. This was their child but this was Mary's reflection. They had come into the world together and had a bond unlike none other. Lovette cried louder and stronger because of this. She knew that Mary didn't understand now but she would be torn once she finally realized the seriousness of the situation.

****

"Papa, Joyce isn't dead. Why would you say something so mean like that? Do you know how that would make her feel if she heard you say that? That's just cruel and mean! She ran away today but she doesn't deserve for you to say things like that!" shouted Mary. The tears began to roll down her face and spilled onto her lap.

This is what Joseph was scared of. He knew it had to be done but he didn't want to hurt his child. Lovette cried along with her daughter while Joey stared as if he was tired of it all. He had missed Joyce too but he knew that she was gone and there was nothing anyone could do about it.

"Mary, Joyce is dead. Do you remember when we rushed her to the hospital? Do you remember the funeral?" questioned Joseph. He had mourned his daughter's death every single day but up until this moment, he had yet to shed a tear. Crying as if Joyce's death just happened at that very moment, Joseph couldn't hold it in any longer.

He cried for Joyce. He cried for Mary. He cried for his son. He cried for his wife. He cried for everyone but himself because he had felt like he could've done more to save his child. He placed blame on himself even though he had known Joyce's condition wasn't his fault.

"Papa! Joyce was just in the car with us! Go up to her room and see! She's up there!" shouted Mary through the tears. She had been breathing in short breaths and could hardly get her words out.

She didn't understand why he was being so mean all because Joyce tried to run away. Running up to their bedroom, Mary pushed open the door to see Joyce's bed had been empty. Running from room to room, checking under beds and searching closets, Mary still couldn't find her sister.

She had watched her get out of the car and walk up the stairs but Joyce was nowhere in the house. Joseph waited for Mary to come back into the living room. She needed to see things for herself and then, maybe she would realize the truth when she was unable to find her sister.

"She must've snuck past us and ran away again. She was in the car. Everyone saw her. You saw her. Mama saw her. She's not dead. She's not dead. She's not dead," repeated Mary. Lovette couldn't work up the courage to say anything. She had felt like this was partly her fault as well because she had convinced Joseph to not force Mary to accept things for what they were.

Mary was happy the way things were and Lovette didn't want her to feel the pain that she had felt. So, if pretending that Joyce was still alive and Mary was content, Lovette had planned to just go along with it.

"See! Tell them you aren't DEAD!" screamed Mary. Everyone had looked up to her talking to the empty blue chair. "Papa has gone nuts," she snickered, sniffled and wiped her nose with the back of her hand.

Chapter 9: The girl next door.

"Mike is a sweet person and I love him but, something is telling me that he's cheating on me. He's been acting really weird lately and everything just feels different," said Lovette.

She had been hanging out with Joseph at his house. They had become close friends ever since the incident at the school dance. She had apologized again the next school day and he had asked her if she wanted to hang out some time.

Graduation had just passed and she had wanted to hang out as much as possible before college started. Mike and Lovette both had decided to go to school in North Carolina but now she had started to second guess going to school together.

Lovette's parents had no idea that they both had been accepted into the same school or they wouldn't have agreed to pay for her education. They still couldn't get over that she had chosen to be with a black boy but they also figured going off to college would eventually break them up anyway.

Joseph had become like a best friend to her. At first, Mike didn't like that his girlfriend was hanging out with one of the football players but he actually took the time out to get to know Joseph and they had become cordial. This made it a lot easier to accept their friendship as well as trusting Lovette and Joseph.

Excusing himself, Joseph told her that he was going in his bedroom for a second. Lovette stayed seated in the living room and waited for him to come back.

"You know I like Mike. We haven't always been cool but he's actually not like what most people think he is. I see why you love him. Did you ask him what was going on? Don't beat yourself up assuming things. Just talk to him. Maybe you should give him a call now," said Joseph.

Joseph was always patient with Lovette and had been there whenever she had needed him. She had also helped him when he had issues with his girlfriend, Maddy.

Joseph had started dating Maddy only a couple of months ago and Maddy couldn't stand Lovette. She had been jealous that Joseph was spending any of his time with another female. Also, she had felt like Lovette was prettier than her. Joseph tried to get Maddy to be Lovette's friend but it just wouldn't happen.

Maddy couldn't see past Lovette's beauty and just knew that there had to be more going on. But, she had really like Joseph and didn't want to let him go. Regardless of his friendship with Lovette, Maddy had wanted to believe she could trust him. But, she didn't trust Lovette.

"You're right. Can I use the phone? I just need to get it out of the way and call him now," said Lovette. Nodding his head, Lovette entered the kitchen and snatched the phone from the wall. Dialing his number, she had expected for his mom to answer. She had always answered the phone.

Before she could greet his mother, Lovette had heard an unfamiliar voice giggling and then it sounded like the phone was being thrown around.

"Would you hand it here?!" She knew that voice had belonged to Mike. The giggling continued and Lovette knew the laughing had belonged to a female...and it wasn't Mrs. O'Conner.

"Mikeeee! It's in YOURRR bedroom, so why can't IIIII answer it?!" squealed the unknown female voice. "I bet you your girlfriend doesn't make you feel that good, huh? Does she touch you like this?"

The giggles started again and the phone started to sound as if they were fighting over it. Lovette had become so upset that she could no longer take hearing what was going on and hung up the phone. Mike had allowed another female to touch him in ways Lovette thought she was only allowed to. Apparently, she had been wrong.

Mike was cheating on her and she had felt it. He had probably been playing her this entire time. Lovette could feel her blood boiling and felt as if steam had been pushing out of her ears. Slamming the phone back into its cradle, Lovette stormed of back into the living room where Joseph had been sitting.

She didn't understand. Lovette and Mike had just had sex a couple of days ago and was supposed to hang out again later. Mike had another girl over and was cheating on Lovette as if it were nothing; this infuriated her even more. The bastard wasted no time sleeping with the next girl! So many thoughts had flooded her mind and each one had made her madder than the last.

pg. 109

"Ummm, Lovette? What's going on?" inquired Joseph. He had never seen Lovette so upset before. Her eyes looked like they were about to pour at any moment now.

"That slime ball is actually cheating on me! He had the NERVE to be over there laid up with some girl and he was JUST with me! That's it; I'm going over there," said Lovette. The heartache she felt at the moment had taken over her ability to think straight. She had needed to see this for herself.

"You sure you want to do that?" asked Joseph. "Is it really worth you going over there to start a fight? If you have all of the evidence that he's cheating, why even go over there? It sounds like he wants the both of you to fight over him and you're better than that."

Lovette knew he was right. She wouldn't give Mike the satisfaction of knowing how bad he hurt her. If he could do this to her, he didn't deserve to know how bad he had hurt her. He had proved he only cared about himself and at that moment, she knew she would never speak to him again.

"You're right. I'm so glad I have a friend like you. Had I been around Penny and Kristina, they would've been just as mad as me and we would've all been banging on his door to whoop his ass," said Lovette. The both busted out laughing but this had been nothing less than the truth. She had two of the best friends ever and they would've done anything to make her feel better.

Joseph had started to look nervous and he had hoped Lovette didn't notice. But, she did.

"What's the matter? You look like you're about to throw up," said Lovette. Joseph was the reason she was able to calm down. He had always known the perfect things to say at the right moments.

"Yea, we're friends but…is that how you always see me? I mean, have you ever thought about being more than just friends?" The lump forming in his throat made it hard for the words to come out. His forehead became sweaty and he just knew he would pass out at any moment.

Lovette was shocked. Yea, she had heard a few rumors that Joseph had liked her more than a friend but he had never shown that side. People just always assumed things and she had figured the rumors were started because so many girls liked Mike. She was positive they had wanted to break the two of them up. But, Joseph was dating Maddy and he had seemed to really like her.

The silence had made Joseph even more nervous. He had basically told Lovette that he liked her and she hadn't said a word yet. He knew speaking on this would jeopardize their friendship and he didn't want to lose Lovette. She meant too much to him.

"Joe, you have Maddy…and I…Well, I don't have Mike anymore but…I just never knew. You never said anything. You never did anything to make me think you thought of me in that way. I'm just surprised." She really had been surprised.

"Maddy wouldn't exist if you had or have any feelings for me. She's a nice girl but she's not you. No one comes close to you," replied Joseph.

*He had meant every word he had just said. Joseph
had always thought she was pretty but he never knew much
about her. Starting a friendship with her had made him fall
in love with her.*

*But, there was Mike. Joseph really did think Mike
was cool but he couldn't help his feelings for Lovette. If she
would allow him, he'd make her happier than Mike could.*

*"You know I've never said anything about Mike but
today, he's shown you who he really is. You didn't deserve
to be treated that way. I'd never do that to you," said
Joseph.*

*Lovette had begun to hurt all over again. For a split
second, she had convinced herself that she didn't care
about Mike any longer. She didn't want to feel for someone
who didn't care about her feelings.*

*Then, here was Joseph saying all of the things that
she never even imagined he would say...and she had liked
them. She didn't want to feel anything at the moment. She
didn't want to hate Mike and she didn't want to like the
things Joseph was saying.*

*Before she could say anything else, Joseph leaned
over and kiss her on the lips. This instantly made her feel
revengeful. She had wanted Mike to feel how she had felt.*

*Giving into Joseph, Lovette kissed him back. She
didn't know exactly how she felt towards Joseph beside
their friendship but at this moment, she had a plan and was
sticking to it. Removing her t-shirt and her pants, he led her
into his bedroom.*

****

June 14, 1982

Mike had been calling Lovette's house for the past few days but was constantly told that she was either busy or not at home. This was strange because even though her parents didn't approve of them dating, they knew they couldn't stop them from seeing one another until Lovette left for school. Her parents had let them talk on the phone, so he wasn't sure why she was so busy and unavailable all of a sudden.

It had been 4 days since he last saw and spoke to Lovette before he had decided to just visit her house. His parents had bought him a car for his graduation gift. It was a cherry red 1979 Pontiac Firebird and had become one of the most precious things to Mike.

Pulling up to her house, Lovette had been sitting on the porch with Joseph. He had called her phone 15 minutes prior to pulling up at her house and once again, her little sister Iris had told him that she wasn't there. He had gotten tired of the lies and needed answers.

Both Joseph and Lovette had watched him pull up to the side of the house and neither one of them moved to greet him. Joseph sat on the bottom step with a smug look on his face and Lovette had felt the sudden urge to just go in the house and lock the door. She knew this would turn sour quick and wasn't in the mood for it. Mike was her past now and she didn't want to hear anything he had to say...but then again, she did.

"Why haven't you been taking my calls, Love?

What's going on?" questioned Mike. He had gotten out of the car and was standing on the grass in front of the staircase. Lovette hadn't bothered to turn and look at him. She had been fighting back her tears because she had refused to let him see how hurt she had been over him.

"She doesn't want to talk to you, so just leave," replied Joseph. He had stood up and was now in between Lovette and Mike. Joseph disliked seeing Lovette pine over Mike when he knew that he was the better choice himself. Lovette said nothing and remained quiet.

"I'm sorry. I didn't know your name was Love. Next time, try shutting up when this doesn't have anything to do with you." Mike was already aggravated but now, he was upset.

He was angry that he hadn't heard from his girlfriend in days and now he was angry that Joseph felt the need to add two scents into their business. Whatever they had going on was between them and he didn't appreciate Joseph answering for her. Before Joseph could reply, Lovette spoke up.

"Joseph, I got this. Can we talk later?" she said. Almost going against her wishes, he turned around and nodded. Walking up the steps to reassure her that he would be back if she needed him, he hugged her and then kissed her on the lips. This had sent Mike in a range. Running up the steps and grabbing Joseph by the back of the neck, Mike shoved him into the screen door.

"HAVE YOU LOST YOUR DAMN MIND PUTTING YOUR LIPS ON HER?!" screamed Mike. He had Joseph pinned up against the door with his forearm into his neck. Struggling to get free, Joseph had been the bigger man but was no match for Mike's adrenaline and strength.

"'MIKE, STOP! YOU'RE GONNA KILL HIM!'" screamed Lovette. Her parents had been gone for the evening and she was glad. Had they been home, her father may have killed Mike for breaking the house's glass door. Plus, they didn't want her dealing with Mike anyway. Breaking his focus, Joseph had gotten free and jumped down off of the porch.

"Had you not been a cheating bastard, you'd still have her as your girlfriend. She's not yours anymore. Lovette, I'm not leaving you here with this maniac," said Joseph while struggling to breathe. He had been embarrassed that Mike had overpowered him so quick and had refused to make eye contact with Lovette.

"Call me another name and I'll rip your throat out!" seethed Mike. "I wouldn't dare hurt her but you've only saw a glimpse of what I can and will do to you!"

"Joe, just go! We'll talk later. I'll be fine." She just wanted to get this conversation with Mike over so he could leave. He had been pacing on her front porch in an attempt to calm himself down. Joseph must've taken Mike's threat seriously because he headed down the driveway towards the road.

"What in the hell are you doing kissing him?! Is this why you haven't been taking my calls?! Because you want to be with HIM?? I trusted you! You told me that there was nothing to worry about with him and now, look!" shouted Mike. This had been the first time Lovette saw him angry.

He had never yelled at her or even engaged in an argument. He had always been the levelheaded one.

"You have some NERVE! You started this whole thing!" shouted Lovette. She had become even more enraged at the fact Mike was trying to play the victim. He had clearly wanted his cake and to eat it as well but had the audacity to get mad at her for moving on.

"What are you talking about?! Started what?! I haven't seen you in 4 days! We've never gone this long without seeing one another and talking. Now, you're talking about I started this?!" As soon as it clicked into his mind what she could've been talking about, Lovette had already started to reply.

"Don't act like you weren't just laid up with another girl! I heard EVERYTHING! I bet you your girlfriend doesn't make you feel that good, huh?" mimicked Lovette. She was just about done talking to him about this.

"Oh shit, Love. I swear I didn't cheat with her. I've been calling you for days and had you taken any of my calls, I was going to tell you about it." He now felt bad for not coming over sooner. Maybe this would've all been avoided had he just come over to let her know what had happened.

"The girl next door, Stephanie, knocked on the door and told me she was selling raffle tickets to help support children in foster care. I told her she could wait in the living room while I went into my bedroom to get my wallet. She just kept smiling, giggling and acting weird. I gave her the money and told her that I had to go, hoping that would make her leave. The whole thing was just weird."

"Right when I was turning around to give her the money, she had walked into my bedroom. She kept smiling, giggling and stuff. That's when the phone rang. She jumped to answer it. The girl is just weird as hell. I had been trying to get the phone from her and I swear I didn't know it was you that had called. Please, believe me, Love. I didn't touch her at all and wouldn't dare. Have you seen her?!" explained Mike.

Lovette wasn't convinced. She had heard every word he had said but she just knew he was fooling around. She had the gut feeling before she had made the phone call to him and this only confirmed what she knew was true; Mike was a cheater AND a liar.

"Mike, not only are you a cheater but you're going to sit there and lie to my face! You don't even have the balls to tell the truth! She said she touched you! Not one time did I hear you deny it! You just kept on asking for the phone back!" Lovette had been in full blown tears at this point. "You can go to hell! You need to leave! I don't ever want to see you again!"

Lovette's words had severely stung Mike in the chest. She had never talked to him like this before. She had been a little argumentative here and there but she was never this harsh to him. It hurt even more that she didn't believe him and he had been telling the truth. He had never cheated on her or even thought about doing so.

The worst part of it all is that he wasn't sure if Lovette and Joseph had been cheating behind his back the entire time. Was this her way of not feeling guilty about what she had been doing? So many thoughts had begun to *flow through his mind and all of a sudden, he started to feel sick to his stomach.*

"Lovette, I never touched her. I never even thought about touching her. Then you sit here and kiss Joe in my face before you even knew my side of the story. I bet he convinced you that I was the bad guy and you fell for it, huh? I've never lied to you before and I have no reason to start lying now. Ya know what? Were you already foolin' around with Joe?" Mike needed to know if she had used this as a way out.

"WHAT?! I've NEVER cheated on you! And with JOE?! Don't turn this around on me because you got caught in the act! Joe was the one who suggested I give you a call because I had the feeling you were cheating!"

"He was the one saying he understood why I loved you and how you were a good person! He had taken up for YOU! And for what?! For you to turn out to be the lying cheater that you are! I wasn't expecting for him to kiss me just now but you can't say anything; we're DONE!" shouted Lovette.

"Done? Love...done? No, I swear. We can even go over to Stephanie's house so she can clear this whole thing up. I didn't do anything with her!" Mike paused for a second and whispered, "Wait...did you do anything with Joe?"

The look on Lovette's face had displayed nothing less than guilt. She shifted from making eye contact with Mike and started to cry again. He had known exactly what this meant.

"Wait, so...you're telling me that you went and fucked Joe because you thought I had cheated on you?! You...are...INSANE! Who does that?! You hadn't even talked to me yet and you just couldn't wait to get back at me, huh? Couldn't wait to get back at me for something I didn't even do! You know what, you're right; I should just leave." Not waiting for a response, Mike stormed off the porch.

"Mike, you've been acting weird for the past month! You've probably been cheating this entire time and you have the nerve to make it seem like I'm so wrong!" This made him stop in his tracks. He stood there for a few seconds and said nothing. For a moment, he had thought about just leaving and letting her continue to assume things. Turning around and facing her, he spoke.

"You wanna know why I've been acting weird for the past month? My mom just told us that she was diagnosed with breast cancer. I didn't know how to tell you or even talk about it. If you felt like I was seeing someone else or something was going on, you could've asked me instead of assuming. But, you chose to listen to a dude that's wanted you this entire time."

"Yea, I've always known he wanted you but you cherished the friendship and I trusted you. The first moment he got, he slid in and convinced you that I was the bad guy, huh? So, I guess that makes me the dummy, right? Bye, Lovette." Getting into his car, Mike slammed the door and sped off down the dirt road.

Lovette had become speechless. Mike was right; all she had to do was ask him why he was acting strange. She *knew he wouldn't lie about something as severe as this and it made her feel even worse that he had been suffering in silence this whole time.*

Now, Lovette had to face the reality that Joseph was a factor. She cared for him but she acted out in revenge. Mike was the one she had been in love with. Knowing it was best to give him a few days to cool off, Lovette had decided she would call Mike to apologize. Hopefully, he would forgive her and things could go back to how they used to be.

Chapter 10: Joey

Sitting up straight in his bed and gasping for air, Joey was awakened from his nightmare. He dreamt of Mary and his mother visiting the shed every night for the past week but hadn't worked up the nerve to tell his father about the dreams. He took a deep breath and began to count to 10. Somehow, this would calm his nerves before he needed to do anything. Reaching into his nightstand, he opened his medicine bottle and swallowed a pill.

Walking to his father's office downstairs, Joey knew he could usually find him there. Knocking on the door and pushing it open, he was greeted by both of his parents. His mother had been sitting across from his father at the desk and they both had turned to see who had entered the room. Lovette smiled and motioned for him to sit next to her.

"Hey, mom…dad. Mom, do you mind if I talk to dad alone?" said Joey. Lovette instantly had a look of concern on her face. A feeling of slight disappointment came over her due to the fact he didn't want her a part of the conversation.

Joey had never asked to speak to his father alone and this had somewhat alarmed her. But, she knew that her husband would tell her what was said between the both of them later on. Standing up to kiss him on the cheek, she replied.

"Sure. Is everything okay?"

"...yea. Just guy talk, ya know?" Joey was a horrible liar and Lovette could see right through him. He knew that his mother knew he was lying and began to sweat under his arms. If anyone knew he wasn't telling the truth, it would always be his mother. Leaving the room and closing the door, Joey had turned back around to face his father.

"Dad, I've been having these weird dreams. I know we aren't really supposed to talk about this but I'm scared," said Joey just a notch above a whisper.

"Walk with me outside." Joseph had a feeling what this had been about. He had forbidden his son to talk about it inside the house or around anyone besides him. Walking out of the office, Joey followed his father outside. Silence filled the space between the both of them until they had both reached the edge of the lake.

"What's this about, Joey?" asked Joseph. It had been awhile since they had talked about anything private. Joseph loved his wife and would do anything she had asked him to do but there were certain things he had wanted to make sure she didn't know about. Certain things he felt could ruin everything between the two of them.

"It's Mary. I think she knows something about the shed. I can't put my finger on it but I just know it. I keep having nightmares about her going there and pulling up the door," said Joey. He had felt a great deal of relief lifted from his shoulders. Keeping this to himself had made him nervous about what he should do.

"A nightmare?" Joseph was confused. "You think she knows about the shed because of a nightmare?? Joey, we've talked about this. No one knows about the shed. It's an abandoned building that has been there for a long time now. Have you been going there?" questioned Joseph.

****

August 1, 1998

"I'll be back. I just have to run by the office and pick up some stuff. Go ahead and head up to bed without me," said Joseph. He had hugged his wife and headed out. He didn't like having to lie to her but this was the only way he could protect what had belonged to him: Lovette.

Pulling off of the dirt road, this time he wouldn't walk. He hadn't been in the mood to travel on foot. Driving towards the building in the grass, he was tired of doing this. He was tired of lying and sneaking around. But, it had to be done. When the time was right, this would all be over and done with. He needed to get in and out before anyone saw his vehicle going in or out.

Just as he had gotten done inside the building and was headed back to his car, he caught a glimpse of a figure walking across the grass. Ducking down behind his car, Joseph prayed that he had been undetected. It had been dark outside and hopefully, the person didn't see him on the porch.

But, there was also a random car sitting next to a random shed. He would get rid of his car tonight and have a new one by tomorrow afternoon.

"Dad, is that you?!" shouted the shadow. It had been Joey.

He had no choice but to get up and muster up an explanation for his son. Dusting the dirt off of his pantsuit, Joseph got up and walked around to the other side of the car. Joey had already walked up.

"Joey, what are you doing out here this late?! We thought you were upstairs getting ready for bed. And why are you walking through this field?" questioned Joseph. Instead, he had decided to drill his son about his whereabouts instead of talking about why he was out at the shed this late in the day.

"Sorry, pop. I was headed back from Jaxon's house. I had left my backpack over there earlier," replied Joey.

"What's going on? Why are you at this old shed?" Joseph's plan hadn't worked. He thought his son would be too scared about being caught to even think about why he had been there.

"Don't worry about it. Get in the car," demanded Joseph. There would be no need to get rid of his car. He knew his son would keep things to himself.

****

"Did you hear me, dad?" said Joey. His father had spaced out in his thoughts for a moment and had gotten quiet. Ever since the day Joey caught him at the abandoned shed, he had regretted using his car instead of walking from the dirt road as usual. Joey would've never found out and nothing would be compromised.

"Yea…no. I'm sorry. What did you say?" replied Joseph. He had been so caught up in thinking about the past that he hadn't heard a word his son said.

"I said I've been going but please don't be mad at me. I haven't told mom anything. I just go to…," stammered Joey.

Joseph was angry inside but he had to always remember that Joey had a special condition. He had lashed out once before and he didn't want to make the mistake of doing it again. His son had improved with his behavior tremendously and Joseph didn't want to be the reason his son would stop making progress. Taking a deep breath, he replied.

"Why did you go back?"

"Well, I was just curious, I guess. The last time I went, the lock had been changed. Did you do that?" sad Joey. He began to get angry as well but he didn't want his father to see it. This would only cause them to clash over the topic and he wanted his father to trust him with this.

"Yes, I changed it. I figured you would have at least gone back there once. Remember the talk we had the night you saw me there?" asked Joseph. Joey nodded his head in acknowledgement.

****

August 1, 1998

"Are you mad at me for seeing you there?" asked

Joey. His dad hadn't said a word during the car ride back home. Joseph appeared to be in deep thought and had even forgot his son was in the car until he spoke. He knew he would have to tell his son the truth...or at least some of the truth.

"No, but I didn't want you to find out this way and this soon. You're growing into being a young man but you're still a child. Sometimes, I still wish you were a small child. Things were a lot easier back then. We could protect you more. Now, you're a teenager. You need a little space and privacy. That's still kind of hard for me to accept," said Joseph. He had started to rant about missing the past and almost forgot what the initial topic was.

"I'm not mad. You were going to get your backpack but you still should've let someone know. Your mom could've driven you over there or you could've called Jaxon to let him know you'd stop by tomorrow to get it. It's late and things happen at this time. Bad things happen around this time," continued Joseph.

"Anyway, do you remember my coworker, Will?" asked Joseph. Joey nodded his head and his father continued talking. "Well, we have a very important business. A business that most people shouldn't know about."

"The business has been in the family for some time now. You know that. But, I plan to be the one to step away from it very soon. I want to do other things in life. Always remember to be your own man. Don't ever feel the need to follow behind me or anyone else because you think that's what they want you to do. You're a smart young man and

*whatever you choose to do, I know you'll be great at it,"
said Joseph.*

*"Me and Will have rules to our business and its
time you know them. I need you to always remember them,
okay? The business is run by the men in our family and
close friends we can trust. I'm trusting you, son. This is a
part of being a man; being trusted with valuable
information that not too many people know about."*

*Joseph was nervous and even thought about
backing out of the topic but he had dug himself deep at this
point. His son knew about the shed and he wanted to test
his loyalty.*

*Joey had been confused. He begin to think his father
must be a drug dealer. He had heard about drug dealers all
over the world and what kind of lifestyle they lived. His
parents owned a big house and a nice car but he would've
never thought they sold drugs. To him, their possessions
hadn't been "drug dealer type of nice".*

*"Dad, I promise not to say anything. Is it drugs?"
blurted out Joey. Joseph had smirked at his son's guess. He
was a smart kid and although it did sound like he sold
drugs, Joseph shook his head.*

"No. We don't sell drugs," replied Joseph.

*Joey was proud that his father wasn't a drug dealer.
He knew that most drug dealers would get caught and end
up in jail; something he didn't want to happen to his father.*

*Also, he knew the things drugs did to people's
bodies and he had hoped his father didn't have a part in*

contributing to this. So, to him, whatever his father was doing couldn't be worse than selling drugs and knew he'd definitely keep his secret.

"There are certain rules to our business. The first one is: the citizens in this county are off limits. Majority of us have grown up together and our children play together. We wouldn't want anyone involved here. The second rule piggy backs off of the first one: family members are to be kept separate."

"You're a growing boy and I know you have urges, but I need you to stay away from dating girls of people I work with. Fortunately, I only work with 4 other people in Shawford, whom you've met and you know who their daughters are. Just stay away, okay?"

Joey nodded. He felt a great sense of proudness because his father had trusted him with some details of the business he ran. He knew no matter what, he would keep his father's secret safe. Plus, Joey had thought that the men his father worked with all had unattractive daughters, so not dating them would be a piece of cake.

"The last rule is: no matter what you see and hear, you aren't allowed to repeat to anyone or anywhere. If you need to talk to me, ask and we can go somewhere private. My business doesn't concern your friends, girlfriends, sisters, grandparents or anyone else. I'm the only one you're allowed to talk to about anything. Not even your mother."

"I love you from the depths of my soul but right beside that same love lies a pit of anger that would be released if you ever broke any of these rules. This doesn't

mean I don't love you but I need you to understand how serious this is. I can't have you unleash that," said Joseph.

Joey had never seen his father become angry before and he felt that since he wouldn't break any of the rules, there would be no need for him to ever get mad. There wouldn't be a soul that Joey would tell about any of his father's information.

"Oh and son? Your mother knows about the business but she doesn't know about the shed. I need you to keep that between the both of us. I want to be the one to tell her. She needs to hear it from me," said Joseph. The whole ride home, this had been his main concern.

This had been the only thing that made Joey feel. He wasn't a good liar and Lovette could always detect when he wasn't telling the truth. But, he would still keep his father's secret to himself and avoid his mother if she ever questioned him. As soon as they had pulled up to the house, it were as if Joseph had read his son's mind.

"I won't tell her. I promise," replied Joey.

****

"Dad, I'm sorry but it's just a lot that I'm confused about. I know I should've come to you first and asked you but you're always busy and well, sometimes I feel like you don't have much time for me…much time for us," said Joey.

Joey had loved his father and Joseph was his hero. He had made sure him, his mother and siblings had gotten everything they asked for. But, he had wished that Joseph had been around more to do things with him.

"And for that, I'm apologetic. I know I work a lot but I promise it's for a good cause. When this is over with, there'll be more time for us to hang out and do stuff. I don't want you feeling like I don't care to spend time with you because I really do. You kids and your mother mean the most to me and I want you all to be happy," replied Joseph.

"As far as the dream goes, maybe you've had this nightmare because you know no one is supposed to know about it. I know Mary can annoy you sometimes and I think that's why she was the one in the dream. Don't worry about it. As long as you keep everything between us and stop going there, everything will be fine. And, I mean it," he continued.

"I know you mean well but you don't want to mess up the plans that are in store. You going there could jeopardize a lot. That's why I had the lock changed. Promise me that you're done going there." Joseph gave his son a stern look until he spoke."

Taking a deep breath in and ejecting a long sigh, Joey replied. "I promise." This time, he had meant it. He had trusted his father and didn't want anything bad to come of his actions. The shed would be on his mind daily but Joseph had expressed how important this was and Joey didn't want to disappoint his father.

"Good. Let's go back in the house. I know your mother is upstairs wondering why you only wanted to talk to me," laughed Joseph. "You know you're her number one baby and it's probably driving her up the wall. Listen, we'll just tell her you wanted to have a talk about your man parts, okay?"

Both of them laughed and walked back towards the house. Kissing his son at the top of his head, Joseph needed to remind him that he was his number one baby as well...no matter how old he got.

Chapter 11: Falling for you.

"I found this in the bathroom trash. Either we are going to be big sisters or you have some explaining to do," whispered Iris.

Lovette had done a poor job of covering the test up with toilet tissue. But, it was only a matter of time before her sister had figured things out anyway. Iris had always noticed little yet important things that many kids her age didn't notice. Sometimes, Lovette felt like they had been closer in age due to how mature Iris had been.

"Look, I'm going to tell them soon. Just don't say anything. I just found out myself and I'm scared as shit," replied Lovette. Iris could hear the fear in her voice. She hadn't planned on ratting Lovette out. Iris had never done it before and today wouldn't be the day that she would start.

"I KNEW something was different! You've been a little pudgy around the waist," said Iris while busting out laughing. Getting up from Lovette's bed, she pinched her sister's love handles and laughed even harder.

"Oh, plus, mom and dad didn't know how disgusted you were when you smelled the pot roast last night!" Iris had been tickled to death while Lovette sat there taking it all in.

"Okay, enough of the jokes. I don't know what I'm

going to do. We're supposed to be starting college soon and I just don't know," Lovette had been scared out of her mind to tell her parents that she was pregnant. She already knew how they would react...especially her mother. As soon as the thought of what she would say or do came to mind, their mother pushed up Lovette's bedroom door.

"Dinner is ready. What's wrong, honey? You don't look like you're feeling well," asked her mother. She was staring at Lovette with genuine concern.

"I'm just hungry. That's all," lied Lovette. In fact, it was the complete opposite. She had started to smell the aroma from the kitchen and couldn't handle the thought of eating fried chicken for dinner. The smell of the burning cooking oil had begun to make her nauseas and before she could swallow the vomit, she gagged and it spilled onto her brand new silver sandals.

"Oh, my Lord! Lovette! Honey?! Iris, go get her a cold washcloth and a water bottle!" hollered Trudy.

Pushing past her mother and slamming the bathroom door shut, Lovette finished dry heaving over the toilet bowl. She hadn't eaten today and the bile had tasted like poison every time it pushed through her throat and shot out of her mouth. Knocking on the bathroom door, Trudy was frantic.

"Lovette, open the door! Do I need to call the doctor?! What's wrong? CLARENCE! Get up here and help me!" she shouted.

"Mom! I'm fine. Just go away for a second. I think it's a stomach bug. Don't call the doctor, please. It's not

that serious. I feel better already," yelled Lovette through the closed door. Trudy had continued fussing and banging until Lovette had worked up the strength to open the door.

"See, I told you I'm fine," she replied tiredly. Her father had just made his way upstairs and was sweating from having to run up them so quickly. He was a heavy set man who didn't exercise at all, so this better had been a good reason why he had to rush up the steps.

Lovette instantly felt the need to tell them and get it over with. Iris had been sitting in the chair in the corner and hadn't reacted to the situation. She felt the same way Lovette had; there mother was going to lose her mind once she found out she was going to be a grandmother. Everyone had been in her bedroom and Lovette didn't feel like delaying the conversation any longer.

"Well, no...I'm not fine. Mom...dad? Can we talk?" said Lovette. Her hands had been shaking and her palms were sweating profusely. Every time she wiped them on her jeans, within seconds they were wet again.

"Lovette, tell us what's going on," said Trudy. The look on her mother's face put her at ease for a second until she remembered what she was about to tell them. She knew her mother would instantly turn into a tornado and everything would go downhill from there. Her father normally didn't react until he saw how his wife felt about things first. He didn't have much of a backbone.

"I don't know how else to say this but to just say it. I'm p...p...pr...pregnant," stuttered Lovette. Relief had escaped her body because she no longer had to hold the secret in but she instantly felt scared due to how her mother *was about to react. The room was filled with loud silence. Trudy had turned towards Iris and she knew that was her cue to leave the room.*

"Before you both say anything, I know how upset you are. I know how disappointed you both are in me. I also know that I've hurt both of you with my actions. I didn't do this on purpose and I didn't expect for it to happen. I didn't want this to happen...at least nowhere near this soon. I'm really sorry if I let you down...I really am," cried Lovette. She hadn't expected to say these words to them; they had just come out of nowhere.

"Come here," whispered Trudy. Lovette stopped crying and looked at her mother with suspicion. She had already hit her once and Trudy had apologized for doing that but she didn't want a repeat of what happened a few months ago.

"I said come here," repeated her mother. Walking towards her, Trudy opened her arms as if she wanted a hug. Confused with her actions, Lovette allowed her mother to wrap her arms around her body.

"You've been a really good daughter to me and for that, I thank you. You've hardly ever been in trouble and you've always done well in school. People make mistakes. You're human; you're going to make mistakes. This doesn't make me love you any less or change how great of a person I know you are. Am I shocked? Well, definitely. You've made so many plans for yourself and while they can still happen, it's just going to either take a little longer or just be a bigger challenge."

Clarence had been sitting on his daughter's bed in

complete shock. He hadn't said a word yet and let his wife do all of the talking. The only thing he could think of was a little boy running up to him and calling him "pawpaw". Smiling to himself, the thought warmed his heart. He had been the only man in the house and had desperately wanted a son. When Trudy had given birth to Iris, she had been adamant on not wanting any more children.

Lovette had been blindsided by her mother's kindness. She hadn't even thought about the option of her parents accepting that she was pregnant and unmarried at 18 years old. They had loved her without a doubt and also wanted the best for her but she just knew in her gut that they weren't going to handle it the way they just did. As soon as the question entered her mind, Trudy pulled away from Lovette's embrace.

"Please tell me the father is Joe," she said.

"Mom! Yes! I'm not a slut. I mean, I understand how this looks but I've thought about all of that. I promise, it's Joes," swore Lovette. The thought of Mike had crossed her mind and she started to cry all over again. He hadn't accepted any of her calls since the altercation between the three of them a few weeks ago.

"Thank God," whispered Trudy. She had overheard her daughters talking about the breakup with Mike and how Lovette was seeing Joe now. Trudy had loved Joe as if he were her own son. He had come from a wealthy family, was a smart and respectable young man and she knew he had loved her daughter the first time she met Joe. He was everything she had wanted for Lovette.

Lovette rolled her eyes at her mother's insensitive

comment but said nothing in return. She had handled the situation well and didn't want to upset her by having a smart remark. Meanwhile, Clarence had stood up and decided to pitch in on the conversation.

"Your mother is right. We just want the best for you. I can't act like I'm not slightly disappointed. You're my baby and I just want you to get the best that life has to offer. Joe is a good guy and I know he will do the right thing," said Clarence. Hugging is daughter and giving her a smile, he left the bedroom and went back downstairs.

"Now, we need to make some arrangements. Have you talked to Joe? Does he know? What about his parents? We can have small and intimate wedding with just us and his parents. The whole word doesn't need to know just yet," said Trudy. The thought of helping decorate a wedding had excited her.

Lovette had looked mortified. Marriage?! A WEDDING?! Her head begin to hurt and she sat down on her bed. She hadn't even thought about these things. She wasn't even certain that she was even ready to become a mother right now. She liked Joe as a friend and he was always there for her but...she didn't love him.

Lovette was still very much in love with Mike and she could only think of how much all of this would hurt him. Even though he hadn't spoken to her, she knew this would be another thing to make him angry all over again.

"Mom, wait. This is a lot. We haven't talked about other options and stuff. Joe is a cool and I like him but I don't love him. You and dad have always told me that I should marry someone that I'm in love with," said Lovette.

"Other options?! What do you mean 'other options'? What other options are there?! You're pregnant with my grandchild and it's going to need a stable environment with BOTH parents around. I HOPE you aren't talking about adoption because there's no way in Hades someone else is going to be raising my flesh and blood!"

"The damage is done and we are going to spin this in a positive way. Joe is a good young man who will grow to be a great man...and he loves you. You may not be in love with him now but you care about him and you can grow to love him," replied Trudy.

Lovette was stuck on her mother's words. Never in a million years did she think she would marry Joe or even raise a family with him. It had been Mike she wanted these things with. For a moment, she thought about going back on her words and telling her parents that Mike was the father. She had desperately wanted him to be the one she would raise this child with but she knew that he wasn't. Changing her mind back, she said nothing and just wept.

"Honey, everything is going to be alright. We'll handle all of the arrangements and we can go over to talk with the Marks tomorrow or within the next few days. They need to know as soon as possible, okay?"

Kissing her daughter on the forehead and giving her another hug, Trudy continued. "Get some rest. I'll bring you up some soup and crackers. It should help ease your stomach. You have to eat a little more now. It's not just about you anymore. Feed my grandbaby, child."

****

"Hello, Mrs. O'Conner. How have you been?" said Lovette with a bit of hesitation. She hadn't called Mike in over a week because his mother had nicely told her that he didn't want to hear from her. Mike's mother really liked Lovette and was a bit disappointed to learn that the two of them had broken up. Mike didn't tell her all of the details but he had been torn up about it.

"Hey, honey. I'm doing as best as I can...considering, ya know. Things get tough here and there but I'm still here. How about you?" she replied.

Trying her best to talk as low as possible on the phone with her, Mike had been home and she didn't want him to have any clue that it had been Lovette calling. For a moment, she just knew Lovette was going to start begging to speak with Mike and she began to regret talking to her.

"I'm okay. I know Mike doesn't want to hear from me but...this is pretty urgent. I'm not calling to get back with him or make him upset. I just need to tell him something really quick," pleaded Lovette.

The long pause that followed had made her feel like Mrs. O'Conner had hung up on her until she had heard whispering in the background. Just when Lovette had given up hope with speaking to Mike, a voice came back on the line.

"What do you want?" said Mike angrily. He had specifically asked his mother to tell her that he didn't want to talk to her. He thought Lovette got the clue when the calls had stopped. Although he did miss her, he couldn't bring himself to forgive how she betrayed him before even knowing the truth.

"Mike, I know you probably hate my guts and I understand you don't want to talk but there's something I think you should know...something you should hear from me," said Lovette. She had started to feel the tears form in her eyes because of how hard starting the conversation had been. This would only make Mike hate her even more.

"Lovette, whatever it is, just say it. I'm kind of busy right now," lied Mike. He had been laying around the house doing absolutely nothing. The thought of running into Lovette had forced him to stay inside for a while. He couldn't handle seeing her just yet.

"I'm pregnant," whispered Lovette. She couldn't hold back the tears any longer. Covering her mouth while silently crying and refusing to make any noise, she waited for what Mike had to say. This had been more nerve-racking than when she had to tell her parents.

"Mike, did you hear what I said?"

"Look, everything is confusing right now but I plan to do the right thing. You won't be in this alone. I'll do what I have to do and be there for you." Taking a deep breath in and letting out a heavy sigh, he continued.

"Have you told your parents yet? I know they don't too much like me but we can tell them together. I don't want you having to go through that alone."

Letting the phone drop to the floor, Lovette didn't realize Mike would think he was the father. He had known she slept with Joe but he hadn't questioned who the father was. Getting dizzier by the second, she could feel vomit threatening to come up. Taking a deep breath and forcing it *back down, she picked up the phone.*

"Hello? Hello? Love? You there? What happened? Everything okay?" inquired Mike. Hearing the phone drop and silence had him worried until he heard Lovette's voice again.

"Yes, I'm here. Mike...you aren't the father. It's Joe's," she confessed. She felt even worse that she had to mention his name. Feeling empty inside and worthless, Lovette couldn't control her crying. She had messed up bad and now fully realized the damage she had done. Even if Mike really didn't cheat on her, seeking revenge had been on her mind and now, she was in an even bigger mess.

"Wait...JOE?! Are you kidding me?!" yelled Mike. He was even more furious than when he found out they had slept together. Now, she had been carrying his child. Even though he was angry with Lovette, he still held on a small piece of hope that one day they would fix things.

Mike was hurt by her actions but a part of him felt like she would come to her senses and that they could eventually make things right. Delivering her news, reconciliation was no longer an option for him.

"Mike, I know I messed up and I know how this looks but I just wanted to be one to let you know. People talk and I just didn't want you to find out from anyone else." She was just as torn as he had been. Her mother had forbidden her from adoption and termination. There was no other choice for her but to prepare to become a mother.

"...and all of this started because of stupid Stephanie! You just had to go sleep with him because you

thought I cheated! I've never lied to you and I've always been honest with you even when I felt like your feelings just might get hurt. Joe has been planning to get with you since day one and you convinced me that it was all in my head! I believed you when you needed me to but you couldn't do the same for me."

"You never deserved me. You judged me before we even started dating and when I proved you wrong, you still showed me just how much you didn't trust my honesty. Do me a favor and don't call back here ever again. I swear, Lovette. I mean it."

Before she could respond, Mike had hung up the phone and ripped it out of the wall. His mother had been in her bedroom listening in on the other end of the phone the entire time; she was holding her hand over the mouthpiece to silence any unforeseen background noises.

Mike's emotional wellbeing had been up and down for the past week and she knew that this would do even more damage. He had been experiencing his real first teenage heartbreak.

Finding out all of this had made her instantly dislike Lovette. She was nothing like what she had thought. Her son wasn't perfect but he had grown to be a great young man. He deserved better than what she had given him.

Since Mike wasn't the father of Lovette's child, this was on the brighter side of things. He had a bright future with possibly becoming a professional basketball player and this could've ruined it. Now, she had been glad Mike was rid of her and could go on with his life.

****

Trudy had taken Lovette to the doctor and had confirmed that she was indeed pregnant. The at home test told her she was pregnant but she had hoped and prayed that the test was giving a false positive; she prayed the doctor would tell her the complete opposite. This alone made her even more depressed.

But, Dr. Gore hadn't. Her gut told her that her plans would never be accomplished. Trudy had already told her that she wouldn't be able attend college in the fall because "there was no way she was taking her grandchild to another state."

The ride home from the office visit had been a silent one. Trudy was quiet because of all of the wedding ideas spinning in her head and Lovette had been quiet because of the plan she had set in stone as soon as she entered the house.

"Don't look so sad. Everything is going to be okay. Go on up and wash up. I'll start dinner and you can help me if you're up to it," said Trudy. Getting out of the car, both of them entered the house and went their separate ways.

As soon as Lovette knew her mother was preoccupied in the kitchen, she headed upstairs and towards the back of the hallway. Standing with her back against the wall beside her parent's bedroom, she took a deep breath and took off as fast as she could charging at the stairwell.

As soon as she got to the top step, her body came

crashing down hitting her head on the vanity. Running and jumping had been the last thing she remembered when she had regained consciousness in the hospital.

****

As soon as she had opened her eyes, Joseph had been the first person she had seen. Her mouth had felt dry and she had desperately needed a drink of water. He was sleeping in the chair beside her bed and her mother had been lying down on the couch on the opposite side of the room.

"You're up! Nurse! She's up! Thank God! Honey, you had us worried sick taking an ugly fall like that," cried Trudy. She had been a total mess when she heard the noise and found Lovette knocked out on the staircase. Her head had been pressed up against the wooden leg and there seemed to have been blood everywhere. Since her daughter was now awake, she cried even harder. For a moment, she thought she had lost her.

"Mom, why is Joe here?" mumbled Lovette. He had still been in a deep sleep and hadn't budged even through all of her mother's yelling. As soon as she had asked this, two nurses entered the room and started examining her.

"I'm okay. Just stop...give me a minute please?" asked Lovette to both of the nurses. They both had been hesitant to leave the room before examining her but Lovette had refused to let them touch her. Leaving out and closing the door, one of the nurses told her that they would be back in 10 minutes to check on her.

"Lovette, you didn't have to be that rude. And, what

do you mean why is he here?! He's the father of your child for crying out loud. Speaking of father of your child. Why would you lie to us and say that you told Joe and his parents?! Do you know how humiliating it was for me to have to call them today and explain all of this?!" said Trudy. She had given Lovette time to tell Joseph and her family but instead, Lovette had lied and told her that they had known.

"Because I wasn't ready! You keep rushing me to make decisions when I don't even know how I feel about things yet! THIS ISN'T YOUR BODY AND THIS ISN'T YOUR LIFE!" shouted Lovette. She had finally reached her breaking point. Her mother had already decided things for her but hadn't once asked her how she felt or what she wanted to do about anything. Every morning, Trudy was at her door with new and overwhelming ideas about the baby, her future, Joe, the wedding...just everything.

"First of all, you better watch your tone. You might be considered an adult now but you're still MY child. You understand me? Second, I'm your mother and I'm supposed to always look out for what's in your best interest. Did I get angry with you when you told us you were pregnant? NO! I told you it would be okay and that we would figure all of this out together. You can always tell me how you feel," replied Trudy.

Joseph sat up in his chair and waited for the two of them to finish their argument before he said anything. He hadn't been at the hospital that long before he fell asleep but had been up all night hanging out with friends. Lovette noticed he had woken up and felt embarrassed that he had to find out about the pregnancy this way.

"Now, I'll give the both of you some time alone so you can REALLY talk this time. Oh, and the doctors said the baby is just fine. They want to keep you overnight just to make sure you're okay," said her mother. "I'm headed to the cafeteria. Do either of you want anything?"

Hearing the news about the baby had made Lovette dizzy. Her whole body had been in pain from the fall and she just knew that the baby wouldn't make it through. This had been her only option to free herself from what she knew she didn't need at the time.

Feeling overwhelmed, she shook her head no to her mother's question. As soon as she had exited the room, Lovette cried so hard that her body began to ache even more.

"Lovette, what's wrong?" asked Joseph. He had found out that he was going to be a father and his unborn child's life could possibly a risk all in the same sentence. His feelings had been up and down until he had finally reached the hospital. When they had gotten the news that the baby was fine, he felt a sense of relief but was still concerned because Lovette had still been unconscious.

"I didn't want you to find out this way. I wanted to be the one to tell you," lied Lovette. She hadn't had any intentions on telling him. She had regretted telling Mike the other day and wish she would've waited until after she had executed her plan.

Now, none of that mattered. She was still pregnant. Figuring the pregnancy would miscarry after the fall, she had hoped Mike would at least talk to her and they could eventually get back to where they used to be. This wouldn't happen now.

"I understand. It's not something that's easy to tell someone but you do know that I'm here for you, right? I always will be and I'm not going anywhere," said Joseph.

He had meant every word of it, too. He had been deeply in love with her and had always felt like he would never get a chance with a girl like her...until now.

Hearing how he felt had actually made her feel a little better. She had heard of stories when females get pregnant and how the male abandons them with a child. Lovette knew that she didn't want to be one of those stories. Even though Joe wasn't the person she wanted to have a child with, knowing that he was going to be supportive comforted her a little.

Chapter 12: Mary

"If everyone could pass their homework assignments from last night to the front of the classroom, please. Did anyone have any difficulties they'd like to discuss? If so, we can talk about them now or we can meet after the final bell if you need extra help. I'll be after school for about an hour and a half," said Mrs. Blotney.

"You should stay after school to explain to Scary Mary how her sister is dead. I'm sick of her whispering to herself!" shouted out Brennen. The whole class laughed as if what he were saying was true. He had always said weird things to other kids but this was it. He wouldn't be shouting out another word after today.

"Brennen! That was unnecessary and just mean. Now, apologize and go straight to the front office," Mrs. Blotney said sternly. Although this had made me feel a little better, I was still going to say what I had on my mind.

"It's okay, Mrs. Blotney. Brennen, I wouldn't be so quick to flap those rotten gums of yours. While you're worried about me and my sister, you should be worried about why you're two years older than everyone in here. You're an idiot and both of your parents are idiots for giving birth to an idiot. Your mom should've swallowed you instead."

I had heard this from Joey and his friends. I had an idea what it meant but wasn't entirely too sure. When

Joey's friend, Jaxon, said it, everyone started laughing and that's exactly what the whole class did when I had used it.

"Mary!! That wasn't nice either!" screamed Mrs. Blotney. "The both of you report to the front office immediately!" She had picked up the phone to tell the principal that we would both be on the way to the front office. Meanwhile, Brennen had a look on his face as if he were about to cry from embarrassment.

"Gather your things and go!"

Taking my time, I chose to add on to my comment. We were already in trouble, so there was no harm and finishing what I had wanted to say.

"I shouldn't be getting in trouble for this. You're the teacher and the one who TAUGHT us that every action has a reaction. Had this fool kept his mouth shut, I would have never said anything about him. He got what he deserved."

"We are kind to those even when they are cruel to us. Don't ever lower yourself down to someone else's level. You could've used kind words to uplift Brennen instead," she replied.

"Well, you just admitted to how low of a person he is, which is pretty funny. Also, being nice to someone who was mean first just sounds as dumb as Brennen's learning ability. And you're supposed to be a teacher?" The "ohhhs" and "ahhhs" spread around the classroom and Mrs. Blotney's face turned redder than the ink she grades the low score tests with.

"Get out of my classroom! NOW!" she shouted.

Laughing at her comment, Brennen and I both walked out of the classroom and headed towards the principal's office.

Our classroom was located back of the school in one of the trailers. I can't stand having classes out here. The trailers were always colder than the actual building and the floors always felt like we were going to fall through if we jumped on them. They could've just added on to the school instead of stick us out here in the cold. Walking a few steps ahead of him, Brennen broke the silence.

"You didn't have to be such a jerk. I know that I'm older than everyone..." he said. "I was out of school a lot because I was sick. Anyway, why do you keep talking to Joyce? She's dead, ya know?"

"It's not my fault you were sick. Why are you minding my business anyway? She's MY sister for ME to talk to. Not yours. I don't bother you and you didn't have to embarrass me like that in front of the whole class. What did I ever do to you, huh?" Turning around to face him, he had stopped walking and looked confused.

"Don't act like you don't know what you did to me, Mary," he said. He actually looked calmer than he did in the classroom and now, he began to look sad.

"I don't know what you're talking about. I haven't done anything to you." This was getting annoying. He must've gotten me confused with someone else because I had no idea what he was talking about. Rolling my eyes and turning around to head back towards the front office, he kept running his mouth.

"In kindergarten, you smashed my blocks over and one hit me in the lip." Kindergarten? He was mad about that?! I barely even remember being in the same class as him then but, just as fast as I thought that, I knew exactly what he could be talking about.

"That wasn't me. It was Joyce." The only people who could really tell me and Joyce apart were mama, papa, and Joey. Everyone else would always ask which one we were before we started talking. Even our grandparents couldn't keep up with who was who sometimes. Sometimes, we even switched classes to see if we could get away with it. This one day he was talking about, we must have.

"Why would you say something about your sister like that?" Brennen had a look of disgust on his face. Before I knew it, he pushed past me and took off storming towards the office again.

"No, seriously. I didn't do that to you. Sometimes, we would trade places. Whenever we traded places, we would have to pretend to act like the one another. She must have taken acting like me overboard." Joyce didn't tell me that she had kicked over someone's blocks that day. I guess that explains why I had silent lunch for two whole days after that.

"Really?" he replied. The look on his face told me that he didn't know what to believe but he wanted to think what I was saying was true. Dropping down to one knee and placing his book bag on the floor, he tied his shoe.

"I thought it was you this whole time. I mean, you weren't the nicest person back then but I kind of always liked..." whispered Brennen. Stopping himself and getting up from the floor, he started walking back towards the front office.

"Liked what?!" I screeched. If he was about to say what I thought he was going to say, I felt as if I were about to vomit. Funny thing was my outfit today was a pea green t-shirt with the same color pants to match. I'm sure the throw up would go right along with today's fit.

"Mary, don't go acting all weird on me now. I mean, I think you're pretty and I did like you but I just didn't know that was Joyce instead of you that day. Plus, you're always acting weird and talking to Joyce when you know she isn't here anymore. Why do you keep doing that?"

My head started spinning. Within the same breath, this idiot just told me that he liked me and that I was crazy for still talking to my sister. Who does that?!

"Listen. Just because YOU can't see her doesn't mean I'm crazy. You got that? For a second, I thought you might've been nice and you just snatched that away, fool." Pushing past him, I walked towards the office and this time, I didn't stop. Brennen didn't say anything else and just followed me there.

Opening the old raggedy door, Ms. Guild sat at the front desk and frowned when she saw us walk in. The woman was already unpleasant to look at and she had the nerve to make an even uglier face which made me giggle. My laughter upset her even more.

"Mary, this is no laughing matter. Both of you have a seat and Principal Greene will be out shortly to talk to you both." Ms. Guild was one of the women that would come over and hang out with mama. Mama would sometimes have these annoying little parties filled with women who complain about their husbands, their jobs, kids and anything else they could find to complain about.

Ms. Guild and her husband got divorced because she gained too much weight and he didn't like that. I would sometimes listen by the door when they would come over until mama came out shooing me away.

Rolling my eyes and plopping down on the old wooden bench, the principal walked out of his office and waved for us to both come into his office. This had been the first time I had seen the inside of his office. I smiled feeling surprised that I hadn't seen it much sooner.

"I hear there was in issue in class today. Who wants to go first and tell me what happened?" said Mr. Greene.

Mr. Greene was a small white man that had a mustache that curved upwards. I don't see how he didn't get bothered from it touching hi nose all day. There was a picture of his family sitting next to his keyboard and oh man! His wife looked as if she could eat him alive. Then, she had the nerve to be sitting her big behind on his lap. Laughing out loud during another serious moment instantly made me stop. I didn't feel like hearing mama's mouth today.

"Would you like to tell the both of us what is so funny, Mary?" questioned Principal Greene. Brennen was staring at me with a smirk and turned red as if he were holding in gas.

"No, Mr. Greene," I said.

"Okay. Once again, would either one of you like to tell me what happened in class? Or do I just need to ask your teacher and suspend you both?"

Suspension? I had never been suspended before. Yea, I had to flip my behavior card a few times, a few silent lunch sessions and had my play time revoked but suspension?! That was taking things too far and mama would for sure have my behind.

"I said something mean about Mary and it upset her. If it wasn't for me, she wouldn't have said the things she said. I'm sorry, Mary. It won't ever happen again," whispered Brennen. I hadn't been expecting for him to say that and it only made me stare at him.

"Is that what happened Mary?" asked Mr. Greene. Nodding my head and still staring at Brennen, Mr. Greene continued talking.

"Okay. Thank you for apologizing, Brennen. In this school, we don't say or do mean things to hurt people. Whenever we feel angry or upset, we talk to teachers to help us sort out our feelings. Okay? Now, I want the both of you to return to class and apologize to Mrs. Blotney for interrupting her class. Also, you both will be staying after school today for detention."

Walking out of the office and heading back towards class, I broke the weird silence between us.

"Did you really mean that? About being sorry?"

"Well, yea…I shouldn't have said it at all. You weren't wrong to get upset at what I said. I really am sorry." The way he started to stare at me made me feel funny. Maybe he wasn't such a bad person after all.

"Well, just don't say anything else about my sister." Nodding his head and walking back into the classroom, we apologized to Mrs. Blotney. The look on her face told me that she had wished we did get suspended.

****

The final bell had blared through the hallways and I was dreading having to stay after school for some mess Brennen had started. Mrs. Blotney had called our parents to let them know they had to pick us up later. I could hear my mother sucking her teeth on the phone from across the room.

"Mrs. Blotney? Can I use the bathroom before I do my jail time?" I asked. Rolling her eyes and dismissing me, I headed out to empty my bladder. I couldn't remember if I had used the bathroom at all today.

"Can you believe she still thinks that Joyce is alive? What a creep, right?" The giggles echoed throughout the bathroom and the three faces turned white as if I were a ghost when I came around the bathroom corner. The burning feeling that left my body from earlier when Brennen mentioned my sister's name had now returned. Only this time, the water had boiled over.

No one said anything. Everyone turned back towards the mirrors they stood in front of and kept packing on more and more of the roll on lip gloss just about every girl in school had. I had thought I knew everyone's name in school but I hadn't a clue who these three girls were. I had never seen them before, so they were bold to be talking about my sister. This pissed me off even more.

I matched their silence. Standing directly behind the girl in the middle and looking over her shoulder into the mirror, my palms began to sweat.

"See, this is what happens when people don't mind their business," whispered Joyce. "Teach her how to mind her business."

"Umm, are you going to continue being a creep behind me? Like, I can literally feel your breath on my neck," sassed the blonde. Both of her sidekicks laughed as if they would pee on themselves any second now. All three of them turned around and continued to laugh in my face.

Before I could let them laugh at me for another second, I had a fist full of blonde hair. Ramming her into the sink and slamming the back of her head into the mirror, the sounds of a million pieces had hit the floor.

Little pieces of my reflection were staring back at me when I looked down. The blond was unconscious and when I turned to run out of the bathroom, both of the girls snatched me back in and began attacking me.

"WHAT'S GOING ON IN HERE?! SOMEONE, HELP! CALL AN AMBULANCE!" screamed the deep voice. As soon as I heard the screams, the beating to my body stopped. The pieces of mirror were digging into my back and I could feel the tiny stings all over my body.

****

"Your principal said that Jane's parents weren't going to press charges but you've been suspended for a week. Oh, and don't go near her again. How are you feeling?" asked mama.

Jane. Blondie has a name now. Mama didn't sound as mad as I thought she would. She had been more concerned about how I was feeling to make a fuss. The hospital had kept me overnight and my body had been hurting in places it had never hurt before.

"Mama, they all started it. They were talking about me and Joyce when I went into the bathroom and then she called me a creep. If it wasn't for that, I wouldn't have hit her. Did the other girls get in trouble? They did attack me, too."

"The other girls did get suspended too but you did start the fight. Trust me, I understand. In high school, I had to show a girl a thing or two the night I met your dad. I was at a school dance, she said some things and I said some things back. She poured a drink on my dress and, oh man. I wanted to beat her senseless but I just pulled her down to the ground and dumped my drink on her. I wish you could've seen her hollering and wiggling all over the dance floor like someone was kicking her around," she said.

As soon as I busted out laughing, I was reminded of the blows I had just taken the day before. One of the sidekicks pulled out some of my hair in the back, so there was a small bald spot where it really didn't matter; I had always worn my hair down anyway. My lip was busted, there was lump on the right side of my forehead and my ribs felt like they were on fire.

"Take it easy, baby. They put a good hurting on you. From the looks of it, you didn't get a hit in on the other girls, huh? You sure you're really my child?" said mama while laughing. Sucking my teeth and trying to sit up in bed, she gently pushed me back down.

"No, you lie down. You need your rest. I was only kidding. You don't look too bad. You'll be your regular self in no time."

"Mama, am I crazy? Because…" and before I could finish talking, she gasped and cut me off.

"NO! Oh, no. You aren't crazy, baby! You're just having a difficult time with certain things. That's all. People are going to say cruel things in life. It happens. It doesn't make it okay but just know that you can't control what people say. You aren't crazy at all. We're getting you help and you're going to be fine. I promise. Okay?"

"Okay." My head was pounding and my ribs felt like they were definitely broken. Rubbing my stomach and trying to sit up again, my body gave in and I fell back against the pillow.

"Yea, you're my child. Hardheaded as ever. You need to relax," said mama while laughing again. "I'm about to go make some pies for Mrs. Blotney. I heard about class today, too. You just had an eventful day, huh?" said mama while giving me the side eye.

"I promise he started it, too. Also, I think he likes me." I had forgotten all about Brennen.

"Well, you're a beautiful and smart young lady. I'm sure all of the boys like you. Sometimes, they just don't know how to show it. That's why some people might be mean to you…because they like you. I know it sounds weird but boys don't always know how to show you they like you. All they'd have to do is just tell us but you'll see how backwards men are later on in life."

Getting up from the bed and kissing me on my forehead, she left out of the bedroom. My body ached from top to bottom. I hadn't felt like this since Joey slammed me all around the bathroom floor. As quick as he came to mind, he pushed in the door and sat down on my bed. Saying nothing but leaning in to hug me, he held on for a few seconds and left back out of the room. If anything was ever awkward, the moment he just hugged me would be on the top of the awkward list.

Chapter 13: "Well...Do you?"

October 1983

Joseph watched as Lovette sank her teeth into the double cheeseburger she had asked him to buy; she had specifically asked for extra tomatoes. Lovette had only been a few months pregnant and her cravings were already through the roof. He had taken the year off from school to stay with her and monitor her pregnancy closely. The fall she had taken down the stairs had Joseph concerned every single day.

Trudy and Clarence had suggested that Joseph move into their house due to how much space they had for them and the baby. His parents hadn't been too happy about their son moving out but Joseph jumped at the chance of being with Lovette daily. They would be married within the next couple of weeks and he had loved the idea of her becoming his wife.

Lovette, on the other hand, wasn't excited at all. She had cared for Joseph but she didn't think they were ready for marriage. In fact, she knew that they weren't ready. The whole summer had passed and all she could think about was Mike. He had been on her mind a lot lately but she knew not to contact him again. He had to have been enjoying college and to hear from her would only upset him.

Watching the cheese hit her chin had made him grin. He couldn't believe that the woman he loved was now about to be the mother of his child and his wife. Joseph felt as if he hit the biggest lottery in the world. No other moment had made him feel happier than this. He couldn't wait to be her husband and show her that everything would be perfect.

"Why are you smiling so hard?" said Lovette through a mouthful of food. Wiping her chin with the napkin, she looked at Joseph sideways. He had been acting weird lately. He'd been happier than usual.

"I'm just happy things are working out. That's all. That burger must be good, huh?" replied Joseph. Lovette nodded her head and both of them laughed together.

The wedding had been mostly planned by Trudy. She loved these type of things and was always willing to take on the lead role. Lovette had tried to convince her that the wedding could wait but Trudy had her mind set on putting her daughter in the white gown before her belly had gotten too big. Lovette had already gained a little pudge but nothing more than people thinking she had just put on a few pounds.

"Don't you think my mom is kind of rushing things? I mean, I get that we're about to be parents but we just graduated from high school. We're going to be parents regardless, so why is a wedding needed right now?" asked Lovette. She didn't know any other way to bring up the topic without hurting Joseph's feelings and she could see the disappointment spread across his face.

"I mean, I understand but I guess she just wants us to do things the right way. The way that she was raised to do things. Your parents are happily married and mine are, too. I want that. I know things are a bit weird right now but

we'll figure everything out along the way. Okay? Do you not like me or something...?" This direction the conversation was going in was what Lovette was afraid of.

"Of course, I like you, Joe. You're one of the closest people to me. I just never thought we would be here doing this especially so young. We never even really had the chance to date one another. It just went from having sex to a baby and now, we're getting married. Everything is moving really fast and I'm trying to wrap my mind around it while not trying to cry over not being able to attend school this fall. You understand that, don't you?"

"I totally understand it," said Joseph. "I get it. But as I promised, things will work out and I'm going to make you happier than you thought you'd ever be. As far as dating, I have just the romantic date planned for us this weekend. Don't worry about anything. I'm gonna date you until you get tired of going on dates and then I'm still gonna date you."

Just when Lovette had felt down about things, Joseph did have a thing for saying the right things at the right time. She didn't know how true it was going to be about him making her happy but she tried not to focus too much on that and geared towards thinking about the baby.

Every day, every single moment, she had wondered what type of person her child would be. After throwing herself down the steps, she had felt bad for trying to rid herself of him or her. The idea of her holding her baby and kissing him or her nonstop didn't seem too bad. She could now feel tiny flutters and such a feeling reassured her that this little person would love her just as much as she would love them.

Would she have a girl? This warmed her even more. Lovette loved her mother but Trudy was a tough cookie. She knew that her parents had only wanted the best out of life for her but the way they went about some things were just hard to deal with. The main issue: their racism. Her mother wouldn't have gone all out like this had Mike been the father of her child. Lovette was sure her mother would've suggested an abortion had the baby been his.

A girl. She knew that she would love her daughter differently than her mother had shown her love. Of course, she would be strong for her but she would also show her daughter love with no conditions. Lovette would make sure her daughter was surrounded by love and always felt accepted. Her daughter would know what it feels like to really be happy.

What if she had a boy? One thing was for sure, he'd have a great male role model. Joseph might not have been who she wanted to marry but she knew for sure he would be a great dad. He was raised in a great environment and their child would have the same.

The thought of having a boy also made her happy. The thought of a chubby little boy running up to her and hugging her legs made her smile. Biting into her burger and shoving a fry into her mouth, Lovette was convinced that the sex of her child didn't matter. She was just happy with the thought of loving a tiny human that could do no wrong.

"What are you smiling at?" questioned Joseph. Lovette had got so into to her own thoughts that she forgot

he had been sitting across from her. They were outside of her parent's house on the picnic bench by the water. The weather was perfect and it couldn't have been a nicer day.

"Just wondering what our child will be like. You think he or she will have my red hair? Or, will they be tall like you? It's just funny the possibilities of what they can look like." The more Lovette thought about the baby's characteristics, the happier she became. Joseph wasn't all that handsome to her but she had hoped the child inherited his personality. He was a lot nicer of a person than she had been.

"With my looks and your great personality, we are for sure going to make one hell of a person," she continued.

"Great way of telling me what you think of my looks," snickered Joseph. He knew he wasn't the most handsome guy around town but all that mattered was that he had Lovette and planned to keep her.

"Oh, you know I didn't mean it like that. I was only kidding," said Lovette. She really didn't want him thinking he was ugly. He wasn't that bad; just not handsome. Joseph was rather plain compared to Mike.

Mike. She had to stop comparing them. Mike was over with and Joseph is what she had to focus on now. Changing the subject, she started talking again.

"So, tell me more about this date you're taking us on. Ya know, gotta include the baby in everything now?" laughed Lovette.

"You'll see when we get there. That's the point of some dates right? Element of surprise. Well, I haven't been on that many dates but that's what the books and movies tell us." They both laughed, he watched her finish the last bite of her meal and toss the trash into the bag.

"That was the best burger I've ever had in my life. I could've eaten three of those. This child is going to make me bigger than this house," joked Lovette.

"And, you'll still be the most beautiful house anyone around here has ever seen," replied Joseph. He had meant every word and would always love her no matter how big she became. Although, he had hoped deep down inside that she wouldn't stay the size of a house after giving birth but he would always be with her no matter what.

Opening the screen door and standing on the front porch, Trudy waved for them to come on in the house. Almost instantly, they both got up and walked towards her. Lovette had the bag of fast food trash in her hand and almost forgot how obsessed her mother had become with her health.

"Now, I know you didn't go giving my grand baby that greasy food when I've been in this kitchen preparing you a good ol' home cooked meal," fussed Trudy. *"You have to be careful what you put into your body. You don't want the baby coming out all messed up because of what you did while pregnant,"* she continued.

"Mama, I'm sure a burger won't make my baby come out with seven arms or something," joked Lovette. *"...and if so, that means they have more arms to hug me with and I'm gonna love them anyway."*

****

September 18, 1982

Lovette had been standing in the mirror satisfied with how pretty she looked. Her mother and sister, Iris, had helped her choose her gown. The arms were made of soft yet detailed lace that draped a bit over her hands and the entire dress was fitted for her shape. The glistening stones neatly lined across her bosom shined in her reflection. The dress's train made it even more elegant. The dress had been altered a bit loose a few weeks ago because of her growing belly and now, it fit perfectly.

Before she knew it, Lovette started to cry. Every reason that she shouldn't be getting married at this exact moment came rushing to her again.

"Awww! No! Don't cry! You're gonna mess up the makeup," whined Trudy. "Elle spent forever on you girl's faces. Iris, hand me a tissue."

She tried her best to hold back the tears but they continued for a few seconds longer. Joseph and Trudy were the only ones truly happy about this day and Lovette realized that she felt forced to go through with it. All of the guests that loved them both had arrived and the thought of them sitting in the church pews waiting on her made her cry even harder.

"Honey, what's wrong? Talk to me," whispered Trudy while hugging her. "I understand that today is an emotional day but you look gorgeous. The church is set up beautifully and you have a good man out there waiting on you. Let's clean you up. Everything is going to be okay."

"Mama, what if this isn't the best decision? Like, what if I'm making a huge mistake?" questioned Lovette. Her stomach began to feel as if it had a million knots in it and she knew it wasn't the baby making her feel nauseous.

"This IS the best decision and you will see that. I promise you. You two are going to get married and have a healthy baby. We can talk about the rest later on. Things will be okay. Trust me. Okay?" Trudy replied.

Lovette wiped her face and nodded her head. She wanted to believe her mother so bad but her gut had refused to. Thinking about her parent's marriage and Joseph's parent's marriage made her stop crying. Maybe there was some type of hope that things would change. She already liked Joseph as a friend, so maybe there was hope that she would grow to be in love with him.

Holding back the rest of her tears and cleaning her face, Elle came back in the dressing room and fixed Lovette's makeup.

"All done. Now, keep it together until after the reception," playfully said Elle.

"Alright, everyone! Let's take our places. We have 5 minutes before its time to walk down the aisle! 5 minutes!" yelled Trudy. She had planned out a wedding for anyone in Shawford to attend. Since it had been a small town, they were expecting about 200 people to show up.

Lovette could hear the music. The sounds soothed her. Taking several deep breaths in and releasing them, her nerves had calmed a little. She knew that Joseph was a good man, so this must've meant that everything would *eventually be okay.*

"Did you hear me? Are you ready, hun?"
whispered her mother. "I have to go take my place but I'll
walk you out with the other girls really quick. Let's go
everyone!" she shouted.

Turquoise, gold and white. The colors had been
picked out by her mother. Everything had except for the
final decision about her dress. Lovette didn't argue
because her mother had wonderful taste and everything
came together well. All of the women had walked to the
main church doors and were greeted by the groomsmen.
They were all dressed in black tuxedos with a gold tie and
turquoise handkerchiefs in their jacket pockets. The men
were close friends and family members of Joseph's.

The bridesmaids were Iris and a few of Lovette's
cousins that she really didn't hang with too often. Each one
of them wore a turquoise dress that had one shoulder piece
and a gold pendant attached. Each bridesmaid beside her
groomsmen made Lovette crack a smile. Her mother sure
did know how to put things together.

5 minutes must've passed because before Lovette
knew it, the doors had opened and her little cousin Jade
was walking in and proceeded to drop flowers with every
step she took. Each couple entered together one by one and
before Lovette knew it, her father was tapping her on the
shoulder and whispering that it was her turn to walk.

She had been so consumed with her thoughts that
she hadn't realized he was standing next to her. Slipping
her arm into his and rolling her shoulders back while
straightening her posture like her mother had reminded
pg. 168

her, Lovette walked up to the entrance with her father.

Everyone had been on their feet and had been staring at her as if they had never seen her before. The tension had been great and for a moment, she was thankful for the veil. It had been a barrier between her and the audience. They could see her face's figure but they couldn't see the worry. She had an aisle's length of a walk to calm her nerves again and to make sure her face matched the calmness.

Stepping one foot on to the white carpet rolled out for her, Lovette and her father slowly and gracefully walked down the aisle. While the music played, everyone echoed their "oohs and ahhs" as she passed them one by one.

Joseph. His face was serious and yet red at the same time. Lovette figured he had been just as nervous as she had been. Within a few more steps in, his face softened a bit and for a second, Lovette felt as if he would cry.

Joseph indeed felt as if he would cry. He had always thought Lovette was gorgeous but this moment topped all of the times he's ever seen her. She was beautiful and carrying his child as well.

Wiping a tear away before it could drop, Joseph felt like a man. He made a promise to always protect Lovette and their child no matter what. He knew that there was no possible way that he could ever love anyone more than her. He was beyond proud.

Reaching the altar and kissing her dad, Lovette had now been standing face to face with Joseph. She could see happiness written all over his face and was determined to fake the feeling for his sake. Raising his hands to peel back her veil, Joseph was more than pleased at his wife to be. To him, she was perfect in every single way.

"Dearly beloved..." Lovette turned towards the minister. He was around the same age as her father. A tall older man who had salt and pepper in his beard. Turning back towards Joseph, he had gone back to the serious stare.

Every now and then, both she and Joseph would take turns repeating what the minister told them to say. Both had decided against writing their own vows. This was more so Lovette's idea due to wanting the process to be quick and over with as soon as possible.

Lovette never thought she would be doing this at this very moment. Had it not been for her trying to get even with Mike, none of this would be happening right now. She would still be going off to college and maybe...she would have gotten back with Mike.

"...Lovette. Well...Do you?" repeated the minister. Apparently she had become lost in her thoughts and forgot that she was supposed to be focusing on the wedding. She could see the embarrassment in Joseph's eyes and felt bad for zoning out.

"Um, yes. I do," replied Lovette. Her mouth started to feel dry and she could feel the sweat gathering in her armpits. There were more words spoken and a moment for anyone who objected to the union.

Deep down, she had wished Mike would bust

through the church doors and object. She had watched one too many love stories and before she knew it, it was time for them to kiss to seal the deal. Holding her breath and leaning in, their lips met and the church erupted with a round of applause.

****

The wedding reception was a great distraction. They had decided to host it in a hall that was suggested by Joseph's mother. Lovette was surprised that Trudy even allowed her to have an input due to how much she wanted to have control of the wedding.

Everyone had wanted pictures and dances with the both of them so much that Lovette had started to feel exhausted. The time had passed and Lovette wasn't only physically exhausted but mentally as well. Her feet had been hurting from her shoes and everyone seemed to having a better time than she had been having.

Sitting at the bride and groom table, Lovette was glad that the day had come to an end. She had enjoyed the father and daughter dance and was now watching everyone slowly but surely head home. She wanted nothing more than to get out of her dress and get into her own bed. As if he could read her mind, Joseph joined her back at their table and asked her was she ready to head home.

"You have no idea how much I've been waiting for you to say that. I've never taken so many pictures in one day before in my life! Did you see how drunk Will got? Your friend drinks more than a fish in the sea," replied Lovette. Joseph laughed and agreed.

Their limo had been waiting outside the building when they stepped out into the night's inviting air. The slight breeze made her skin bump up but felt good at the same time. Joseph took the lead walking down the steps and opening the door for his new bride. Lovette made her way down as well, stepped into the backseat and slid over for Joseph to get in.

Chapter 14: "Who got away?"

Joseph had been sitting in his office for several hours and this had concerned Lovette. The only time he would be in there that long is if something had gone wrong. When she had left to go to the grocery store and a few other places, he had still been in his office when she had returned home.

He was aware of what happened in school with Mary and Joey had been doing well for a while now, so she knew it had to be business related. Walking up to the office, Lovette put her ear up to the wooden door and tried to listen as hard as she could.

"What do you mean she got away?! How could this have happened?? We have used the SAME precautions for years now and nothing like this has happened before. I swear, you better fix this ASAP!" yelled Joseph angrily.

Lovette knew her husband had worked for a distribution company and the whole spill of it had been boring to her. He had eventually gained a position in his father's business. Joseph had brought in more than enough money to support their family.

Lovette had a large savings account, which she hardly ever touch. She didn't care to know too much about his job until she had heard the pieces of the conversation he had just been having. Waiting for a few more moments to make sure he had been done on the phone, Lovette knocked a few times and pushed open the office doors without waiting for a response.

"Hey. You okay? What was that all about?" she had questioned. His face was bright red and there was sweat dripping from his forehead. The house temperature was comfortable, so she knew his perspiration had everything to do with the phone call he had just been on.

Looking up from his desk, Joseph had begun to sweat even more thinking of how much of the conversation his wife had heard. She was supposed to be at the grocery store and the kids were with his parents for the night. He had been too busy yelling that he hadn't heard the car pull up to the house.

"Umm, everything is okay. Just mistakes happening at the office. Everything is okay though. How are you?" asked Joseph. Wiping his forehead and taking a few deep breaths, he had to get his self together or she would keep questioning him about what she thought she heard.

"Just making sure. Did you call your parents and check up on the kids? I know they are spoiling them but just making sure Joey isn't giving them a hard time about spending time with them. The boy thinks he is so grown already," said Lovette.

Joseph's parents adored the children but Lovette tried not to send Joey over as much. They knew about his condition and felt like if they gave him whatever he had wanted, he would behave in their presence.

Lovette had tried to explain to them time and time again that if Joey had taken his medicine the way he was supposed to, he would be no threat to them or anyone else. Although this had been explained to them several times, she could tell that Joseph's parents were still walking on eggshells around her son.

"The kids are fine. Mom is just cooking her usual large dinner and dad was in the garage showing the kids is tools for the millionth time," laughed Joseph. Lovette loved her in-laws and felt like they had become more of her actual parents throughout the years. Although, no one could ever replace her own.

✷✷

"Mama, we're going to be fine. He is my baby, ya know?" said Lovette as patiently as she could. Her parents had booked a weeklong vacation at the mountains and now, Trudy was having mixed feelings about leaving Lovette and Joseph so soon when Joseph Jr. had just been born.

"Well, he is my grandbaby, too. I just want to make sure you're going to be fine while we are away. What if you need me?" replied Trudy.

Trudy was genuinely concerned about leaving her alone so soon. Lovette had been doing a great job with everything but her mother felt as if she would be abandoning her too soon. Her oldest child was a mother now and it was her duty to make sure she had as much help with her son as possible.

Baby Joey had been born on March 9, 1984 and Lovette had felt complete. Joseph had made sure her pregnancy went as smooth as possible by providing any and everything Lovette ever needed. Her parents also made sure she got everything she needed. Joseph had been at every doctor appointment and made sure she knew that she wasn't alone. Although she had wanted some space sometimes, she still appreciated how much they were around to help.

"Trudy, leave them alone. We have been helping every single day for the past 8 weeks. Plus, we've been her for the whole pregnancy. Now, I'm gonna miss my little man but we wanted to go to the mountains and woman, that's where we are going. He's going to be here waiting on us when we get back. Joseph and Lovette need some alone time anyway. You two, just hold off on making any more grandkids for a while," joked Clarence.

Sucking her teeth and rolling her eyes, Trudy did as her husband said and went to go finish loading up their car for the trip. She had gotten so attached to Joey and loved him dearly. The way Lovette and Joseph both cared for Joey child made her happy with decision about them getting married.

Lovette had loved her child but deep down inside, she had been suffering silently. She didn't exactly know what it was but there had been times when she just wanted to run away. Run away from her husband, run away from her parents and...run away from her baby. Her soul had ached for some alone time the last two months.

Joey was the sweetest baby that Lovette had ever known. He clung to her most of the day while Joseph would be with his father learning the ropes of their family business. When Joseph would come home after work, Joey would cling to his father as if he missed him all day.

But, the crying spells would make Lovette feel like she couldn't help her only son. Holding him would do no justice when the cry fits would start. Trudy and Clarence still worked during the day, so when Joseph left, she was all by herself. Spending normal working hours with her child alone had become some of the hardest times of her life.

Whenever the crying spells would start, so would Lovette's. Many of times, she and Joey would cry together. She cried because she couldn't figure out what was wrong with her son. Often, she would think that he just didn't like her. Maybe she didn't give off enough of a love vibe for him to feel comfortable with her. To top things off, she had yet to witness a time when Joey would cry with his father the way he had cried with her.

"Now, you have the number to where we will be staying. I'll call as soon as we get there. Don't hesitate to call me, either. If we aren't in the cabin, you better leave a message. I told Iris to call just in case she thinks she has to. I know you do a good job but I just want to make sure everything is okay. I'll be calling daily a few times to check up on y'all, so make sure you answer that phone or I'm sending the police out here," laughed Trudy. Lovette knew she was joking and yet serious at the same time.

"Go have fun. You both deserve it. We'll be fine. Iris is a big help as well. I'm sure she's probably in her room writing down all of the emergency numbers and plans God forbid anything happens. You know she thinks she's my big sister," replied Lovette. As if she heard her name, Iris walked into the living room holding Joey and smiling.

"He just woke up from his nap. The kid likes to talk. Should've heard him up there going on and on," said Iris. Sitting on the couch and bending down to kiss him on the forehead, Iris played with her nephew. Moments like this had added to the love Lovette had for being a mother. She and Joe had created life that added more love to those around them.

Everyone walked Trudy and Clarence out to their car and said their goodbyes. For Lovette, it was bittersweet to see them go for a week but she also knew that they deserved some alone time as well. Joseph loved his in laws but also felt like he had wanted more time with Lovette by himself.

Watching them drive down the long rocky road, Lovette had the urge to flee after their car and tell them to come back. She had a gut feeling that something was off and couldn't tell if she was having one of her moments or whatever it had been. Fighting against her gut, she had convinced herself that she would be okay with Joseph, Iris and baby Joey.

****

Lovette hadn't been satisfied with her husband's answer of everything being okay at the office. She knew him and she knew that things weren't okay. But as usual, he had always tried to protect the family from worrying about anything.

She didn't like to pry too much when he had been displaying frustration because sometimes, that only made him more frustrated. Joseph had always felt like anything that occurred at work was his responsibility to fix and that was it; he never wanted Lovette getting involved.

Leaving him to himself, Lovette left and closed his office doors. Since the kids were gone, this had been the perfect time for her to sit on her porch and have a glass of wine…or a bottle instead.

A few months ago, Joseph had a company come install a screened in porch and Lovette was in love. No more Alabama bugs to buzz by her ear while trying to enjoy her porch.

Sitting down on her bench, Lovette sighed heavily and propped her feet up. She had missed sitting in this same exact spot while watching her father fix up his car in the driveway.

****

Lovette was starting to worry. Pacing back and forth, she was supposed to hear from her parents by now. They were staying in Boone, North Carolina and was supposed to check in hours ago. It was now dark and she still hadn't heard from them.

Joseph had convinced her not to call just yet and maybe the traffic had held them up. He knew that all it took was one phone call from Lovette and that Trudy would turn her car around to head back home.

"Joe, I can't keep waiting. She was supposed to call as soon as they checked in no later than three o'clock. It's eight-thirty! I don't care what you say, I'm calling them!" shouted Lovette.

He knew once his wife made up her mind about

something, there was nothing he could do to stop her. He understood her worry but at the same time, he didn't want Trudy coming back thinking that they couldn't handle taking care of their child on their own.

"Hello, my name is Lovette Veasley...ehh, I meant Lovette Marks. My parents were supposed to check in around three o'clock. I'm just calling to see if they ever made it there. Okay, I'll hold," said Lovette. The elevator music started to play and automatically, she sucked her teeth and tapped her foot with a great deal of impatience.

"Yes, their names are Trudy and Clarence Veasley," said Lovette into the phone. Waiting a few more seconds for the receptionist to find the information for their room, she continued to tap her foot.

As soon as Lovette let out a gasp, Joseph knew that they hadn't made it to the hotel. He instantly felt bad for making her wait so long to check up on them.

Hanging up the phone and plopping down on the couch to cry, Lovette started to panic. She felt something was off earlier and now wished she had told them to turn back around. Instantly switching her thoughts, she began to think about all of the possible things that could happen.

"Joseph, they never made it! Anything could've happened to them. Oh my...what if..." cried Lovette in between sobs. Joseph instantly stopped her from going off the deep end.

"Listen, maybe they just got lost. You know they had to drive a good amount of time to get there. Clarence gets lost easily. Remember the time he tried driving to the

beach and he kept taking 'shortcuts' because he thought he knew where he was going? I'm sure everything is fine. Don't do this to yourself," he said.

He did have a point. Her father had the confidence of ten confident men and didn't like using maps to get where he needed to go. Clarence would get them to their destination but could've avoided the longer drives had he used a map in the first place. This calmed her down some and she decided to wait a while longer before thinking the worst.

Deciding to distract herself, she focused on getting Joey ready for bed. Picking him up from his bassinet, Joseph followed her upstairs to run his bath water. Joey cooed in her ear and settled her nerves her even more. She had wish he was this content every second of the day; it would make her life a whole lot easier.

Peaking her head inside the bathroom, Iris saw how happy Lovette and Joseph were to be washing the baby together. She had planned on asking if they needed help but decided that they needed this time together. Leaving them to their baby, she went into her room and closed her bedroom door for the night.

****

Peeking out of his office window, Joseph saw Lovette sitting on the porch and drinking her wine. It had been a while since she had done this, so he knew a lot had to be on her mind.

Lovette was one to avoid issues as much as possible by trying to distract herself from thinking about things way too much. Feeling someone looking her way, Lovette looked over her shoulder and saw her husband smiling at her through the window.

****

Walking down the steps behind her husband, Lovette bumped into the stairwell vanity. She had no idea why her mother had put the thing there and was tired of bumping into it. The both of them had been awaken by loud knocking at the front door.

Before either one of them could get to the door, they had seen the red and blue lights flashing through the window curtains. The same gut feeling Lovette had before, it had just returned.

"Shawford Police!" said the voice along with more knocking came from the other side of the door. Part of Lovette wanted to run back upstairs, jump into their bed and hide from what she felt like was about to happen. Standing still at the bottom of the last step, she let her husband continue to the door by himself.

"Yes, officer. How can we help you?" asked Joseph. He had been just as nervous as Lovette had been. He'd convinced her to go to bed for the night and if her parents didn't call by the morning, they would go put in a missing person's report. But, it was almost midnight and the police were now knocking on their door.

"Sorry to wake y'all up but does Lovette Veasley or Iris Veasley live here? If so, we need to speak to one or both of them," said the tall figure in uniform. Hearing her name unglued Lovette from her spot near the steps and she

walked towards the both of them.

"I'm Lovette. My little sister is sleeping. Speaking to y'all will only freak her out. Um, you can come in," said Lovette while motioning the officer in. She hadn't noticed the second officer until he stepped from the side and entered with the first one. Everyone had walked into the family room and was now seated.

"Would anyone like anything to drink?" asked Lovette. She struggled to get the words out and had hoped they both would say no. She had just wanted them to tell her why they were there and get this over with. Both declined and the taller officer started talking.

"No, thank you. I just wanted to be the one to deliver the news to you all. At approximately nine thirty-two tonight, the dispatch center in Atlanta had received a call about a suspicious vehicle in a well-known but not so good neighborhood. Officers were dispatched and their findings were that of vehicle registered to Clarence Veasley that is attached to this address."

"When officers approached the car, two subjects were found deceased in the car from several stab wounds. A female had been in the passenger seat and a male had been in the floor of the backseat. We checked the purse and wallet that was in the vehicle and they came back to Trudy Veasley and Clarence Veasley. We are positive that the bodies found are the same subjects on the identification cards. From what we've concluded, it appears to be a double homicide. I'm truly sorry for your loss," he finished.

Joseph instantly grabbed his wife and held on to her. Lovette had been frozen. She had heard every word the officer had said but refused to believe that this had happened to her parents. What if someone had stolen their car and it wasn't really them? Depending on how bad of a murder scene it was, it could've easily been someone else...right?

"The bodies will be transported back to Shawford and we will need you or your sister to identify them," said the second officer.

"MY SISTER?! She's a child for crying out loud! Why would I let her see a dead body?!" screamed Lovette. Instantly covering her mouth, she had been shocked by her own outburst. The thought of her parents being dead had started to settle in and before she knew it, her whole body was shaking from crying so much.

"I understand and I'm sorry for the insensitive comment my colleague gave you. I'm going to leave my card with you. Is there anything you need for us to do?" said the first officer while giving his partner a stern look. Both officers gave their condolences once more and left their house.

Murdered? Lovette was overwhelmed with the word. Who would want to murder her parents? They had tons of friends who loved them and were good people. Why would someone choose them out of all the people in the world? Her parents?

The more questions she had, the more she felt like weights were being put on her chest and the harder it became for her to breathe. She had still been crying and hadn't even felt Joseph's touch. He hadn't said a word and just held on to her for as long as she would allow him.

"What's going on? Lovette, what's wrong? DID YOU HIT HER?!" screamed Iris. Before Joseph could reply, she had been in his face waiting on an answer. "Because if you did…"

"NO! I'd never hit her. I need you to calm down for a second and have a seat. We need to talk to you about something, okay?" Instantly calming down, Iris believed him. Joseph was one of the sweetest individuals ever and the thought of him hitting Lovette didn't seem valid but she walked in on her sister crying and that didn't sit well with her.

Lovette had stopped shaking long enough to tell her sister exactly what the officers had told her. When she had finished, Iris sat beside her and they both wept together. Lovette had felt like things were her fault. Had she gone with her gut instinct, her parents would be safe and alive in their own home.

Upstairs, Joey had begun to scream out of hunger. Kissing both girls on the forehead, Joseph went upstairs to tend to his son.

On the way up, he started to get even sadder at the thought of anything happening to him before his son was old enough to remember him. It worried him to think about Lovette having to raise her son alone.

****

The horrible way her parents were taken from the earth would always raise the same questions in Lovette's mind. She didn't know if it was because of the wine or because the kids were with Joseph's parents…his living parents.

She had such a short amount of time with her parents that sometimes, she felt jealous that Joseph was still able to laugh with and talk to his. Lovette loved them but nobody could take her parent's place in her heart.

"I just came out here to check on you. I see wine and I know wine means mama's heart is hurting in some way. I haven't made you mad lately, so I know it isn't me. Let me guess: you miss the kids, huh?" said Joseph with half of a grin forming across his face.

"Do you mind if I join you?" he asked while pulling a wine glass from behind his back.

"Sure. Come sit down. Of course, I miss the kids but I actually was thinking about my parents," whispered Lovette while sliding over for him to sit down.

He instantly felt sad for her because he had known the thought of his parents spending time with their children made her sad. Lovette's parents had eight weeks with Joey and that was it. He knew that they would've been perfect grandparents to their children had they still been alive.

****

Lovette's house had been filled with guests in every room on the bottom floor. A lot of people had come over after the funeral and there had been such a huge spread of food. She knew that she didn't have to cook for the next few days and for this, she was thankful. The last thing she felt like doing was cooking in the kitchen...without her mother by her side.

Opening one of the kitchen drawers, she got a glimpsed of the checks. They had been sitting in there and she had refused to deposit them. She knew that she would have to do it eventually, but she didn't know when.

It almost felt as if she were exchanging the envelopes for the missing presence of her parents. They had been worth way more than $750,000 and she would exchange the envelopes at any given moment if that meant bringing her parents back.

Slamming the drawer shut, it pinched her finger and made her wince. Walking back in the living room, she sat in the corner and watching everyone fuss over holding Joey. Lovette zoned out and replayed the story of how her parents died over and over in her head.

Clarence had been driving and Trudy was busy bossing him around in the passenger seat. During their trip towards the mountains, their car had gotten a flat tire and they had to pull over and change it. Clarence had told Trudy to stand well off of the highway into the grass but as usual, she had to be helping him do anything he attempted to do alone. He loved and disliked this about her at times.

A man by the name of James Roads had been walking along the highway and offered to help change the tire. Both of them had advised him that they were just finishing up and Clarence had just started to lower the car back to the ground when the tire was secured.

Somehow, the man had managed to hold them at gunpoint and demanded that they both get in the vehicle and drive to the nearest bank. He made Clarence go inside to withdraw cash and told him that he would shoot Trudy in the back of the head had he told someone to call the police.

Listening to his every demand, he then forced them to drive to another location. When they got there, the man attempted to make them both get out of the car and into a house. The police had suspected that Clarence had refused to get out and turned around in an attempt to disarm him.

During the struggle, the man pulled out a knife and stabbed Clarence in his stomach multiple times. Brought back to reality through Trudy's screams, he felt the need to silence her as well due to her being a witness. Slitting her across the throat, blood shot out everywhere in the front of the car.

James Roads had then pulled Clarence to the back seat and proceeded to drive around the city with both bodies in the car looking for heroin. During some time while driving, Clarence had made a noise in the backseat confirming that he wasn't deceased. James then pulled over to a discreet location and continued to stab Clarence until he was sure he was dead.

Finally finding what he had been looking for, he parked the vehicle outside of an abandoned house and proceeded inside to use the drugs. Apparently, he had gotten so high that he forgot that the bodies were outside of the building in plain sight. One of the neighbors across the street had called the police about the car and told them that it looked as if someone had been sitting in the front passenger seat for a very long time.

When the police had arrived on scene, there had been traces of blood from the car to the front steps of the abandoned house. James Roads had still been in the house and was unconscious from an overdose. Medics arrived and transported him to the hospital. His version of the story was that Trudy and Clarence attempted to abduct him and that is why he had to kill them.

"Lovette? Honey, did you hear me?" said Joseph's mother, Lorraine. Lovette had been replaying the story so many times and still couldn't believe how things ended. All her parents had wanted to do was spend some alone time together. The worst part was that had he simply asked them for some money, they would've given it to them. They didn't deserve to die that way and that alone made Lovette begin to cry again.

"Aww, I didn't mean to make you cry. Come on, let's go outside away from everyone and get some fresh air," said Lorraine. Helping her daughter-in-law up from the couch, they both walked outside arm in arm towards the lake.

****

"What I still can't accept is why it had to be my parents, ya know? Like, why would he just walk up on two innocent people and take their lives? No one deserves to die that way," said Lovette.

They both continued to drink their wine and talk about life and how cruel it could be. Joseph tried his best to console his wife and watched everything he said because she hadn't broken down crying yet. This was the growth in her. She had now been able to express her feelings about her parents without crying and he didn't want to be the one to make her cry.

"He was once a married man and has children; that really blows me. You would think he would've been more sympathetic towards a married couple but he didn't even show remorse when it was time for him to go off to jail. I feel for his children but I'm glad he's going to rot in that place."

"The world is better off without people like him roaming around. There's no telling if he even had done this before and gotten away with it. Sorry, I'm ranting babe. It's just been awhile since I've talked about this and this wine is making my lips a little loose," said Lovette.

"Now you know you can always talk to me about this an unlimited amount of times and an unlimited amount of rant miles. You're my wife and you come first. This is what I'm here for. Never apologize for expressing yourself. Okay?" replied Joseph. He had a serious look on his face and had wanted her to know how much his words meant.

Placing her wine glass on the front porch, she slid closer to her husband and laid her head on his shoulder. These were moments that she loved the most. He was such a good listener and always paid attention. Joseph positioned his head on top of hers and they sat this way for a few minutes.

"Joe? Who got away earlier?" questioned Lovette. She had told herself that she was going to drop it for the time being but the question shot out of her mouth faster than it came to mind.

"Huh?" replied Joseph. He was lost in his thoughts for a second and was thinking of ways to help his wife heal. He meant what he said about always being there to listen but sometimes, he felt as if maybe a professional would be able to help more.

"I heard you yell on the phone earlier and you told someone that 'she' got away. So, who is she?" said Lovette. She had always trusted her husband to tell the truth.

"Oh that? We had bought a dog for the office because someone kept attempting to break in. Just an extra piece of security besides the camera footage. Criminals can cover themselves from the camera but it's kind of hard to outrun a dog."

"Will had went to the office and one of the dogs ran past him and right on out the front door. You know he can't catch a dog let alone catch a slug if it got away from him. I'm pretty sure he was drunk," said Joseph.

Joseph did tell her that they were having issues with someone trying to get into the building and at one point, they did believe someone had gotten in. This is why they had gotten a security system. Lovette dropped the subject and picked up wine glass back up.

"You feel like running to the store and getting another bottle?" she asked.

Chapter 15: Iris

May 31, 2001

Lovette had dropped Mary off to her counseling session, Joey was hanging out with his friends and she had the evening to do with as she pleased. Joseph's parents were going to pick them up after and drop them off at home after dinner.

Iris had come back home to attend Joey's graduation and they both were headed to do some shopping before dinner time. Lovette had been stoked that her baby sister had come to spend time with her.

"I'm so glad you're finally here! It's been forever! Tell me everything and don't leave out any juicy details. Love life? Work drama? I want to know it all!" said Lovette excitedly.

Iris had always been her favorite person. Not only because they were sisters but because Iris was always honest with Lovette. They had a bond that couldn't have been any better.

"Sheesh, you sound like you haven't seen me in 20 years or something. It hasn't been that long," replied Iris while laughing. "We talk on the phone all the time. Everything is pretty much the same." That was nothing less than the truth but somehow, seeing her sister in the flesh made things that much more exciting.

Although she had completed high school at the top

of her class, Iris had struggled to do so after their parents had died. When Harvard had sent her letter of acceptance, she was relieved that her hard work paid off. She had graduated from school and was now a neurosurgeon. Lovette couldn't have been prouder of her sister. One of the best parts was that Iris didn't owe a penny towards her education.

"So, nothing new at all? Now, I know you better than that. Something is new, so spill the beans, missy."

Lovette had been right. Something was new with her sister but Iris didn't know how to tell Lovette out of fear of being judged. She hadn't told anyone yet and was waiting for the right moment to let the cat out of the bag.

"Ok, well…promise me you won't judge me or get mad. I just…I just don't need that right now," confessed Iris. Taking her eyes off of the road for a moment, Lovette saw how serious Iris's face had become. This alarmed her. Iris never had any bad news.

"You know you don't have to worry about me judging you. I'm here, so whatever it is, you know you can tell me. There's nothing that would make me love you any less or look at you any differently. Unless…you didn't kill anyone did you?!" joked Lovette. They both busted out laughing while Iris shook her head at her sister's wild guess.

"Of course not. I've worked my butt of to become a doctor. I refuse to lose that. But seriously, I've been seeing someone for a while now," said Iris. She was fiddling with her fingers and Lovette knew there was more to the story.

"Okay. Seems like you really like him. There must be a catch coming up. What? Is he like 20 or something? Ahhh, he's a youngin', huh?" laughed Lovette. Iris hadn't changed her facial expression and turned to look out of her windows.

Iris had despised the highway. This was the place where her parents had been forced to get into their car by a maniac who only wanted to get high. This had been part of the reason she hardly ever visited home. She was too afraid to travel by a plane because she now lived in New York. Also, the house seemed to haunt her as well.

"He's married," whispered Iris. Without breaking her stare from the trees beyond the car window, she heard her sister gasp as quiet as she could manage. Judgement. She had always felt safe with talking to Lovette about anything but this was the first thing that Iris had come out in the open with something that would be perceived as wrong. She had always been so "perfect" and nobody really expected anything less from her.

"I heard that gasp, so go ahead and say whatever it is that you want to say. I'm ready for it," continued Iris.

"Oh no! Don't think I'm mad at you. This is your life. No one is perfect; not even you. Yea, you're the better sister between us two but things happen. People make mistakes in life and do things they never thought they would do. Things happen and we move around them. It's a part of being human and you'll grow from it," replied Lovette.

She was shocked and felt bad for her initial reaction but she hadn't been expecting for her sister to tell her that she was dealing with a married man.

"Thanks for not beating me over the head about this. I've been holding it in for so long and just needed to get it out there. I didn't want to tell my friends because they would've just pointed the finger at me, especially since all of them are married," replied Iris. She could feel herself getting emotional; she loved the man so much but wasn't sure how to go about things.

"Let's start with you telling me about him. How did you meet him?" asked Lovette. Although sleeping with a married man wasn't good at all, she wanted to hear her sister's full side of the story before she had to say everything she needed to tell her. Jumping down her throat about her life's decisions would only push her away and possibly make Iris never want to visit her again.

"He's my boss," said Iris. She was now staring at the side of her sister's head while she continued to steer the car around the mall's parking lot looking for a space. She needed to see her every reaction to everything she was about to tell her. This was a portion of judgment. Lovette was good with words but she was no good when it came to controlling her facial expressions.

Lovette raised any eyebrow and said nothing. Waiting for her sister to continue talking, she pulled into the nearest space of the mall's entrance and parked the car.

"Okay…What else?" she said.

"Well, he has two children that are ages ten and thirteen. He's been married for 15 years but says he's unhappy and wants to leave his wife for me," said Iris.

Lovette turned towards her sister and gave her a look of sadness.

Lovette had wanted to be honest with her baby sister. There was absolutely no one that loved Iris more than Lovette, so she knew it was her duty to tell her sister exactly how this would go.

"How long have you been seeing him?" she asked.

"About a year now," replied Iris. Her stomach began to growl as soon as she opened her mouth. She just realized that she hadn't eaten all day and this conversation was definitely one that would take a while to fully get through.

"Okay, listen to me. I love you deeply. You're one of my favorite people in the world, so don't take anything I say as if I'm attacking you, okay?" said Lovette. Iris nodded and waited for the blow that she knew was about to come next.

"That man will never leave his wife for you. He's probably said the same thing to his first few side pieces and won't stop. He doesn't care about you. Want to know how? Because he doesn't care about cheating on his wife. The woman he's been with for 15 or more years and has given him two children."

"The woman who has stuck by his side through whatever he's put her through because every marriage goes through SOMETHING. If this man can cheat on his wife with you and go back to her as if nothing is going on, he has no heart," said Lovette.

"You're beautiful and can get anyone you want. Don't settle for this. Don't waste your time on someone who is feeding you filthy lies about leaving his wife just to continue to get in your bed whenever he feels like it. If he were a real man, he would've handled his business and left his wife before even starting a 'relationship' with someone else. You don't even like children. Suppose he did leave his wife. That means you're going to be playing step mommy to some children that are old enough to form their own opinions and probably give you hell for thinking you stole their dad away from their mother," Lovette continued.

"He's trash and you're a diamond. Don't make yourself dirty with him when you can eventually be with someone who has good intentions. This creep only cares about himself and how he can get as much out of a woman as he can until he finds a new one. You're better than this," said Lovette with tears in her eyes.

She didn't mean to get so emotional but she didn't want to see her sister get hurt. But, it was inevitable. Iris had fallen in love with a married man and either she had to be strong enough to cut him off or he was going to string her along with his promises to leave his wife.

"...but he loves me," whispered Iris. She was staring at the car floorboard and had refused to make eye contact with Lovette. She knew that she had been crying due to the sniffling at the end of her spill on things.

"Hun, he tells his wife that he loves her but you see what he's doing to her. He didn't just have a one night stand with you, felt bad, confessed to his wife and promised to never do it again. This man has been dealing with you for a whole year now and is telling you these lies about leaving her. I can just about guess the lies he's told."

"I'm sure he's with you with excuses like the divorce is going to be expensive…he's trying to stick around a little longer because he doesn't want to hurt the kids. He's scared of child support. Oh, his wife might try to hurt herself if he leaves right now because she's emotional. Stuff like that, right?" said Lovette.

The tears that dropped on top of Iris's red Prada bag Lovette had given her for Christmas last year had confirmed that these had been the lies he fed her. She had eaten each and every lie.

Every time Iris would bring up him leaving his wife, he had a new excuse. Every time she wanted to go out and do something together, he reminded her that he couldn't do it just yet out of fear of being caught. The only time she saw him was at work and in her bed a few times a week.

Wiping her face and lifting her head, she knew her sister was right. It felt better to hear it from someone who genuinely cared about her and wouldn't tell her anything to hurt her. Had she told her friends, she would've thought they were just being judgmental without considering her feelings.

"You're right. I don't know why I even started this thing knowing he was married. I'm so glad I have you, Vetty Betty," replied Iris while laughing. She hadn't called her that in years and it felt good to say it out loud.

"Oh, Lord! You done brought up the world's worst

nickname ever! But, seriously, this is just a bump in the road. Like I said before, you're human. Don't beat yourself up over this. Let his ass go and continue on with your life. It'll be hard because you both work together but just do your job and keep it at that. Maybe you could ask them to transfer you in the hospital somewhere else or under someone else," said Lovette.

"Well, I actually got another offer from another hospital but it's a couple of hours away. I'm really considering taking it. I had been looking at other options prior to this thing with Chris but maybe this was just the shove and a sign that I needed to start over," replied Iris. "Plus, the pay is a lot better than the coins Justice Memorial was pushing out."

Lovette was relieved that Iris wasn't angry with her words. She had never wanted to hurt her but Iris had needed to hear the truth. Never in a million years did she imagine that they would be having this conversation.

"Good for you! You deserve it. You know what would be even better? If you came back home and worked here. You know they would hire you instantly," said Lovette cheerfully.

The look on her sister's face was the complete opposite. Iris had been so ready to get out of Shawford and had no plans on coming back to stay. She loved her sister but she didn't love Shawford.

"Now, Lovette. You know damn well I'm not coming back here. Period…" said Iris. Gasping and almost choking on air, Iris coughed until she could breathe normal again.

"What is it, Rissy?" questioned Lovette. They both were still sitting in the car and Lovette was sure Iris had seen something suspicious. Looking around the parking lot, there were couples and teenagers walking into the mall but nothing seemed off. "What's going on?" asked Lovette, again.

"I didn't get my period this last month…or this month," confessed Iris. "Work has been so hectic and I lost track of my cycle. At first, I just figured it was stress and totally forgot about it. I don't know how I missed something like this! What am I gonna do?!" she cried.

Lovette was shocked, sad and happy all at the same time. Iris had made it clear that she never wanted children and always had a strong focus on her career. On the other hand, that meant that Lovette would never be an aunt. Joseph was an only child, so she wouldn't even have and nieces or nephews on his side of the family.

"Lovette, please say something. I'm freaking out here!" yelled Iris. An elderly couple had just walked near the car and heard the shouting. The old man grabbed his wife's hand and the both of them attempted to run towards their car as fast as they could.

"Okay, calm down. You done scared granny and paw paw over there. Listen, everything is going to be fine. You don't even know if you're pregnant yet. It could still be stress, Iris. Let's just go get some tests and go from there," rubbing her sister's shoulder and giving her a hug, the gestures seem to calm Iris down a bit.

"Now, you know the shopaholic in me has to ask if you still want to go inside this mall. We don't have to but I sure do need a new pair of black pumps," said Lovette. Taking a few deep breaths and opening her door, Iris got out of the car.

"I know one damn thing: as soon as we leave this mall, you're taking me to buy one of each pregnancy test in the pharmacy. Oh, and don't say a word to Joseph or the kids. I don't want anyone knowing any of this. Okay?" said Iris.

Bringing her hands to her mouth, Lovette pretended to zip her lips and throw away the key. She'd respect her sister's wishes and not mention it to anyone.

****

"You want to know what's so funny?" asked Lovette. They had done enough shopping for the next two months. The plan was to just buy a pair of shoes but as usual, she bought way more than that. She picked up a new shirt and tie for Joseph to let him know that she had thought about him as well.

"Are you really going to stand on the other side of the door and talk to me the entire time I take these tests?" asked Iris ignoring Lovette's question. They had stopped at the pharmacy on the way home and just like Iris had demanded, Lovette had bought her 12 pregnancy tests just to make her feel better.

"I sure am. Anyway, like I was saying. It's not 'ha-ha' funny but it's just that now, I'm on the opposite side of the door this time," chuckled Lovette. For a moment, she forgot that it was a possibility that her sister was pregnant by a married man. For this, she apologized.

"I'm sorry, Rissy. I know this isn't the position you wanted to be in but whatever you decide to do or whatever happens, you know I have your back."

Iris loved Chris but she didn't love him enough to have his child. Children were never supposed to be a part of her plan. She had been on the pill but they weren't consistent with using condoms. She instantly slapped herself on the forehead for being so careless. Now, here she was sitting on her old home's toilet with a dozen pregnancy test waiting to see what they would say.

"Don't get quiet on me now. I didn't mean to make a joke during a moment like this," said Lovette softly.

"Would you shut up already?! I'm not mad at some corny joke. I'm over here trying to read the boxes while not passing out from confusion. I'm a damn doctor and apparently can't even do a pregnancy test correctly," replied Iris. Barging in the bathroom, Lovette had plopped down on the side of the tub.

"Give it here. I'll help you." The more she thought about the possibility of her sister being pregnant, the less she cared about being an aunt. Her prior feelings had been a bit selfish and she knew that this wasn't what Iris had wanted. Taking the time to do the first 4 tests, the both of them sat in silence in the bathroom. Iris remained on the toilet and didn't bother to move until she knew the results.

The anxiety levels began to rise inside of Iris. What was she going to do with a baby? Abortion was an option but did she have it in her to go through with it? Would that be karma on her behalf for making such a decision?

If she was pregnant and had the baby, what would she tell Chris? She would have to eventually explain being pregnant to him since they see one another daily. Or, she could switch jobs and never say anything to him at all. After all, he had a whole life that included children already.

Iris instantly felt bad for thinking she could possibly keep someone's child away from them. But, what about his wife? They would have to tell her. All of the possibilities made it clear that if she was indeed pregnant, she wasn't going to have this baby. The decision was final.

"Iris! Look!" shouted Lovette. The four tests that she had just taken had all come back negative. Iris instantly felt a huge amount of relief. As if her body knew she was still curious about not having a cycle in so long, she looked between her legs and drops of blood had been falling into the toilet bowl's water. Seeing her own blood had never made her happier.

"Can you both hurry up?! I hear you in there talking! I have to pee!" shouted Mary. Hearing her voice brought them both back to reality and they both jumped up scurrying around the bathroom to hide the mess they had made. The last thing they needed was for Mary to go telling her father about anything she had found.

"Girl, its other bathrooms in this house! Now, get away from the door!" shouted Iris in between laughs. She adored Mary but the child had a mouth on her.

"It would've been nice to use my own bathroom!" Mary shouted back while storming off to one of the other bathrooms.

Chapter 16: "No crying."

June 2, 2001

Lovette had invited everyone who wanted to come to Joey's cookout. The sun was blaring its heat and shined perfectly on their property. Today had been a good day from morning up to the exact moment of the cookout.

The family had gotten to see her first child and only son walk across the stage and accept his diploma. He had improved drastically with time and proved that he was ready to go off to college. Lovette still worried from time to time but she knew that if he continued to take his medicine, he would be okay.

People were spread out throughout the yard and within the house. The small kids were splashing around the little pools Joseph had bought for them and couldn't have been having more fun. The cheap things would break before the evening but it was worth it seeing the kids having a ball.

"Come here, son. I've hardly had a chance to see you since the party started. I know you're trying to hang out with your friends as much as you can before you leave for school but can a mom get a moment of the celebrity's time?" said Lovette while pulling Joey in for a hug.

"Of course, mom." For the past few months, Joey had done a tremendous job on working on his appearance. He made sure he had kept his hair clean and cut, his clothes were always neat now and he smelled as if he had a hot date every night. Every time Joseph or Lovette would question him about the change, he would deny it had anything to do with a female love interest.

"I'm so proud of you. You've always been a smart kid but I'm really proud of the progress you've made. Your dad I are lucky to have you as our son and we love you beyond the moon and all of the stars out there," said Lovette.

She had managed to keep her tears tucked away during the graduation ceremony but reality had finally set in that her baby was growing up and moving on with his life. Tears formed in her eyes and she tried to hold them back as she continued talking.

"You know that we will always be here for you, right? You can always call us anytime of the day or night if you need us. I know you haven't left for school yet but I just want to make sure you know all of this. We have your back," continued Lovette.

Joey had grown to be even taller and looking so far up to him made her even more emotional. The baby that was once small enough to sleep on her chest was now a man.

"Mom, don't cry. I promise I'll be right back here during some weekends and the holidays. It won't even feel like I'm gone," replied Joey. He had been excited about college but nervous as well. This would be a big change for him. He would be going to school in North Carolina. Another decision that made Lovette feel bittersweet.

She was overly happy for her son but the thought of

her and Mike always came to mind when North Carolina was mentioned. She never got the chance to attend college but was still happy her son would.

Pushing Mike out of her thoughts, she brought her mental state back to the present. Mary had been sitting on the porch with one of her classmates playing with her Gameboy. Lovette was glad that the summer-time was here. She could focus on doing more things with Mary and accepting what had happened to Joyce.

Joyce. It had been a long time since she had allowed herself to grieve over Joyce. She always tried to be strong for everyone and never really took the time to feel what she had been suppressing.

She had missed Joyce's laugh, affection and silly ways. Although Mary had been her reflection, they were two totally different people. Somehow, seeing Mary daily wasn't a reminder of Joyce. They were their own individual people.

"Mom, did you hear me? I'm gonna go back to hanging out with my friends. That's if you don't mind. They kind of came to the party for me. Hate to leave them hanging," said Joey.

"Oh, yea. Sure. Go have fun. We'll talk later," replied Lovette. Now that she had thought about Joyce, she wanted to be alone for a while. This was Joey's day, so trying to shake her current feeling would be a task but she would do it for her son.

Joseph had been sitting on the bench by the lake, talking to Will. Lovette hadn't seen much of his friend lately and didn't really care to. She was friends with his wife, Caron, and he had finally moved in with Brenda making things official.

For months, Caron would come over and cry over the loss. One day, it were as if a light a light bulb had been turned on. She had quit pining over him and went out to find her a man. Although both of them had moved on, Lovette still disliked Will for what he did to her friend. Sneaking up behind him and pinching his shoulder, he jumped from the sudden touch.

"You don't mind if I borrow my husband for a few, do you?" asked Lovette. Will was beyond drunk and look as if he was going to fall asleep standing up at any moment. It had been a party for her son but Will definitely made sure he was drunk enough at every event.

"No, no, no, no…of course. Take your wife. I mean your husband," Will slurred and hiccupped. Stumbling off towards the house, Lovette watched him walk away in disgust.

"When is he going to get some help? The man is a walking distillery and smells like one, too. You ever worry about him drinking on the job and stuff?" questioned Lovette. She didn't care if he really got help or not but she didn't like him stumbling around the kids.

"I'll talk to him about it. He claimed that he would only drink so much because he wanted to be with Brenda but now that he's with her, nothing has changed," replied Joseph. He was clearly exhausted.

"You look tired. You've been working so much.

Maybe we should go on a family vacation. It's been awhile and you deserve it," said Lovette.

Rubbing his back, she felt a sudden need to look over her shoulder. It felt as if someone had been staring at her. Scanning the yard and looking at the small kids playing, Joseph's father cooking on the grill and all of the adults conversing with one another, she saw nothing out of the ordinary.

"You're right; it has been awhile. We'll look at some spots we can go to later on tonight if you're up for it," said Joseph. It wasn't just work that had him tired; it was home, too. Mary hadn't been making any progress with her therapist and it worried him.

Another worry he had was that he had used the upstairs bathroom and found a pregnancy test under the cabinet. He knew that it couldn't possibly belong to Mary and felt that it had either belonged to his wife or his son had brought a girl in the house scared she might be pregnant.

Joey was acting different with his hygiene. They appreciated how much better it was but it was still suspicious. Taking a deep breath and bringing up one of his concerns, he chose to talk about the test he found.

"There is something that has been on my mind that I think we should talk about," said Joseph. He paused for a second to think about how he wanted to ask her. The last thing he wanted to do was sound insensitive or hurt her feelings but he didn't want to bring another child into this world. Especially after what happened to Joyce.

"What is it? You know you can talk to me about anything," said Lovette. She started to worry for a second because Joseph didn't have too many serious moments with her. It couldn't have been too bad or else he would've waited until after the party to say something to her about it.

"Umm, well. I found a pregnancy test under the bathroom sink," he confessed. He loved her and wanted to give her everything she ever wanted but another child hadn't been one of those things. Letting out a huge cackle, Lovette slapped her leg and continued to laugh.

"You thought that was MINE?! Oh, sheesh! Is that what you were over here worrying about?! That was for..." she asked while continuing to laugh. For a moment, she almost forgot the promise she made to Iris and had to catch herself. Now that she told him it didn't belong to her, she had to come up with something quick as to why it had been there in the first place.

"For...?" asked Joseph. The most important part was that it didn't belong to his wife. The thought of a crying baby coming into their lives now had him more scared than anything.

"Caron had told me about a girl who needed one down at the youth center. I was already at the pharmacy earlier and told her I would pick one up. You know she helps teenagers out and the girl was scared to talk to her parents about it. Since she just turned eighteen, by law, Caron isn't required to report it to anyone," said Lovette.

The way Lovette had spit the lie out so quick, she had almost believed it to be true herself. She didn't like lying to him but she had made a promise to her sister.

Believing her, he shook his head and laughed.

"For a moment, my second thought was that Joey had a situation on his hands and was trying to handle it himself. I don't want any more children but I'm definitely not ready to be a grandfather," said Joseph while laughing some more.

He had been the only one laughing. Catching the insensitivity he displayed, he instantly felt bad. The look on her face had clearly been one of disappointment.

"Oh, no. Lovette, I swear I didn't mean it like that. It's just you know…the things we've been through and stuff…" stammered Joseph.

The thought of his disappointment had she been pregnant had hurt her feelings. She didn't want another child either but the test could've very well been hers. Deciding that this was one of the battles that she wouldn't pick at, she knew that her husband's intentions were pure.

"I know. It just caught me off guard. We're good. I promise." Holding out her pinky and waiting for his, they linked fingers. Kissing him to seal the deal, he felt better knowing that she wasn't mad at his remark

****

The party had been a success and all of the guests had cleared out for the night. Lovette, Iris, Joseph and Mary were now in the living room having family game night. It had been a while since they had all had a game night together. The funeral had been the last time Iris had come back home.

Joey had been sitting in the recliner and was holding the spinner for the game *Twister*. It was Mary's favorite game and she had been even more excited to play it now that her aunt was in town. Flicking the arrow, he told everyone the next color and position for them to play.

"Put your left hand on blue." Following his directions, everyone wiggled around one another to attempt the command. As soon as Lovette slid her hand under Joseph's back, she tickled him and he fell to the floor.

"Hey! Cheaters never win, ya know?!" he said while picking himself up from the floor. Lovette had known her husband didn't really like playing this game and that Joseph didn't want to tell Mary no, so she decided to help him get out of the game early. Winking at his wife for the easy way out of the game, he made his way out of the family room towards the kitchen.

Joey had always chosen the role in games that required the least amount of participation from him. He had liked the family moments but actually playing the games hadn't been much of his thing. Flicking the spinner once more, he read out the next game play. "Right foot on red."

Mary's left foot was on green and her left hand was on blue. Sliding her right foot on to the color red, she fell into a split. Kicking the floor and pouting, Mary never failed to show how much she couldn't handle losing.

"Awww, don't be such a sore loser! It's just me and you now, Vetty Betty," said Iris. Sucking her teeth and sliding off of the game mat, Mary got up and plopped down on the couch across from Joseph. Lovette was a competitive woman and she had refused to let Iris win.

****

*"On your mark...get set...GO!" yelled Joseph.
Taking off towards the end of the street, Iris made sure she
let her nephew feel as if he were running faster than her.
He had just turned three years old and felt as if he were
invincible. If anyone had been the fastest runner ever, Joey
knew it had to have been him.*

*Letting him get a few paces ahead, Iris was proud
to be his aunt. She had been struggling with her parent's
death and Joey had made it easier on her. There were times
she felt as if Lovette and Joseph were better off without her
around and then Joey would remind her of how much she
was needed. Everyone always made her feel loved but
somehow, she still felt as if it weren't enough.*

*Until Joey added his input. He had been so
articulate and smart for a child is age. Most parents had
thought that their children were different and special
against other children but it was truly something different
about Joey.*

*One time, he caught Iris crying in her room over the
death of her parents. He sat down on the bed beside her
and wrapped his arms around her neck. Iris knew that
something was indeed special about her nephew.*

*Almost reaching the end of the road to see who
would win the race, Joey made an instant right in the grass
and ran towards the huge oak tree in the middle of their
front yard. It had taken Iris a few seconds to catch on and
when she finally did, she turned around and jogged
towards her nephew. Lovette and Joseph watched from afar
as they waited to see what their son had been up to.*

Finally catching up to Joey, he stopped in front of the tree and looked up as if he had been searching for something inside of the branches. Not saying anything, Iris waited to see what he would do next.

Pointing up and smiling, Joey whispered "Granny and paw." Turning towards Iris, he smiled.

"What did you say?!" questioned Iris. Her nerves were on edge. She had heard exactly what he said clear as day but needed him to confirm what she had heard.

"Granny and paw. 'No crying'," said Joey. Feeling as if she had heard the words from her mother's mouth herself, Iris dropped to the ground beside Joey and began to weep. As soon as Lovette saw the scene unfold, both she and Joseph ran towards the tree to see what had happened.

Lovette began to panic. "What's going on?! What happened?!" Joey was patting his aunt's shoulders as she cried uncontrollably. He had gone from smiling to looking terribly sad thinking that he had said or done something wrong.

Once she had gotten her crying under control, Iris had repeated everything to Joseph and Lovette. Letting out a sigh of relief, Lovette and Joseph then calmed down themselves.

Iris had dreamt of her mother on numerous occasions. Each dream, Trudy would end by telling her that they were at peace and to stop crying. Iris hadn't been big on dreams and just thought they were the underlining meaning of her deepest desire for them to be at peace.

But, hearing her nephew confirm the almost exact same words had brought her a great deal of peace. Iris would always miss her parents and would never consider herself "over" their death. She'd always miss and mourn them but Joey had made things that much easier on her.

****

Flicking the spinner, Joey was in a trance as he watched it spin around and around. His head moved in circles as he waited for it to stop. When it finally had, he was stuck staring at its final position.

"Umm, Joey. You plan on telling us the next move before I collapse on my face?" asked Iris. She had been halfway stuck under Lovette, who couldn't keep from laughing because she knew she would win the game soon.

"Joey?!" repeated Iris. Shaking his head and looking up, he forgot that he had been playing the game.

"Left foot on yellow." As soon as Iris slid her foot on to yellow circle, Lovette got shaky and fell onto the floor. Iris had won the game and it had been her very first *Twister* victory.

"You know I let you win, right?" said Lovette in between laughs as she rolled over off of the game mat. They had played the game every time Iris came back home to visit and she had finally been beat by her little sister.

"Yea, yea, yea. Take your loss and don't be a sore loser like your daughter over there pouting," replied Iris. She got up and walked over to Mary giving her a playful pinch on the belly and kissing her at the top of her head.

"We can play again before I head back home, Bug. Okay? Just me and you," continued Iris. This instantly made Mary smile and she ran up to her room filled with excitement.

As soon as Mary left the room, so did Joey. He loved his aunt but couldn't deal with just her and his mother together. They would start laughing and cackling louder than anyone he knew. Leaving them to themselves, he headed upstairs to get dressed. He had plans to hang out with his friends later tonight.

"I know I've said it before but oh well, I'm going to say it again anyway. I'm glad you're here. I've missed you so much and just wish you would think about moving back home. Can't you see yourself doing this more often? Doesn't it feel good being with family?" said Lovette. She had started her rant but Iris knew it was coming. And, she had to admit-it did feel really good being home.

"If I said, 'I'll think about it', will you stop harassing me already?!" Iris replied while folding up the game mat and placing it in the box. She knew that if she moved back to Shawford, Lovette would only insist that she lived in their house and that wasn't something she could do. Iris was able to stay a few nights and enjoy her family but what she couldn't do is live there. She hadn't been mentally ready for that.

This had been enough to satisfy Lovette for the time being. Nodding her head while smiling, she dropped the topic and put the game away in the hallway closet. Iris would be headed back to New York in the morning and she would miss her terribly.

Chapter 17: Happy Anniversary

September 15, 2001

Joseph and Lovette had invited their closest friends to their wedding anniversary party. They had decided to rent out a nearby venue instead of doing the usual events at home. Even though all of the planning had been done by Lovette, she was promised a cleanup crew and it gave her relief knowing that she wouldn't have to do so the after the party.

Lovette and Joseph had danced the night away. Both of them were now sitting while they continued to sip their champagne. Joey was in the corner hanging out with his friend Jaxon and Mary was in another corner leaned up against the wall as if she were ready to go.

Just as Lovette was about to suggest they wrap the party up, a petite female walked past Mary towards the bathroom. Feeling herself boil with rage, Lovette proceeded to follow after the woman.

****

September 16, 1988

It had been Joseph and Lovette's 6 year anniversary. It was an adjustment for the both of them being married but an even tougher time for Lovette. For the first two years, she couldn't shake the feeling that Mike should've been the one she was married to. Shortly after, she gave up the thought and let it go. Joseph had grown on her and she had actually fallen in love with him.

Parking her car and walking into the store, Lovette had her usual long list of items that she had to buy before their party. She usually didn't make it a habit to wait until the last minute but Joey had just gotten over from being sick and planning a party was the last thing on her mind.

The anniversary party was being hosted at their house. Lovette had wanted to go all out due to her actually being in love with her husband now. It had taken some time but Joseph had always remained consistent with the type of father and husband he was. He had made her happy and Lovette knew that he was good for her.

Gathering her items one by one and strolling down each aisle making sure she didn't forget anything, a woman walked towards her with a basket on her arm wearing the prettiest lipstick she had ever seen. Her face was beyond captivating and Lovette just had to ask her where she had gotten her lip color from.

"Excuse me. I couldn't help but notice how beautiful your lipstick is! Do you mind if I ask what name and brand it is?" asked Lovette. She didn't normally talk to strangers but she just had to know where this particular lipstick had come from.

The lady smiled and before she could open her mouth to respond, a voice from the next aisle over called out a name.

"Monica...Where'd you go that quick, woman?! This is why I don't go shopping with you," he said. Lovette had known that voice. Before she could react, the voice

along with its flesh came walking around the corner onto the aisle she was on.

He stopped in his tracks and looked from one woman to the next. Repeating the same movements once again, the lady with the red lips cocked her head to the side with suspicion.

"I'm right here. I was just about to tell her where I had gotten my lipstick from. You look like you've just seen a ghost. Am I missing something?" she asked him while looking back and forth between him and Lovette. "Because, obviously you both know one another," she continued.

"Um...Monica, this is Lovette. Lovette, this is Monica," said Mike. He felt butterflies throughout his stomach and it felt as if his knees were going to give out at any second.

"Lovette? THE Lovette? Ahhh. The woman who hurt my man," replied Monica while looking Lovette up and down. The smile that was on her face was long gone and had been replaced with a stale impression.

"Um, I have to go. Never mind that color. I can tell it's only made for bitches!" sneered Lovette. She had known this woman for all of 30 seconds and she had been rude to her off of the strength of the things Mike's had told her.

"Oh, HELL NAW!" shouted the woman. Stepping back to hand Mike her basket, Monica started taking off her earrings and walking towards Lovette. Mike snatched her up by the waist before she could get any closer.

"Let me GO!" she shouted over and over again. Lovette laughed a mad woman's laugh and turned around to leave before the owner of the store had kicked them both out. Leaving her basket in the middle of the aisle, she left and decided it was best that she did her grocery shopping elsewhere.

"It was nice seeing you, Mike. Oh, you can do better," said Lovette over her shoulder. This only made the woman holler even more. Lovette continued to laugh all the way to her car.

****

As soon as Lovette had almost reached the exit, Mary stopped her complaining of a stomachache. "Mommy, I want to go home. My stomach is killing me and this party sucks," she whined. Stopping her from reaching the exit, Lovette turned around and bent down to feel Mary's head.

"You feel okay. Wait right here for one second. As soon as I get out of the bathroom, we can leave. Okay?" Mary nodded her head and waited for her mother to return.

****

September 17, 1988

Everyone that was invited to Joseph and Lovette's anniversary party had showed up with plenty of gifts. Lovette had told everyone that there was no need for gifts but she was very pleased to see that people still felt the need to bring them.

Joseph had been on the grill and was wearing a

custom made apron that Lovette had gotten as one of the many anniversary gifts. It was all black and had "World's #1 Dad" printed in white cursive on the front. Joseph had loved the cheesy meaningful gifts like these and Lovette loved giving them to him.

Lovette had been on her third glass of wine and was enjoying the party. Scanning the yard, everyone had a smile on their faces and this satisfied her. It made her happy to know that everyone was enjoying themselves.

Taking a bite of a piece of chicken fresh off of the grill, Lovette closed her eyes and savored the flavor. Joseph knew how to work a grill and the chicken she had just bitten into had been the evidence. Feeling someone plop down beside her on the bench, it startled her and the plate on her lap fell to the ground.

Opening her eyes, it was Stephanie. She had no idea who invited her or when she even showed up but Lovette had been two seconds from losing her cool. Not wanting Joseph to feel some way about her getting angry over the past, which had included Mike, Lovette calmed her nerves and greeted her.

"Hey, Stephanie. I'm guessing Joe invited you…?" said Lovette. She had been giving her the side eye. She couldn't believe her husband had the nerve to invite the girl who possibly had slept with her old boyfriend causing them to break up. He wouldn't do something like that.

"Well, no," she replied. She had aged terribly. Her hair was in a messy ponytail and her dress looked like it had been worn one too many times. She took a long swig of the beer she had in her hand, let out a loud belch and

wiped the corner of her mouth with the back of her hand.

"I came with a friend. Y'all invited umm...what's his name? Kyle? Yea, I met him and he was giving me a ride but said he needed to stop here first to congratulate y'all on the anniversary," replied Stephanie.

"You know, I don't see how you stayed married to Joe after what he done went and did to you," she continued. Lovette was confused and waited for her to finish. She was a drunk mess but Lovette still wanted to see what she had to say.

"You seemed like a good man...I mean, woman. I feel so bad for going over there and starting up that mess. I didn't like Mike in that kind of way. You need to know that, I promise."

Lovette began to steam inside. She felt like she knew what Stephanie was getting at but she needed her drunk lips to reveal a bit more before she reacted in the way she saw fit.

"What are you talking about?" she replied.

"That day I had went over to Mike's house and told him I was selling raffle tickets, Joseph had called me and told me to go next door and wait for the phone to ring. He told me that he would pay me to act like I was fooling around with Mike. I asked him 'Why?' and he told me to do it if I wanted to make some money," said Stephanie.

The fire from her feet rose and shot out of Lovette's ears. The day she had been in his house confiding in him as a friend, he had taken advantage of that moment. She had remembered him going into the other room for a moment but she didn't think anything of it. Unsure if what she was saying was true, Lovette took a deep breath and questioned her further.

"How do I know you aren't making this all up, huh? Why come here on our day and tell me this now? You had every damn opportunity to tell me this YEARS AGO!" shouted Lovette.

Everyone had turned to see where the yelling was coming from, including Joseph. Seeing the sight of Stephanie sitting side by side with his wife made his stomach feel as if it were sinking into the ground beneath his feet.

Storming over to where Lovette and Stephanie had been sitting, Joseph took Stephanie by the elbow and attempted to take her as far away from his wife as possible. He hadn't been able to move fast enough before Lovette continued her scene.

"Oh, no. Where do you think you're taking her? What is this talk about you sending her over to Mike's house to pretend to be having sex with him?!" Lovette spat out. She was filled with rage and could feel every single tiny hair on her body standing at attention.

Stopping in his tracks with his back still facing Lovette, Joseph let go of Stephanie's arm. He dropped his head and remained that way for a few seconds.

"I know you hear me!" shouted Lovette. Everyone had their full attention on the event unfolding before them. Some people started gathering their children and leaving *while others stayed glued to the lawn.*

Kyle scurried over to get Stephanie, yanked her by the arm and pushed her into his car. Speeding off down the dirt road, Lovette wished she had stopped him from taking her so that she could explain to Joseph exactly what she had told Lovette. But, judging from Joseph's guilty demeanor, she had already known what Stephanie had said was true.

"Honey, let's not do this here. Right now...in front of everyone. We can talk about it later. Okay?" This had only made Lovette even angrier.

"Fuck later! How could you do something so low?! You took how I was feeling and manipulated me that day!" shouted Lovette. One of their neighbors had taken Joey in the house and started shooing everyone away to leave the party. "You were my friend and I trusted you! Why would you do something so messed up like this?!"

"He wasn't good enough for you," Joseph confessed. "He didn't care about you the way I did and still do. I've been in love with ever since we started hanging out and I knew it was meant to be. Don't you see that? Look at everything we've built, Love."

Love. No one had ever called her that but Mike. This had been the icing on the cake. Before Lovette knew it, she hopped on towards Joseph and was windmilling all over his head.

The anger that she had been holding in the last few minutes had erupted and was now being unleashed on him. In her mind, he had deserved every single blow that she had delivered. Doing nothing in return, Joseph allowed her to release her emotions.

He deserved it. He deserved every ounce of anger she had been feeling at the moment. Lovette hadn't been his from the start and he had intervened with something that could've been great. But, he had loved Lovette and no one else was supposed to have her.

Joseph allowed her to continue the attack until she had gotten too tired to go on. It was the least he could do. Bill, their neighbor, came running out of their house in attempt to calm Lovette down but she had already finished the smallest part of her anger.

"Go home, Bill. This is between me and MY husband," whispered Lovette. Her tone was low and dark. She had completely sobered up and had contemplated on attacking Joseph again. The hurt and betrayal she had felt was threatening to come out again.

Not saying a word and turning to leave towards his house, Bill understood. There had been rumors in the past about what Joseph did to get with Lovette and he had been surprised that she hadn't learned about them sooner. He didn't feel bad for Joseph but he did hope that the poor girl just didn't kill him.

"Lovette, I'm sorry. I know it's hard to accept right now but I'm really sorry. I never meant to hurt you. You have to believe me. I didn't mean..."

"I should've known you were up to something. You hit on me right after that damn phone call. You couldn't WAIT to sink your teeth in to get a taste, huh? All of that *friend shit was to just get closer to me just so you could find the opportunity to get in good," said Lovette cutting him off.*

She had now been pacing in the yard back and forth. She had been too angry to realize that her knuckles on both hands had been bleeding. A few more paces in, she began to feel the stings on both hands.

"You're bleeding. Let me help you," said Joseph while walking closer to her.

"If you touch me, I swear..." said Lovette while backing up. She had never expected Joseph to hurt her in this way. She had finally accepted their life together and actually loved him. To find this out at this moment, she had been confused. He wasn't perfect but he had been a great husband and father. What was she supposed to do? The irony of it all was that Mike was in town.

Mike. The rage in her had been from her husband's betrayal. She had just noticed that her anger hadn't been from what could've been with Mike. It had been so long since she had thought about him that everything she had once felt for him, some of it started to return. He had been telling the truth about Stephanie this whole time and Lovette hadn't fully believed him.

Turning away to storm off towards the house, Lovette went inside to grab her purse and keys. Joey had been sitting at the bottom of the stairwell and she immediately felt bad for him. This had been the first time she had lashed out in front of him...and in front of guests.

For a moment, she thought about not leaving

because of Joey. Bending down to sit next to him on the step, she kissed him at the top of his head.

"Mommy is so sorry for screaming like that. If I scared you, I'm sorry. It won't happen again. I love you. You know that, right?" Nodding his head and hugging her, she walked him in the family room and turned the television on.

"Daddy is in the yard and will be in here as soon as I walk at the door. I'll be back."

Deciding that her anger wasn't done with, she walked out of the house and walked towards her car. Before placing the key in the door, she turned to Joseph. He had been standing in the same exact spot with the world's most pitiful look on his face.

"Joey is watching TV. You might want to clean up and go in there with him. Explain to him how his father is a lying bastard. Don't look around for me. I'll be back when I get back," said Lovette. Just seeing his face made her even angrier.

Saying nothing and walking into the house, Joseph had felt like he had just lost his best friend and the love of his life. He knew she would come back because of Joey but he wasn't sure if she would come back for him.

The thought of her leaving him was too much to think of at the moment. He wasn't sure if this day would ever come but his happiness with her had allowed him to forget it even happened. He hadn't even known Stephanie was there.

Pulling out of the yard and driving down the dirt road, Lovette was headed to Mike's mother's house. She had gone back and forth with her feelings on going over there unannounced. She didn't know or even cared if it was a smart decision but she had need to see Mike.

Parking on the street in front of Mr. and Mrs. O'Conner's house, Lovette's stomach started to knot up. She had seen his parents throughout the years and they had always been cordial to her but this was different than randomly showing up on their front doorstep. Ignoring the angel on her shoulder, she listened to the opposite and got out.

Before she could reach the door, Mike came from the side of the house wiping his hands on his pants. He was covered in oil and appeared to have been working on his car. Lovette realized her coming here had been a mistake and that she would've looked foolish knocking on their door. But, Mike had caught her and it had been too late to turn back around.

Standing at the end of the driveway, Lovette stared back at Mike who had been standing at the edge of the house. She was stuck and didn't know what to say or do next. Not being able to make a move, Mike walked towards her.

"What are you doing here?! Do you see what my girl almost did to you yesterday?? You're bugging. You need to leave," whispered Mike through clenched teeth. He had been so close to her face that she could see the veins on the right side of his temple pulsating.

"Mike, I didn't start that yesterday. I didn't even

know you were in a relationship, I didn't even know she knew you and I definitely didn't know you were back in town. I just came to speak my peace and that's it. I've left you alone all these years. I didn't come to bring any trouble," she replied. She had meant every word.

The look on his face softened a bit and he could tell she had been telling the truth. Scratching the side of his head and looking over his shoulder, he waited for her to continue.

"Well, I came here to ask your mom or dad if they could give me your number or give you my number. I know what I'm about to say doesn't matter anymore and I promise I'll leave you alone but I just want you to hear me out. Okay?" Tears had started to form in her eyes but she managed to keep them from falling...for now.

The sun had gone down and they had still been standing in the driveway waiting for the darkness to approach at any second. Lovette had been so busy with focusing on Mike that she hadn't realized that there were no cars in the driveway. Mike had been home alone.

"Love, whatever it is, just say it." Mike had called her the only named she cared to hear from his mouth. It had been so long since she had heard him say it that it caught her off guard. "Love" coming from his mouth had been music to her ears.

"Well...today, the girl who used to live next door to your parents showed up to our anniversary party drunk and blabbing her mouth," started Lovette. The thought of Stephanie made her ears burn.

"Okay, and??" said Mike with a bit of aggravation. Stephanie's name would always have a bitter taste. Had she not shown up and trying to seduce him, he would've still had Lovette. He hadn't seen her in years and still hated her for what she did.

"Joseph was the one who sent her over here. We had been hanging out in his living room and I was telling him about how I felt something was off between me and you. I thought you were cheating. I didn't know your mother had personal things going on and it never crossed my mind that something like that could be happening."

"He was the one who told me that I shouldn't assume things and to just call you. Apparently, before he gave me that advice, he went and called Stephanie. He told her to come over here and do all of that because he knew I was about to call you. He knew I'd accuse you of cheating."

"That's not making an excuse for what I did. As soon as I told him what had happened on the phone, he hit on me. I never even thought he looked at me in that kind of way, ya know? We were just friends, I swear. I never looked at him in that way either. I did what I did thinking it would make me feel better about what I thought you did to me and it only made things worse," continued Lovette.

The softened look Mike had previously displayed turned right back into an angry one. He was livid. Turning away from her and walking back down the driveway towards the house, he stopped a few steps in and turned back around.

"You know what? The worst part of this was that I

told you from the beginning that he was in love with you. But, no. I let you convince me that he didn't view you in that kind of way. Then this fool turns around and manipulates you into being with him."

"I told you that I didn't do anything with that girl. You see her now? A damn crackhead who's slept with everyone in the damn city. I still hear about what goes on here. You think I didn't see that coming years ago?! You think I would risk losing you over a slut like her?" continued Mike.

"I've never lied to you. You made assumptions about me before you even met me. I cleared up those assumptions, loved you to the best of my ability and I can say I did a damn good job at it. Even after all of that, you still made assumptions about me from what you THOUGHT you heard on the other end of that line."

"Excuse me if it sounds like I'm just angry with you because you better believe that I want to drive over to your house and bash your husband's skull in. The only thing stopping me is your son needing his father," said Mike.

Turning around to head back towards the house, Lovette chased after him and gently grabbed him by the elbow. He stopped but didn't resist her touch. It had been years since he had felt any of her and even if this meant that this was all he was allowed, he'd accept it.

"I know that I should've talked to you. I'll apologize a million times for it if that makes you hate me any less. We were teenagers and I just didn't know what to believe," said Lovette. She had wished she would've been slower to react.

"I don't hate you, Love. I hate Stephanie and I hate your husband. I hate that you didn't believe me when I needed you to but I don't hate you," replied Mike. He had thought about calling her for years to tell these exact words but couldn't bring himself to start a conversation about something he didn't cause.

Hearing him say these words had forced out her tears that threatened to come down before. All of the hurt, betrayal and rage that she had been feeling had all evaporated into a mist of sadness.

"Look, my mom and Monica are out of town overnight at a conference promoting my wife's make-up line. My dad is playing poker with some friends. Come inside and get cleaned up," said Mike walking towards the side door of the house. Lovette didn't think twice about following him.

She hadn't been inside of his parent's house since before they had broken up. A few things had been the same but a lot had changed. The kitchen had been remodeled and there was new furniture in the living room and dining area. All of the same pictures had been hanging on the walls.

"What happened to your hands? You look like a cat attacked you," said Mike. Not waiting for her to answer, he left the living room and went to the back of the house. As soon as she heard him enter back into the living room, she answered him without looking up from her lap. She wasn't sure if she was ready to be in such a close proximity to him and look him directly in the eyes at the same time.

"Nothing attacked me. I attacked Joseph," whispered Lovette. She was still shocked that Mike wasn't *angrier with her. Forcing herself to look up at him hoovering over her holding a first aid kit, he had taken off the work suit and was now in a white tank top with some gray sweatpants.*

Sitting down on the couch beside her, Mike opened the box and picked up her left hand. Gently wiping it down while applying peroxide and antibiotic ointment, he placed a bandage around her knuckles. Taking his time to do the same with her other hand, he placed everything back in its box and put it on the living room table.

"Did the man even try to block any of the hits?" said Mike breaking the silence. Both of them busted out laughing.

"Yea, but you should've seen me out there like a looney bird. Honestly, I didn't plan on hitting him. I've gotten mad before but I've never hit him before. When he called me...when he called me 'Love', I just snapped," replied Lovette.

He knew that he was the only one to call her that. It even made him a little upset to know that Joseph had the nerve to use it on her. That was his "thing".

"Anyway, I just wanted to clear the air as much as possible. I didn't mean to come over here like this. I know I look a mess," said Lovette while wiping her face. The perfect curls that she had taken the time to do had now fallen and looked flat.

"Stop. You're beautiful," Mike instantly replied. As fast as he had said it, he had regretted it as well. Not that he didn't mean it but he knew it wasn't the right thing to be

saying at the time. Plus, he was in a committed relationship.

"Love, I'm sorry. I shouldn't have said that."

"It's okay. Thanks though. I worked all morning on this hair and I let the fool mess it up by jumping on him like a maniac," she laughed. Pushing her hair behind her left ear, Mike hadn't dropped his stare once. She still looked exactly like she had when they were teenagers.

"I sure would've loved to been a fly on the wall during that," he replied. He didn't like the idea of anyone being violent in a marriage but because Lovette had attacked her husband for the horrible lie he had created, Mike was turned on. She still cared about him.

And, he had still cared about her.

"Come. Let me show you something," said Mike. Standing up and taking her by the hand, he led her towards his bedroom. Pushing the door open, everything had looked the same as it had while he was in high school. His mother didn't replace a thing.

Going to his closet and reaching for the top shelf, he pulled down a Nike shoe box. Opening it up, it had been filled with their old love notes, pictures, movie tickets and all of their memories. He had kept every single thing they had done together.

Moving things around one by one, she was surprised that Mike had really kept a whole box of their time together. She was shocked that he hadn't ripped everything up or thrown it out when they had their breakup.

At the very bottom of the box was the ticket to the dance they went to and the receipt for the food they ate at Baker's after the dance.

"Wow! I can't believe you have the receipt for Baker's! I remember that night like it was yesterday," said Lovette. She had been sitting on his bed and he walked up and sat beside her.

"Yea...well..." said Mike while rubbing the back of his head. "I couldn't bring myself to throw this stuff out. Our last time seeing one another was a bad one but it didn't top all of the good moments we had with one another."

He hadn't fell of a beat with how he talked to her. The strongest part of it all was that he had meant it all. It wasn't game he was running and it wasn't lies; Lovette still had somewhat of a hold on him. Taking her by the chin and turning her face towards him, Mike had a serious yet soft look on his face.

"I've never stopped caring about you. I was just hurt. I know you understand that now. I've never stopped thinking about you either," said Mike. His touch had sent a current through her body and Lovette realized how much she had longed to feel this way again.

He didn't have to say another word. Lovette was sold and he hadn't even been pitching her a sale. Straddling his lap, she could see the worry in his face.

"Take me by the waist and flip me on the bed," was all she said.

"You know once we start, there's no coming back from that. I want you now more than I have ever wanted you. Tell me. I need to hear you say it," whispered Mike. She felt him throbbing beneath her and she knew the words that would make him cross the point of no return.

Placing her mouth on his ear, she whispered, "I want you."

Taking her by the waist and flipping her on her back, Mike knew there was no going back. The hold she had on him had resurfaced and was now stronger than it had ever been.

Removing her shirt and sliding off her pants, he stood up from the bed and admired her. It had been years since he had seen her in this state and she had been more gorgeous than before. Everything had still been perfect and her hips had spread more. This had only added to her beauty.

Lifting his shirt above his head and dropping it to the floor, Lovette returned the admiration. This had been the best silence of her life. Letting every moment and every feeling do the talking, no spoken words were needed.

Lacking absolutely nothing at all, his image was the definition of perfection. Untying his sweatpants and allowing them to drop to the floor, his boxer briefs came next. Lovette squirmed. She felt her breathing increase and tried her best to control it.

Crawling back on the bed and inching closer to her, she felt as if she were panting. His face had finally met hers and deciding she couldn't wait any longer, Lovette pressed her lips onto his. Mike could feel the moisture through her black satin and lace underwear. He couldn't hold back from what he needed most.

Planting kisses from her neck and down to her waistline, Mike used his teeth to remove her underwear and tossed them to the floor. She knew exactly what to do. She had remembered everything.

Grabbing him and placing it at her entrance, he plunged in and felt his knees go weak. There had been a significant difference in size between Joseph and Mike, so Lovette had enjoyed the return of pain mixed with pleasure.

****

Pushing open the bathroom door, the female had her back facing towards the door and was pulling paper towels out of its holder. Lovette had felt that same rage from years ago return. She had the nerve to show up at another anniversary party. As soon as Lovette was about to tell her about herself, the female turned around. It hadn't been Stephanie.

"Excuse me, but do I know you? This is an invite only event and I'm a bit confused," questioned Lovette.

"Sorry, I was invited to an event next door and was only stopping by to drop off a gift. I got the rooms confused and was in a rush to pee. Hence the baby in here," she said while pointing to her stomach. Picking up the gift back from the sink, she smiled and moved around Lovette to exit the bathroom.

****

September 17, 1988

Mike and Lovette had laid up together for a couple of hours talking about the past and catching one another up on things. He had met Monica in college and they had been together ever since their sophomore year. She did a lot of traveling to different cities and states to promote her make-up line she had started in high school. According to Mike, she had been doing pretty well with sales.

After college, Mike had a hard time landing a job. A year had passed and he still hadn't found anything. Deciding not to waste any more time waiting for people to call him back, he and a friend from college, Brandon Weigh, decided to start a cleaning service named "Con-Weigh's Cleaners."

"That's amazing. I'm proud of you," said Lovette. This alone had made he wonder about her own future. She had loved being home with Joey every day and Joseph being able to support them but sometimes, having her own "thing" would be nice, too.

"Thanks. We're just getting started and have other business plans in the works," said Mike. Even though it wasn't what he had imagined for his future, he made decent money and was proud of what they had built and would continue to build. He was still young and still planned on eventually using his degree.

"We plan to open up one in Shawford. I thought about moving back home...at least for a while."

Mike had missed Shawford. He missed his parents and he missed the feeling of knowing someone wherever he had gone in town. He hadn't felt as important in North Carolina and had recently talked to Monica about moving back home. This same trip back to Shawford had been partly business and partly to show her how good of a place it had been to live.

The slam of the house's side door had cut the conversation short. Jumping up from the bed and rushing to put their clothes on, Mike knew he was a dead man. His girlfriend was one of the sweetest people ever but she didn't play. He knew she was about to come in the room swinging like Mike Tyson any minute now.

There was no point in hiding or denying. He had been guilty and was ready to face whatever consequences that came his way. They both had finally gotten fully clothed and had waited for her to enter. When it felt as if an eternity had passed, Mike peeped his head out of the door anticipating a blow.

When nothing came, he had been confused. He and Lovette had clearly heard the same sound of the door slamming and it sounded as if no one was in the house. Deciding it was best that she left, both of them quietly walked to the front door.

"Lovette, tell your husband to get that taillight fixed for you. You shouldn't be driving around with that thing busted out like that," said Mr. O'Conner casually. Both of them turned around to see him standing in the kitchen with a beer in his hand as if seeming them together had been no big deal.

"Yes, sir. I'm uh...well, you have a good night," stammered Lovette. She and Mike both turned around and

walked out the front door leaving the awkward moment behind.

"Why was your dad so calm about that? Your mother would've flipped her shit had she seen me leaving your bedroom just now," said Lovette. Mr. O'Conner's calmness made her feel a bit uneasy and she had wondered if it was low key threat to tell her husband that she had just cheated on him.

"I've never cheated on Monica before and well, he owes me one. The man isn't as faithful as everyone thinks. Plus, he keeps telling me that I'm single until I'm married," replied Mike.

"To say 'I'll call you' would be cliché and insensitive. Plus, I don't have your number anddd your girlfriend would attempt to kill me. Home girl tried to attack me in the store," laughed Lovette.

The silence between them had appeared and even though Lovette knew what they had done was wrong, she didn't regret it. Mike, on the other hand, did feel regret. Noticing the serious look on his face, Lovette removed the smile from hers.

"I didn't mean to make you upset or anything. Hey, look. We both knew what we were doing in there. It happened and I don't feel bad about it. I get why you would feel bad but I don't. Joseph did one of the worst things ever and I just can't see myself feeling bad right now," said Lovette.

"I didn't come over here with intentions on doing any of this. I just wanted to speak my peace and it just *happened. We don't have to see one another anymore and Monica doesn't have to know," she continued.*

Initiating this agreement to him had hurt her own feelings. Of course, she didn't want to be the reason why anyone's relationship failed but what she and Mike had, it was different.

Before Monica had tried to attack her in the grocery store, Lovette would've been more sensitive to the thought of her being cheated on. Since she had been rude to Lovette, majority of her conscience didn't care about Monica at the moment.

"Can I be extremely transparent right now?" asked Mike. This question alone made Lovette anxious. She wasn't ready for the rejection he was about to throw at her but she had no other choice. Nodding her head, he continued.

"I'm a bit upset at myself for betraying Monica. She's been there for me through some tough times and she's a good girl. She doesn't deserve what I just did to her. But, what also happened in there made me feel more alive than I have felt in a long time. I've thought about you just about every single day. Wondering if Joseph was treating you right and if you were genuinely happy with him. I managed to push my feelings for you aside throughout the years as much as I could."

"When we were in the grocery store, I held Monica back only to protect you. I knew that if she laid a hand on you, I would've been angry with her instead. That probably would've made me want to end things with her. I love still love you, Love. And, I can't help that," finished Mike.

pg. 240

Lovette had thought he was about to dismiss her after what they had just done and go back to just being with Monica as if nothing ever happened. She didn't think he would say everything that he just had and even though she had Joseph at home, in her mind, she had Mike at the moment.

"You don't have to say anything in response to that. Especially now and after what just happened. We can revisit this another time because, Love? This?" said Mike pointing from himself and then pointing at Lovette. "This right here isn't done. You know it and I know it."

The last comment had made her want him all over again. If Mike's father hadn't been home, she would've found the strength to drag him back in the house for another round. Leaving him standing there, she got in her car and headed home. Mike watched her car until he could no longer see it.

Lovette had been too busy replaying the night's events over and over in her head that she didn't realize that she had been home. She could've gone straight through red lights and stop signs for all she knew because the drive from Mike to home was a complete blur. Now, she had to face her husband. Well, he had to face her too.

All of the lights in the house were off except for the family room and Joseph's office. Lovette knew he had been in either one waiting for her to come home. It was almost one o'clock in the morning and this was the latest she had ever been out. Especially being out and Joseph not knowing where she was.

Taking a deep breath and stepping in the house,

Joseph was in his pajamas on the couch and snoring. Lovette had decided that he was going to stay there for the night. She would sneak upstairs to check on Joey, take a shower and go straight to bed.

As soon as she stepped out of the shower, Joseph was sitting on the bed with a pitiful look on his face. The exact same look he had when she left earlier. Ignoring his presence, she walked around him to the other side of the bed and opened her dresser to retrieve her nightclothes.

"Lovette, we need to talk about this. I know how it looks and I'm so sorry for even starting this mess. I can't take it back and if I could, I would. It wasn't the right way to go about letting you know how I felt about you. It was stupid and foolish of me to do. I'll apologize a million times if I need to. Whatever you need me to do and whatever you want from me is yours. Just don't give up on me because of this," he pleaded.

A part of her had felt bad for him. Their whole friendship and marriage, he had treated her amazing. He put her on a pedestal the first time he laid eyes on her and she had remained there. There was nothing she could do to make him feel otherwise. Even if that meant her leaving.

Lovette said nothing and continued to apply her lotion and slipping into her night gown. She had taken in every word he said. Her hands began to sting again from the lotion over her cuts and reminded her of just why she had been angry. Joseph had crossed the line.

Sitting on the opposite corner of the bed, she stared at the side of his head. His head was hanging so low that it looked as if it would drop down in his lap at any second.

pg. 242

Joseph felt Lovette staring at him but couldn't bring himself to look her in the eyes.

"What you did was fucked up on so many levels? I would NEVER do that to someone. No matter how much I cared for them or loved them; I could never lie to get someone. That's exactly what you did to me. You know exactly how I felt about us in the beginning and not once did that make you feel bad...not once did it make you feel guilty. You had Maddy..." said Lovette.

"Maddy?! You think I cared about that girl at all?! She was nothing compared to you. I only started dating her thinking you would see how good of a boyfriend I could be and want the same treatment in return. I took the first chance I got with you because that's how bad I wanted you. I've never cheated on you or even thought about it," said Joseph. He tried his hardest to say it with the least amount of anger but just hearing Maddy's name upset him for a reason he wasn't sure of.

"Don't get an attitude with me because you got caught in a lie. This whole marriage is based off of a lie!" shouted Lovette. The anger she had started to feel again was directed towards the love she had grown for Joseph. Her mother had told her that everything would work itself out and somehow, it had. To know that Joseph started the whole thing from being grimy had hurt her.

"I'm sorry. It's just that no one compares to you. I wanted you for myself and I didn't go about it the right way," said Joseph while lowering his tone. Sliding closer to her, he continued. "Just don't throw away everything we had built together because of this, please."

The feeling of guilt had returned and Lovette instantly felt as if she didn't want to continue giving him the cold shoulder after what she had done. She felt how sincere his apology had been. He had never really done much to upset her and had always gone out of his way to make sure she was happy. Fully forgiving him wouldn't be easy...or a guaranteed outcome but she would try.

Joseph had slid all the way beside Lovette and was now looking at her. But, she couldn't look at him. Mike had been on her mind heavy and all she could think about was what she had done. Kissing her on the cheek, Lovette didn't move. Feeling as if this was a green light, Joseph continued.

He wanted to feel his wife and show her how sorry he had been. Lovette had wanted to feel Mike. The needs of both of them couldn't have been more opposite. Besides while pregnant, she had never denied Joseph. Lying back on the bed, she imagined it had been Mike in her bedroom and let her husband have his way.

Chapter 18: Mary

December 14, 2001

"How's everything at home?" asked Ms. Carle. The same questions every time! I found out what mama and papa paid this woman and she hardly asked anything new. They could ask me this stuff for free! She was wearing a pair of dark green flats today and this had been the first time she had worn a pair of ugly shoes.

"Were those shoes a gift this time, too?" I asked. If she wanted to always talk about the same stuff, so would I. She annoyed me and I annoyed her. We were even.

"No. I actually picked them out myself," she said. Ms. Carle became like an aunt to me. Except, she had been a lot more annoying than my actual aunt.

"You should stick to letting people give you shoes as gifts," I said with a smirk on my face. She had been trying her best not to roll her eyes at me.

"Fine. Anyway, tell me how things are going at home?" she asked again. "I know it has to be a little tough now that Joey is away at college. How does that make you feel?"

I actually did miss Joey. Well, a little.

****

"Now, Mary. I want to try something new. We've been having sessions for a while now and while we have

made some improvement, I want to be able to help you a bit more. I've talked to your parents about it and they agree that we can move on to the next step. Sit here for me and lie back," said Ms. Carle.

"Why didn't you ask me if it was okay to move on to the next step? My parents aren't the ones sitting in this room and talking to you all the time." Sometimes I liked her and other times I didn't. Everybody always thought they knew what we best for me instead of asking me first.

"Okay, you're right. You're older now and you are more mature to discuss things. I apologize for not taking your opinion into consideration first. If this doesn't work, I'll come to you first next time. Deal?" she asked. Now, she was talking. Nodding my head, she continued.

"Good. So, I want you to lie back on this couch near the window. I know you were probably wondering why I have another couch. This one is for you to take in the sun's warmth while we talk. Good. Now, close your eyes and just listen to everything I say," she said.

Looking at her for a second, I had no idea why she had wanted me to close my eyes. If she tried some weird stuff, it would be my last time coming. Staring at me as if I were wasting time, I closed my eyes. The couch was really comfy and the sun did feel really good. I could hear the birds outside chirping, car doors slamming, and Ms. Carle's heavy breathing.

"Imagine that you are on a beach. You're sitting in the sand and the sun is shining on your skin. The sand is between your toes and it's squishy. What are you feeling?" she said.

"I'm happy because I'm at the beach and not at school or in therapy," I said. Whatever this new thing was that she was trying on me, it wasn't going to work.

"Okay. It's good that the beach gives you comfort. Tell me somethings you see on the beach."

"Other kids are playing. There are a bunch of seashells all over the sand." Wiggling my toes, there are clumps of sand stuck between them. Picking my foot up, there's a piece of something stuck at the bottom. Gum. Who spits out gum on the beach?!

Joey. He has his headphones on and those stupid sunglasses he always wears. His skin is red. I'm pretty sure he didn't put on suntan lotion like mama told him to. He's gonna be a piece of bacon in a few.

Mama and papa are in the water. Mama has the prettiest pink bathing suit on. It has a bunch of sparkling pieces on the top and the bottom. Papa doesn't have a shirt on. His hairy chest looks gross.

Putting her hands in the water and scooping some up, she throws the water in papa's face. Laughing at the top of her lungs, she does it over and over again until he picks her up and runs through the water.

"I'm gonna toss you in the water! I'm gonna do it!" he shouted.

"PUT ME DOWN, JOE!" mama screams. "I SWEAR, IF YOU THROW ME IN THIS WATER!" she threatened.

Putting her back down in the water, she scoops up

some more water and throws it on him. Moving fast out of the water, mama runs towards me. Laughing the whole way, papa chases after her. Pulling me into her arms, she soaked me with water. I had just dried off.

"Come get in the water! You're just sitting here watching everyone," said mama.

"Mary? Did you hear me?" Sitting straight up, I was back in Ms. Carle's office. The back of my head was throbbing a little and she was sitting with a strange grin on her face.

"Huh? What did you do to me?" I ask.

"I didn't do anything. I asked you a few questions and I let your body do the rest. I never moved from my chair. I promise. Now, tell me what you saw, heard, or how you feel," she said.

✳✳

"Umm…home is okay. Nothing different really. I started hanging out with a couple of girls from school. They aren't so bad. One talks a bit much but she has a cool room. Her parents buy her whatever she wants and when I hang with her, they buy me whatever I want too." As soon as I said it, I knew what she was about to say next, so I beat her to it.

"I don't hang with her just for gifts. It just happens when we do hang out. Her parents have a lot of money and they just don't want me to feel left out if they buy her something while I'm there. They do the same thing for everyone that is around at the time. Not just me."

This had changed her facial expression. She thought she could read me so well but didn't realize that I had been coming to her for so long now that I could read her, too.

"I'm glad you said that. Friendships aren't just about the material things people can do for us and I'm glad you know that. Have you ever thought about doing something nice for....what's her name?" she said.

"Brittany. She's nice, I guess." We met on the first day of school and the teacher told us to form groups to get to know one another. Me, Brittany, Lonnie and Sheena were in the same group.

"It's good that you've made some new friends. I'm proud of you," said Ms. Carle.

Everyone was proud of me for making friends as if it were so bad that I just wanted to hang out with my sister all of the time. Mama acted as if we had won the lottery the first time Brittany, Lonnie and Sheena came over to hang out. The way she screeched when they walked in the door was the most embarrassing day of my life.

"Do you feel comfortable doing a window session today?" This is what we had called them. Window sessions. She had said exactly what it was called but I couldn't remember it; the word was funny. Plus, window sessions had sounded better anyway. Nodding my head, I lie back on the couch. Comfy.

"Whenever you clear your thoughts, we can begin," she said. The sun feels good again. Ms. Carle's office always had the best sunlight. It shined through as if the sun was made for her window. There's a baby crying outside. A car door slams and then the cries stop. Silence. I nod.

"You're at home. You're dressed in your favorite pajamas and you're snuggled up under your blanket. It's early in the morning and you're just waking up."

Bacon. It smells so good and I can't wait to get a taste. Nobody cooks as good as mama. Nobody.

It's cold. Throwing the blanket behind me, a breeze hits me. I shiver and push my purple toenails into my fuzzy blue bedroom slippers. Walking towards the door, I hear a noise. Reaching for the doorknob, it's freezing. Pulling the door towards me, it squeaks.

Papa. He's standing in the doorway of the guest room Joyce is sleeping in. Walking closer to him, I can see her body moving around in a weird way and…there's blood. Lots and lots of blood.

"JOYCE! MAMA, JOYCE NEEDS HELP! PAPA, DO SOMETHING!" There's so much blood. She's choking. The quilt grandma Trudy had made was on top of her. There were so many squares decorated in different designs. Blood had covered the top row of squares and the white was now ruined.

We're in the car. Mama's screams won't stop. Joey looks scared and Joyce's body is hardly moving. Her head is rested on my shoulder. Mama is now in the backseat and holding Joyce. Papa is driving so fast. The car moves from lane to lane and my stomach starts to hurt. I feel as if I want to throw up. I smell the blood.

The tall men wearing all blue clothes are talking to

mama and papa. They ask them to sit down. There's more crying. Papa is holding mama while me and Joey stare at one another. Do they know that we are here? What is going on?

Mama says we have to wear black today. It's time to say our final goodbyes. I get to wear the special gold hoop earrings and necklace. She won't let me wear it every day because she think's I'll lose the jewelry. It's pretty like me. I don't lose pretty things.

There's knocking at the door. Mama ignores it and papa goes to see who it is. He shouts that the person has the wrong house. He apologizes to them and says how he is about to attend a private family matter. He is going to show them how to get where they are going but it has to be quick. He tells mama that he will be back in 10 minutes.

Papa comes back and we are in the back of a long black car. When I asked mama if we could ride in our car, she told me to hush and ride. Joey is staring out of the window and won't say anything.

The building is big. Like, really big. Mama is holding my hand and squeezes it really tight. She hands me a rose and then, she hands Joey a rose. Just one rose. A pretty red rose. Pulling it towards my nose, I sniff. They are so pretty but I wish they had smelled as nice as they looked. My head tilts back and I sneeze.

Mama takes a few steps and pulls my hand. My feet feel heavy and I don't want to move. She tugs again and bends down whispering that we have to go. People are waiting.

"We have to go. Now," she repeats.

The box is shining. The wood glows. Reminds me of the tree in the front yard. Papa says that the tree isn't feeling well and should be cut down. It's not healthy. It's time for it to go. There's a hole in the tree that has the same color as this. There are lines of gold. I put my finger on it and follow its path.

Mama tells me to say goodbye and put the rose inside. Joyce puts her head on my shoulder and sighs. I look inside and…she looks like Joyce. She looks as if she's sleeping. Her face looks as if someone made her look sticky and put some plastic over it. She's not smiling.

I remember. Papa stands at the microphone and says some words. There is a loud screech and he pulls the microphone down some. His deep voice whispers how much he misses her. He says that he wishes he could have done more and how he feels like things are his fault.

We're back outside and people are still crying. Papa says it's time to lay her to rest. This is where she will be for forever. Whenever we want to visit her, we will come here and talk to her. Mama hands me another rose. This time, the rose is white. Mama says that this one represents peace.

We've talked about what I should do when it was time to say goodbye. My thoughts are supposed to lead me. When it's time, I drop the rose on top of the shiny box. I close my eyes and let my heart tell me what to do.

"Get in."

Leaning over the box, I try to get in. There is

someone pulling at my clothes and it presses against my neck. I can hardly breathe. I'm supposed to be with her. I'm supposed to go, too. Turning around and swinging fast, my hands hit hard things. I can't stop swinging. I'm supposed to go with her!

"Mary! MARY! LISTEN TO MY VOICE!" she screams. My chest hurts but the sun feels good. I don't want to open my eyes. The back of my head begins to throb again.

"Can you hear me? Are you okay?" says Ms. Carle. Turning to my side, she's wearing the same ugly green shoes. Looking up at her face, she looks worried.

"I guess," I say. Sitting all the way up and placing my feet on the floor, the clock's bright red numbers are staring back at me.

"It's 4 o'clock. Session over. Hopefully, I'll see you again never time," I said while attempting to stand up and leave.

"Whoa! Take it easy, missy. That was pretty intense. Do the thing I taught you," she said. Breathing in and out, I close my eyes and count out loud.

"16...17...18...19...20. I'm done. I feel okay. Can I go now?" My head had started to hurt but had I told her this, she would make me lie back down. She would say that I needed more time to rest before I could leave.

"Yea, sure. Write down everything in your journal. Everything you saw and felt. We can talk about it during our next session. See you later this week. Be nice to your teachers, do your homework and don't curse. Have a good rest of the day," said Ms. Carle. She heard me curse one time and now she feels the need to remind me not to curse every other session.

Most of the time, mama or papa was waiting downstairs in the car. Today, it had been mama and she looked extremely happy. She looked as if she just stepped out of a magazine. She's so beautiful.

"Get in! We're going shopping!" Those had been my favorite words. Whenever we went shopping, she let me get just about whatever I wanted. Mama had a big weakness for cute shoes. Especially cute shoes for me that matched hers.

Rushing to get to the car, I tripped over one of my shoelaces. Bending down to tie it, I look up to a flat tire. She must not know.

"Mama, the tire is flat."

Jumping out of the car as if it were on fire, she ran around towards me and let out a scream. Throwing her hands up in the air and fussing, she sat down on the curb beside me and called papa.

When he had finally got to us, mama had been crying as if it were the end of the world. I tried hugging her and letting her know that papa was on the way to fix it but she wouldn't stop crying. It was just a tire.

"We'll go shopping another day. I promise. Okay?" said mama in between sniffles. Nodding my head, she sat in the passenger seat while papa drove and didn't say anything else.

I saw papa reach over and squeeze mama's hand. She was still crying as if the tire was that big of a deal. Papa had fixed it and we were on the way home. Going shopping was fun and all but it wasn't that serious. We could go tomorrow.

"It's okay, babe. It's going to be okay. Let's just order Chinese food tonight and relax. Take you a bubble bath and I'll handle everything else," he said to mama.

"It's just that…they were killed because of a stupid flat tire. What if that would've happened to me and Mary today, huh?" blurted out mama. If she could see the size of my eyeballs, she would've told me to put them back in my face.

"Who could've killed us? And, what are you talking about?!" I shouted. If anyone was about to kill us over a flat tire, I see why mama was crying as hard as she was. My hands began to sweat and before I could help it, I was crying right along with my mama.

"Whoa! Whoa! Relax! Nobody is going to kill anyone. We should've told you this story already but just relax," said papa. Mama had stopped crying and was reaching in the backseat trying to get me to calm down. If people were out here killing people because they had a flat tire, well, they should've been told me this.

"Your grandparents, Trudy and Clarence, were taken from this earth because of a very bad person. They had a flat tire and he forced them into the car and did some very cruel things to them. You and mom are safe, okay?

That isn't going to happen to you because you both have me. Alright? That coward is in jail for the rest of his life and he can't come anywhere near any of us. Everything is okay."

Papa kept looking in the mirror in the backseat to see if I believed him. Wiping my face and nodding my head, I believe him.

"I didn't mean to scare you, baby. Your father is right. Something bad did happen to my parents but it doesn't mean it will happen to us. Sorry for scaring you like that. I just had a moment of being scared myself. Everything is okay. I promise," said mama. I nodded my head at her, too. She smiled and turned back around.

"I'll definitely take you up on the Chinese food and bubble bath," said mama. She had returned back to her usual self and was now happy again. I never understood how she could just turn off her tears like that and go back to acting like nothing had ever happened.

Anyway, I needed to tell them about today's window session. Mama had always acted weird when I tried to talk to her and papa mainly listened. They never really knew what to say but Ms. Carle told me that I should talk to them about the sessions, too.

"I saw Joyce in the coffin today."

I could see the smile on mama's face drop. Both of them were staring forward and I could feel it. The same thing was about to happen. She started squirming in her seat and turned to look out of her window.

"Explain," said papa.

"Well, she looked like Joyce but couldn't have been. Joyce was standing next to me. Next to all of us. The girl in the coffin looked like she was sleeping. I remember the roses. We all had to put a rose in. Right, mama?"

I could hear her sniffling. She was trying to hold back her tears. She always did this. Surprisingly, she turned her head around and looked at me with a sad look but trying to force a grin at the same time. Papa pulled down the driveway and parked the car in front of the house.

"You're right. I did make everyone put the roses in the coffin. Joyce loved roses. I wanted everyone to give her one last rose so that she could be with them forever. It was Joyce, baby. Joyce was in the coffin. Sometimes you see her because she was a part of you. You both have the strongest bond in the world. Nobody could ever break that, not even after her death. What you both had and still have is very special and no one can ever take that away from you. But, she's no longer here with us. It was Joyce laying in there. That's who you saw," said mama.

Chapter 19: "Round 2"

December 14, 2001

"I'm proud of you. I wasn't expecting you to say all of that to her because, well…you don't say much about it," said Joseph.

The both of them had just gotten in bed for the night. To satisfy whatever everyone had a taste for, he had ordered just about one of everything they loved on the menu. The dining room table was filled with takeout boxes and Mary had even offered to clean the table afterwards.

They talked here and there about what had happened in therapy for the day. When Mary finally detailed the whole event, Joseph was glad that the new approach had been working for her.

It had taken a while to get to the point that they were at but he was glad that there was progress. He had been skeptical at first and felt that the sessions would do damage to Mary but at the same time, he was desperate to get his daughter the help that she needed.

"I didn't expect myself to say it either. I don't know. I think it kind of just flew out of my mouth. When Mary became confused as to why I was crying and it upset her, I instantly felt like I should be doing more for her. I should've been saying more. Joyce was my baby but she was also a part of Mary. I felt them inside of me and they have been side by side since day one," whispered Lovette.

It had been so long since she had thought about being pregnant with them. Every kick, every hiccup, those little legs stretching in the morning…she had felt all of this.

Lovette enjoyed her last pregnancy way more than the first. Despite carrying more than one child the second time around, the pregnancies were almost identical. Morning sickness, backaches and even the cravings were just about the same. Joseph catered to her as usual but the second pregnancy enlightened her soul more.

****

November 4, 1988

Lovette had been throwing up non-stop for two days and had finally taken Joseph's advice about having Dr. Oar make another visit to their home. A horrible stomach bug had hit their household and she was the last one to get it. Joey and Joseph both were feeling back to their usual self and Lovette had now been feeling the pain they had felt.

Joseph had offered to stay home and take care of her while she had been sick but as usual, she shooed him off to work. He had been home for three days and was the worst person when he was sick. She felt for him but at the same time, men were some of the biggest babies while they were under the weather.

Every move Joseph would make would be attached with a moan and the complaints were nonstop. If she had to spend another day with him home all day, she would lose her mind. He was just as worse when she was sick. Following her around like a puppy wouldn't speed up her recovery.

Hunched over the bathroom toilet, Lovette's knees were in pain and red from the tiles. This had been her second time vomiting and it was only the beginning of the afternoon. Running into the bathroom with one of his action figure toys, Joey pretended as if it were flying.

"Look, mom!" he shouted while turning in circles. Gathering the strength to somewhat entertain her son, she lifted her head to see what the excitement was about. Joey had been spinning in circles and this alone made her dizzy. Swiveling her head back around towards the bowl, she threw up again.

"I'm not feeling well, baby. How about you got downstairs and pull out the bread, peanut butter and jelly? Let me get this out of my system really quick and I'll make you lunch. I'll be down in a few," said Lovette. Nodding his head, Joey ran downstairs.

Letting her head hang, Lovette sat on her knees until she felt as if the vomiting was done. Their family doctor would be over any minute now to check on her. Getting up from the floor, she washed her hands, brushed her teeth and threw cool water on her face. Feeling ten times better, she went to make Joey his lunch.

Walking into the kitchen, Joey was sitting on the floor with his action figure and had been eating his sandwich. There was an empty banana peel sitting beside him. Instantly feeling bad, Lovette squatted down beside him and crossed her legs.

"I'm so sorry I took so long. Mommy hasn't been

feeling good. Did you make the sandwich all by yourself?!"
joked Lovette. Looking up at her and smiling, he had jelly
stuck to the corners of his mouth.

"I did! All by myself! I know you don't feel good
and I wanted to show you how growed up I am," said Joey.

Her feelings instantly switched to proud. She had
been so used to doing everything for him and barely
thought to let him do things on his own. Joey was now in
kindergarten and she still had a hard time seeing that her
baby was growing every day.

"Well, I'm proud of you but 'growed' up isn't the
right way to say it. You wanted to show me how much you
have grown and I see. You did a good job and you also
added in a healthy snack," replied Lovette. Kissing him at
the top of his head, she got up from the floor as soon as she
heard the wheels roll over the rocks in her driveway.

Dr. Oar. He had been their family doctor and would
remain their doctor for as long as he worked. He was one
of the nicest people she had ever known and had a passion
for helping others.

"I heard mama bear caught the bug, too. Is that so?
How are we feeling?" said Dr. Oar. Slamming his car door
and wobbling up towards the front porch, Lovette was
happy to see him. Waving him inside, he placed his
equipment on the chair and turned towards Lovette.

"Well, you look good. Tell me what's going on," he
said.

"I've been vomiting for a few days now," said

Lovette. Pointing to the chair, Dr. Oar waited for her to have a seat. Pulling out his thermometer, he checked her temperature. After a minute or so passed, he spoke.

"You don't have a fever. Have you had the shits?" he questioned. Lovette instantly cackled and he joined her. Dr. Oar felt more like a family member than he did an actual doctor. He knew his stuff but he also knew his patients personally and dealt with each individual with care.

"Nope. Just can't stop vomiting," replied Lovette. She was still wearing her house coat and it was making her sweat. Taking it off, she felt relieved and sat back in the chair.

"Well, I'm no doctor...yes I am...but it sounds like it's not a stomach bug but possibly a baby bug. When was your last cycle?" said Dr. Oar. Lovette instantly sat up straight and got nervous.

"I'm guessing that's code for 'baby bug is a possibility', huh?" he continued.

It was definitely a possibility. She hadn't been on any type of birth control and condoms were never used in her marriage. Lovette didn't get a cycle in October but she ignored it due to the stress her marriage had been going through. Now, it was only the first week of November and nothing had shown up.

"Getting back on track within her marriage." The sentences echoed in her head so much that it made her head hurt. The past two months have been filled with her and Joseph trying to make things right after Lovette found out he had sabotaged their whole relationship. Things weren't perfect but she had been trying to make their marriage work.

"I'll take the silence as this was unplanned. Would you like for me to go pick up a pregnancy test for you? I don't have anything planned for the rest of the evening, so I really don't mind," he said.

Shaking her head, Lovette wasn't ready for anyone to know if she was indeed pregnant. Not even Dr. Oar.

"No, thank you. I'll go get one myself," she replied.

"Go take that test and if it's positive, make you an appointment with an OBGYN first thing Monday morning. I hope you get to feeling better. Tell Joseph that I said hello," As soon as he started packing up his things, Joey ran into the living room.

"Did you fix her?" Joey asked. He still had the same action figure in his hands but this time, it was covered in peanut butter.

"Mommy is going to be fine. She just needs a little rest. Make sure you be her big helper and does what she tells you to do. Okay?" said Dr. Oar. Joey smiled, nodded and ran out of the room.

Lovette watched the doctor's car drive down the rocky road and was consumed with tons of different feelings. She knew that one day she wanted to have another child. But, was she ready?

****

"I know you only want what's best for the kids. I'm glad you said those words to her today. She needed to hear that from you," said Joseph. He had slid all the way under the comforter and looked as if he was about to fall asleep any second.

Lovette, on the other hand, was wide awake. She was in the mood to talk to him and wanted him to be in the mood to listen. Sitting straight up, she continued talking. Joseph took the hint and sat back up with her.

"I agree. From now on, I'm going to listen to her more. The therapist told me that Mary feels as if we don't really listen to her. While I don't fully agree with this, I'm going to try to do more to let her know that we're listening. I know how I can be sometimes and I just want her to heal as much as possible," said Lovette.

Everything she had been saying had been true. She loved Mary and wanted her to fully understand what happened and how they can get through the healing process. Lovette knew that she wouldn't completely get over the loss of her sister but the plan was to get her as much help as she needed.

Closing her eyes and imagining she was pregnant, Lovette felt at peace. All of the pieces to her puzzle are present inside of her.

****

November 5, 1988

Yesterday, Lovette had avoided going to the market to pick up a pregnancy test. She hadn't worked up the nerve to go find out the truth. She wasn't ready to know if she would be bringing another life into the world this soon.

Instead, she decided to hang out with Caron for the day and maybe it would distract her. Both of them had been standing in the kitchen and was catching one another up on the latest gossip.

"Girl, this is why you need to get out more. Being stuck up in this big ol' house all the time. The only time anyone really sees you is when you have a party or something," said Caron. Her daughter, Frankie, had been upstairs with Joey playing.

"You're a wife and a mother, too. I don't see how you have so much time to do anything else. I get out sometimes. I love throwing parties. My friends can come to me. Plus, I love being in this big ol' house," replied Lovette.

"Yea, yea, yea. Anyway, we're going out sometime in the next few weeks. I don't want to hear any excuses either. I know you can't turn down a shopping date. Seems like that's all I can do to get you to leave this place," joked Caron.

Both of them laughed but it had been some truth to what she was saying. Lovette knew she needed to get out more but the underlining problem of her parent's death had her tied to home base. She had been scared to go out too often.

Although Lovette had convinced herself to keep the pregnancy topic to herself for now, she had been dying on the inside to tell someone. She had called her sister this *morning but decided against telling Iris. Iris was her favorite person in the world but she had her own life and was doing so amazing in college. Lovette didn't want to distract her. Instead, she asked her how school was going, talked about random things and hung up the phone letting Iris think it had just been a check in call.*

"Caron, I need to tell you something," said Lovette. She had been staring out of the kitchen window and was drinking a glass of ice cold water.

"You're pregnant," said Caron. Throwing back the rest of her wine, she grinned. She knew Lovette like the back of her hand and had been waiting on her to confirm the truth. Lovette spit out her water and it hit the kitchen window. Swiveling around as if she were on fire, she stared back at Caron who had now been laughing.

"How do you know I was about to say something like that? What are you? A witch, woman?!" said Lovette. This only made Caron laugh even harder.

"Girl. Do you really think you can hand me a glass of wine and pour yourself water? Since when do you drink water whenever we hang out? I was just waiting on you to spill the beans. Plus, you look pale. Have you told Joseph yet?"

"No. Actually, I don't know if I'm pregnant yet. I've been feeling like crap these last few days but I figured it came from the bug Joseph and Joey both had. Dr. Oar came over and I didn't have a fever and I haven't been letting it out from both ends like they did. Just vomiting. I wanted to go buy a test but I chickened out," replied Lovette.

"And you want me to go get you one, huh?" asked Caron. She knew whatever Lovette needed from her, it would happen. They had been friends ever since Will and Joseph introduced them to one another and their friendship couldn't have been any tighter.

"You know I got you," she continued. Pulling her purse off of the kitchen counter, she smiled, hugged Lovette and kissed her on the cheek.

"I can see the worry all over your face. Relax. Everything will be okay. I'm going to go get the test right now and we're going to sort stuff out right now. Drink some more water and be ready to pee when I get back," said Caron.

Caron had always come through for Lovette. She was scared to be seen buying a pregnancy test before talking to Joseph about what was going on.

Joseph. He fussed over her when she was pregnant with Joey and even the mention of a possible baby would instantly make her sit down and elevate her feet. Lovette appreciated the concern but as of now, there was nothing for him to fuss over. She didn't know if she was ready for this right now.

Where was Caron? Did she run into someone? What if they thought the test was for her? Lovette began to get impatient and her thoughts ran wild. Pacing back and forth in her kitchen, she could hear the kids upstairs playing. Frankie and Joey had a brother and sister bond that was the sweetest thing ever. But, Lovette didn't know if she was ready for him to have an actual brother or sister yet.

The store was right up the street from them. What had been taking her so long? Lovette had been tapping her foot and was now nervous more than ever. Looking at the time on the wall, only 20 minutes had passed. Maybe the line was long or maybe, Caron had a hard time deciding which brand to buy. Yea, that was it.

Finally, Lovette heard the screen door slam shut. Walking into the foyer, it was Joseph. She felt the blood drain from her face.

"What are you doing home so early?" she questioned. He had already started to undo his tie and could tell he had a lot on his mind.

"I don't feel too good. Is that Joey and Frankie upstairs? I'm going to shower and get in bed," he replied. Giving her a kiss on the cheek. Wrapping her arms around his neck and giving him a hug, he hugged her waist.

"Yea. I'll try to keep them quiet. Caron ran to the store to get more wine. Girl's day. I'll bring you up some soup and tea," said Lovette.

As soon as she heard their bedroom door shut, Caron had pulled up in their driveway. Lovette felt as if she could breathe again.

"Looks like Joe is home. Good thing I brought another bottle of wine AND the test. Just in case the results are negative," said Caron while laughing.

Lovette playfully snatched the test and went into the downstairs bathroom. Her bladder had been itching to release its contents. Lovette peed on the stick, laid it down on top of a napkin and cleaned herself up. Refusing to look at it, she joined Caron in the kitchen and handed it to her.

"Too chicken to look at it, huh?" she joked. Lovette managed a smile but deep down inside, she wasn't really in the playing mood. It had only been a day since she saw Dr. Oar but she had prayed for her period who still refused to make its entrance.

For some strange reason, her parents came to her mind. Lovette tried her best not to think of them because when she did, it was mainly about their deaths. Joseph had told her to try and focus on the good moments and not the horrible one. This method would work at first but then, it would always end with how they died. Either way, she would end up dwelling just like she had started to now.

"You hear me?" said Caron. Lovette had guided off with thoughts of her parents and hadn't heard one word her friend had said to her. Shaking her head, Caron repeated herself.

"Your oven is empty, mama. You can breathe now," said Caron. Lovette felt her knees go weak and needed the countertop for support. Her nerves were at ease. Before she realized it, she had tears coming down her face.

"Whoa, now! What's going on? Are these sad tears? Happy tears? Say something before I drink this wine bottle by myself," said Caron.

"No, no. I'm okay. I was just scared. Another baby wasn't planned right now. I want more kids, eventually, but I wanted the next go round to be planned. A bit of relief, ya know?" said Lovette. Caron nodded her head and hugged *her friend. Whatever made Lovette happy, it made her happy and vice versa. Caron had been the big sister that Lovette wished she had.*

Relief. Lovette had her relief and could now go see her OBGYN about what else could be going on. She knew it was probably stress and her doctor would tell her to take it easy but she would confirm so that Joseph could be at ease as well.

★★★

"What is your favorite memory of Joyce?" asked Lovette. She rubbed her feet together and felt the warmth of the blanket. They had just bought a new one a couple of weeks ago and she had fallen in love with how good it felt.

"The beach. Remember the first time we went? The girls were about to turn 3. Mary was so bold. She ran towards the water and didn't even know how to swim. We both started to run after her but I stopped to turn around because Joyce was tugging at my shorts. She was scared. The shells on the beach had scared her for some reason."

"You went after Mary while I tended to Joyce. I picked up a shell and showed her that they were nothing to be afraid of. The whole trip, she was timid of everything but once I showed her that that she didn't have to be afraid, she let her guard down. That made me feel like I was her person. She trusted me and she trusted my judgement," said Joseph.

She felt his sadness. This wasn't her intent. Lovette had wanted to strike up the conversation with good intentions but she had done the exact opposite.

"I didn't mean to make you sad. I just wanted to talk about her. I know it seems like I avoid these feelings but I'm just trying my best to show you that I still think of her and I'm getting through this as well," said Lovette.

Joseph knew she meant well. The guilt he carried still lingered around from time to time. There was no telling if the feeling would ever die down and he had tried his best to live with the feeling.

"I know, baby. I know. But, it is my best memory of her. She relied on me and even though I love them equally, I love them differently. Mary is so fierce, independent and ready to tackle things, like you. Joyce was a daddy's girl and I felt as if she needed me."

This had been the truth. Mary had Lovette's exact personality and Joyce had been the opposite. She understood his pain and wanted nothing more for him to rid the feeling of guilt. Nothing had been his fault and he had always been a good father.

****

November 15, 1988

"8 WEEKS! HOW IN THE…?! What in the…?! But…" shouted Lovette. The doctor had been removing her white gloves, tossed them in the trash and was now washing her hands in the sink as if her shock hadn't mattered at all.

"I'm assuming this wasn't planned. Based off the time you had your last menstrual cycle and the ultrasound, 8 weeks sounds accurate. Would you like to talk about your

options?" said Dr. Jenkins.

The irony. Options. Nobody wanted to discuss options when she had found out she was pregnant with Joey but now, options were available. Instantly, she felt bad for thinking these thoughts. Her mother, Trudy, had a lot to do with Lovette becoming a wife and mother. Even though things were hard at first and not what she thought she had wanted, Lovette was grateful that her mother had been right all along. Well, somewhat right.

"I mean...I took the at home test and it said negative. I don't understand," replied Lovette. She had been expecting the doctor to tell her to reduce her stress, eat healthier, exercise, or something else but she hadn't expected to be pregnant.

"Believe it or not, this is very common. You're early in the pregnancy and sometimes, some test don't detect the pregnancy right away because of the hormone levels. I gave you one today and the test lit up with a positive result almost immediately."

Lovette had still been in disbelief. More children were part of the plan but not at the moment. Remembering the time she had thrown herself down the stairs trying to terminate her own pregnancy, a feeling of guilt washed over her. Joey had been her entire life and there was no way she would try to do something like that again. Saying nothing else to the doctor, Lovette gathered her things and headed to the car.

She wasn't ready to drive home. She wasn't ready to tell Joseph the news. Even though another baby wasn't what they had planned at the moment, she knew that there *was no other option than to suck it up and go through with it. After what she did, there was no way she would try to block another one of God's blessings. Everything would be okay.*

Forcing herself to think on the brighter side, Lovette pictured how much happier Joey would be. He had been lonely at times and the thought of a little brother running after him had made her smile. They had enough money and a huge house to fill. She had Caron as a supportive friend and most importantly, she had Joseph.

Starting up her car and backing out of the parking lot, her nerves had calmed and the knot in her stomach had released. Lovette had felt better about being with child and she knew that Joseph would be supportive as he always had.

8 weeks. Rubbing her belly with one hand while steering the car with the other, Lovette slammed the brakes. 8 weeks ago was around her anniversary.

Mike. She had placed herself in almost the exact same position as before. Only this time, she didn't know who the father of her child was. Horns blared from behind her and she gassed the car while crying all the way home.

Chapter 20: Mary

January 11, 2002

"Tell me the truth because I'm sick and tired of being confused. I just want the truth, Joyce." We were sitting on the front porch and she was brushing my hair up into a bun. I was going on my first "date" tonight and Joyce insisted I wear my hair up with a pair of gold hoops mama had bought me.

His name is Eric. I'm not sure if I like him but he seems nice and he's cute. The only reason mama and papa agreed to let me go was because Ms. Carle suggested I get out and "do things that pre-teenagers do."

Eric had just moved next door with his uncle, Bill. His father wasn't able to take care of him anymore because of his health. His mother was never around, so it had been just them two. At least this is what he told me.

"What outfit are you going to wear? You put two on your bed and still haven't picked one. Your date starts in 45 minutes and you don't even know what you're going to wear. Better stop acting up or you're gonna see Eric with another pretty girl on his arm," said Joyce.

This is what she did. Whenever I wanted the truth, she ignored me and talked about something else. Jerking my hair from her hands, the brush dropped and clashed on the porch.

"Answer me. I'm done playing with you. I'm sick

of everyone telling me one thing and then you won't even tell me anything at all. I swear if you don't tell me right now…" This was it. The last time I would let her try to weasel out this. Staring her in the eyes, she knew I was serious.

"Okay but if I tell you, you can't tell anyone I said this. Not mama, not papa, not Joey, and not Eric. No one," said Joyce. If the look on her voice wasn't creepy enough, her voice sure was. Nodding my head, crossing my heart and adding "hope to die", she knew that the secret was locked between us.

"I can't leave until everything is done. He told me that there is something missing and we need to finish it. I'll return back to Him when this is done but you have to help me get back there so I can stay. You'll know when it's time to tell and when you do, only tell mama. Take papa's keys and go to the shed," whispered Joyce.

The shed. We hadn't been there in years. The thing had to have fallen to the ground by now. Joey used to hang out there when he was in his "bad boy" phase. It's been a while since I had even thought about the old thing.

"Who is 'He' and what do you mean 'help you get back there'? Get back where?" I asked. She sounded crazier than people telling me that I really couldn't see my sister and it was all in my head.

"Don't worry about all of that. Just focus on what needs to be done. We have work to do," said Joyce. She was looking over her shoulder as if someone was about to come out of the front door.

And, someone did. Papa. Placing her finger over her mouth and shaking her head, we stopped talking.

"I thought someone had a hot date tonight," said papa with a big grin on his face. He snapped his fingers and pointed at me. I hated when he tried to be cool.

"You're going on that date. Don't let papa get suspicious. You can go to the shed tomorrow," whispered Joyce.

"I was just, ummm…brushing my hair and trying to figure out which outfit I wanted to wear," I said while picking up the brush.

"Well, you have about 20 more minutes before it's time to head out. I'll be taking y'all but Eric's uncle, Bill will be picking you both up after the movie. Oh, and you should wear the blue outfit," said papa.

I was definitely going to wear the red one. Papa had barely any sense of fashion and to wear an outfit he thought was the best choice, this meant I would have to go with the exact opposite. Mama would agree.

Getting up from the porch to get ready for my "hot date", Joyce stayed glued to the bench. Papa smiled at me and sat down beside her.

Leaning back and resting his head up against the window, Joyce smiled at him and whispered, "I love you, papa."

"I love you too, Mary," said papa.

"I didn't…" Joyce had put her finger over her

mouth again for me to be quiet.

****

"Look at the most beautiful girl in the house! No offense, honey, but she has you beat tonight!" shouted papa.

I told mama about papa choosing the blue outfit and she had agreed that the red choice was the smart decision. The red shirt sat off of my shoulders and was long sleeve. My skirt and stockings were black. The red flats on my feet sparkled and were so pretty. The bun Joyce had suggested made the outfit look even more amazing.

Walking down the stairs, both of them smiled back up at me hard. Mama was one smile away from popping all of her teeth out of her mouth from grinning too hard. You would have thought I was going to prom or something the way they were fussing over me.

"Please, stop," I said. As soon as Eric heard the shouting, he came from around the living room corner and smiled up at me. He had the prettiest teeth I had ever seen. Most boys my age didn't even brush their teeth.

His skin reminded me of Ms. Carle's. Smooth and dark. He was wearing a white long sleeve button up shirt and black slacks. His shoes shined as if he just polished them. This boy was really dressed. His uncle, Bill, wasn't much of a dresser. Bill mainly wore overalls and spent most of his time working on cars around his house.

But, Eric? Eric had it going on. Must've gotten it from his dad. Yea, this was officially a date.

The stairwell vanity. I needed to check my face one last time. Looking over my shoulder, I bent down and looked at myself. My skin is brown.

"WHAT THE HELL?!" Turning around to face everyone, they all had confused looks on their faces. I was brown. What happened to my skin?

"Mary, watch your mouth! What is going on with you?" said mama. She was standing beside papa with one hand on her hip. She always did this before she fussed someone out. It was me. I was about to get fussed out.

Turning back towards the mirror, my skin was back to its normal color. Something was wrong. Rubbing my eyes and looking into the mirror again, it was still the same me. I just saw brown. I know I did.

"Girl, what are you doing?! Get down here! Eric is waiting on you and here you are making a weird impression on him," mama said. Papa had his hands in pockets and was tapping his foot.

"Sorry mama...papa...Eric. I saw a spider on the mirror. My bad," I lied. I had really turned brown for all of 10 seconds. I don't know what kind of evil mirror mama had in this house but the thing always had made me feel weird.

"Just get down here so your daddy can drop y'all off," said mama. Rolling her eyes and hugging me, she continued. "What movie did y'all decide on?"

"Well... I was going to talk to you about that. Can we just go get something to eat instead? I don't want to sit in a movie theater. We already asked Bill and he said he didn't mind. I meant to tell you earlier," I said.

"You're always last minute. Yes, this time," said papa. "Here's an extra 20. Have fun," said papa while handing Eric the money.

"It's okay, Mr. Marks. I have enough to cover whatever Mary wants," said Eric. He was so well mannered. He'd be my boyfriend by the end of the night. I knew he would.

Papa must've been impressed because he looked at mama, smirked and then put the money back into his wallet. Mama smiled back at him. Grabbing his coat and hat from the rack, he turned around towards us.

"Y'all ready?"

Before I could answer, Eric grabbed my coat from the rack and placed it over my shoulders. This boy just knew how to keep adding on cool points. Kissing me on the cheek, mama shoved us out the door. She probably felt as if I was going to change my mind but there was no way I was cutting out on Eric.

Pulling up to Baker's, I remember mama told me this was where she had her first date. Eric got out of the car, ran around to my side and opened the door. Oh, yea. This is definitely about to be my boyfriend.

"I'll be back in two hours. Oh, and Eric? Keep all body parts to yourself. The cook is a good friend of mind, so I have an extra set of eyes," said papa. This moment couldn't have been more embarrassing. Rolling my eyes and slamming the door shut, I walked off towards the door.

"Yes, sir," said Eric turning around to catch up to me. Beating me to the door, he grabbed the handle, and stepped aside for me to walk in.

French fries. Not only did Baker's have the best burgers but the fries were to die for. The smell filled up the restaurant and made my stomach growl. Surprisingly, there were only 2 other people in the place. Taking my hand, Eric led me into a booth. Butterflies.

"Are you comfortable? You can use my jacket if you want," said Eric flashing those bright white teeth. His haircut looked as if he had just gotten it done and he smelled amazing. I knew he was cute but tonight, he looked even better.

"I'm okay." Looking around, Baker's needed to update the place bad. I'm sure it was the same inside and out when my parents were my age. It was clear Mr. Baker didn't want to change a thing.

"Soooo...What do you like to do?" said Eric. No one had ever asked me this before. I had no idea what to say.

"Tell him that you like playing video games, reading, and watching TV," whispered Joyce. Did she really have to do this right now?! "Tell him. I know you don't know what to say."

"Umm...I like playing video games, reading and watching TV," I said. Shit. Here I go listening to her again. I like video games but I can't even remember the last book

I read.

"What was the last book you've read?" Really? He would ask me the one question that I had no answer to. Looking over to Joyce, she had her hand over her mouth and was laughing.

"It's been a while since I've read. I can't remember." The truth was easier to say than I had thought it would be. Before he could ask another question, a waitress came to our table looking as if she were ready to quit her job any minute now.

"What'll it be?" she asked. She had a notepad in one hand and a pen in the other. Tapping it on the table, her fingernails were dirty. I couldn't resist.

"Is Mr. Baker back there?" I said while smiling. There was no way I was letting this girl touch my food. Her hair even looked dirty. She let out a sigh and turned around to walk back towards the kitchen. Minutes later, Mr. Baker came to our table.

"Heyyyy! There's my favorite girl!" He would always say this when he saw me. Every time our family came here, he acted as if he hadn't saw us in years.

"Hey, Mr. Baker. Do you mind taking our orders and bringing it out? Shelly over there looks like she hasn't washed her hands in years. You know, mama would have a fit had she saw that," I said.

"I keep telling her about her hygiene. She's a good kid though. I'll get on her about it. And who is this fella here?" said Mr. Baker smiling at Eric. He knew who he was. Papa told him we would be here.

"I'm Eric, sir," he said while standing up to shake Mr. Baker's hand. Mr. Baker smiled. He likes him. Everyone likes Eric.

"Nice to meet you, young man. What are y'all eating tonight? Oh, and it's on the house, so eat up! Don't walk out of here until y'all are nice and full," said Mr. Baker. He had always been in a good mood and today was no different.

"I'll have chili cheese fries with jalapeños and a cheeseburger with ketchup and mustard. Oh and a water, please." Shit. I just ordered the one meal that was guaranteed to mess up my shirt. God, please don't let any chili fall on my shirt or hit my chin. This boy is going to think I eat like a baby.

"Relax. He'll think that the way you eat is cute," whispered Joyce.

"Would you just shut up?" I said. Mr. Baker and Eric instantly looked at me as if I had three heads. If their eyes were any bigger, they would fall out of their faces.

"Sorry, I didn't mean to say that."

"It's okay," said Eric. He still looked confused but he continued to order his food. "I'll have 2 franks...I mean, 2 hotdogs with chili, onions, ketchup, mustard and sauerkraut with a side of fries and a vanilla milk shake." I wouldn't be the only one getting my clothes messy. Let's see how white his shirt would be when we left.

"I'll bring everything out in a few. Have fun!" said

Mr. Baker and he disappeared towards the back of the restaurant.

"Sauerkraut?! Who eats that?! I've never even seen anyone eat that stuff," I said.

"Whatttt?! It's the best thing ever. It adds the extra that a frank needs. Well, hotdog. I'm still getting used to the down south talk. You should try some when he brings the food out. You'll like it," said Eric. He was so fine.

"Okay." I was a lucky girl to have him living next door. This must be what all of the other girls and school gossiped about. I hadn't liked anyone yet and he actually wanted to go out on a date with me.

Mr. Baker brought our food out and before I could taste my own, Eric had picked up his hot dog and pushed it towards my face.

"Here. You take the first bite." Doing as he said, I did. Amazing. Sauerkraut is amazing. Nodding my head and smiled, he smiled back at me.

"I told you that you would like it," he said while shoving the hot dog into his mouth. Looking down at my own food, I wish I had ordered what he had. Taking a bite of my chili cheese fries, the thought went away. It was so good.

"Ask him a question," whispered Joyce. She was working a nerve. I'd pinch her if Eric wouldn't think I was being weird. I had already shouted once before and I didn't want to scare him off. Giving her the side eye, she sat back in the booth and zipped her lips.

"What do you like to do?" I asked. Even the way he chewed his food was cute. He swallowed what was left in his mouth and wiped his lips with a napkin.

"I like video games. I love working on cars with my uncle. Oh and you might laugh at this one but....gardening," he said. I hadn't been expecting that last one. I've never heard any boy our age say they like gardening. Deciding that I shouldn't laugh, he continued.

"It gives me time to think, ya know? Plus, the ending results are pretty cool. A small seed turning into something so big is just...just wild. It's pretty cool," he said.

"Sounds cool. Maybe I can come over and help you one day," I said. Instantly feeling weird, I wish I hadn't said it.

"You should. You'd like it." Smiling and eating some more of his food, I was convinced. He said I would like the sauerkraut and well, I did. Gardening. Watching him eat, I almost forgot that I had my own food.

****

"How was your date?" asked mama. She had come into my room and was now curled up in bed with me. Looking up at her, she kept talking.

"That smile lets me know it went well. Do you like him?" she asked.

"I guess. I think so. But, don't tell papa," I said. Even though I told her not to, I'm pretty sure that she would. "Do you mind buying me some flower seeds?"

"I saw that boy gardening outside last week. You must really like him to be asking for some flower seeds when you know nothing about gardening," said mama while laughing. I'm sure my face was redder than her hair. She caught me.

"It's okay to like him. It's normal. Just make sure you keep it appropriate. Which means, you two can hang out but no grown folks business. There always has to be an adult present when you two hang out. I'm glad you had fun. Tell me more about him," she said.

"He told me that he never knew his mother and how it was just always him and his dad. He said she left right after giving birth to him; she wasn't ready to be a mother. That's so sad. I can never imagine not knowing you. I wonder if he could find his mother. Maybe she is sorry for leaving," I said.

"Well, baby. It sounds like she doesn't want to be found. If Eric and his dad were living in the same place this entire time, she could've come back. Try not to dig too deep into his mother, though. You don't want to make him sad and y'all are building a friendship."

"Let him come to you, that's if he wants to tell you. It's like building trust. And, thank you. I can never imagine not knowing you too," said mama. Kissing me on the forehead, she tucked the blankets around my arms.

"Okay. But, another thing. How can I tell if he likes me?" It was clear to her that I liked him but I didn't know if he liked me or not.

"He's the one who asked you out, right? He likes

you. Also, what's to not like about you? You came from me, girl. Watch out or he'll be in love before you know it," said mama while laughing. "Get you some sleep. I love you. Good night."

"I love you too. Good night, mama."

Chapter 21: You're mine to keep.

November 30, 1988

When Lovette had delivered the news, Joseph had instantly felt excited. Not noticing her demeanor, posture and facial expression, he instantly picked her up and spun her around. They were having another baby and to him, now had been the perfect time.

"Joe, put me down, please. I'm not done talking. Plus, you're making me nauseous," said Lovette. It had been a couple of weeks since she had found out she was pregnant and she had gotten tired of hiding it from him. Between the new cravings, missed periods, and her becoming exhausted all of a sudden, she had to come clean.

"What is it?" he replied. Now looking Lovette in her face, he could tell that something was off.

"I don't know else how to say it but to just say it. During our anniversary party, after that whole spill, I went over to Mike's parent's house. Before I say any of this, you need to know that I didn't plan any of this. Mike and his girlfriend had been in Shawford that weekend and I had run into them at the grocery store. This is how I knew he was in town," said Lovette.

"After finding out the truth about how we became what we are now, I was angry. When I left here, I drove straight to his parent's house. I just wanted to get his phone number or something to let him know I was sorry for not believing him," she continued.

Joseph hadn't been angry. He had hurt the woman

he loved the most and knew that it would take some time to heal the wounds he had cut open. Lovette hadn't left him for the betrayal and he was forever in debt to her. She was being patient with forgiving him and trying her best to not be angry with him. If she had went to talk to Mike, he understood.

"When I got there, he was there. No one but him. I told him what I had to say, we caught up on old times and...it just happened," whispered Lovette

"What 'just happened'?" asked Joseph. One of his eyebrows were lifted as he looked at his wife suspiciously. The 'just happened' part had taken him by surprise.

"It. I didn't mean for it to happen. I was just so hurt and angry with you and before I knew it...everything just happened so fast," said Lovette. She had been sniffling and trying her best to hold back the tears.

"So, let me get this straight. You left here, went over there and had sex with him? Correct?" questioned Joseph. Her words had cut Joseph but for him to repeat it back to her in the exact words that needed to be said, he had hurt himself even more.

"Yes but you need to know that those weren't my intentions when going over there. I didn't even know he would be there," pleaded Lovette.

"...and you came home and fucked me the exact same night?!" hollered Joseph. This had been the very first time he had raised his voice at Lovette. Lifting her head in a bit of confusion, he had never yelled at her. Joseph had always been so kind and soft spoken, so to hear him scream

at her, she didn't know exactly how to handle it.

"Joseph, I didn't plan it. I swear, I didn't" said Lovette. When she had imagined this conversation with him, it didn't include her pleading. She wanted to tell the truth and move on from there. They both had done wrong.

"So, this all relates to you being pregnant in what way?" said Joseph. He needed to hear it from her mouth. At this point, he had refused to tell her story from his lips. She would say exactly what needed to be said this time. Her silence had angered him even more.

"SAY IT!" he screamed.

Lovette jumped from the bass in his voice and spoke. "The baby might not be yours," she said. She had wiped her face and had now been staring him in the eyes. There was no more dropping her head and hiding behind her hair. He would see her every expression from now on; the way it should have been from the beginning.

Joseph instantly began to cry. He and Lovette had plans. They had plans of having another child or several children. She had grown to love him. He knew that she didn't at first and he was never her first choice but she had grown in love with him. Everything had been so...perfect. Everything had grown to be perfect...until Stephanie showed up.

He had convinced himself that this was his fault. Had he not lied about everything, there wouldn't be an issue. The way she had now been in love with him, it could've been possible for her to love her on her own. He went behind her back and had been conniving. This was his fault.

"Are you still messing around with him?!" asked Joseph. It was one thing if she had slept with him once but it was another if she was continuing to see Mike. He wanted the answer to his questions but at the same time, he didn't. He hadn't been prepared for any of this, including her next answer.

"No. We only slept together once. The next day, I got in touch with him just to let him know that it couldn't happen again. He agreed and we left it at that," she said. Hurting him had hurt her as well. He had been her best friend and there for her every step of the way she had needed him...and she betrayed him.

Although, he was wrong for the way he had started their relationship, that was years ago and she had vowed to be faithful towards him. Plus, she had been on the path of forgiveness for what he had done to her.

Joseph had felt a sense of relief. The last thing he wanted to hear was that his wife had continued to see the man that was her first love. Weirdly, not knowing if the child she was carrying was his or not didn't disturb him as much as it would've to know she had continued to have an affair with Mike. This would've been the blow he wouldn't be able to handle.

"I don't know what to say besides I'm sorry but...I want this baby," said Lovette. "I didn't know if I wanted another child just yet. Not because I don't know which one of you the baby belongs to...it didn't cross my mind until after I had an appointment and the doctor confirmed how far along I am. I just didn't want to take any attention away

from Joey just yet."

"Anyway, I'm not terminating this pregnancy. If this means you want to divorce me, I understand but..." continued Lovette.

"DIVORCE?! Whoa! Slow down! Who said anything about a divorce, Lovette?! You're going so fast with this. Just...stop for a second," said Joseph. His head felt as if were about to explode from taking everything in all at once.

Lovette was Joseph's life. He lived for her. She could do no wrong...almost. He had felt as if he were nothing without her and even after her confession, she was still his. There was no future without her and to hear the word divorce...he couldn't bear what it would be like to live life without her by his side. He needed her.

"Mommy. I'm thirsty," said Joey. He was rubbing his eyes and wearing his all red footy pajamas with his blue blanket draped over his shoulder. Neither one of them had known how long he had been standing in the living room doorway.

"Go on back up to bed and I'll bring you some water. Okay?" said Lovette. He hadn't been satisfied with her response. Not moving from the doorway, he stared at them both.

"I want it now. I'm thirsty," he whined.

"Joey, mommy said she is going to bring it up to you. Now, go back to bed!" shouted Joseph. He had raised his voice at their son and this had been the first time. He

was hurting from what they had going on and it stemmed off towards Joey. She didn't like it at all.

Joey's eyes teared up but he didn't say another word. He turned back around and headed back up to his room.

"Joseph, you didn't have to yell at him like that. He doesn't have shit to do with this," said Lovette. It was one thing for him to yell at her because maybe she deserved it but he wasn't going to yell at their child when he did nothing at all.

"You're right," sighed Joseph. "I'm going to take the water up to him and apologize. Can we finish this later?"

"Can we finish this tomorrow? I'm just as exhausted as you are with it. I just want to take a shower and head to bed," replied Lovette. Not waiting for a response, she got up from the couch and walked towards the steps.

****

December 5, 1988

Two separate heartbeats were heard. Twins. Lovette had been carrying two babies. As if the thought of having one more child wasn't a bit overwhelming enough, their doctor had confirmed that she was carrying twins.

After confessing to Joseph about her infidelity, she felt better and worse at the same time. She hadn't talked to Mike about it just yet and each day passing had creeped closer and closer towards her due date.

pg. 292

Joseph had the idea to wait until the babies had been born and to not say anything to Mike but that idea just didn't sit well with Lovette. He deserved to know the possibility of him becoming a dad ahead of time. Leaving the doctor's office, Lovette decided to break the car ride silence.

"I was thinking I would give Mike a call today. This has gone on long enough. He needs to know. Keeping it from him isn't fair. If he is...the father...he deserves the chance to know a head of time," she said.

Joseph was afraid of this. He was afraid that Mike still loved Lovette and would be the first thing smoking back to Shawford to woo his wife back into his arms. Joseph wouldn't allow this to happen. No matter what it took, he would keep his wife. And, no matter what he needed to do, Mike would never have her.

Waiting a few moments to speak, Lovette knew he didn't agree with her decision. Her mind was made up. It was the right thing to do.

"You can sit beside me the entire phone call if it makes you feel any better," added Lovette.

This statement gave him a bit of emotional pleasure. She was still his. Lovette still and would always carry the title of being his wife but she was still attached to him emotionally. He needed to know that she still cared about him and this gesture had made him feel a bit at ease.

"Okay," he agreed. Going against her wishes would only put more of a strain on their marriage and this was something he hadn't cared to do. Things were going to

get better between them. They had to.

Pulling up to their house, Joseph's parents were there. They hadn't been expecting them to stop by. Neither one of them had been sitting in their car or waiting outside, so Lovette assumed they had let themselves in with the "emergency only" key they had given them.

"Oh, there you two are! Y'all haven't been answering the phone for days now and we started to worry! Don't scare us like that!" screeched Joseph's mother, Sarah. She coming from upstairs carrying a laundry basket of Joey's clothes.

It bothered Lovette when she came over and instantly started cleaning. She loved her mother-in-law but it made Lovette to feel like she wasn't a good enough cleaner. The annoying part was that the basket only had a few items in it.

Sarah had to be doing something all the time. She was about to start a whole load of clothes for a couple of shirts and a couple of pants. Lovette reminded herself to jokingly slide her the water bill once it came in the mail.

"Sorry, mom. Between work and home, things have been a little hectic. We meant to call you back. Is dad here?" said Joseph. He didn't mind his mother letting herself in. It had only bothered Lovette. If he could, he would have his parents live right next door so they could be closer.

"Naw. He told me to stay home and mind my business. You know he doesn't worry like I do. What time does Joey get home from school? I want him to see maw

maw waiting at the bus stop for him," she squealed.

Lovette instantly let go of the aggravation of her letting herself into their home and smiled. Sarah was such a wonderful grandmother. Since Joey was too young to remember his grandmother, Trudy, it made her sad but she was grateful that Sarah had done such a great job of loving her son as grandmother should.

"3. You should stay for dinner. Give him a bath and read him a bedtime story. You know he'd love that. Tell dad to come over," said Lovette.

"Oh, see now you just want me for my good cooking but you know since I love you so much, I'm gonna do just that!" said Sarah. She loved Lovette like the daughter she never had. "I'll make my lasagna. Joey loves it! Oh, and what's so hectic around here that y'all couldn't call me back? Trouble in the marriage? You know I counsel..."

"Everything is okay around here, mom. I promise. Do you need me to go to the grocery store and pick up the ingredients?" said Joseph. The less his mother knew about the pregnancy, the better. He knew she would judge her if she ever found out that Lovette had been unfaithful. He also didn't want her to find out exactly how they became a couple and this would come out as well.

"I'll go," his mother replied while giving him the side eye. He knew she didn't believe him and that this topic was going to be brought up again. Looking Lovette up and down, she continued. "Lovette, you're looking kind of pale. You feeling okay?"

Lovette immediately felt guilty. She was nowhere

*near ready to tell her anything about her pregnancy. Even
though no one could replace Trudy, Sarah had been the
closest thing as a mother to her and Lovette didn't want to
disappoint her.*

*"I'm okay. Just a little tired. Just gonna go take a
nap before Joey gets home," said Lovette. Taking the
basket of clothes from Sarah, Lovette took it back upstairs
to Joey's room. She wouldn't be adding to the water bill
today. Sarah waited for her to get all the way upstairs
before she began her whispers.*

*"You think she's really okay? She seems a bit off
today," said Sarah. "And, she's looking a bit heavier."*

*"She's okay. Just tired. She does so much around
here. I've been thinking that maybe I should book her spa
date. Something relaxing. You think it's a good idea?" said
Joseph.*

*"You know what would be an even better idea?
Booking that date for two. I can join her. Mother and
daughter date," said Sarah. She laughed but Joseph knew
she was serious. That's exactly what he would do.*

*Picking up her purse and heading for the grocery
store, Joseph watched his mother drive down the long
rocky path towards the main road. Standing still in the
screen door, he took the time to reflect on how he actually
felt about everything.*

*First and most important, Lovette was his to keep.
No matter what happened between them, he was willing to
work around it and fix it. He had worked hard to build and
keep the strong family bond that they had and no one would*

come between them. Even if this meant the babies weren't his.

The babies. The thought of one baby possibly not being his didn't hurt as much as knowing more than one child was coming into this world. Mike had a dark complexion and Lovette was part African American herself. This meant that there was a great chance that the babies could come out with a darker skin tone and well...people would know that the children weren't his.

Maybe he could convince her that now wasn't the right time to have another child. They had been focused working on their marriage and right now, that mattered most. She made it clear that she wanted the pregnancy but maybe something had changed in her. Maybe the thought of two babies had overwhelmed her. This was a possibility. He would bring it up.

No he wouldn't. This would make her hate him. She had already told him that she wanted the pregnancy and if he mentioned anything close to an abortion, she would look at him differently. This would only push her away and...he couldn't have that.

The next day, Joseph waited for Lovette to come out of the bathroom to approach her with his feelings. He had tossed and turned all night deciding what was best for the both of them. Stepping out of the bathroom with a towel around her hair and body, she had never looked more beautiful.

"I've decided that I don't need to hear your conversation with Mike. We've had trust in our marriage and if we want things to get better, I have to remain to trust *you. I've messed up and you have as well. Now, we can only move forward from there. We just have to figure things out as they go, I guess," said Joseph.*

Lovette was relieved to know that he trusted her to do the right thing. She had planned to be responsible with or without him around.

"Thank you for saying that," she replied.

"Also, I got you something," said Joseph. Holding up his hand and shaking the keys, Lovette's eyes widened. "Since there are more babies on the way, we need another car. I don't care if the babies aren't mine. We are going to figure this out because you're my wife and that's how it's going to stay."

Wrapping her arms around his neck and hugging him tightly, she sobbed. She wasn't sure if it were the hormones or feeling overwhelmed by everything but she couldn't hold back the tears. Lovette had her own time to think things over and it felt as if he had only ever done one thing wrong to her. And, that was the start of their relationship. He had been faithful, loving, supportive, and she still trusted him.

"Thank you!" she managed to push out in between sobs.

"Get dressed. It's in the driveway. You don't have to thank me," replied Joseph.

Rushing to get dressed, she almost raced him downstairs to see her new car. It was early in the morning, so she was clueless as to when he had time to even go get it. It didn't matter. She was just excited to have her very own first car.

A bright red Audi! She had mentioned to him a while back that she had wanted a red car. Since she knew little about cars, she didn't really care which kind but wanted it to be red. He had done a good job of listening and remembering. Another thing she loved about him.

Hugging him over and over, Joseph playfully broke away from her grasped and told her he needed to head over to his parent's house. He had to meet with his father before work.

Sarah would be picking Joey up from school today and he would be spending the weekend with them, so the day was open for whatever Lovette had wanted to do. She was excited to drive her new car around and to be seen in it. The places she would go!

Kissing him goodbye and running back up into their bedroom, Lovette fished for a better outfit to wear. Something to match her new car. Walking past her nightstand, she stopped in her tracks and picked up the house phone.

Tapping the first three buttons, Lovette dropped it back down into its resting place. She took a chance on calling the O'Conner's house the last time to tell Mike that they couldn't ever see one another again. She got lucky when Mike had picked up. If Mrs. O'Conner picked up, there would be too many questions asked and no turning back from there.

"Dial the number, Lovette," she whispered to

herself. Picking up the phone, the dial tone sounded as if it were a horn blaring. To silence it, she punched in the first three numbers. Taking a few seconds to dial the rest of the number, she punched in the last four digits and took a deep breath.

"Hello." It was Mr. O'Conner. Lovette let out the breath she had been holding in and spoke.

"Hey. Mr. O'Conner, it's. Lovette. I didn't call to stir anything up but I really need Mike to give me a call. It's pretty urgent," she said. The silence on the other end of the phone had made her want to hang up.

"You can just give him my number," said Lovette. She read her number out loud and hung up the phone. The feeling of stupidity washed over her. Mike deserved to know the situation that was at hand because it affected his life in a major way if he had fathered her children.

Lovette had been sitting on the edge of her bed for some time and was stuck in her thoughts. All of the possibilities of what outcome could come about bothered her. The phone began to ring and had shaken her from all of her "what if" scenarios.

"Hello," said Lovette. Silence. There was breathing but no background noises were heard. It had to have been Mr. O'Conner calling her back.

"Look, I'm sorry for calling you like that but I just needed to talk to Mike. This is really important. I don't want anything from him. He just needs to know something," said Lovette.

"This is Mike. I just need to know what?" he said.

It felt as if a million butterflies had submerged into her stomach. Or was that the babies? Stay focused, Lovette.

"Hey. Are you free to talk right now? This might take a second," said Lovette. Her chest had felt heavy. Why was it still possible for him to activate so many different feelings in her? No. "Stick to what you're calling him for and that's it," the voice echoed in her head.

"What? You're pregnant?" asked Mike while laughing.

"Actually, I am. And, I'm carrying twins anddd they might be yours. Still funny?" shot back Lovette. He had hurt her deeply by laughing. She knew it wasn't to make a mock of her but at the same time, it felt insensitive.

"Wait. What?!" whispered Mike. He was only joking and had never expected Lovette to call him about being pregnant...with his child...two children?! Grabbing the side of his couch, he sat down and the words rung in his ears.

"Not so funny anymore, huh? The doctor dated everything back to around our anniversary. My anniversary. That night...I slept with you...and Joe," said Lovette shamefully.

"Why would you do that?! It was already bad enough we slept together but you went home and did the same thing to your husband?! Why? What sense does that make?! After finding out what he did to you?" shouted Mike. He was filled with rage. This time it had been at her.

"I don't know! He had wanted to work things out so bad and I guess if I turned down his gesture, I felt as if he would know something was up! It just happened! I didn't call you for a fucking screaming match," cried Lovette.

Mike had been soft with her the last time they saw one another. He had showered her with affection and made her feel like he had when they were teenagers. She had missed the feeling. Hearing from him made her feel as if that same Mike would return but it hadn't.

"Why are you like this?! Why are you so irresponsible?" questioned Mike.

"Irresponsible?! I didn't have sex with myself! I didn't force you to do anything! Last time I checked, we BOTH wanted it! How dare you call ME irresponsible?! What gives you the fucking right?!" screamed back Lovette in between tears.

"Let's just slow this down for a second. Look," said Mike. He had calmed his tone down and felt bad for the things he had said to her. "I'm sorry. I just freaked out for a few seconds. This is a lot to take in. Please, Love. I swear, I'm sorry."

Love. No. This wouldn't sway her this time. It was her weakness but not at this moment. She wouldn't let up so easy.

"You're freaked out?! Try thinking about how I feel?! I'm the one carrying not one but two children and don't know who THEY belong to! I didn't ask for this but guess what? It's happening Mike! You don't ever get to judge me, either! You were there. You were part of this!"

she continued to shout.

"I know, I know. Just calm down for a second. Have you told Joseph?"

"Of course, I told him. He isn't jumping for joy about it either but we're trying our best to work things out," said Lovette.

"So, you're keeping the babies? And, don't get mad. I just need to be caught up to speed. How long have you known you were pregnant before telling me?" asked Mike.

"Not that long. And, yes. I'm keeping them. I'll just have to deal with whatever when we find out who the father is. Joseph has already come to terms and no matter what, he wants to stay married and work things out."

"Are you sure it's only between me and him that could be the possible father?" questioned Mike. He had spit out the question before he thought of how she would react.

"Are you kidding me right now?! You know what...GO TO HELL!" screamed Lovette. Slamming down the phone into its cradle, she wept. Mike had really had the nerve. She wasn't a slut! Mike and Joseph had been the only two men she had ever slept with! How dare he?!

The phone instantly started ringing again. It was him. Lovette had been too distraught to pick up the phone and just wanted everything to disappear. For a second, she felt as if life would've been better had she never found out that Joseph had been sneaky and sabotaged things.

Everyone would still be happy and she would've never cheated on him. If she still would be pregnant right now, she would know her babies belonged to Joseph for sure. The phone continued to ring back to back and she knew he wouldn't stop until she picked up.

"WHAT?!" she screamed after picking up the phone. The constant arguing back and forth had started to make her nauseous. Joseph was the man she was married to and not even HE upset her like Mike had.

The whole conversation had gone opposite of how she had hoped for. She started to think that maybe she shouldn't have called at all. Joseph was going to be there and they could've raised their family together without telling Mike....

"Look, don't hang up! I just wanted to make sure. That's all. Love, we need to talk in person. This phone thing isn't doing it for me. I'm going to book a flight tomorrow. We'll talk when I get there because I've obviously messed this up. Okay?" said Mike. He waited a couple of minutes for a response and when he was only left with her tears, he hung up the phone.

Lovette couldn't speak. She had been too consumed with crying and just wanted everything to go away. This would've been the perfect time for her to wake up from a nightmare. Everyone was going to think she was a whore and this is something she hadn't been. She had been unfaithful one time and this decision was going to cost her.

But, she still couldn't abort her babies. They were a part of her and would always be.

Chapter 22: Push

April 13, 2002

"He actually has my baby out there digging in the dirt," said Joseph. Mary had been spending more time with Eric the last couple of days and while they were grateful she had been socializing more, Joseph hadn't been ready for Mary to find a bigger interest in boys.

Eric was a good kid and he appreciated him making friends with his daughter...but he knew they were more than friends. Joseph didn't know what to feel about his daughter growing up so fast. Lovette walked up behind him, peaked out of the kitchen window and laughed.

"She's almost 13. It was bound to happen. Pre-teens and teenagers do the things boys like to do in order to impress them. I've done it," she said. She had instantly regretted saying it. Joseph knew that his wife had been referring to Mike.

"Sorry," whispered Lovette.

"It's okay," said Joseph. And, it had been. "I think we should go visit Joey at school next week. Surprise visit," he continued.

"That's a good idea. I miss my baby. He acts like he doesn't want to come home sometimes," said Lovette. "He hardly ever calls and when he does, it's only for a few minutes. He better be going to class for all the money we've dished out."

"That's because you keep using words like him being your baby," joked Joseph. Joey had gone to college a few hours outside of Shawford in a town called Hempshire. It was still located in Alabama and for that, Lovette was grateful. He was still able to have his distance but not too much.

"He is my baby," whined Lovette playfully. "So is Mary. Everything is just moving too fast."

****

December 9, 1988

"How did Monica take it?" asked Lovette. She was sitting across from Mike at her kitchen island. He was here. In her house. And, they had been alone. Ridding herself of the thought, she guided back to why he was here and only that.

Lovette and Joseph had talked about Mike's visit. The plan was for them to talk in a public setting but at the last minute, Lovette asked him to come to their house. She didn't want to be seen in public with Mike and start up the rumors.

But, Lovette failed to tell Joseph that he would be coming to the house. He was at work and she felt as if she could say what needed to be said and he would leave. She would tell him later and if he got upset, she would deal with it then.

"She didn't..." said Mike.

"And I'm the irresponsible one?" laughed Lovette. She rubbed her stomach for a brief second. It felt as if she

were already showing. She couldn't wait for the pregnancy to be over with so that they could know what to do next.

"I just don't know how to tell her yet. She thinks I'm on a business trip. Another lie I have to confess. I didn't think it would get to this point," said Mike.

"What do you plan on doing? Just waiting until the babies are here and we get them tested? What if they are yours? Just gonna go home and be like, 'Surprise. Here are two babies that I made when I cheated on you with Lovette?'" she replied.

The sadness spread across his face. He had messed up and now, it had caught up to him. The saddest part was Monica had gotten pregnant their senior year in college and lost the baby early in the pregnancy. She had taken it extremely hard. Knowing that Lovette was possibly pregnant by him would tear her apart.

But, deep down, he had a burning desire for the children to be his. He cared for Monica...but he had still loved Lovette. It was wrong of him to cheat but he couldn't help but thinking that everything had been happening for a reason. Lovette was supposed to be his and he knew these babies would belong to him.

"I don't know yet. I'm still trying to sort through everything. Life is just happening so fast. We're still young and all of this is happening. On top of all of this, Brandon and I decided to sell Con-Weigh's. Things have been rough lately and it was just the best thing to do. It wasn't up that long, so I guess it was best to quit now before we got way into debt. Another thing I have to tell her," said Mike.

"Sorry to hear. What do you plan to do now?" said Lovette.

"Probably go back to college. Get my master's degree. I'll be looking for a job soon, too. Monica is going to take it pretty bad. The girl is high maintenance," said Mike. He laughed a little but Lovette knew better. She knew this had hurt him deeply and that he was trying his best to find something to keep her happy.

"That sounds like a good plan," said Lovette. "Can I ask you a question?"

Mike's heart started pounding. He knew it would be a question that he didn't want to answer. Nodding his head, he stared her in the eyes.

"Do you love her? Like, really love her?" asked Lovette. She had been wanting to ask him this question ever since they had slept together but she hadn't been ready to hear his response.

"Not like I love you," said Mike without even as much as a blink. The way his life had been going at the moment, he didn't care what came about from saying this to her. He already figured Monica would leave him and at this very moment, it hadn't been his most important care.

Lovette's knees began to feel as if they were made of jelly. Leaning up against the countertop, her palms were sweaty and slid off of the sides. Almost losing her balance, she stared back at him.

"She's smart, caring and loves me. I feel like I owe her something. But, I also feel for you. You...us...we were *different. We are different," said Mike.*

She had wanted him. At this exact moment. In her kitchen. Right on the island. He was supposed to have been with her. He was supposed to be in Joseph's position as her husband. Joseph. Bringing herself back to reality, she had regretted asking the question.

"Mike, I think you need to leave. This has gone too far and we weren't supposed to meet here anyway. I can't do this right now," said Lovette.

"You also can't tell me you don't feel anything for me, huh? Joseph isn't me. Monica isn't you. But, whatever. I'll leave. Let me know when you're in labor," said Mike. He had been pissed off by her response.

Snatching his jacket from the back of the chair, he stormed out of the kitchen. The sound of the screen door slamming had made Lovette jump. Fighting the urge to stand still, she unglued herself from her kitchen floor and ran after him.

"Mike! Wait!"

"Wait for WHAT?! I'm fighting against everything in me that wants to tell you everything about how I feel and you asked me to leave. You were right. I'm going about all of this wrong. I have to figure out things for myself and you should do the same because you're obviously just as confused as me."

"I'll be sending you money and checking on you and the babies but I won't be back here until it's time for you to deliver. You aren't mine to have and I can't be alone *with you." Getting into his car, Mike slammed the door and drove off.*

Lovette was stuck watching him drive away the same way she had the last time he left her house when they were teenagers. She wanted Mike...and she had wanted her family with Joseph. She wanted everything to be okay but she knew that one or both people would eventually be hurt.

****

"Have you ever, um, kissed someone before?" asked Eric. He had been wanting to ask Mary this for a few days now but hadn't worked up the nerve to say it. Taking his gloves off and sitting them on the ground, he stared at the side of her head waiting for a response.

"Tell him you have," whispered Joyce. Shrugging off her sister's voice, Mary answered with honesty. She had lied to him before and ended up almost looking stupid, so she had refused to put herself in that position again.

"Well, no. Have you ever kissed a girl before?" she asked. The whole conversation had started to make her nervous. She couldn't tell if it were a good nervous or a bad one.

"Yea, a few times. So, you must be a virgin too, huh?" asked Eric. "Sorry, I shouldn't have said that. Ignore it. It was stupid."

"A virgin is someone who hasn't had sex yet," said Joyce.

"How do you even know?!" replied Mary.

"Huh? I don't. I shouldn't have asked that. My bad. Want to go get something to drink?" asked Eric. Mary had her weird moments but he really did like her. A few girls from school had told Eric things about Mary talking to her deceased sister but he didn't mind. She was nice and didn't act like the other girls. The other girls put lip gloss on all day, bragged about who had the nicest clothes and only wanted to talk about themselves.

"Sure." Getting up from the ground, both of them brushed off their pants. Before heading into his back door, Mary caught a glimpse of her parents staring at her through the kitchen window. Rolling her eyes and throwing up her hands, she followed Eric into the house.

"She's going into his house," said Joseph. Bill had been home but he decided he would head on over to make sure he was awake and monitoring their every move. "I'll be right back."

"No, you won't! Leave them alone. Trust her a little. They are probably just going inside to wash up or something. See, look. They went inside to grab drinks and are coming back out. Don't you feel foolish?" laughed Lovette.

****

June 11, 1989

   Lovette had Iris call Mike's house posing as a potential business partner. She knew Monica loved money and would deliver the message to Mike. When she called, Monica had told Iris that he wasn't home and she was expecting him home shortly. When Mike called back, she delivered the news about Lovette being in labor.

Everything had been rearranged in the living room for her comfort. In the middle of the floor, Lovette was in a pool of water with only a bra on. Joseph was sitting on one side of the pool beside Lovette and Iris was sitting on the opposite side. There had been a lady standing over Lovette with light blue scrubs on. Another woman in the same outfit came from the kitchen area and placed a washcloth on Lovette's forehead.

Joseph had finally told his parents about the situation with the babies and Sarah had been distraught. Joseph had called her one last time and she still had refused to attend the birth of the children. Calling him all types of foolish and naïve, she had refused to be a part of the birth. The only thing she had agreed to do was keep Joey for a few days because "he was actually her grandson".

"I'm going to check your cervix now," said one of the birth coaches. "Feels like you're right at 5."

"You sure? Because it feels like I'm about to shit out these humans any minute now," whined Lovette. Contractions. She had felt them what seemed to be all over her body; especially, in her back. Joseph reached in the water and rubbed her stomach.

"Want me to get in there and yank those things out? It'll cut this middleman business out" said Iris. Lovette chuckled a little and returned back to her low and deep groaning.

"Breathe, babe. Breathe. You're doing so good,"

said Joseph.

Lovette couldn't take her mind off of Mike. She had felt weird the night before and thought it was just the usual throw down between the babies. Seemed like they fought one another every night before she could fall asleep. Had she had Iris call last night, he probably would be here by now.

"What time is it?" she asked.

"Almost 4' o clock," said Iris. "Why? I hope you didn't make any plans." Iris and her jokes. Even in the middle of Lovette holding it together trying to prevent herself from having a mental break down, Iris always had jokes.

"Shut up," replied Lovette. Focusing back in on her thoughts, Mike better had been on the way. Iris had talked to him this morning and he told her that he was booking the next flight out that was departing at 1 o' clock. He should be there within the next hour or two but Lovette had the greatest feeling that he wouldn't make it in time.

"Can someone check me again?!" she said just a level about a whisper. The pressure in her bottom had her easing lower in the water.

"Whoa, mama. Somebody jumped up to 7 centimeters. You're moving fast," said one of the coaches. Removing the plastic gloves, she tossed them into a nearby trash.

Lovette tried her best to hide her disappointment. She wasn't even sure if the babies had belonged to Mike or *not but she couldn't help feeling like he needed to be there. Hearing the screen door shut, Lovette sighed in relief that he had finally made it.*

"Hey, everyone! I came as soon as I could! I'm sorry that I'm late. Catch me up to speed." Lovette instantly began to cry. It was Caron. She loved her friend and totally forgot that she had called her but she had hoped it was Mike walking through the living room.

The disappointment of her voice followed by Lovette's tears, was also followed by a strong contractions.

"Ahhhhhhhh...oooohhhhh," she moaned.

Joseph was staring at Lovette concerned. He had been dealing with her labor this time better than he had the first time. Saying little reassurances here and there, Joseph didn't say much of anything else. He had actually been somewhat glad her labor was moving along kind of fast and that...Mike hadn't made it yet. He didn't want to see him and he didn't want him in their house. But, he agreed because it had been what Lovette wanted.

They hadn't talked about boy names because Lovette had been set on the babies being girls. She told Joseph that she had felt they were going to be girls. They were naming them Joyce and Mary. The oldest being Mary.

"I don't think I can hold on anymore. I feel like I have to push now!" shouted Lovette. Both birth coaches were by her side and was soon as one slipped her hand under the water, her eyes widened.

"I feel the head. It's time. Do what we taught you.

Push as hard as you can when you feel that contraction," she said.

"AHHHHHH!" she screamed. Most was due to pain and some had been due to Mike missing this moment. He was supposed to be here.

"Come on, push!" chanted both of the birth coaches.

After 20 minutes of pushing, one of the ladies pulled the first baby from the water. The area between Lovette's legs gushed with red liquid and she tossed her head back in relief.

"It's a girl!" one of them squealed. "Dad? You want to cut the cord?" Reaching for the scissors, Joseph made the snip and she handed the baby off to the other life coach. The very first cry had been heard. Another relief.

As quick as she had just saw her baby, she started screaming again. Baby number two was coming. A couple of minutes later, the baby was out and Joey had cut the cord again.

"It's another girl!" she squealed. Both nurses rushed to tend to both babies and before anyone could get anything settled, Lovette began screaming right along with the baby she had just pushed out. Caron dropped down by her side to see what was happening.

"Is she pushing out the placenta already?!" she asked.

"AHHHHHH!" screamed Lovette. Handing the babies off to Iris and Joseph, both of the ladies rushed to be

*by her side to see what was happening. Something was
wrong.*

*"The placenta shouldn't be coming out just yet.
Something isn't right," said one of the coaches. Placing
her hand in the water to feel under Lovette, her eyes looked
as if they were about to fall out of her face.*

*"It's another baby!" she shouted. Pointing to
Caron, "You! Go get more towels and supplies! Come on,
Lovette. Push!"*

*Everyone had been stuck in their spots with their
mouths hung open. Twins. They had been expecting twins
and now, there was another one coming.*

"NOW!" she shouted at Caron.

*Caron rushed around the house to gather more
supplies while Iris and Joseph had been stuck with their
mouths wide open watching their sister and wife deliver
another baby. They had been told how dangerous it was to
deliver twins at home but now, Lovette was about to push
out a third. A couple more pushes and screams, the birth
coach lifted the baby out of the water.*

"It's...a...boy!"

*Lovette had been exhausted. She knew that she
heard someone say that another baby was coming and she
knew that she had just pushed something out but she was
out of it. How did the doctor miss this?! They constantly
told her that she was carrying bigger than normal but from
her understanding, this had also happened the more
pregnancies a woman had.*

Everything seemed as if it went into fast forward mode and before Lovette realized, she had been holding two babies in her arms and one on her lap. All four of them were now fully dressed in the middle of her king size bed.

Mary-Anne Marks had come first. The leader of the pack. She was pressed up against Lovette's left breast and was sound asleep. Joyce Marks and been the exact same way in Lovette's right arm. Both girls had a head full of jet black hair.

And him. He was on her lap with his face toward the ceiling. His already tanned skin had started progressing while his sisters remained pale. Light brown skin...with red hair and freckles. He was her twin.

A light knock on the door and push; it was Joseph.

"I know you wanted a moment with the babies but Dr. Oar is here and we need to um...get started," said Joseph. It had been hard for him to bring it up but the sooner it had been done, the sooner they would know.

Lovette was stuck staring at her baby boy who had yet to be named. Mike still hadn't made it. She hadn't even heard from him and it was now almost 10 o'clock at night.

"I'll leave you and him to that. I want to sit on the porch for a while, anyway," said Lovette nonchalantly. Not waiting for his response, she put the babies on their backs in the middle of the bed and left the bedroom.

Going into the downstairs guest bedroom, Iris had been snoring as if she were the one who just pushed out three babies. Putting the blanket over here, Lovette sat beside her and picked up the phone. She was calling Mike and didn't care if Monica answered.

"We're sorry. The phone number you have reached has been disconnected or is no longer in service." Hanging up the phone and redialing the number, Lovette figured she must've hit a wrong digit.

"We're sorry. The phone number you have reached has been disconnected or is no longer in service," the robotic voice repeated. Disconnected?! Slamming the phone down, Iris jumped up, rolled out of the bed and fell to the floor.

"What in the hell?! What is going on?" questioned Iris while rubbing her forehead. Lovette had been sitting on the edge of the bed and her whole body had been shaking. "What's wrong?"

"The bastard didn't show up and now his phone is off! Why? Just...Why would he do this? I mean, I know there was a chance that the babies weren't his but he knew that and promised to be here," cried Lovette.

She had been hurt. The disappointment of Mike not showing up and now, his phone being disconnected had been the icing on the cake.

"Maybe something happened. Just calm down. You know Mike isn't even that type of person. Relax. You look crazy. Are the babies upstairs with Joe?" asked Iris. Lovette nodded her head and wiped her cheeks.

"Let's go outside and get some air. Everything is going to be okay. Just chill."

Chapter 23: Mary

April 14, 2002

"You need to go. You've wasted enough time. Just go," said Joyce. She had started getting so pushy and had been so annoying. "You spend so much time with him and haven't even been to the shed yet! Just go already. Shoot! You can even take him with you."

"You're the one who was so excited about me hanging out with him and now you want to complain. Make up your mind. You're the crazy one. Not me." The more she talked, the more I became angry.

"Are you going to go tonight? Mama and papa are already sleep. They won't even hear you leave out," said Joyce.

"It's dark as crap out there and you want me to go through the woods?! Have you lost your mind?! Yea, you're definitely the crazy one," I said.

I had been hanging out with Eric all day at his house. He showed me pictures of people in his family, we rode our bikes, messed around the garden and talked on the bench. It was the best day ever and he actually liked me. He finally told me.

"Take papa's big flashlight and you'll be able to see good enough. Mary, we need to do this. He told me to tell you. I'm tired. We have to do this," said Joyce. She had always talked about this "He" man and things just didn't make sense.

"If I go, will you shut up about it from now on? I'm sick of hearing about this raggedy ol' shed Joey used to hide out to drink beer and smoke cigarettes in. After I do this, you better not mention it again. Deal?"

"Deal! We have one problem. He told me that the keys are with papa in the nightstand," said Joyce.

"What keys?! The shed barely has a door. You know we don't need keys to get in there." Getting out of the bed and changing my clothes, I had refused to go alone. Eric would definitely be down to come along.

"Just do it. You have to be quiet," she said.

As soon as I had been standing in front of their bedroom door, I wanted to turn back around. Joyce had always listened to me. Not the other way around. Now, here I was about to go to some stupid shed because she said so. Not only was she "tired", but I was, too. Tired of hearing her complain. Tired of hearing her voice. I'm going back in my room.

"Did you get the keys?" asked Joyce with a huge smile on her face.

"No. I'm not going. I want you to stop." Looking her in the eyes, I meant it. I wanted all of this to stop. "I want you to go away."

"We need to do this. This has…"

"No, no, no…you aren't listening. I need you to go away. I'm sick of feeling like a freak. I'm sick of people looking at me weird when you're around. And, I'm sick of you just popping up when you feel like it! They're right about you. You are dead, huh?"

I had hurt her feelings. I knew this look and I knew this awkward quietness between us. Her feelings were crushed.

"JUST DO THIS SO WE CAN BE DONE! You won't see me again! I promise! I don't even want to be around you anymore! I wish I had never told you to go out with Eric because you've changed!" cried Joyce.

Between therapy, our parents, and school, I was tired of this. No one could see her but me and this needed to end. Eric was nice enough to put up with a few of my outburst but how much longer would he continue to deal with it before he thought I was a creep like everyone else had thought?

Leaving Joyce crying in the room, I had been sad that I had said those things to her. I would apologize later but now, I needed to get the keys and go wake Eric up.

Twisting the doorknob as quiet as I could, mama and papa were laying on their sides facing the window. Papa was snoring loud, as usual, and mama didn't make a peep.

The nightstand. Tip toeing over towards it, the floor was squeaky. But, neither one of them moved yet. I needed to hurry. Opening the first drawer, it wasn't there. Nothing had been there but a few papers.

Opening the second drawer, nothing was there but a Bible. She said the key was in here and it wasn't! Picking up the Bible to see if the key was under it, the book fell and hit the floor.

Papa instantly flipped over on his side and was staring me in the face. Neither one of us moved. I was waiting on him to fuss at me for being in his things but he never did. He closed his eyes as if he didn't see me there, laid back down and went back to snoring.

Picking up the Bible, of this was silly! I was done. No more searching for a key that wasn't here.

"Mark 15:37," whispered Joyce. She snuck up on me so fast, I almost threw the book at her.

"What?" I whispered.

"Go to the page. You know how to find it," she whispered.

Turning to the page, there it was. A small gold key. She had been right all along. But, that still didn't mean anything. People hide things all the time. I hide things, too.

Placing the Bible back in the nightstand, I backed out of the room. Both of them were sound asleep and I just wanted to get all of this over with so Joyce could be happy.

"Go. Hurry up before they wake up," whispered Joyce.

Putting on my slippers and hoodie, I was going to get Eric. I wasn't doing this alone. Papa's flashlight was right beside the front door. Grabbing it and letting myself out, I picked up some rocks in the driveway and headed next door. He opened his window right after the first rock hit it.

"What are you doing, Mary? It's almost midnight," whispered Eric. "Also, why didn't you just tap on the window? You do realize that we don't have steps, right?"

Oh, yea. But, I had saw this in movies and wanted to try it out for myself. So much for looking cool.

"Sorry but I need you to come with me somewhere. I don't want to go alone. Is your uncle sleep? Whispering was starting to get on my nerves. "Put some clothes on and let's go."

He turned around and closed the window. Really? This jerk really was about to ignore me. Turning around to leave, I'd just have to go by myself. He had another thing coming if he thought I was going to hang out with him anytime soon. I'd be slamming the front door in his face just like he closed the window in mine.

The darkness. I didn't mind it in the house but the dark outside was different. The noises the bugs and animals made at night had always made me feel weird.

"PSSSS! Mary! Wait up!" Eric. He was jogging towards me. "You didn't even give me time to get dressed before you left."

"Well, maybe next time you should say something instead of closing the window like you weren't coming," I said while rolling my eyes.

"You're right. My bad. Where are we going? And, why didn't we go when it was daytime?" he said.

"We just need to check something out. It's an old shed. We won't be long," I said. Holding the light up to his face, he instantly turned away.

"Well, I'd like to not go blind before I can see what was so important to come out this late," he said while rubbing his eyes. I grabbed his hand and pulled him towards the woods.

The talk on the way made the trip go by faster. Eric told me what his mother looked like from the pictures he had saw of her. He said he looked just like her. This had been the second time he had talked about his mother. Mama was right. He would trust me and talk about things on his own time. Before I knew it, there it was. The shed.

"This is what we came to see? As if Shawford doesn't have tons of raggedy sheds that are about to fall over any second. What's going on?" said Eric.

If I told him, he would think I was crazy. I couldn't bring up Joyce without him feeling like everyone else. He knew that no one else could see her but me and he still liked me. If I told him that she told me to come to the shed, it would for sure freak him out.

"I just need to see something. I didn't want to walk out here alone." It had looked even older than it did the time me and Joyce had come. I couldn't believe it was still standing. Eric was right behind me as we walked up to the porch. I could feel how nervous he was.

The steps had been so messed up that we had to stretch our legs to the very top of the steps in order to get on the porch. Almost losing my balance, Eric caught me and pushed me up on to the porch. He stepped up and I helped pull him up the rest of the way.

Walking inside for the very first time, it smelled worse than it looked. Only this time, someone had come and removed what small stuff was inside. Except...the rug. It was still the same old dusty brown rug. Pulling it back and tossing it to the side, the door.

"Mary, what's going on? You're starting to freak me out," said Eric.

I knew it was coming. I knew he was going to turn into everyone else and think that I was crazy.

"Look, we just need to see what's in here and that's it," I said. Putting the key into the lock, I twisted it and it popped open.

"You have a key?! Where did you get that from?" he asked. Crouched down on the floor, I turned around and looked him in the face. I was tired of lying. I'd tell him the truth and if he wanted to leave, he could.

"Something is going on in here and I have to know what it is. I know this is weird, so if you want to stand outside while I do this, you can. I don't actually know what's in here but that's why we're here. Joyce sent me," I said.

"Why'd you tell him that?! Now, he's going to think what everyone else thinks!" shouted Joyce. She had been standing in the corner and was staring down at me. Perfect timing for her to show up. Ignoring her as if she wasn't there, she continued. "I know you hear me talking to you. I know you saw me. You can't pretend like I'm not here!"

Yes, I can. And, yes I will. She was beyond annoying and I just wanted to get this over with.

Eric had a confused look on his face but he still crouched down beside me and we lifted up the door. Pushing it back, the loud thud against the wood felt as if it were about to make the whole house fall over. Shining the light down into the hole, it was complete darkness.

"You sure you want to go down there? It's dark as hell down there. What are we looking for?" asked Eric.

"I don't know. I guess we will know when we find it. Do I need to go first or do you want to?" I said.

Looking at me as if he were insulted, he took the flashlight and walked down the steps first. Following behind him, the steps felt smoother than the ones outside. They didn't creak like the rest of the shed had. Looking down, the steps were concrete.

It felt like we were going down forever. When Eric shined the light on the wall, it had been just two sides covered in concrete, too. Reaching the bottom of the stairs, it had been another door. Eric shined the light all around us and the small space was completely covered in concrete. From the wall to the floor...concrete. Except for...the door.

"I'm guessing we have to go through this door, too, huh?" I could tell he had wanted to go home and was tired of being here. Nodding my head and reaching for the door handle, the flashlight shut off. And, of course, I didn't think to bring batteries.

"You have got to be kidding me!" said Eric while

hitting the side of the flashlight. Nothing. We had been in complete darkness and was about to go into another door with no way of knowing what was on the other side of it.

"We have to keep going. I promise, once we find out what we need to know, I won't ever ask you to do anything this crazy again," I said. I couldn't see his face but he was close enough that I could feel his breath.

"You didn't drag me out of bed for nothing. Let's see what's down here," said Eric. Feeling for the handle, I placed my hand on top of it and pulled slowly. Peeping through the slit, the bright light came through. Eric pulled the door up the rest of the way and there were a short set of steps with a door at the end. At least there was light this time. Hopefully, this would be the last door because I had been tired of the door game.

Pushing the door open, it looked as if it were a living room. There were two couches; each one across from another. There was a painting of horses above one of the couches. And, there was a rocking chair. It had been moving.

"Someone is here," whispered Eric. He had noticed the same thing I had. "I think we should leave, Mary."

Going further into the living room, there is another door. Slowly pushing it open, I gasp.

Chapter 24: Matthias

June 17, 1989

It had been six days since the babies were born and Lovette had been exhausted. They refused to sleep all at once and she felt as if she couldn't keep up with breastfeeding each of them. Her nipples were sore and her breasts were a whole size bigger than before. Getting up from her bed and heading to the nursery, she was sure that he would be hungry.

Matthias. He had been nameless for hours until Lovette saw his face the morning after their birth. The only thing she could think about was how he looked like his named should be Matthias. He was light brown...and his sisters weren't. She was sure the babies had belonged to Mike.

Mike. She still hadn't heard from him. Each day that passed, the more she felt as if she would never hear from him. Lovette didn't know if this was a good or bad thing. She had wanted her marriage to work and still loved her husband but she still couldn't help but to feel as if the babies should belong to Mike. Confusion had never been at an all-time high.

Iris had still been helping out around the house and had been doing a great job with the babies. Lovette dreaded the day that she had to return back to school. Walking past the nursery, she decided to go thank her. Matthias hadn't made a peep yet from his nap and Joey had just gotten back from being with Joseph's parents.

Lovette peeped into the living room to see Iris

holding one baby, another laying in the bassinet and Joey was sitting beside her reading. She had wished she had a camera to capture the moment but she knew that she would never forget this. Joey caught Lovette spying and ran around the corner to hug her.

"Where is Matthias?" he asked her. Iris looked up at Lovette, smiled and continued to rock her niece to sleep.

"I'm about to go get him from his nap, feed him and bring him down to the best big brother ever so that you can read to him. Sound like a plan?" asked Lovette. The biggest smiled spread across Joey's face. He nodded and ran back to sit down next to Iris.

Lovette turned around to a rush of wind from Joey running past her. He had Matthias in his hands.

"What's going on? What are you doing?" questioned Lovette while running after Joseph.

"He's not breathing! I went to check on him and he's not breathing! Go back in the house! I'm taking him to the hospital!" shouted Joseph.

"WHAT DO YOU MEAN HE'S NOT BREATHING?! WHAT HAPPENED? I'm going with you!" shouted Lovette.

She watched Joseph get into the driver seat and placed Matthias in the passenger seat. His body was wrapped up and he hadn't been moving.

Running around to the passenger seat, Lovette pulled on the car handle. It was locked. Rage had fully taken over her body. Running back to Joseph's side of the *car, she banged on the window.*

*"Open the damn car door! I'M GOING WITH MY
FUCKING CHILD!" screamed Lovette. Rolling down the
window in a hurry, Joseph spoke while putting the car in
drive.*

*"NO! I'll call you. You just had 3 babies and don't
need to see any of this! Everything will be fine. He will be
okay! Let me go get him some help, Lovette. He started
breathing a little when I put him in the car. Go back in the
house," he demanded. Pressing on the gas, Joseph sped off.*

*He had left her. He had taken their child and
refused to let her be there during a time when Matthias had
needed her most. Yea, he was only a few days old but she
should be with him.*

*But, then again, Joseph was right. She didn't need
to be distraught in a hospital while she had 3 other
children at home. Her mind had been racing and she
couldn't make it stop. Looking at her car sitting next to the
house, she changed her mind and ran in the house to go be
with her baby. Matthias needed her.*

*As soon as she stepped inside, one of the girls were
crying. Looking down at her chest, her breasts were soaked
with milk. She was hungry and Lovette knew that the other
would be hungry right after. Crying as if she felt like she
had no control over her life at the moment, she joined
Lovette in the family room.*

*"What's going on? Why did he run out like that?
And, what was all of the screaming about?" questioned
Iris.*

"Matthias isn't feeling well, so Joe took him to get checked out. Everything is going to be okay," said Lovette while wiping a tear from her face. She looked over to Joey who had immediately gotten sad. He had been looking forward to reading to his baby brother.

"Hey. Don't be sad. Your daddy is gonna go get Matthias checked out and he's going to be all better when they get back. Then, you can read him as many books as you want. Okay?" said Lovette. Iris handed over Mary so Lovette could nurse. As soon as she latched on, Mary had been content.

"Do you want me to drive to the hospital to sit with him?" asked Iris.

"Would it be selfish of me to ask you to stay? I'm scared shitless and I just can't be alone right now. I really need you here to help me keep my head on straight," cried Lovette. Iris wiped her face and nodded.

"You sit back and feed Mary. Me and Joey are gonna go start cooking dinner. Relax. Baby Matthias is going to be just fine. You know Joseph wouldn't let anything happen to him. I'm sure he's going to call soon and tell you everything is okay," said Iris.

Playfully punching Joey on the shoulder, Iris continued. "Come on, bud. We're making pizza tonight. I'll race you to the kitchen." Joey's eyes lit up and he took off running out of the living room.

Looking down at Mary, she and Joyce had both been identical and looked just like Lovette. They didn't have her freckles or red hair but both looked just like her.

Bringing her hand up and putting it on her eyelids, Mary had started to get full but had been too greedy to unlatch. She began to fall asleep and eventually let go. The milk had been sliding down her chin and slid onto her bib. Picking her up and pulling her towards her shoulder, Lovette patted her back until she had released a burp.

Putting her down to rest, Lovette sat back down on the couch and stared at both bassinets in front of her. She had been expecting two children. She knew she would be giving birth to two girls but then, a bonus baby came. Matthias was just as cute as his sisters but had Lovette's red hair and freckles. She had fallen in love with her bonus baby and now, she didn't know if he was okay or not.

Interrupting her thoughts, there had been a knock at the door. For a second, she thought about asking Iris to get it but she had been in the kitchen with Joey. He was happy to be making pizza with his aunt and Lovette didn't want to interrupt that. Finding the strength to get up from the couch, she headed to the front door. Opening the door, she was face to face with Mike.

"I know you're probably mad at me but let me explain. Please," he pleaded. Lovette was refilled with rage. He hadn't showed up when he said he would or even bothered to pick up the phone and now, he had the nerve to be on her porch looking sad.

"You said you were coming. Iris called you and you said you would be here. You knew the possibility of the babies being yours and you told me you would be here. But, no. You backed out at the last minute. And, it's funny how I couldn't even get in contact with you. Go to hell, Mike,"

said Lovette. She had been talking just above a whisper because she didn't want Iris to hear her.

"I swear, I didn't back out. Monica felt like something was off and contacted the phone company. She had them tell her what the number was from the mysterious business offer that called for me and she traced it back to you. She changed the number," started Mike.

Stepping outside and closing the door behind her, Lovette had had enough of his excuses. "I don't care! You should've been told your girlfriend about all of this!" shouted Lovette.

"Wife," said Mike. He dropped his head and refused to make eye contact with her.

"Excuse me?" said Lovette. With everything going on around her, she just knew that she was hearing things. Wife?

"She's my wife now," said Mike. "When I finally confessed everything, she broke down. She left for a few hours and when she came back, she told me that if I wanted to keep her, I would marry her. I know all of this is crazy right now but I swear I wanted to be here."

"So, let me get this right. Instead of attending the birth of babies you might be the father of, you go and get married? The day I give birth? And, now what? What if you are the father? You think I'm going to let that bitch play step-mother my children?!" said Lovette. She had decreased her tone but increased in anger.

Mike had wanted to say, "You slept with two men in

the same night and have the nerve to call me stupid. That was a stupid thing you did." But, instead, he let it flow through his thoughts and decided that it was best he kept it to himself.

"You know what? It was stupid. Very stupid of me. I care about her and I panicked. She's always been good to me and I felt as if I owe her something. I wanted to call but she has literally been by my side 24/7. She took off from work and has been home all week. Today was the first time she let me out of her sight and I left. I'll deal with the consequences when I get back but I should've been here. I knew you wouldn't hear me out over the phone and...you deserved better than that. So, I'm here," said Mike.

Although she had been angry with him, she couldn't resist the feeling of being glad that he showed up. But, the fact remained that he had gotten married. Married? She knew that the two of them couldn't be together but it hurt to know that he went and married someone he wasn't in love with. She was twisted with her emotions and kept going back and forth on how to feel.

"How are the twins?" he asked while staring at the floor. He had felt bad that he missed their birth. If the babies were his, he would feel guilty for eternity.

"Triplets," said Lovette.

"What?!" shouted Mike.

"You aren't the only one with a surprise announcement. Triplets. Two girls and one boy," said Lovette. As soon as she said the word "boy", she instantly felt bad. Running back in the house, she had needed to call

the hospital to check up on Matthias. Not knowing what was happening, Mike ran after her into the downstairs guest room.

"Polk-Jones Hospital. How can I help you?"

"I'm looking for my husband. Well, my son. He was checked into the hospital. Yes. Joseph Marks should've brought in an infant named Matthias. Okay," said Lovette.

The hold music began to play and Lovette began to get more and more impatient. The hospital in Shawford never seemed to be that busy, so what was taking so long? Mike had been staring at her for answers and Lovette had been staring up at the ceiling in an attempt to keep herself from crying.

"Hang up the phone, Lovette," said Joseph. He was standing in the doorway staring at her and Mike as if he were in a trance.

"What's going on in here?" questioned Iris. She was standing behind him with Joey by her side.

"Iris, please take Joey upstairs," whispered Joseph. His tone had been low and Iris immediately knew it wasn't something for Joey to hear. Taking him by the hand, she led him upstairs.

"Hey, bud. Let's go play with Legos until the pizza is done," said Iris.

"Where is Matthias, Joe?" whispered Lovette. Hanging the phone up, she and Mike waited for him to answer. Unsatisfied with how long he was taking to answer her question, she jumped up and ran into the family room.

He hadn't been there.

Returning to both men in the hallway, she knew something was off. Joseph looked as if he had been crying.

"WHERE THE FUCK IS MATTHIAS?!" screamed Lovette.

"Baby, let's go sit down and talk," said Joseph while trying to touch her arm.

"I don't want to sit! Tell me where my child is now!" demanded Lovette with tears pouring from her eyes.

Mike knew. He could feel it. He had yet to say a word.

"He didn't make it. They tried to do everything they could but...it was too late," said Joseph. "I'm so sorry, babe. I tried. I swear, I tried."

Lovette felt her knees get weak and fell to the floor. She didn't know that she would be bringing three lives into the world but she had accepted it. Now, Joseph was telling her that her baby boy was gone.

****

June 23, 1989

Lovette had decided she didn't want to see him. She wanted to keep the memories of his sweet little face as she held him close. Her surprise baby.

Joseph had handled everything and Lovette was appreciative. He had handled her with care and was patient with how she had been grieving. It was hard for her to look at Mary and Joyce some days. They were missing a link. Also, Joey had been sad. His only brother never came home and it was hard for Lovette to deal with the fact she told him Matthias would be back.

Mike had stayed in town a few days so that Dr. Oar could submit his DNA along with the babies, Lovette and Joseph. When Monica showed up at his parent's house the next day, his time with the girls had been cut short. She had called Lovette's house threatening to come over if he didn't get to his parent's house immediately. He knew his wife would come over swinging, so he took her word and headed over there.

"I just put the girls in their crib. Both of them are out like a light," said Iris. "What can I do?"

Iris had been so strong for Lovette. She knew her baby sister was grieving along with her but not once did Iris lose it. She had been the glue to Lovette's emotions. Iris had a thing for keeping things intact.

"You've been great, sis. I need you to take some time to relax. Do something for you. Go out and go shopping, see a movie or get your nails done. You haven't left this house one time yet," said Lovette.

"You know I'm fine. This is what I'm here for," Iris replied.

"I'm not asking you. I'm kicking you out," laughed Lovette. "Go do something. Please. That's what you can do for me. Go and treat yourself to something. And, take my card. Have fun and get whatever you like."

Iris laid her head on Lovette's shoulder and they sat this way for some time. Neither one of them said a word. Nothing needed to be said. They were one another's best friends and nothing could ever come between their bond.

"Okay. I'm done being sappy. I'll be back in a few. I'm picking you up some cute stuff, too. You deserve it for pushing babies out of that thing. Super woman has nothing on you," said Iris.

Lovette smiled and waved her off. Deep down, she couldn't wait for Iris to return so that they could have a mini fashion show together. She knew her sister would pick out the best things for her.

"Hey. You ready to eat lunch?" said Lovette walking into the family room. Joey had been sitting on the floor and was playing with his race cars. He looked up at her, didn't say anything and went back to playing with his toys.

"What's wrong?" asked Lovette.

"I don't want lunch. I want my brother," said Joey. He hadn't taken his eyes off of his toys.

It hurt Lovette deeply that he had been feeling so much pain. Matthias hadn't been around long but had gained the title of Joey's best friend as soon as he found out he had gained a little brother.

"I know, baby. I want him, too. We all do. But, sometimes, things happen and people go away. The older you get, the more you will understand. It's sad that he had to go and we will always miss him so much. But, you need

to eat something. You want to stay strong and healthy for your baby sisters right?" said Lovette.

"Okay," said Joey. Getting up from the floor, he walked into the kitchen and sat down at the island. Lovette made him a sandwich with chips on the side and went upstairs to check on the girls. Just as she had suspected, one of them would be waking up and the other would follow seconds or minutes later. Joyce was up.

Sitting in the rocking chair, she latched her on and stroked her hair. The jet black curls had already started forming in both of their heads and Lovette couldn't get enough of twirling her fingers in each coil as she fed them. A tap at the door had shifted her attention. Joseph.

"What's wrong with Joey? I tried talking to him while he ate lunch and he didn't have much to say" he whispered. Lovette explained the conversation that the two of them had just had. Nodding his head, he peeped in Mary's crib. She had just started shifting around.

"How was grocery shopping?" laughed Lovette. She had given him a list and he had been stressed out trying to fill her shoes.

"I don't see how you do it. Special thanks to you because between choosing brands, long lines, and actually sticking to the list, I had enough. Just admit it. You're a superhero, huh?" said Joseph.

Lovette laughed and passed Joyce to him. Picking up Mary, she sat back down and nursed her, too.

"My mom wants to meet the babies. She feels bad

for not being here and the things she's said," said Joseph. This had been what he wanted to talk about. He had needed to feel Lovette out before he brought up the topic of his mother. With everything that had been happening, he didn't want to upset her.

Everything inside of Lovette had wanted to tell her husband to tell his mother that she could go sit on a stick and swivel but at the same time, Lovette knew that someone would feel some type of way about the babies. If she hadn't cheated on Joseph, none of this would be happening right now. Instead, she chose to let it go and move forward.

"She can come over whenever she wants," said Lovette. The words felt like vomit coming from her mouth but she let the sentence glide off of her taste buds and roll out of her mouth. He smiled, carried Joyce out of the room and went to check on Joey.

****

July 8, 1989

A couple of weeks had gone by and Mike had finally decided he would visit the babies. He had wanted to be active as much as he could until they found out who they had belonged to.

They had the biggest argument over him secretly visiting the first time and Monica had threatened to tell his parents about the babies if he ever went to visit them again. At first, he allowed her to hold the threat over his head but he had had enough. Calling her bluff, he told her to "do it" and booked his flight to Shawford.

He was greeted by Iris and Joey running around in the yard. As soon as Iris saw him, she ran over to Mike and gave him a hug. He had felt like a brother to her and even though she loved Joseph like a brother as well, Iris had always wanted Mike and Lovette to work out. Joseph peeped out of the window to see his sister-in-law hugging the man who had felt like the enemy.

"Your skin is so cool. It's the same color as my best friend, Quincy. I wish I had cool skin like that," said Joey. He ran away towards the house leaving Mike and Iris with their laughter.

"Cool kid. They say anything that comes to mind. Is everyone home? I know they were expecting me but I forgot to call and tell Love I was on the way over," said Mike.

"Now, you know she's here waiting on you," laughed Iris. Cutting herself short, she apologized. "I didn't mean to say that. Don't tell her I said it or I'll cut you," she joked.

"It's already forgotten," said Mike. He felt proud knowing that Lovette had been waiting on his arrival. He was ready to see the babies he knew deep down inside were his.

Chapter 25: "Do I make myself clear?"

April 14, 2002

"What's going in here?" asked Joseph. He had been staring at the back of two short figure's heads. Both of them were dressed in sweatpants and hooded sweaters. Pulling the gun from his waist, he aimed it at the one on the left's head. Both of them turned around only to face the barrel of the gun.

"DAD!" screamed Mary. Jumping back as if she had been electrocuted, she fell to the floor and scooted against the cage.

"WHAT IN THE HELL ARE YOU DOING HERE?! Do you realize what kind of position you've put me in?! Do you?!" screamed Joseph. Putting the gun back in its holster, he tried his best to evaluate everything that could fall apart because of them being here.

"What's going on? Why…why are they here? And, why are their mouths covered up? And, why…"

"Mary, I need you to shut up for a second. I get up out of bed and when I do, I damn near trip over the dresser drawer. Funny thing is, I never leave it open. Then when I go look into my book, the key is gone," said Joseph.

As soon as Eric felt Joseph hadn't been focusing on him enough, he tried to make a run for the door. Catching him by the collar and tossing him against the cage, Eric fell to the floor and groaned in pain. Crouching down in Eric's face, Joseph wanted to make himself clearer than day.

"If you even think about moving again, you'll be right in these cages with the rest of them," he said. Standing up and straightening his jacket, he drew is leg back and forcefully kicked Eric in the stomach.

"Let that be a reminder," said Joseph. Eric screamed out in agony and clutched his abdomen.

"WHY ARE YOU DOING THIS?!" shouted Mary. She had begun to cry as she watched everything unfold before her. This wasn't her father. This was a monster.

"Like I was saying. I found my key missing and when I went to your room, you had been missing. Now, who told you to come here?" asked Joseph.

"…Joyce did," she cried.

"Joyce? Of course, she did. I knew we should've put you in a mental institution the day you told us you saw Joyce after she had died. After Matthias was gone and Joyce died, I knew it would only be a matter of time before something happened to you. Who really told you? Did Eric tell you about this? Did he have you steal the key and bring you here? TELL ME!" shouted Joseph.

Who was Matthias? Did her dad kill Joyce? Was she next? So many questions attacked her back to back. She knew something was off about her dad but this moment had confirmed everything.

Mary had been pressed so hard up against the gate, she had started to feel pain in the back of her head. Looking up to her father, he was capable of hurting Eric and he was capable of hurting these people, but he wasn't capable of hurting her. She was his child. Getting up from the ground, she walked towards him and stared him in the face.

"No." Staring at Eric in the corner in pain, Mary wouldn't allow her father to bully her.

"What did you say to me?" asked Joseph. One brow was raised while he was towered over her. Mary was so much like her mother and at this very moment, it slipped his mind that she had only been a child.

"I said no. What are they doing in here? Tell me or I will tell mom what's going on." That had been the icing on the cake. In his mind, she was no longer his daughter. She had no more worth. Mary had become the enemy.

"If you think for one second that you're about to ruin anything I have going on here, you're sadly mistaken. If only you really knew how much I can and will do to you, you would've thought twice about threatening me. You'll be eating those words later," said Joseph.

The smile he had been wearing seconds after made Mary feel uneasy. But, she had refused to let him know that. Running over to Eric, she squatted down to make sure he was okay. Helping him sit up, she continued her rant.

"You're the crazy one! How could you do this?! What did they ever do to you?!" shouted Mary.

Joseph walked over to the first cage and opened it. He stepped inside and removed the mouth covers.

"Stand up and go stand right there," ordered Joseph. The female stood up and did exactly what was told of her.

Saying nothing, she waited for her next orders.

"You see, Mary. Her hands were never tied. This gate, it was never locked. But, she knew to keep her mouthpiece on. They all know to have it on unless they are eating, drinking and talking to me."

"They are aware of consequences. Something we failed to instill in you while you were younger. Had we done that, you wouldn't be standing here today minding my business and you definitely wouldn't have puffed your chest out to me just now," said Joseph.

"Does she look sick to you? Doesn't she look miserable?" asked Joseph. Mary said nothing and let her father continue to talk as crazy as he looked. The lady smiled so hard that her face looked as if it were paused. Joseph tapped his foot and the smile went back to a normal stare.

"What's going on here is something you have no control over. This," said Joseph while pointing to everything around him. "This is happening. And, you? Just be thankful I'm allowing you to step out of here tonight. Your friend? He's staying. Let's see what happens to him when you tell your mother."

The fear had been written all over her face. He had threatened to do harm to the only boy she had ever liked. It was one thing to threaten her but now, she had no control over what he could or would do to Eric.

He read Mary like a book. Displaying a half grin, he handed the female back the mouth cover. Placing it back over her lips and snapping the button shut behind her head, she walked back into the cage and pulled it shut.

Mary stared at the woman as if she were an idiot.

"How can you do this?! How can any of you let him do this to you?!" screamed Mary. "SAY SOMETHING!"

"They know better and you…you don't. But, you will," said Joseph. He had been so focused on Mary and Eric that he failed to realize one of the 10 gates had been empty. Fear entered his body and settled into his soul.

Turning around so fast, he almost lost his balance. Where was he? Running out of the room and back into the main room, the exit door had been cracked. Opening it, he got a glimpse of his heel trying to escape.

"WHERE DO YOU THINK YOU'RE GOING?!" shouted Joseph. Running behind him and grabbing the boy by the ankle, Joseph drug him back down the rest of the stairs and slammed the door shut.

"SEE! Look what you've started, Mary! You just had to come snooping and now everyone has to suffer from your actions!" Taking the squirming boy by the back of his red hair, Joseph drug him back into the caged room.

Dragging him past Mary, she felt a pull and gravitated towards him. Leaving Eric in the corner, she banged on Joseph's back in an attempt to free the boy.

"Let him go! He doesn't want to be here! Let him go!" repeated Mary. Joseph pushed her down, tossed the boy into the cage, and grabbed Eric. Placing him inside with the boy, he popped open a box and pulled out handcuffs.

"No, no, no. Please, don't. Don't do this! I won't tell anyone. I won't say anything but please don't make me stay here!" pleaded Eric.

Joseph ignored the begging and proceeded to handcuff Eric to the gate. Walking backwards out of the cage and slamming it shut, he reached into his pocket pulling out a small gold lock and placed it on the cage.

"Every once in a while, this one likes to go against the grain. It's in his blood," said Joseph in between Eric's screams for help. He knew that he would have to make several calls and arrangements before things got too out of hand. Joseph had the perfect plan and was ready to put it into action.

"Eric. Listen to me. If you don't stop screaming, you will die. Simple. Okay?" said Joseph. Eric immediately shut up and cried in silence.

"This is my last warning. If you talk about this to ANYONE, Eric will die. Do I make myself clear?" said Joseph while staring down at Mary as if she were a peasant. Nodding her head, she couldn't believe what was happening.

"Now, get up and let's go home. It's late. If your mother is still sleeping, you're lucky. If she is awake, you need to tell her that you snuck out to go hang with those little friends you made at school and that I came to find you. That's it. Got it?" Mary nodded her head and continued to cry.

"And, stop all of that damn crying. Well, we can work with the tears, too. We'll say I hollered at you and that's why you cried. Stick to it or you will never see your little friend over there again," said Joseph. "Let's go."

Chapter 26: Oblivious

June 17, 1989

Joseph waited until he heard Lovette go downstairs and slid into the nursery. Matthias had been napping and now had been the perfect time to execute his plan. Picking the baby up and wrapping him in the blanket, Joseph stared at the door and made a run for downstairs.

"What's going on? What are you doing?" questioned Lovette while running after Joseph. He was trying his best to make sure she did catch up to him before he could get into the car and lock all of the doors.

"He's not breathing! I went to check on him and he's not breathing! Go back in the house! I'm taking him to the hospital!" shouted Joseph.

The terror written all over her had almost made him feel guilty enough to get out of the car and go back into the house. But, this had to be done. There was no turning back from there.

"WHAT DO YOU MEAN HE'S NOT BREATHING?! WHAT HAPPENED? I'm going with you!" shouted Lovette.

Placing Matthias in the passenger seat, he needed to leave in a hurry but Lovette had been hollering and running around the car. He didn't want to just leave her in this state, but he had to.

"Open the damn car door! I'M GOING WITH MY CHILD!" screamed Lovette. Rolling down the window in a

hurry, Joseph spoke while putting the car in drive.

*"NO! I'll call you. You just had 3 babies and don't
need to see any of this! Everything will be fine. He will be
okay! Let me go get him some help, Lovette. He started
breathing a little when I put him in the car. Go back in the
house," he demanded. Pressing on the gas, Joseph sped off.*

*Joseph pulled up to his work office and slid into the
back door with Matthias. He knew that no one would be
coming in today. Picking up the phone, he called Dr. Oar.*

"I have him. Do your part," said Joseph.

*"Are you sure you want to do this? We haven't even
gotten the results back yet. Lovette is part black. That gene
could've carried over and made the baby's skin complexion
darker. The results will be in soon. These things can
be...complicated," said Dr. Oar.*

*"Are you questioning me? Because, last time I
checked, you worked for me now. Doing your part isn't an
option. I'll pick the papers up tomorrow evening," replied
Joseph. There was a few seconds of silence between the two
and finally, Dr. Oar spoke.*

"Everything will be in order."

*Leaving his office, Joseph headed to the shed. When
he had finally made it down to the lower level, he handed
the baby off to the female in the first cage.*

*"Nurse him. I'll be back with some stuff," said
Joseph. Taking the mask from over her mouth, she
hesitated when he handed her the baby.*

"Please...no. Please, don't make me," she cried. Matthias started to cry and milk leaked from her chest onto the baby's blanket.

"Do I need to teach you a lesson?" asked Joseph. Shaking her head and wiping her tears, she placed Matthias up to her breast and attempted to make him latch. After several attempts, he had refused to eat.

"Bebe know I not he mother," said the female with a heavy accent. Taking her by the throat, Joseph squeezed tight until she was red in the face.

"Make him eat!" he demanded. Releasing his hold, she gasped for air. She tried several times to make him latch and finally, he did.

Leaving the shed and getting into his car, Joseph felt like he was way in over his head. He had violated the rules that were set in stone but this needed to be done. He was a boss, so this was an exception.

****

"Pop, I have everything under control. I swear," said Joseph. He had stopped over his parent's house and confessed to what was going on.

"Do you realize how much you're risking? You're in charge now but..."

"You're right. I am in charge now, so I need you to trust me. This will all go away and no one will ever know," replied Joseph.

Guy trusted his son but at times, he felt like he

didn't think about how much he was putting the family business in jeopardy. This wasn't acceptable.

"You may be the boss now but I can always come out of retirement. Don't you ever cut me off again," said his father.

"My apologies," said Joseph.

"Now, what is your plan for this baby? Joyce and Mary blend in even if they come back to not be your children. Why didn't you just kill him?" asked Guy.

Joseph loved the money from the business and in fact, he made so much money that he had to hide bank accounts from Lovette so that she wouldn't become suspicious. He would soon get out and start legal businesses. This needed to be done.

But, one thing he couldn't do was kill a baby. He wasn't exactly sure what he was going to do but he knew that he wouldn't kill Matthias. At least not yet.

"The hospital, Dr. Oar, everyone will be paid for their services. Everything is taken care of. I promise," replied Joseph.

"Just trust him," said Sarah. "We're out of this and he wouldn't do anything to get us caught up in something."

****

July 8, 1989

It had been a few weeks since Joseph had taken Matthias from the home. It hurt him to see the pain he had caused Lovette but it had been for a reason. He was sitting at his desk and continued to look over the DNA results and was in complete shock.

Peeking out of his office window, Mike had just arrived and was outside talking to Iris and Joey. This had been his son and his sister-in-law. This was his family and somehow, Mike still had his charm and it worked on everyone he came in contact with.

Joey ran into the house and upstairs into his room. Before long, Lovette invited Mike inside and he could hear everyone in the family room talking from his office. Once in a while, he would hear one of the babies fuss and Joseph knew in his gut that Mike was consoling his daughters.

He had planned to tell Lovette the results today and couldn't wait. This would end her communication with Mike and it was long overdue. He would sit in his office and stare at the results as long as he needed until he cooled off.

"The doctor's told Joseph that he had been gone before they arrived at the hospital. It was nothing they could do. I named him Matthias," said Lovette.

She instantly felt overwhelmed all over again as if it were the day it happened. Not once had she ever thought about losing a child and wish she could do something to ease the pain. Lovette had shunned the thought of talking to a therapist and felt as if it would do her no good.

Mike had been holding Mary and Joyce. Placing them both in their bassinets, he felt her pain. He never got to meet Matthias but it hurt him to know she had been in pain over this loss.

"I'm sorry I couldn't be here. Believe me when I say I really wanted to be here for you but..."

"It's okay, Mike. I know you would've been here if you could've," said Lovette. She wasn't sure if she fully believed the words that had come out of her mouth but she wanted to believe that he had wanted to be there.

Patting him on the knee, she went into Joseph's office. As soon as she opened the door, he shoved some papers in his desk drawer and slammed it shut. Guilty.

"What's up?" asked Joseph. He was nervous and knew she would ask about him pushing the papers in the drawer.

"Nothing," said Lovette suspiciously. "Was just checking in on you. You okay? Mike is here."

"Yea. Just need to get some air. I think I'm going to take Joey to the park just to get out of the house," said Joseph. Pulling his keys from his pocket, he placed one inside the drawer and locked it.

"Okay. Me and Iris are gonna get started on dinner while Mike is here with the kids. Speaking of...have you heard anything back yet?" asked Lovette.

"I'll take a stop over there and see what the holdup is," lied Joseph. He needed more time to prepare himself for what reaction he felt he would receive from her. She would either hate him or believe him. There would be no in between.

"Okay. Well, have fun. He's upstairs," replied Lovette. Joseph kissed her on the cheek and went upstairs to get Joey. Within minutes, they both were back downstairs and on their way out the door.

Standing on the porch, Lovette waited until she could no longer see Joseph's car and went into his office. Pulling apart the family picture of her, Joseph and Joey, Lovette peeled back the picture and removed the spare key her husband didn't know she knew about. Opening the desk, Lovette pulled out the stack of papers her husband tried to hide.

The first paper had been their joint account bank statement. Nothing for him to be shoving in a desk to hide. Shuffling through several other papers, they contained receipts from work, bills, and...

The results they had been waiting on. Joseph had been sitting on the results and didn't say a word to her. Lovette was livid.

She was hurt that her husband felt the need to hide them from her and she was confused as to how it could even be possible. She had never heard of anything like this. It had to have been an error.

Storming out of the office and into the downstairs guest bedroom, Lovette called Dr. Oar. Mike saw how furious she had walked off and left the girls with Iris to follow her.

"I'd like to speak to Dr. Oar. It's important. I DON'T GIVE A DAMN IF HE'S WITH A PATIENT! Tell him Lovette Marks is on the line right fucking now!"

screamed Lovette.

"What's going on, Love?" asked Mike. Closing the bedroom door behind him, he waited for a response. Holding her hand up in a gesture to give her a moment, he stood there while she continued to talk on the phone.

"Yes. Do you mind telling me what the hell these results are about? Like, how is this even possible?! This has to be wrong," said Lovette.

"Believe it or not, the test were done many times just to make sure we were looking at the correct information and it's true. Mary and Joyce's biological father is Joseph Marks and...Matthias's biological father is Michael O'Conner."

"This has actually happened before. It's not quite common but it happens. If the female party has had sexual intercourse with both male parties in a certain time frame..." Dr. Oar continued.

Lovette dropped the phone. She had been prepared for the children to belong to one or the other but not both. This had been all her fault.

"What is it, Love?! Say something already," said Mike. He had been worried about her actions. She was just in the living room with him smiling and now, she had seemed as if the world was about to end.

Mike could hear Dr. Oar on the line constantly saying "Hello?" and when he had gotten enough, he picked up the phone and hung it up.

Lovette instantly thought about Matthias. Did

Joseph kill her son? He knew that Matthias belonged to Mike and he had been in a rush to get him out of the hospital. She couldn't believe he would do something so evil!

"Matthias is yours. The girls belong to Joseph," said Lovette. She shoved the paper of evidence into Mike's hands and walked out of the bedroom as if everything that had just happened had been casual.

"Whoa, whoa, whoa!" said Mike as he ran after Lovette. "What do you mean "he's mine" but the girls aren't?! Since when has shit like this happened?! Is this for real?!" he questioned.

Lovette ignored Mike and ran up to her room to change her clothes. She couldn't sit around and wait for Joseph to come back to confront him. She was about to drive around to every park in Shawford to find him.

"Where are you going? It doesn't even matter. I'm coming. Iris, can you um…"

"Go ahead. I have the girls," said Iris. Mike had shown her the papers and Iris had been shocked herself. She had a feeling the kids belonged to Mike but would've never thought that the results would be what they were.

Lovette took all of 2 stops before she found Joseph sitting on a bench and watching Joey play at the park with the other children. She wasted no time throwing the car in park and jumped out with Mike on her heels.

"JOSEPH! YOU SON OF A BITCH!" screamed Lovette. She was running towards him at top speed and *couldn't wait to pounce on him.*

Joseph jumped up just in time to move out of the way of his fired up wife. Mike grabbed Lovette and held her until she calmed down.

"What's going on?!" asked Joseph. Looking over to the playground to check on Joey, he had still been playing as if he didn't hear his mother shouting.

"You know what's going on! How could you?! Tell me the truth RIGHT NOW!" screamed Lovette. Mike had still been holding her back from attacking Joseph.

"What are you talking about?! What is she talking about?" asked Joseph. He had refused to incriminate himself by admitting anything until she told him exactly what was going on.

"I found the paperwork in your desk! When were you going to tell me...tell US what was going on?! Did you not think for one second that we wanted to know?! I knew I should've taken my ass up there but noooo, I trusted you to handle everything!" shouted Lovette.

"Matthias! What did you do to him?! Were you that jealous of Mike that you had to go and hurt him?!" she continued.

The assumption alone made Mike angry. He had given Joseph a lot of credit for sticking with Lovette through her cheating and actually supported her through the whole pregnancy. Joseph had been good to her even though he wasn't sure if the babies were his.

But, hearing Lovette throw out the fact he could've

caused his only son...his deceased son to perish, Mike was instantly filled with anger.

Letting Lovette go, Mike had been on top of Joseph in a flash. Wrapping both hands around his neck and squeezing as tight as he could, Mike watched Joseph's eyes bulge from his eye sockets.

Finding the strength to knee Mike in the groin, the pain was enough to make Mike release his grip. Falling over in the grass, he rolled around in agony.

"I just found out today," said Joseph in between trying to catch his breath. "I swear, Lovette. I found out today and I was going to tell you but I didn't want you to think I did anything to hurt Matthias. I swear I didn't lay a finger on him."

"Bullshit! You have always been jealous of Mike and you let it get in the way of an innocent baby! Why, Joe? Why would you do this?" cried Lovette.

"I can prove it! We can go to the hospital and get all of the official paperwork. I swear, I didn't do anything to him. Why would you think I would hurt a baby?!" said Joseph.

Was he telling the truth? Lovette stopped for a minute because she had never known Joseph to be cruel. Matthias was innocent and if he found out today, he had no way of knowing who the babies belonged to. If that was the case, why didn't he cause harm to the girls as well?

The wheel of questions kept turning and turning in her head. Lovette had been in a trance and hadn't noticed

Joey pulling at shirt.

"Mama, mama, mama," repeated an irritated Joey.

Finally realizing the scene that was unfolding in front of her child, Lovette tried her best to calm herself. Mike had finally gotten up from the ground and was sitting on the bench. Joseph was standing in the grass and kept a close eye on him in case he tried to attack again.

"Yes, baby. Sorry. I need you to go get in the car," said Lovette. Joey was about to argue with his mother about leaving the park but instantly knew she hadn't been in the mood. Walking over to his father's car, he got in and put his seatbelt on.

"Mike, take my car and take Joey back to the house with Iris," said Lovette.

"Have you lost your mind? That's my son and if he leaves with anyone, it should be me or you. I know you're upset right now and I get how all of this looks but he's not leaving in the car with him," said Joseph.

"He's going with Mike. And, you? You're taking me to the hospital right now to get every damn document they have on my son. I want to talk with the front desk receptionist, everybody that was there that day, I want all of the damn camera footage to show you arrived at the hospital WITH my son, I want to speak with the coroner and every damn body who had signed anything pertaining to my child!"

"I'll take you to do whatever you want to do to prove that I didn't hurt Matthias but Joey is coming with

us." Joseph left the both of them standing there and went to start up his car.

"You can drive my car back to the house. We'll be back soon," said Lovette.

"I'll be at my parent's house," said Mike as he stormed off. He knew everything hadn't been her fault and held himself accountable as well but he wanted answers.

Mike felt terrible for missing the birth of his only child and never got to meet him. He never got the chance to hold him and now, it had been a mystery as to how Matthias passed away.

Chapter 27: Insanity

April 17, 2002

Joseph, Lovette and Mary had all sat down for dinner and it couldn't have been thicker tension in the atmosphere. After Joseph practically drug Mary from the shed a few nights ago and demanded she kept her mouth shut, he was no longer a father in her eyes; he was the devil.

"What's wrong, hun? Why aren't you eating your food?" asked Lovette. It had been taco night and it was Mary's favorite.

Joseph's threats to kill Eric had echoed in her head and she thought about it day after day. After seeing how he had kicked him and talked to her, she didn't know exactly what he was capable of.

"What's up? You know you can tell us anything right, sweetheart?" said Joseph.

Sweetheart? He was trying to mock her and prevent Lovette from suspecting anything was going on. Mary decided that she had had enough of his games for the last time and that was the icing on the cake.

"How about you tell mom "what's up", sweetheart," whispered Mary.

Joseph was taken aback at the fact she had the nerve to whisper something so slick. He nervously swallowed his food and avoided eye contact with Lovette. He refused to break his stare from Mary's eyes.

"Huh? What's going on?" questioned Lovette. She had been looking back and forth between the both of them and felt left out of the loop. Whatever it was, Mary had clearly been upset about it for a while now.

"She's probably just upset Eric is missing. I'm sure he probably tried to go back up north to be with his father. People are looking for him, honey. We'll find him," said Joseph. The side grin he gave her almost made Mary want to crawl across the table and shove her fork into his eye.

"Oh, I know you're still worried about him but your father is right. He's probably just acting out because he misses his father. Bill has been looking all over for him and even filed a police report," said Lovette.

"See. Even the police are looking for him," mocked Joseph. "Finish your food. You don't want to go to bed hungry."

Picking up her taco and looking at it as if she were examining it, Mary moved it up and down...and up and down. Joseph and Lovette looked at her as if she had lost her mind. Making a noise as if it were an airplane, Mary drew her arm back, aimed and used all of her strength to crash it into Joseph's face.

"Mary! What is wrong with you?!" shouted Lovette as she and Joseph but jumped up from the table.

"Let's just calm down for a second. Sit down, Lovette. Mary is clearly acting out because she's confused as to where her friend is," said Joseph while wiping the sour cream and lettuce from his clothes.

"Wrong answer! You know EXACTLY where he is! Mama, papa is lying about everything! He has Eric locked up in some weird underground shed with a bunch of other people! They are in these cages and…"

"Whoa! WHAT IN THE HELL IS SHE TALKING ABOUT?!" screamed Lovette while staring at Joseph.

"You know she likes to make things up when she doesn't know how to handle someone disappearing. It's the exact same thing she did when Joyce…" said Joseph. He whispered her name and instantly stopped talking.

Lovette knew that there could be some truth to this. Mary had had a very difficult time with Joyce's death and now, maybe, she was probably thinking her friend was going to end up the same way.

"He's lying! I swear, mama! He's a lying bastard and I can't wait until he dies!" shouted Mary. She hadn't noticed she was crying until several tears dropped on the wooden table.

"Everybody just calm down a second!" said Lovette. Mary had her moments of acting out but she had never wished death on her father.

"Mama, I swear! Joyce kept telling me that I needed to go and see what this shed was about. She said it would reveal who papa REALLY was. That's why she wouldn't go away. She told me that we had to finish it so she could go be with Him for good," said Mary.

Joseph stood with his hands crossed in front of him and had a stale face while his daughter continued to rant.

He told her what the consequences would be and now, he would allow her to finish what she needed to say. He knew she would eventually crack and tell her mother everything.

"He had a key in the Bible and Eric went with me to the shed. You can even ask Joey about the shed! Me and Joyce followed him there years ago!" said Mary.

"Mary, you haven't dealt with your sister's death the way we had hoped and now, it's gotten worse to the point where you have made up imaginary things. This isn't healthy. I love you and always want the best for you but you leave us no choice but to seek more help for you," said Joseph.

"No," said Lovette. She whipped her neck around so fast and stared Joseph in the face. She knew exactly what he meant and there was no way she would allow him to take the last child living under their roof away.

"Lovette, we've been avoiding this for some time now. Ms. Carle clearly isn't able to give her the help she needs. We've paid this woman all of this money and for what? For Mary to sit here and get worse? Just look at her," said Joseph. "Is this the life you want for her?"

"Mama, I can show you! He's such a liar! I can show you where he is keeping people locked up! There was even a kid in there my age! Eric is down there mama," pleaded Mary.

The whole conversation had started to make Lovette's head spin. Joseph had been denying everything but her child had gone beyond a child's imagination with this story. Something wasn't right.

"Okay. Lovette, you can call Joey and ask him. Mary, if it makes you feel any better, we can all go together to this mystery shed. You show us how to get there and we will go," said Joseph.

Mary felt only an ounce better. She knew that her father was evil and had something up his sleeve. Even if he had taken everyone out of the shed, she would still be able to back up her story about the cages. The whole place could be empty but at least her mother would know that she hadn't made it up.

Leaving the dinner table, Lovette went into the downstairs guest room to call Joey. The phone rang a few times and he finally answered.

"Hey, baby. How's it going?" said Lovette.

"It's going pretty good. How is everyone?" replied Joey.

"Everyone is doing okay," she lied. "I know you're probably busy based off of the laughing and loud talking in the background but I just have a question really quick. Do you know anything about your father having a random shed?"

The shed. It had been forever since he had been or even thought about it. Joey had wanted to show his father just how much he had become a man and did as he was told; he stayed away from the shed and hadn't returned.

"No...not sure what you're talking about. Hey, mom? I'm in the middle of a video game with my friends. Can I call you back?"

It was only a matter of time before he rushed her off of the phone. Saying their goodbyes, Lovette returned to the dinner table and found only Joseph sitting there.

"She went upstairs to get cleaned up and I'm doing the same. We're going wherever she needs us to go before it gets too dark. I want her to show us whatever it is that she's so fixated on. Then, we can be done with this," said Joseph.

He left Lovette standing there alone. Joseph was acting as if everything going on was no issue and that sending her off would be the answer to everything. Meanwhile, it was true that Mary showed little improvement. And, now, they had to deal with this.

As soon as everyone was settled into the car, Lovette still couldn't believe what they were getting themselves into. Mary said that there was this cage that sounded like hell. And Joseph? Here he was saying that he had no idea what she was talking about.

Mary believed her father had been the one holding Eric captive along with several others. Lovette didn't know what to think. But, she knew her husband wasn't capable of such an extreme thing. He hadn't been perfect but this wasn't like him.

"You plan on telling us which way to drive or do I have to drive around town for some random shed?" asked Joseph. Since she had started this game, he would play along with her.

Mary couldn't believe her father had the nerve to act like he didn't know where his own torture chamber had been. But, if she wanted to get this over with so that Eric could be free, she acted right with him.

"Stop here. We have to get out, walk between these woods and into the field," said Mary,

"Mary, I've had enough of this already. I'm not getting out of this car and walking in these woods just for something to chase me out of it!" said Lovette.

"Mama, no! It's right in there. We have to just walk a little. It's not that far," whined Mary.

"Oh, no. We came out here to find this mystery shed and that's what we are going to do. I want an end to all of this and this is a start," said Joseph. Getting out of the car, he continued talking. "You gonna get out and show us the way?"

Both Lovette and Mary climbed out of the car and Mary took the lead. Letting her get a little way ahead of them, Joseph took the time to finish what he had wanted to say to Lovette.

"This is the final straw. She needs help that we or Ms. Carle cannot give her. I'm done repeating myself. We're out here in the woods walking to a shed, Lovette. Don't you see how out of hand this has gotten?"

Lovette knew her husband was right. She had tried her best to help Mary adjust to life without Joyce but now, she had started to feel as if it also had something to do with Matthias. It had been three children brought into the world and to deal with her grief, she had to pretend as if it had only been twins born. She had suppressed the memory of their baby brother's short life.

"We'll talk more about it later. I promise," said Lovette. Joseph accepted the answer for now but it was only so long before he would hold off bringing it back up.

Finally, they had sorted through the trees and had been in an open field. Nothing had been there. Marry took off running in a diagonal direction and then stopped.

"WHAT DID YOU DO TO IT?! IT WAS RIGHT HERE! WHAT DID YOU DO?!" she screamed. Joseph shook his head and looked at his wife. She was exhausted from the whole night.

Running back over to the both of them, Mary instantly started kicking and punching Joseph. Lovette tried her hardest to hold her back but Mary was like her mother. Once she had gotten to a certain level of anger, no one could contain the raging bull within them.

"Mary! Stop it! Just stop all of this! There's no shed! There was never a shed. Do you see one here?! We followed you out here so you could tell us what you saw but there's nothing here! There isn't even a piece of wood out here to even suggest a shed had been here!" shouted Joseph.

Mary's insanity with talking to Joyce hadn't been anyone's fault. She had legit thought she could see her sister and thanks to that, Joseph used it to his advantage. Mary constantly kicked and screamed while they both practically drug her back to the car.

"I hate both of you! You both are crazy! This whole

time, everyone thought I was crazy but it's both of you! Mama, you're in on this, too! YOU KNEW PAPA WAS IN THERE HURTING THOSE PEOPLE, TOO! YOU KNEW! I KNOW YOU KNOW!" screamed Mary.

When they finally reached the car, Lovette had to sit in the backseat with her and held her down. Mary clawed at her arms, face and legs in an attempt to flee the car but her mother refused to release her hold.

"Mary, I need you to calm down. We are going to take you home. Unless you want to be sent away to the crazy houses you see on TV, you better stop this RIGHT NOW!" shouted Lovette.

It had been enough to make Mary stop her screaming and actually think about being sent away. Were they serious? Would they really make her go to one of those places? All she had wanted to do was get Eric out of there and now, it had come to this.

Chapter 28: Desperation

"Babe, a package is here for you," yelled Monica. Mike had just gotten home from his new job. He worked in a furniture warehouse and between the cold temperatures and weak pay, he couldn't wait to find something better.

When he had finally told her about the business, she hadn't taken it like had thought she would. He was expecting for her to want to end the marriage but to his surprise, she clung to him even more and was supportive.

They had talked about the DNA results and when he told her about Matthias, she actually seemed hurt. Deep down, Monica felt as if she would never have a baby. Although she loathed Lovette, Monica had planned on convincing Mike to file for sole custody. Matthias could've been her baby and everything would've been better in their marriage.

Picking up the box, it didn't have a return address on it and he hadn't been expecting any packages. Opening the brown box, there had been another little white box inside with a blue angel on top. Pulling out of the card, Mike opened it and it read it out loud.

"I wanted you to have this. You would've loved him- Love."

Mike instantly knew was in the box. He wasn't sure if he had wanted to open it. Things were starting to get better between him and Monica and he didn't know how she would react to seeing it.

"Open the box," said Monica. "It's okay. I promise." She smiled at him and laid her head on his shoulder.

Pulling out the white box and opening it, there was a glass box with a tiny blue egg in it with golden angels printed on it. Matthias.

"I'll give you a moment," said Monica. Kissing him on the cheek, she went into their bedroom.

Trying his best to maintain his composure, Mike picked up the box and turned it. He examined it from every angle. This had been the first time he had gotten to hold his son. Placing the glass box on top of the fireplace along with the certificate of cremation, he went into the kitchen and called Lovette.

"Hello." The little voice had belonged to Joey.

"Hey. Is your mom home?" asked Mike. Joey didn't say anything and within the next minute, Lovette was on the line.

"Hello."

"Hey. It's Mike. I was just calling to say thanks for that. Are you sure you don't want to keep him? Because, I don't mind..." he replied

"No, you keep him. I was able to hold him. He belongs with his father," whispered Lovette.

Her words touched him. Mike wished he could be there to hold her. He stopped himself from thinking any further about it before he said something that he probably shouldn't.

"Thank you. And, I'm sorry for leaving like that. After getting into the fight with Joseph and hearing everything…I just…"

"It's okay. Speaking of that, he cleared everything. The only thing I wasn't able to get was video footage. The hospital admitted that they discard them after a certain amount of days. He gave me the death certificate, all if the hospital information, cause of death…everything. Sudden Infant Death Syndrome," said Lovette.

Mike knew Lovette had been trying her best to explain things to him. He could hear the pain in her voice and wanted nothing more than to ease the hurt.

"Tell me something about him. Anything," said Mike.

"Well, he had the cutest red hair, freckles and smooth skin. He was the quietest out of all of them," said Lovette. The lump in her throat almost stopped her from finishing what she wanted to say. "He was…handsome."

"I believe it. How are you feeling?" replied Mike.

"I'm a little better. I try not to think about it so much, ya know?" said Lovette.

"I know exactly what you mean. I've always loved how strong you are," said Mike. It slipped out so fast and it caused him to peep around the corner to see if Monica had *possibly heard what he said. When she hadn't been in the hallway, he released a sigh of relief and went back in the kitchen.*

Lovette smiled as if he could see her. She didn't know what to say in return and didn't want to overstep at the same time.

"Hey, look. I just wanted to call to say thank you and check on you. I have to do a few things, so...can I call you some other time?" asked Mike.

"...yea. Of course. Talk to you later," said Lovette. Without waiting for a response, she hung up the phone.

Mike was the strong one. Lovette had been pretending to keep everything together and didn't want to alarm anyone with how she had been feeling.

****

Lovette had followed Joseph around for months trying to get to the bottom of how she had been feeling. He acted weird and guilty around her and simply asking him wouldn't be enough. She needed evidence.

And, today had been the day that she would get her evidence.

"Hey, um...is Joe home?"

"And, who's calling?" asked Lovette. She was breastfeeding Joyce and trying to balance the phone on her shoulder.

"I can call back some other time..." she said.

"You called my house and asked to speak to my husband and...you know what. He's here. I'll put him on the phone," said Lovette. Yelling upstairs for him, he eventually picked up the other line.

"Hello?" said Joseph. His voice was groggy from his nap being interrupted.

"Hey, it's Janet. You busy?" said the female voice.

"Who is Janet?" asked Lovette. She was still on the line waiting for her husband to answer her question. Lovette heard the phone slam down and his feet running downstairs. He pushed open the downstairs bedroom door and had guilt written all over his face.

"Hello? Hello? Hello?" repeated Janet.

"Lovette. Hang up the phone. We have to talk," said Joseph.

"You can tell me what you want, Janet. I'm staring at my guilty ass husband. So, just say what you're calling for and I can deliver the message," said Lovette. Janet hung up the phone before she could say anything else.

"Your little girlfriend hung up," said Lovette. "How long have y'all been screwing around?"

Joseph knew that if he told the truth, Lovette would leave him. He knew she was already suspicious of Matthias disappearing and this would only deepen it.

"Look, it was only one time," lied Joseph. "After everything went down between you and Mike, I did this just one time. I haven't seen her since and I honestly don't even *know how she got the house number. I'm sorry."*

"That was too easy. You expect for me to believe you two only slept around once and you confess just that easy?" said Lovette.

"Because it was wrong. I should've been told you," said Joseph. A lie about cheating would do him better than the actual truth. Lovette had really cheated herself and if she even thought about leaving because he had done the same in return...

Lovette thought she would be hurt but she hadn't been. She did cheat first and well, there wasn't anything she could say about it. Keeping her family together had been important to her. She promised her mother that she would work hard to keep it together and failing to do so would mean Lovette failed her deceased mother.

"I think you cheated because you wanted to. Not because you wanted to get even. I think that you would've eventually done it but used me as an excuse to fulfill something you've always been wanting to do. Do you want to keep this family together?" said Lovette.

Joseph had been shocked by her response. He had been faithful to Lovette their entire marriage. Him having to lie about having an affair, made him want to come clean about it. He loved her more than he loved anyone, including himself, and because she had felt like he had wanted to cheat all along...he didn't know what to feel.

Lovette knew her husband hadn't cheated on her. Whatever lie he had been trying to cover up, he did it well. He was throwing infidelity around as if it were something to play with; she knew that she wasn't dealing with the average person.

"Of course, I do! You know that. I would never want to be without you. Everything that has happened, it happened and won't happen again. I know you regretted Mike and I for sure regretted her. Janet was more than likely calling for more hush money" said Joseph. He would later make her admit to this lie.

"Ha! And, you paid her off?" she laughed. Joyce was sound asleep. "I'm going to put her down and check on the kids." Lovette left the bedroom and returned empty handed.

"Surprisingly, they are all sleep at once," she said. "Since you clearly want other things and maybe I do, maybe we can do things with other people from time to time. Doesn't seem too bad. We still love one another and want to raise a family together."

Joseph's eyes became huge due to being shocked with his wife's suggestion. He knew exactly what she meant and still, he couldn't allow her to know the truth.

"Lovette, have you lost your mind? I know we've both made mistakes and we are trying to move past it but that is insane. I'm supposed to walk around daily knowing that my wife is screwing other people?!"

"Oh, no. Not just me. You, too. Of course, it won't be a daily thing. We can work out a schedule and only pick one person. Either that or you confess about this whole cheating thing being a lie and tell me exactly what's going on," said Lovette. She calmly called his bluff and was

slightly serious at the same time.

Joseph knew exactly what she had been doing but he couldn't allow his wife to find out the truth. The thought of slitting her throat had crossed his mind all of two seconds but he knew there would be no turning back from that. He loved her too much and his children needed their mother.

"I told you the truth," said Joseph. "I told you that we aren't ever divorcing and I meant that. Is this about Mike?" Joseph knew it was. He could easily make Mike disappear but at the same time, he didn't want to raise any more suspicion within his wife.

Lovette hadn't realized before but today, she had reached a new level in her marriage. Her husband was willing to do whatever she wanted to keep their relationship intact. He would do whatever she wanted before he really told the truth about what he had been hiding.

For this, she would use everything to her advantage. She could have whatever and still keep her family together. Joseph would never really understand what type of monster he had just unleashed.

****

"She's talking about sleeping with other people. Tell me what to do. After Matthias...well, she's been different," said Mike.

"Well. What do you expect? You've taken her child out of the household and have been pretending that he is

deceased. She knows something isn't right but she cannot prove it. You drove her to this point," said Dr. Oar.

Instantly regretting what he said, Dr. Oar began to apologize for his words. Joseph held up his hand to stop him.

"Listen to me. You're a part of this now. If I ever feel like you're going to open your mouth to my wife or anyone else, I'll make you disappear as well," said Joseph.

Dr. Oar knew he was serious. He knew what Joseph was capable of and he knew his family's history only added to the threat. He nodded his head and went back to suggesting his solution.

"I suggest you let her. You say you love her more than anything. Well, let her do what she needs to do in order to feel comfortable with you again. You've managed to keep these secrets from her this far. She knows you're hiding something and apparently, she doesn't think you're capable of cheating."

The look on Joseph's face couldn't have been any closer to disgust. Lovette was his wife and the thought of anyone else touching her made him cringe. But, her finding out the truth about him made him cringe even more. Cheating may be forgivable but his hidden lifestyle wasn't.

****

October 27, 1994

After the guests had left the party, Joseph sat across from Lovette with the biggest smile on her face. He didn't know if she was provoking him or what, but the game she had been playing, he would eventually have his victory.

"How did you like it?" asked Lovette.

"It's different, ya know? Nothing like what we have, of course. But now, I'm glad you suggested it," said Joseph. He had actually been telling the truth. He was against it at first but throughout everything he had put her through, she was still his wife. She had still been his. But, he wanted to remind her that this was all her idea.

"Good. Was this red one different from the last one?" asked Lovette. While they had been in the same room but engaging in different people, Lovette would occasionally glance over at her husband to see how much he had been consumed with the atmosphere.

What started off as her calling his bluff, had turned into something Joseph actually enjoyed. The fact of the matter was that she enjoyed it, too. But, her initial mission hadn't been introduced at all.

"She was okay," said Joseph in a nervous voice. He didn't want to say the wrong thing to have her second guessing herself. The ultimate truth was that Lovette was still and would always be his number one. Any moment she had wanted to stop all of this would've been fine with him.

Ignoring his response, Lovette could only think about Mike. She had wanted him there but knew it would take some time to ease him into their life. Joseph had needed to get comfortable about their new "lifestyle" before she mentioned his name.

Chapter 29: Coping mechanism

Mary was her mother's personality twin. This is why Lovette had a hard time dealing with the things her child had been experiencing. Mary would easily get upset about things she had been passionate about. These same things would trigger her anger if no one believed what she felt had been the truth.

Sliding into her daughter's bed and wrapping her arms around her, Lovette knew Mary needed this. She needed her mother's love and trust.

"Talk to me, baby," asked Lovette.

Mary had been upset and lingered in her room for the last couple of days. She had refused to come downstairs, refused to talk to her parents and refused to eat anything.

"For what? Just so you can believe him and send me away?" sneered Mary.

She hadn't attended school the whole week. Joseph convinced Lovette that it was best she took some days off from school and they consider other options about where she had belonged.

"I'm so sorry that you're hurting. I really am. I want the best for you but sometimes, parents mess up. So, let's start over. I want you tell me everything and what you feel is best for you. I just want to help," said Lovette.

Was she serious? Mary didn't know if her mother was faking it to see what she would say next. But, then again, she had always trusted her mother more than her father. Mary knew he was sneaky and something was different about him. She knew that he never loved her the way he had loved Joey.

"Who is Matthias?" asked Mary.

Lovette's sat up with the quickness. She had never told the girls about the brother they never got to grow up with. Joey had suppressed the death of his brother and acted as if he never existed and because of this, Lovette had done the same.

This had been the beginning of her coping mechanism. She failed to tell the girls about their brother and she had done the same when it came to her parents. If she never mentioned it, it felt as if it never happened. Lovette couldn't deal with the pain of talking about it to her children.

"What?!" questioned Lovette.

"The night me and Eric went to the shed…dad said something about after Matthias was gone and Joyce being dead, he knew it would be only a matter of time before something happened to me," said Mary.

"What do you mean?"

"I don't know. Papa said his name. He was evil, mom. I wish you had been there. He was…different. He made this woman come out of the cage and she acted weird. She acted like she it was okay for her to be there," whispered Mary.

Lovette felt as if she wanted to throw up. It had been years since she had heard her deceased son's name out loud. She had refused to say it and felt as if doing this would make the pain disappear.

Mary learning about Matthias had triggered Lovette. There was absolutely no evidence of him inside the house. The little that had belonged to him was locked away at Caron's house in her garage.

The fact that her husband had the nerve to bring up his name had set fire under her. They had agreed that it was best to not bring him up. The wounds never healed and this is what Lovette had been best at. Suppression.

"If you and Eric went to this shed, tell me what it looked like on the inside. Tell me as much as possible," said Lovette.

Mary felt proud. She felt as if someone had finally decided to start believing in her. This someone had been her mother. There had been no better person to believe her.

"There was a raggedy shed. It was really old. Then, it was a door in the middle of the floor with a bunch of steps going down. When we finally got to the bottom, it was another floor door. When we opened it, it was some more steps that actually had light this time."

"When we got to the last steps, it had a door. When we opened the door, it looked like a small family room," said Mary.

Lovette hugged her child tighter and listened to her story. Whether it had been the truth or her imagination, she had needed to hear it. Mary had brought up her brother's name and now, Lovette needed answers.

"There was rocking chair moving by the door. Eric felt like someone had been there and told me that we should go. We both noticed it but I just had to know. I had to see what was going on inside."

"There was another door. When we opened it, it was another room full of cages. We hadn't been in there that long before papa caught us. He was...insane. He hurt Eric and even said he would kill him if I told you!" said Mary.

Her daughter had been in tears. The energy she had felt between the two of them had been unmatched. Mary had always had a wild imagination but for her to make up this place...something was off. There had to be some truth to what she was saying. But, she needed evidence.

"Did Eric say anything to you about wanting to run away?" asked Lovette.

"No. He missed his dad but he told me he loved it here. He was glad me and him were friends. He wanted to be here. Eric didn't run away, mama. Papa did this," cried Mary.

"You said there was a boy your age in there. Did he say anything?"

"No, but he must've been in the first room that looked normal. He must've gotten out of one of the cages and tried to get out of the shed. Papa drug him back inside," said Mary. "He had the same hair color as you and freckles."

Lovette hadn't realized but she had been holding her breath. A coping mechanism. There was no way it could be him. Could it?

"How about we go back to the field? Search a little more. See what we can find. How does that sound? Just us. Don't tell your papa," said Lovette.

Mary immediately felt better. She had finally gotten through to someone and would prove who her father really was. She hadn't figured out exactly how he managed to move or hide the shed but at least her mother was willing to go back and help her look for it.

****

April 20, 2002

The following morning after Joseph left for work, Lovette kept her promise. She called Joseph at the office just to make sure he was actually there. Satisfied that he wouldn't be making a surprise visit back home, Lovette drove Mary back to the field.

"Mama, is was right here. I swear it was," said Mary. The whole thing only made her that much more frustrated because she knew the exact spot it was supposed to be in. The huge trees that stood on each side of the shed had both been there. She knew it had been the exact same trees because one of them had been leaning over.

Lovette felt that something was off. The grass they

had been standing over didn't match the grass around them. They were two different greens.

"Go over there and look between those trees," said Lovette.

"It wasn't over there. It was here," said Mary in a stern voice.

"Look. I'm trying to help you, so just do as I say," demanded Lovette.

Stomping away, Mary pretending to be doing what her mother told her to do. She knew it wouldn't be in the opposite direction and felt like it had been pointless.

Lovette bent down towards the grass and tugged at it. Just as she suspected, the grass moved. Feeling around for its perimeter, she finally discovered a corner and peeled it back.

Cement. Nothing but cement. Lovette tugged at the grass she knew didn't match and stuck her finger into it. Pulling her hand up, there was dirt beneath her fingernail.

"What are you doing?" asked Mary. Lovette hadn't felt her behind her and jumped. Laying the grass back down on top of the cement, Lovette dusted her hands off and stood back up.

"Nothing. Let's go," said Lovette.

"But, mama…"

"I said we're leaving. We'll talk about this later." Mary said nothing else and followed behind her mother feeling as if she were back at square one.

****

April 26, 2002

"You sure you don't need me to turn around and take care of you?" asked Joseph.

"No. We promised him we would visit this weekend. He knows I don't feel well. Plus, you two are long overdue for a father and son outing," replied Lovette. "Did Mary act up on the way to your mom's?"

"She told me she hated me and that I was the worst father ever. I really think it's time to get her admitted," lied Joseph.

In fact, Mary hadn't said a word to him the entire ride to her grandparent's house. After her mother failed to do anything and her father continued to lie, she was glad to be getting away from the both of them.

"She'll get better. I'm about to get some rest," said Lovette.

"I'll call you later. I love you."

"Love you, too."

As soon as she hung up the phone, she grabbed her car keys along with the set of copies she had secretly made and headed over to Joseph's office.

There was work she had to do. Work that she had avoided doing over the years. All of the suspicions she had but never fully acted on them caused her to have a lot of regret.

Pulling up to the office, Lovette felt a sense of relief knowing that no vehicles were in the lot. It was Friday evening and nobody was supposed to be at the office afterhours. Had it been someone there, her plans would've been ruined.

Pulling out the piece of paper from her purse, Lovette placed the key in the door and stepped inside. Glancing at the paper as if she hadn't memorized the security pin, she punched in the numbers to disarm the system.

Lovette waited for a few seconds to see if a dog would come running around the corner. Nothing. Either they had gotten rid of the security dog or there was never one. She knew it had to have been the latter.

The smell in the office was nice. It smelled as if someone had just sprayed or maybe even lit a candle. The receptionist's area was kept neat and a bottle of blue nail polish sat right next to the phone.

Searching through the desk, all of the files and cabinets, Lovette found nothing. Just a bunch of women's magazines, receipts from buyers and colorful pens. If she didn't know any better, Joseph's newest receptionist was a teenager.

Lovette slowly walked down the hall and peeped into the two office rooms before Joseph. The first one had belonged to Will and the second one had been the security footage room. Deciding she would come back to this room last, Lovette headed to Joseph's office

Twisting his office doorknob, she had expected for it to be locked. Placing each key in the door until one opened the door, Lovette stepped inside and closed the door behind her.

Everything in Joseph's office required a key. The closet, desk, file cabinets, and even a pen box that sat on his desk. Taking out her set of keys, she opened the file cabinet first.

The top file cabinet was filled with office supplies. The second was filled with miscellaneous papers that Lovette didn't too much understand. Opening up the third cabinet, it was completely empty.

"Tuh. All these things are locked for no damn reason," said Lovette out loud to herself. She continued to search throughout the whole office and nothing caught her attention. Deciding to go look at the camera footage, Lovette made sure the office was exactly how he had left it. Turning to leave, the closet's gold lock caught her attention.

Running her hands along the black matte door, she tried the keys until one had been its match. Pulling it open, she was faced with boxes on top of boxes stacked up under the top shelf. Pulling the first one open, there were highlighted tabs filed one after another.

"What in the…" whispered Lovette.

Chapter 30: The plan.

April 27, 2002

"Hey. I'm coming to get Mary. I feel better and I want to take her on a girl's day out," said Lovette.

"You sure? Joseph said you were pretty ill and we love having her over. She's been helping me in the garden. I couldn't get that child to touch dirt a year ago and now, look at her," laughed Sarah.

"Yea, she's definitely growing up. I just really miss her and we haven't gotten a chance to do much together lately. I'll be over in a few. Don't tell Joseph I'm coming. He's just going to make a fuss and I feel fine," said Lovette.

Hanging up the phone, Lovette called around to see what she could do with the information she had found in Joseph's office. His power had now been shifted upon her. He had left her in the dark for so many years and she now had enough of it.

Pulling into her in-law's driveway, Mary had been sitting on the front porch waiting for her. Lovette felt warm inside knowing that Mary wasn't mad at her for not finding anything out in the field.

"I'm only coming with you because I know we are going shopping," said Mary as she slid into the car and put her seatbelt on.

"Fair enough. We have a lot to talk about anyway. I believe you," said Lovette.

Mary's throat felt dry. Finally. She couldn't believe the words that her mother was saying but at the same time, she was glad she had finally heard them.

"Really?" she questioned.

"Yes. Are you hungry?" asked Lovette while changing the subject.

"No. You know Grandma loves to cook and wasn't going to let me out the door before I ate again for the twentieth time today," said Mary.

Lovette laughed because she knew her daughter hadn't been exaggerating. Sarah loved to feed everyone and denying her food would only hurt her feelings.

"How did you enjoy your grandparents?"

"It was okay. Grandpa just yelled at the TV, as usual. Grandma cooked and kept asking me about "the boy she heard I like"," said Mary. Her voice faded out near the end of her sentence.

She had missed Eric and was torn that she hadn't known where he was or what her father had done to him. Mary had gone against what her fathered warned her and for all she knew, he was dead by now.

"Hey. It's okay. People are still looking for him. I went over to Bill's yesterday and he told me that he was going to visit some surrounding states to look around for him. Hopefully, he shows up soon. Try not to think too much about it," replied Lovette.

"So, why do you believe me all of a sudden?" asked Mary. She knew her mother was trying to shy away from talking about it and wanted to know more about what she had recently found out. Pulling into Shawford Mall, Lovette parked the car and turned towards Mary.

"Let's save that for home. We have all night to talk about that. For now, let's shop until our feet hurt. You can have whatever you want. I mean it," said Lovette.

****

Lovette and Mary had just gotten home from shopping and putting everything up. When she told Mary she could have anything she had wanted, she took it literal. Lovette had spent over $5,000 between the both of them and every penny had been worth it.

Placing the chicken in the pan and watching it sizzle, Lovette took a sip of her wine. She turned around to face Mary sitting at the kitchen island.

"I really do believe you," started Lovette. "Your father…my husband…he isn't who we think he is."

"That's what I was trying to tell you! He's a maniac and he needs to pay for what he's done to Eric and all of the other people he had down there," said Mary.

The house phone started ringing, Lovette held up her finger to Mary and ran into the downstairs guest room.

"Hello."

"Hey. It's…Mike. I'm glad you answered. I didn't want to have to explain to Joe why I was calling. I just needed to talk to someone."

"It sounds serious. What's going on?" asked Lovette.

"It's Monica. She's…dead. Well, someone killed her this morning. She was in the parking deck getting into her car and someone shot her," said Mike in a cold and low tone.

"Mike, I'm so sorry! That is terrible! Nobody deserves that. I know it's extremely new but…how are you holding up?" asked Lovette.

"I don't know how to feel besides angry. I just want to find out who did this to her just so I can kill them myself and maybe the anger will subside," said Mike. "I just don't understand why someone would do this to her."

"People are crazy and do crazy shit. She didn't deserve it and you don't deserve this. Is there anything I can do for you?" replied Lovette.

"You've already done something just by listening. I just needed to hear a familiar voice. Sorry if that sounds weird. I just don't know what to do right now."

"It's normal to feel like this. Everything just happened. It's the same way I felt when my parents were killed," said Lovette. Shaking her head, she tried to rid the thought and keep the focus on Mike.

"I understand exactly how you feel. It takes time to sort your feelings out. Don't rush yourself to be okay.

Move at your own speed," she continued.

"Thank you. That really means a lot to me and I'll keep that in mind. Hey, look. Can I call you some other time? Maybe later? It's some things I need to handle," said Mike.

"Sure. I'm here all day. Joseph is going to be out of town visiting Joey until Monday night." Hanging up the phone, Lovette went back in the kitchen to check on her food and finish talking to Mary.

"Mama, he's crazy and has to pay," repeated Mary.

"I know. And...he will," said Lovette. She took a long sip of her wine and begun to feel a buzz. "You cannot tell you father anything. You can't tell your grandparents or Joey either. No one can know about anything we talk about. Okay?"

"Okay."

"I'm serious, Mary. We have got to work together to figure this out. If anyone else finds out, they won't believe us."

"I promise. I won't tell anyone."

Lovette stared at her for a few seconds without saying anything. Mary needed to know how serious the matter had been. When she had felt confident enough, she continued talking.

"I know how we can solve everything, help those people and get Eric back," said Lovette. She had Mary's full attention and now was the time for her to put her plan into action.

"Remember when you said you couldn't wait until your father dies?" asked Lovette.

"Yea, well..." said Mary.

"Well, that's the thing. You were right. He does deserve to die," said Lovette.

Mary's eyes had gotten so wide. She would've never expected for her mother to say such a thing. She had said those things out of anger and wasn't sure if she had really meant it.

"But...I can't be the one to do it. I'll go to jail and you'll never get to see me again," said Lovette.

"Be the one to do what?" asked Mary. She had a feeling about what her mother was getting at but didn't want to think it had been that.

"The one to kill him," said Lovette with no emotion at all. The expression on her face added emphasis to how serious she had been.

"Mama..." whispered Mary.

"Your father has done some awful things and have hurt a lot of people. We have to get rid of him so that we can help people who are innocent. Isn't that what you want, right?"

Mary nodded her head. She wanted Eric back and she wanted everyone to know what kind of person her father had been but she didn't know about him actually dying. She was confused and didn't know how to feel.

"Just listen. Your father is a bad very bad man. This is something neither one of us knew. In order for the good people to stop feeling pain, we have to take him out. You understand that, don't you?"

"Yes, mama." Mary had started to see her mother's side and now felt as if she agreed. Her father was a bad man that had hurt people. People like him didn't deserve to walk around as if they were a good person.

"If I do it, you'll never see me again. Is that what you want?" asked Lovette.

"No, mama. I don't," replied Mary.

"You have to be the one to do it. You're a child. Children don't go to jail," said Lovette.

"But…"

"Joey won't believe us. He told me that there was never a shed. We can't trust him to do this. We can make it fast," said Lovette. "Think about what he did to Eric."

Eric. Lovette saying his name had triggered Mary. Eric had been the one person who understood her and never judged her. He was important to her and she wanted him back. She would do it for Eric.

"Okay," said Mary.

Lovette was surprised at how easy it had been to convince her. She thought it would take more due to Mary always being so set on doing the opposite of what they told her to do.

"I have a plan that will make everything go smoothly. You have to do exactly what I tell you to do. Nothing more and nothing less; exactly what I tell you to do. Okay?" Mary nodded her head. Turning around to flip the chicken, the opposite side had been burned.

"Shit. Well…go order a pizza," said Lovette.

Chapter 31: "You put on a good act."

May 4, 2002

Lovette poured both glasses of champagne and watched one fizz more than the other. Picking them up and walking into the family room, Joseph had been sitting on the couch and was watching *The Green Mile.*

"Imagine having to feel like that just from taking a piss," said Joseph as Lovette entered in the room. "Champagne? What are we celebrating?"

"Oh. Just new beginnings, I guess. Hopefully, things will get better around here soon. Mary seems to be doing better," said Lovette.

"I that case, I'll toast to that. Yea, she does seem to be calming down some," said Joseph while taking a large swig of the drink. Lovette watched him swallow and took a sip of her own.

"How's work been? Did you keep…I mean, meet any new people?" asked Lovette. She watched his brows furrow and quickly release.

"No. Haven't really made any new business partners," said Joseph. "We're doing. We really don't need anyone new. I'm thinking about selling very soon and looking at new opportunities."

Joseph blinked his eyes continuously and rubbed them as if something were blurring his vision. Sitting back on the sofa and rolling his shoulders, he looked at Lovette with crossed eyes.

"Joe. You okay?" asked Lovette.

"Yea. I think I need to go lie down. It's been a long day," he replied.

"Oh, no! I wanted to have a little fun but if you aren't feeling well, just relax for a while and we can watch a little more of the movie together," pouted Lovette. Her disappointment made him lie back on the couch in an attempt to relieve the pressure he had been feeling in his head.

Joseph hadn't been lying down for more than 45 seconds before he had begun to snore. Slowing moving from up under his feet, Lovette headed up to Mary's bedroom.

"Hey. You ready?" asked Lovette.

Mary's face instantly had concern on it. She didn't want to do this...but, she wanted Eric back. She wanted her only friend and to be able to laugh again. If this was the only way, she would have to do it.

"I guess," she replied.

"Everything is going to go as planned. Do it exactly where I told you to. Then, we can go get Eric. I'm sure I know where he is," said Lovette.

Instantly, Mary rose to her feet. Hearing her mother say she knew where her father had been keeping him made her anxious and happy at the same time.

Both of them walked downstairs towards the family room where Joseph had been sleeping. Handing her daughter the knife, Lovette stood back and watched Mary stand over Joseph's head. As soon as Lovette gave her the greenlight, Joseph opened his eyes and coughed.

"Shit!" whispered Lovette. "Just do it!"

"Mary, WHAT IN THE HELL ARE YOU DOING WITH…" shouted Joseph. He was stuck in his position and was too in shock to move.

Before he could finish his sentence, Mary plunged the knife into his chest and twisted it. In and out. In and out. In and out. In and out.

Joseph screamed at the top of his lungs while attempting to get her off of him. Falling to the floor, he continued to scream. Mary ran to the kitchen and sat at the counter like her mother told her to do.

"Lovette. Why? Why would you…" said Joseph in between taking deep breaths and spitting up blood.

Bending down to the floor and crouching close enough to hear, Lovette made sure she didn't touch his blood at the moment.

"Because, Joe. You're evil. I know that shed was there and you had a company clean it out, fill it with cement and placed new grass there. I've seen all of the files. All of the humans you and your sick family have tortured and sold."

"I've seen footage," Lovette continued. "You have everyone wrapped around your finger. Everyone at

Joseph's every command. No one being able to refuse what you want or they end up….like you're about to be."

Joseph continued to gurgle on his own blood as Lovette sipped her champagne and watched.

"The icing on the cake is Matthias. I know he isn't dead and I know what you did. You got rid of him but kept him alive this entire time. Yea, Mary found out about the red head boy who tried to escape from the shed."

"You took my son from me. You destroyed his files but guess who told the truth? Dr. fucking Oar. You knew that Mike would continue to come around and you got rid of what you thought would be a problem. You felt like he was a threat. Competition."

"You put on a good act," said Lovette. Joseph had been on his side with blood still seeping from his nose and mouth. He was no longer breathing but Lovette continued to talk.

"You probably killed Joyce and Mary was next, huh? I mean, the child was talking to her deceased sister and you clearly wanted her away with all of that nut house talk. The doctors searched up and down to find what was wrong with Joyce and well, did you pay them off, too?"

"It's funny how Will, Brenda and Caron all up and moved out of Shawford at the same time. Funny, huh? Because, I don't hear you laughing, Joe. Did they know, too?"

"All of the deceitful shit you've done, threats to people and every single one had obeyed your command.

You deserve to be dead right now. And, to think I actually ended up loving you," said Lovette. Whispering so that Mary couldn't hear her, she continued.

"You're actually going to get your wish."

Lovette put the glass down and screamed at the top of her lungs.

"WHAT HAPPENED?! WHAT THE HELL HAPPENED?!" Falling over onto Joseph and pulling his lifeless body into her arms, she cried and wept over her dead husband.

Letting his body drop back to the floor, she ran to the kitchen and continued to scream. This time, it was towards Mary.

"WHAT HAPPENED?! WHY ARE YOU COVERED IN BLOOD?! WHAT DID YOU DO?? NO!" screamed Lovette.

"What? Mama, what are you talking about?! You're scaring me..." said Mary. This hadn't been part of the plan.

Backing up and going into the downstairs bedroom, Lovette locked the door and rushed to call for help.

"Yes! 911! My daughter just stabbed my husband! He's on the living room floor and he isn't moving! She's banging on the door and I think she's trying to stab me next!" cried Lovette.

Mary continued to bang on the door screaming for her mother to let her in. The frightfulness she had felt had taken over her body. Her mother had acted as if she wasn't the one to tell her to do this and now, she was placing full blame on her.

Minutes went by of continued screams and as soon as Lovette heard the police announce themselves, she cracked open the door.

"PUT YOUR HANDS ON YOUR HEAD! NOW!" screamed the officer. Lovette watched as a fearful Mary placed her hands on her head. Opening the door, Lovette shot out into the hallway brushing past her and running towards the officers.

"Someone please help my husband! He needs help now!" cried Lovette.

"Mama! What's going on?! MAMA!" shouted Mary over and over again.

The first officer proceeded Mary with caution and before Lovette knew it, he had her in handcuffs. Her stomach immediately knotted up and she began to feel guilty. She hadn't realized what procedures were needed to get to the point she knew would happen. Her baby had been in handcuffs like she were a criminal.

Seeing her child being handcuffed wasn't her intentions. Mary didn't deserve this. But, the plan needed to be fully carried out. Lovette would see that she would never see the inside of a jail cell.

"Unit 606 to dispatch. The scene is clear for paramedics to enter," said the second officer.

"10-4," responded the dispatcher.

Mary's screams continued to echo throughout the house until the officer had gotten enough and took her to the back of his car.

"Please, be gentle with her!" shouted Lovette. "She's just a kid. We're going to get you some help, baby," cried Lovette.

Lovette had been crying as if she had come home to this event and had known nothing about it. While one officer attempted to calm her down, the medics rolled Joseph's body out of the front door.

Lovette looked at the sheet covering her husband's body and let out the biggest scream she could muster up. Her knees buckled and one of the officers caught her before she could hit the floor.

"Ma'am, let's go outside and sit on the porch. You need some fresh air," he said.

Doing as he instructed her, Lovette stood on the porch crying while staring at Mary in the back of the police car. How did things get this far?

****

June 11, 2002

"Tell the bitch to go away! She's the reason I'm in here! I don't give a shit about it being my birthday!" screamed Mary while looking up at the camera in the corner of her room.

Lovette had arranged for Mary to stay at a psychiatric ward and was standing outside of her bedroom listening to her daughter scream. Mary was refusing to visit with her but since Lovette had new contacts and could pull just about any string, there was nothing Mary could do to keep her away.

Pushing open the white door, Lovette entered her room and sat down. She waited for Mary to stop her tantrum before she said anything.

"Mary, come sit down. Now."

"Go to hell," sneered Mary. "You told me that everything would be better if I listened to you and now look at me! Stuck in this place with all of these crazy people."

"You won't be here forever. I promise. This is just until you...feel better," said Lovette. "Do you know what they do to people in jail? You should be thankful I've gotten you a very nice set up. Your food is amazing. You get to go outside, use a cellphone, and even have a spa day whenever you feel like it."

"Then how about you switch places with me! You're the one that deserves to be here! I don't know who is crazier between you and papa," said Mary.

"I know where he is," replied Lovette while ignoring her comments.

"You know where who is?" questioned Mary. She had stopped pacing around the room and gave Lovette her undivided attention.

"Your friend," said Lovette.

Her mother had finally found Eric. She had been waiting on the day she could hear those words. Mary rushed over to the table and plopped down in the chair.

"Where is he?!" asked Mary.

"He's at home…with Bill. He's…um, different but he's alive," said Lovette.

"Why didn't he come? Doesn't he want to see me? How is he different now? What's going on?" Mary felt herself getting angry with how her mother wouldn't just come out and tell her everything.

"Whatever your father had done to him or told him, he is denying everything. He's saying that there was never a shed and how he doesn't know what you're talking about. He misses you and wants to be your friend but he's not willing to talk about anything."

"He told everyone that he ran away because he was trying to go visit his dad. He was found at truck stop in a really bad condition and now, his uncle is trying to get him back to feeling normal," said Lovette.

Lovette let the many lies fly from her mouth just as she had rehearsed it. One thing had been the truth, Eric really did miss Mary.

"The receptionist will bring in your gifts. I hope you love them. We'll work on getting Eric to come visit you. How would you like that?" asked Lovette.

Mary softened her demeanor. She had missed him so much and seeing him would change her mood for the better. Nodding her head, she continued to listen to her mother.

Lovette had made sure she covered all of her tracks and everyone knew she was in charge now. With all of the information she now had access to, whatever she wanted would be easier than snapping her fingers.

Whoever she wanted to get rid of or whatever she wanted to do in Shawford, as well as many other places, she could do just that. Including, getting rid of Monica.

Chapter 32: Reunited

February 10, 2004

"Are you sure? Because, if you aren't sure, I won't sell it. It belongs to the both of us and I want to make sure you're on board with everything," said Lovette.

"Lovette, sell the damn thing. After everything that has happened there, I don't blame you for wanting to get rid of it. I can't imagine waking up there every single day and having gone through what you've been through," said Iris.

"Yea, well. You're right about that. Joey refuses to ever come back. Two of my children are gone and they're not releasing Mary until she's 18. It's too lonely here. I can still smell the blood," Lovette replied.

"I know, sis. I know. I'm so sorry you had to go through so much. I wish you would move up here and be with me. Annie sure could get used to seeing her favorite auntie's face every day," said Iris.

Iris had just given birth to her first child and although Lovette would visit, she couldn't see herself moving up north. She had just picked out the perfect house just outside of Shawford and it wasn't too far from visiting Mary.

"Maybe one day," lied Lovette. "How's my niece doing? I don't hear any babbling in the background."

"She's great. Keeping me up all night. Who would've known that a 2 month old would be so demanding? I don't remember Joey being like this," laughed Iris.

"Oh, but he was. Whenever I had to be alone with him, I would cry right along with him. The boy had a set of lungs on him and it got really rough some days," replied Lovette.

"I understand. Annie has her days, too. Her father is useless. But, hey. I already knew that. Stupid me to go back to a married man," whispered Iris.

"Things happen and you are now the mother of a healthy little beautiful girl. Screw him. If he wants to continue to hide his child from his wife, put him on child support. At least make him pay. You deserve some kind of help."

"I don't want to force anything out of him. And, you're right. She is beautiful and I never knew I could love someone this much. She's just…perfect," replied Iris.

Lovette was proud of her baby sister. Yea, she made a couple of mistakes but so did everyone else. But, she had a great career and was already one of the best mothers she had ever known.

"I'm really proud of you, Rissy. Kiss Annie for me and always tell her how she's named after the best auntie in the world. I'll be visiting y'all soon. I'm going to call you later, the realtor is coming outside," said Lovette.

Pressing the "For Sale" sign down into the grass,

Lovette felt a bit of relief lift from her shoulders. This change was going to be for the better and she would be able to heal properly this time.

"Mrs. O'Conner, your house is perfect! It won't take long to sell this at all! I love what you've done with the kitchen, family room and turning the downstairs office into a fancy little mudroom," said the overly hyped up realtor.

"Thank you," said Lovette. Mike walked out of the house right behind her and walked over towards Lovette who was standing in the grass. Looking down at her, he kissed her on the lips as if he had been waiting all day for the moment.

"I'll be getting back with the both of you within the next few hours about what's to come next so be on the lookout for my call," she said. Getting into her car and leaving, she wasted no time speeding down the driveway. This sale would be one of her biggest ones and she couldn't wait to brag about it.

Lovette was relieved to know that she didn't have to stay in the house another night. She had more than enough money to purchase a new house without having to wait on her current one to be sold.

"I can't wait to start my party planning business. At least it's one thing I'm excited about," said Lovette. She wrapped her arms around Mike's waist and placed her forehead against his shirt. Lovette inhaled his scent and fell in love all over again.

"Ouch, Love. I guess being my wife doesn't count,

huh?" joked Mike.

"Of course, it does! It's the best thing to happen to me in a long time. We need to go visit Mary before we head out for the night."

As soon as they both turned around to get into the car, a patrol vehicle pulled into the driveway and parked behind them. As soon as the figure stepped out of the car, Lovette instantly noticed who she was. Jennie.

She hadn't seen her since graduation and never knew what happened to her. After their incident at the dance, Jennie left her alone and made some other girls her bully victims.

"Jennie," sneered Lovette.

She walked up towards Lovette and Mike with a white box in her hands. The box was covered with a brown lid and Lovette could see "Marks" written in the lower corner.

"Can we go inside and talk? It's pretty important," asked Jennie.

"Whatever we can talk about can be said out here. This house doesn't belong to me anymore and I refuse to go back inside. But, I'm sure you know why," sneered Lovette.

"Okay. I understand. I at least want you to have a seat," said Jennie.

Have a seat? Lovette had been accustomed to these three words. It had echoed throughout her head so many times and for so many years. Having a seat was never good.

"No….please…don't tell me…" said Lovette. She felt her body began to shake and Mike pulled her towards the bench to sit down.

"When the staff wen to check on Mary today, they found her unresponsive. She had a bottle of pills that they are unsure how she had gained access to them due to protocol about locking away pharmaceutical drugs in the facility. CPR was administered for over thirty minutes and she was transported to the hospital but unfortunately, they weren't able to resuscitate her. I'm very sorry for your loss," said Jennie.

Lovette broke. Her entire world felt as if it were breaking into a million pieces. Mary was the last of her trio. Despite forcing Mary to take the blame, Lovette had wanted her to get out one day and eventually, they could make amends. She wanted Mary to be able to get out and return to her first love, Eric.

But, this would never happen. Lovette blamed herself. She saw it in Mary's eyes the last visit and failed to protect her from herself.

"If there's anything I can do or the department, please let us know. There are some more items still there for you to pick up at a later date. This is just what they allowed me to bring to you," said Jennie. She slid the box on top of the table.

"Whenever you are up to it, they need you to come identify the body." Jennie got into her patrol car and left Lovette to mourn.

"Baby, I'm so sorry. Let it out. Cry as long as you need. I'm not going anywhere," said Mike.

She had told him about all of the betrayal Joseph had put her through and the things he had done to people. Mike was disgusted. He knew that Joseph was a snake in high school and it hurt him to know that Lovette had to go through so much pain.

The best and worst part was that Joseph was now gone. He detested never getting justice from the man who took his only son away but he was glad that such a monster was no longer walking the earth. Lovette made him promise to keep all of their secrets and although he wanted everyone involved to be held accountable, breaking a promise to her would never happen.

Mike had now had the love of his life back and there was no way he was letting Lovette go. She had been there for him when he lost his wife and he would remain by her side to help her get through the losses she had taken.

Lovette peeled herself from Mike's arms and reached to open the box. She knew what was inside before opening it. Lovette could smell her scent through the box.

The first item was a white sweater Lovette had just bought Mary. The tag was still attached. Mary had refused to wear anything Lovette had bought her. Placing her face into the sweater, she cried even harder.

Mike rubbed her back and kissed the top of her head. After a few minutes, Lovette placed the sweater on the table and reached in the box for the envelope address to Joyce. This alone made her start to cry again.

Opening the letter, Lovette hesitated. She wasn't sure if she was ready to see and feel her daughter's words.

February 10, 2004

Dear Joyce,

I wanted to write to you because I knew this would be the only way you would listen to what I had to say. Things have gotten crazy over the last few months and I wish something different would've happen.

I wish I could hug you. All of the times I was rude or mean to you, I wish I could take them back and say nicer things instead. I wish I could've been more like you.

I'm...different now. You know where I am. These people here make you different. No one is happy and everyone walks around as if they are never leaving. We're stuck. One girl tried to jump on me and when I stabbed her, they told me that I was a threat to everyone.

They make me take medicine. At first, I tried hiding it under my tongue because I knew what they were doing to me. But, one of the ladies caught on and they forced me to swallow the pills.

The medicine makes me feel like I'm spinning and unable to talk. Most of the time, I just go to sleep and hope that the feeling goes away when I wake up. I think everyone here must take medicine. It's just weird. A lot of the people here shouldn't really be here.

I know you probably don't want to hear from me after the way I treated you but I just wanted to let you know that I'm leaving this place. I'm getting out of here and I'm coming to be with you. I miss you more than I've ever missed anyone before.

Mom, I know you're reading this. Give this to Joyce. It belongs to her.

I wish we could breathe in the mirror together just one last time. I've loved us since the belly. I'll love us forever.

Love, Mary.

"What does it say?" asked Mike.

"I'd rather not. I shouldn't have read it. It's for Joyce. Can you drive me to her plot?" asked Lovette through her tears.

Nodding his head, the both of them walked towards the car and he opened the trunk. Lovette placed the box of clothes between two cases. One had been Joseph's ashes and the other had been the actual remains of Matthias.

It had taken Lovette crossing mountains trying to find out what happened to her youngest child. It was unknown how he exactly died but Joseph had covered his tracks almost perfectly.

Lovette had felt she would never get to bring her son's body back home for burial until one day she had received a package in the mail with no return address. It had been his ashes attached with pictures of Matthias's corpse. His skin looked perfect and he hadn't had one bruise in sight.

Lovette knew it was her child because of the red freckles, red hair and his birth mark being so visible on his ankle. He had gotten so big and even though he looked like her, he favored his father.

The thought of Joey hardly wanting anything to do with her after his father's death and now, the triplets were all deceased, Lovette cried even harder. None of this was supposed to end this way and she wished she could go back to fix things.

Death had surrounded them both. When Mike had found out that the box of ashes he had received years ago hadn't belonged to his son, it was bittersweet until Lovette revealed that he was actually deceased now. Life had been so confusing for the both of them.

Pulling up to the gravesite, Mark hung around in the car to give her some privacy. He had been dealing with his own emotions for the day and had wanted a moment to take everything in.

Visiting Joyce's grave had always been tough for Lovette. She would always feel pain knowing her daughter hadn't been able to live a full life. Now, her sister and brother would both be joining her.

Lovette bent down and placed the letter between the headstone and the grass and pushed it down as much as she could to secure it.

"Hey, baby. Mama misses you so much. I need you to look after your brother and sister for me. You and Mary have to shower Matthias with love. He's missed our love and affection for so many years."

"I know you're behaving up there. Keep your sister in check. She's going to need it. I love all of you so much and I'll be back soon to put your sister right next to you. Matthias will be in her arms and the three of you can be together again on earth and in heaven," said Lovette.

She had done so much crying and had felt so much pain throughout the years. At this very moment, not a tear a dropped. She needed them to "see" her having a strong moment. Lovette needed to be strong for them.

Now, she had Mike. The first person she had ever loved and he was now hers again. In a sense, Lovette felt as if her life were incomplete and complete at the same time. Her children were the best things to ever come from her and the greatest love of all.

But, Mike had filled a void that had lingering for so long. Lovette had been able to love Joseph but nothing had compared to what she and Mike had experienced together.

As soon as she got back into the passenger seat, Mike looked as if he had something heavy on his mind as well.

"You feeling okay?" asked Lovette. She tried to stifle her sniffles as best as she could but now, it was time to see Mary and she hadn't been ready.

"I know what you did. I couldn't go another day being married to you without letting you know that I know. I've known about Joseph's family business for some time now and the only reason why he didn't come after me was because he knew he would be destroying a piece of you."

"I know you love me but you better be done with all of that. You've lost a lot of people in such a short amount of time and we are all we have left. Joey will come around one day. Things will get better but you belong to me now," said Mike.

Lovette knew he was serious and took his words for exactly what they were. She didn't know if he was specifically talking about Joseph or found out about Monica as well but she would never admit that unless he revealed exactly what he knew. But, she was done with the power she had stolen from Joseph. She wanted nothing else to do with it and was done. Unless…it chased her.

Nodding her head, Mike squeezed her hand and kissed it. The tears she had been holding back could no longer be contained.

Mike knew she was no monster. Everything she had done had a reason behind it. He had gotten his Love back and now, nothing would ever get in between the two of them ever again.

"Let's go see Mary," said Lovette.

Let's Talk About It!

1. Why do you think the story was told in a first person and third person point of view?

2. What was your initial guess about what was in the shed?

3. When Lovette tells the story about the dance she attended in high school, did it bring back a high school memory for you? If so, what happened?

4. Are you a twin? If so, can you describe the connection you two share?

5. If you were Mike, would you have continued to date Lovette if she insisted on being friends with Joseph?

6. Joey struggles with a few things but maintains his behavior while on medicine. How did you initially feel about his character? How do you feel now?

7. Do you think Joseph genuinely loves Lovette or is it possible some obsession? Perhaps both? Why?

8. Mary feels as if her father doesn't too much care about her. Did you think her feelings were valid this entire time?

9. When Lovette's parents go out of town, she had the urge to chase after their car for them to come back. Have you ever had a gut feeling that something terrible would happen and it did?

10. Joey and Iris were racing one another and he splits off towards the tree. Do you believe that children can see those

who have passed away?

11. Why do you think Lovette continues to ignore issues rather than facing them head on?

12. Do you think Joseph had anything to do with Joyce's death? Why or why not?

13. A lot of time had passed since Matthias had been in the shed. Why do you think Joseph kept him alive? What do you think his initial plans were when it came to what he was going to do with Matthias?

14. Let's talk about Lovette convincing Mary that she needed to kill Joseph. How did that make you feel?

15. Do you believe in soulmates? Do you think Mike and Lovette were supposed to be together?

16. Did the shed contain what you thought it would?

17. What was the biggest plot twist?

A Message from the Author

I just wanted to take the time to thank each and every person who took the time to read this book. Also, thank you to everyone who provided feedback. Thanks to Justus Wilson for taking my author photos and Antonio Douglas for designing the cover of the book.

Most importantly, thank you to my husband, Rodd, who thinks I'm cool for doing this. You've become my best friend and I love you. Even when neither one of us are at our best, I wouldn't want to be doing this with anyone else.

Even though I invested a great amount of time in this book, I know this novel isn't perfect. I'm headed towards perfecting my craft and I can't wait to show everyone what I am capable of. As long as I have breath in my body and I'm able to tell a story, I'll remain an author. I'm at the happiest point in life and I'm forever grateful.

Be on the lookout for more to come and don't forget to leave a review!